From New York Times _and_ U
Thea Harrison comes the first in

Power can change a person…

For months Molly Sullivan endures the inexplicable: electrical surges, car breakdowns, visions. She even wonders if she might be the cause… and wonders if she might be crazy. Then she discovers her husband has cheated on her. Again. Now Molly realizes she is a newly awakening witch and a woman pushed over the edge.

Revenge can shape a person…

Josiah Mason is a Powerful witch and the leader of a secret coven with a shared goal: to destroy an ancient enemy who has ruined many lives. Josiah lost years to this man, and his sole focus is revenge. He's prepared for every contingency—except encountering a beautiful new witch who understands nothing of the immense Power building within her or the attraction she wields over him.

Danger can bring them together…

When divorcing her husband, Molly uncovers a dangerous secret he's willing to kill to protect. She turns to Josiah for help, and they discover a connection between Molly's husband and Josiah's enemy.

As they work together, a spark ignites between them that threatens to become an inferno. But Molly is done compromising herself for any man, and Josiah's mission is his top priority. And the enemy is cunning, cruel, and drawing ever closer.

As the danger escalates, so does the tension between them. Is a lasting relationship possible? *Will either of them live long enough to try?*

American Witch

Thea Harrison

American Witch

ISBN 13: 978-1-947046-17-7
Print Edition

Cover design by K.D. Ritchie at Story Wrappers

Chapter One

MOLLY STARED AT what she had found while she flushed hot, then cold, and the roaring in her ears was the sound of all the balls she'd been juggling for years that were now crashing at her feet.

Her fingers shook as she pulled out the strange pair of underwear from the narrow space between her husband's nightstand and their king-sized mattress. She dropped the panties onto the bed. They were outrageously feminine, a dark purple with lace trim.

They were a size smaller than what she wore.

Her gaze listed around the shadowed, quiet room, a foundering ship in search of a safe harbor. Years ago she had decorated the master bedroom to reflect serenity, but at the moment it felt anything but serene. A storm had rolled in, and the sky was so dark outside it looked like twilight.

Rain lashed against the windows like a wild creature trying to break in. Water ran in rivulets down the glass pane, and thunder growled. Inside, the house felt too still, as if it held its breath, and the heavy, dense air was thick with an electrical charge.

Her attention snapped back to the purple panties. They were a shocking intrusion, the purple violent against the pale cream duvet.

What kind of woman trysted with a married man in his own bed, then forgot to put on her panties when she left? What kind of husband did that to his wife?

Hot tears spilled down her cheeks. Something tightly leashed inside her tore, and her emotions raged uncontrollably.

On the landing at the head of the stairs, the antique grandfather clock stopped ticking. The bedroom plunged into semidarkness with a sizzling electric *pop* that made her nearly leap out of her skin.

From his office downstairs, Austin shouted irritably, "Goddammit, Molly—a circuit blew again. The party's in two hours, and I'm still in the middle of crunching the numbers I need to go over with the other partners tonight. Would you fix it?"

Go ahead, Molly. Fix it.

Go into the basement and reset the circuit breaker.

Then bake the puff-pastry hors d'oeuvres by 5:45 p.m. The chicken should marinate until 6:10 p.m., and then you need to put it immediately into a preheated oven. Check the wine cooler to make sure the white wine is chilled to fifty-two degrees, slice lemons and limes for cocktails, and don't forget you need to ice the sponge cake with buttercream frosting and top it with the fresh fruit that you've washed and left to dry on paper towels.

And you need to shower, put on your makeup, and

dress well so you can do your part and charm your guests tonight.

Would the owner of the purple panties be at the party?

She couldn't feel her fingers. Carefully, she folded the panties and stuffed them into the pocket of her old cardigan. Then she went downstairs, picked up her purse, located her car keys, and walked out of the charming six-bedroom, four-and-a-half-bath Cape Cod house.

The gray sky spat needles of chilly rain as she climbed into her Escalade in the driveway. After starting the engine and cranking up the heat, she took the panties and laid them out on the passenger seat. Then she fastened her seat belt and pulled out.

Her shoulders felt crushed, and her face was streaming. She couldn't get a deep enough breath into her cramped lungs.

She drove to the end of the street and then turned and drove back on the neighboring street, passing large well-tended lawns and equally large familiar houses. Zigzagging back and forth, going nowhere, her mind a blank.

Her cell phone rang. She ignored it. It rang several more times until she put it on vibrate. Then it buzzed like an angry hornet. She didn't want to ever talk to him again. She felt like she could drive for weeks and weeks. Just watch the road as it came scrolling toward her. Why couldn't she do that? When she thought of how trapped she felt, a wave of anguish rolled through her.

Every light on the dashboard of the Escalade lit up, and the engine sputtered. Suddenly calming, she listened as it gave one last cough before it died. Using the SUV's momentum, she steered to a stop at the curb and put it in park opposite a large, landscaped retention pond at the edge of the neighborhood.

She told the absent woman who owned the panties, "Today's Thursday. The cleaning service came yesterday morning. I got home from visiting my mother last night, and I only just got around to straightening the bedroom today. So you were in my bed yesterday afternoon."

"True," admitted the woman in her imagination. "There wasn't any other time it could have been."

Molly could picture her. The woman would be leggy. Perhaps lightly tanned, with golden-blond hair and freshly returned from a trip to the Caribbean. The purple panties would look good on her. She would be intelligent as well as pretty, educated, a knowing expression in her worldly eyes. She might hold her mouth in a slight ironic slant.

She probably looked a great deal like Molly. Austin had a type.

Molly said between her teeth, "You left those panties on purpose. Nobody forgets something like that. You left them for either Austin or me to find. If Austin found them, it would remind him of what you and he did. If I found them, I would learn about your affair. Either way would work for you."

In her mind, the woman smiled and crossed her long legs. "Indeed. What else have you got?"

She clenched the steering wheel with both hands. "Austin wouldn't bring an unknown hooker into the house. If he were going to have a hooker, he would go to a hotel. This is a relationship. You and he have been together before."

The woman gave her a conspiratorial smile. "You're not quite as stupid as Austin thinks you are."

This time when Molly glanced at the panties, the passenger seat didn't seem quite empty. An indistinct, transparent form of a woman appeared to be sitting there, although she wasn't the tall, leggy blonde Molly had been envisioning. She got the impression of a small, curvy figure, dark hair, and a bright gaze.

Her heart kicked hard. Blinking rapidly, she dug the heels of both hands into her dry, burning eyes. When she looked again, the strange hallucination had vanished. The seat was as empty as it had always been.

What the hell is happening to me?

Shaken, she wiped her face. When she had composed herself, she found her phone. Ignoring the multiple text and phone messages, she called roadside service.

It took them almost an hour to arrive. As she waited, she slipped out of the car, and ignoring the light rain, she walked the path alongside the pond while keeping the Escalade in her line of sight.

The wind was chilly, but she barely noticed. She felt like a walking bruise.

Everything in her life had been about Austin's career. Every decision they had made had been carefully plotted out.

They had met in college, and after graduation they had moved to Atlanta where Austin's father had a small law firm. Then his father's firm had been bought out by a larger one. Austin had been made a partner in the new, larger firm while his father had retired.

So they had settled here, making more money as the years rolled by, increasing in influence and reputation, developing important connections, and buying a showcase house with an open floor plan that was perfect for throwing frequent dinner parties for powerful people.

Out of the corner of her eye, bright red flared. Turning, she watched as the lights of a tow truck appeared at the end of the street. While the mechanic parked, she walked back quickly and stuffed the panties into her cardigan pocket.

She waited in the Escalade as he changed the battery. Afterward, she paid with her credit card, and he handed her the paperwork. "That car is less than two years old," he told her. "The battery should have been fine. If I were you, I'd contact the dealership. This is probably still under warranty."

"Understood. Thank you." She watched him climb into his truck.

While he had worked on her SUV, the last of the afternoon light had faded. She was horribly, unforgivably late.

When she arrived home, the house was ablaze with lights. Austin had fixed the tripped electrical circuit. High-end cars lined the side of the long driveway and the street.

His important dinner party had started. The white wine hadn't been taken from the cooler, so it would be too cold. The hors d'oeuvres hadn't been baked, the cake hadn't been iced, and there had been no one to cook the chicken.

She certainly hadn't showered, nor had she put on makeup. She caught a glimpse of her appearance in her side mirror. She looked like a half-drowned rat.

Okay, she thought. What am I going to do now?

I could go in the back way, slip upstairs and clean up, go back down and make my excuses. Austin will be furious, but he'll hide it with warm smiles and a kiss on the cheek.

Afterward, he'll lecture me. He might yell a bit. I could make up some lie about going to help a friend in trouble, tell the truth about my car breaking down, and the whole thing would blow over.

But no. I don't think so.

She strode for the front door, picking up speed as she went, while the frozen lump in her chest melted into something hot and volcanic. Anger felt like a wild animal living in her chest. It made her strides long and powerful.

In the door.

Past well-dressed, startled people. Molly let the rage take over while she hovered high in one corner of her mind, watching.

The colors of the guest's clothes seemed garish, too bright. Many of the women were beautiful, their painted mouths forming words as they stared at her, some catty and judging, others disturbed. Was the owner of the panties here? Possibly.

She stalked past partners in Austin's firm and their significant others. Select clients. Judge Mallory. Somewhere, the new DA, Josiah Mason, would be mingling. A real up-and-comer, people called him. A man to be careful around. A man to watch.

Everyone had drinks. Several people called out questions and greetings, but she didn't answer. She had a single objective.

She found Austin talking to Russell Sherman, the managing partner of the firm, and a tall, imposing man she didn't recognize. When she drew close, the three turned to her. Her sense of disconnection vanished, and suddenly she slammed back into her body again.

Austin's handsome face creased in a smile while his sharp gaze looked murderous. "There you are, honey. What happened? I was getting worried about y—"

As he talked, she reached out and dropped the wadded-up panties in his martini glass. His words cut off, like flying birds shot out of the sky.

"You broke my heart the first time you cheated on me," she told him. "Broke it into a million pieces. I was only twenty-one and a junior in college. You were twenty-two and had just graduated, and we'd only been together for a year. But you were *so* sorry, and oh Lord, my mother was *so* damn insistent. So I stayed and gave you another chance." She turned to Russell and the powerful-looking stranger who stood beside him. "He can be persuasive, can't he?"

Russell stared at her like she had turned into a rattlesnake, while the new, unknown man watched her with an impassive gaze. He had a hard, strong-boned face that was distinctive rather than classically handsome. In her mind's eye, he seemed to shimmer with a dark essence, as if he was a polished onyx that caught the light while all the people around him faded into the background like flat paper dolls in a book that told someone else's story.

"Molly," said Russell with an embarrassed laugh and a sideways glance around the quieting room. "This is neither the time nor the place."

Her voice sliced across his. "This is exactly the right time and place."

Russell turned away, moving his square, bulky body like a weapon. In a low voice, he said to Austin, "Get her under control."

Austin had whitened. His jaw clenched, and his eyes burned with a promise of retribution. Grabbing her arm with hard fingers that bit into the muscles of her biceps, he muttered, "We're going into the kitchen. Now."

Fury erupted, filling her body with a flash fire. She actually saw sparks of light like lightning at the edges of her vision.

Jerking her arm free, she hissed, "I believe the legal definition of assault is laying hands on another person without their permission. Or is that battery? I can never keep those two straight. Touch me again, and I'll call the police."

Red spots of hectic color burned in his taut face. He bit out, "Have you lost your fucking mind?"

Over his shoulder, she caught sight of the antique Japanese Satsuma vase he had given her as a wedding present twenty years ago. They had gone to Japan on their honeymoon and discovered the vase while shopping. It had cost so much money she had walked away from it, but Austin had returned to the shop to purchase it for her.

She had felt so happy then. So full of faith in their future, the shadow of his first infidelity buried well and truly in the past.

She focused all her rage and hurt on that vase. The specks of lightning at the edges of her eyesight flared, and something—*some indefinable, invisible thing*—shot out of her body like a thunderbolt.

Across the room, the vase slammed into the wall and shattered, and the stand toppled over.

Hey, she thought. Wait. I… Did I do that? *How the hell did I do that?*

She stared numbly at the destruction while the rest of the world faded into swirls of people exclaiming and muttering in the background. Some of the dinner-party guests were slipping out the front door while others lingered to stare.

The imposing stranger regarded the fallen vase, then turned to look at her, a corner of his mouth tilting up. Against a deep suntan, his knowledgeable eyes looked yellow like a cat's. Reaching to his forehead with long fingers, he tilted an invisible hat at her.

Austin broke the throbbing tension with a loud laugh. "I guess we should have gotten someone to fix the wobble in that vase stand," he said in a voice pitched to carry across the silent room. "Tell you what, everybody, it's abundantly clear Molly and I are having a rough moment. Why don't you all head to the bar in the other room? Russell will serve you up whatever you desire while my wife and I resolve this."

That snapped her focus back into place.

"Because resolving *this* should only take five minutes or so?" Her acidic retort caused his head to rear back.

"Where is your Xanax?" he muttered.

"You think *drugging me* is the way to deal with this?" Raising her voice, she said clearly, "The second time you cheated on me, I cried for weeks. You didn't know I found out. I was too… something. I don't even know what the word is. There you were, going through your life with your dick hanging out of your pants, and I was too scared or intimidated or heartsick to confront you. I felt like a failure. I thought it had to be at least partly my fault. I had fallen out of love with you by then, but I still tried to make our life together work. I'm not a quitter, I said. I would stick it out. For better or worse, right?"

As she watched, the embarrassed anger in Austin's face switched to uncalculated fury. "You frigid bitch," he spat out. "You don't know the meaning of the word *love.* Everything always has to be portioned out with you, balanced on some kind of invisible scale. I had to earn every fuck I got from you."

His words sank invisible claws deep and tore at her, underneath her unmarked skin. Her face burned with greater fury and humiliation.

She made her shaking lips form words. "The second time you cheated. That was when I knew I didn't want to have children. Years passed, and now here we are. I'm almost forty, you're over forty. And I'm looking back over the past twenty years of my life, and all I can think is what a goddamn waste, and *none* of it was my fault."

He barked out a harsh laugh. "You're delusional."

"Did I ever cheat on you?" she snapped. "*Did I?*"

"Of course you didn't," he growled. "You barely knew how to part your legs."

The calculated cruelty in his words shredded every tender memory they had shared—every tender moment she had thought they had shared—and the depth of his anger confounded her. She felt wounded and bloodied. Was she really that cold and inflexible? That unlovable?

No. She would not let him do this to her.

Pulling herself together, she thrust away the pain, took a step forward and stabbed at his chest. "Quit trying to justify what you did by tearing me down. I was the *perfect wife.* I was great in bed, I took all the right classes, and I worked out and kept my figure. I was patient, and I learned how to cook all the right things. I always put your career first, and for what? You are a goddamn waste of space, and I am done living a cliché."

"Jesus, you two," Russell growled, shouldering his blunt figure between them. "Will you quit burning down your lives in front of everybody and shut the fuck up?"

Awareness pierced the anger in Austin's gaze, and he looked mortified. That did her hurting heart a little bit of good.

"I don't think so," she told Russell. Underneath everything else, she saw the surprise in both Austin's and Russell's eyes that she would dare to talk back to the managing partner. Turning her attention back to Austin, she shouted, "You had that woman in my house. In my bed. *No, I will not shut the fuck up!*"

"Forget about the bar," Russell said to the strange man. "This evening is over. We should be going."

"No, you gentlemen go ahead and stay," Molly said. She glared at Austin until his gaze slid away. "There's a lot of booze in the house, and I'm sure Austin could use some commiseration over his frigid bitch of a wife who won't spread her legs or shut up when she's told to. I'll be the one who leaves."

Turning away, she charged through the people who still remained and jogged up the stairs to the master suite. Moving swiftly, she pulled out her suitcases and threw things in. Underwear, casual clothes, shoes, toiletries…

She needed all her jewelry. There was quite a bit of money tied up in it, and she wouldn't leave a single piece behind.

What else, what else? What are you supposed to take with you when you burn down your life?

Financial documents.

Right now Austin was busy dealing with the important people and contacts in his professional life, trying to smooth over a mortifying situation. But when he had time to think, he would think like a lawyer.

She took her suitcases down the back stairs. She could hear a few voices still talking at the front of the house.

Leaving the cases by the back door, she strode into Austin's office, opened the floor safe, and stuffed everything into a large leather satchel without examining it—investment portfolios, car titles, CDs, cash, wills, advance directives, both of their passports.

He wasn't going anywhere in a hurry. He needed to stay and face whatever happened next.

After she had cleaned out the safe, she shut it and dug the household checkbook out of the upper drawer of Austin's desk. First thing in the morning, she would go to the bank and transfer their liquid assets into her own bank account. He had enough to clean up from the fallout of this evening. Relationships to bolster. No doubt a mistress to complain to. With any luck, he wouldn't expect her to move so fast.

While she worked, wetness streamed down her face

and her emotions raged all over the place, rampant and chaotic. Pain and self-recrimination were a large part of it.

She was almost forty years old and childless, with a patchwork history of working part-time at various socially acceptable jobs and volunteering at socially acceptable charities. She had spent all her adult life trying to fit into the right-sized box.

Somehow she needed to unchain her mind. Needed to discover her authentic self and try to live *that* Molly's life, before it was too late.

Slinging the leather satchel onto one shoulder, she slipped into the kitchen. Just before she pulled her suitcases out the door, she looked around one last time.

The kitchen counters were littered with open bottles, glasses, trays of uncooked pastry puffs, the bare vanilla-berry cake. Austin had a mess on his hands. That, along with work, would be more than enough to distract him while she took care of business in the morning.

All those empty bedrooms in a showcase house, and he had to take that other woman into hers. All those empty, childless bedrooms. One last wave of rage and pain burst through her.

The kitchen lights flickered. As the entire house fell into darkness, she wheeled her suitcases into the rainy night. Nobody approached as she threw her luggage into the back of the Escalade and climbed in. Relief washed over her raw nerves as she drove away.

The SUV's headlights lit the edges of the wet,

burgeoning foliage that hemmed the neighborhood streets. Black pressed on the other side of overhanging branches, turning sights that had been long familiar strange, until it felt as if she traveled down a secret tunnel.

Immense shapes seemed to lurk in the trees. She thought she saw a wolf watching her, and a raven. Each one melted back into leaves and shadows as she drove past it.

Then she broke out of the foliage into an open area by the entrance to the interstate. Massive relief lifted her up, as if she had traveled an unimaginable distance and crossed an invisible border to a new country.

After a single glance back at the forest from which she had emerged, she turned onto the highway and drove into the city.

She thought, I'm almost forty years old and I'm just being born.

RUSSELL SHERMAN WASN'T the type to let go easily once he had his mind fixed on something. He had his mind fixed on forging a connection with Josiah, and he held on like an octopus gripping with all tentacles.

In the end, however, he didn't hold a candle to Josiah's force of will. After finally extricating himself, Josiah drove swiftly, taking a circuitous route as his mind filled with images from the wrecked dinner party, like lurid snapshots of a crime scene.

The district attorney had a two-bedroom loft apartment in an upscale building near downtown Atlanta, and it was filled with carefully curated items. Josiah also owned an old four-bedroom, two-story house outside the city limits that he had bought under a different identity, and that was where he drove now.

The house was located down a quiet country lane that dead-ended at the property. It had a three-quarter-acre yard that bordered a large farm field and a patch of old-growth woods. The isolation and privacy suited him.

This place, too, had carefully curated furniture—just enough arranged at the front window so that the house looked occupied when the blinds were up. Aside from a few lamps that were scattered throughout the rooms and set to operate on timers, most of the house was empty.

Except for the basement.

Pulling into the driveway, he mentally checked the subtle magical spells that he had woven around the perimeter of the property. Nothing had been disturbed. Still, he didn't relax until he had let himself inside and walked through the house to inspect it visually. Only then did he descend the old, bare-wood stairs into the basement.

Months of planning and work had gone into this space. When he had bought the house, there had been a utilitarian bathroom and a large game room in the basement. Now there were two finished rooms, with more protection and obscuring spells layered over the floors, walls, and ceiling and anchored into place by runes made of magic-sensitive silver.

The earth itself was another layer of protection and concealment. You could do a lot of magic in a basement before it began to leak out and became potentially noticeable to outside observers.

This was his real base of operations. One room held a bed that was large enough to be comfortable for his tall frame, a closet filled with clothes, a nightstand, and a bedside lamp.

The other room was larger. At one end it held three computers, several phones, and a monitor for the extensive security system he had installed. The other end held magical paraphernalia—all his current tools—along with a large floor safe that held the more dangerous items. He always locked the safe and the door to the room before he left.

There were two ways to enter or exit the basement. One was the obvious way, by using the old stairs that led up to the large empty kitchen. Josiah had created the other way, which was part of the reason it had taken so long to adapt the space to suit his needs.

After chiseling out a hole in the concrete wall of the basement, he had patiently dug a tunnel that came out under the cover of the thick tangle of old-growth forest behind the house. No one in the basement was going to get trapped in an underground space if he could avoid it.

He owned still other properties in other areas that he had bought under yet other names. Many of those properties had undergone similar adaptations, but none of them were relevant to his current persona as Josiah Mason.

Sitting in front of one of the computers, he conducted an internet search on Molly Sullivan and scrolled through local news articles and photos. Most of the hits were from society pages or charities.

She was right—she *was* the perfect wife, especially for a law partner at a high-profile firm. At least on the surface. In the photos she was cool, elegant, and composed, completely unlike the haggard, angry woman who had confronted Austin with such steely determination.

He picked up one of the phones and punched a number set on speed dial. When the person on the other end picked up, he said, "Change of plans."

"Okay," the man said. "What's up?"

"Build a file on a woman named Molly Sullivan. Blond, blue eyes, five ten or so, between thirty-five and forty-five, wife to Austin Sullivan from Sherman & Associates." At least for now. "Dig into her past and her known associates, but most especially, find out where she lands tonight. She left her husband after a messy, public confrontation at the party I attended. I want to know where she goes and what she does next."

"I'm on it." The man disconnected.

Josiah tossed the phone onto the desk and sat back, the fingers of one hand hooked over his mouth as he studied the image of the beautiful woman on his computer screen.

He had meticulously planned for so many contingencies, but he had not planned for this.

"You're quite a complication, Molly Sullivan," he murmured. "Now I have to figure out what to do about you."

Chapter Two

HOURS LATER, MOLLY had checked into a hotel suite and unpacked what she had stuffed into her suitcases, such as it was.

She hadn't been as clear thinking as she'd thought. She had packed her toothbrush but hadn't grabbed a tube of toothpaste. She had swept her cosmetics into a bag, but her facial cleanser had been sitting by her sink and she'd missed it.

She didn't have the Xanax. She had packed a single shoe, not a pair, but at least she had the athletic sneakers she was wearing. And she had forgotten to grab any of her bras. She had her bathrobe, jeans and T-shirts, a light jacket, and a dove-gray two-piece suit to go with her single shoe.

At least she'd grabbed the most important things. She tossed the leather satchel full of the contents from the safe onto the table, unexamined. Then the fury that had propelled her forward ebbed, and her emotional landscape crashed.

A single comfort existed. It felt good to be somewhere Austin couldn't find her, existing in the cool silence of a strange place. Temporary as it was, this was her space, and she finally felt like she could breathe again.

Calling the concierge desk, she requested an overnight bag of toiletries, then she called room service to order a dinner she didn't think she could eat along with a bottle of wine that she had every intention of drinking.

After that, she wandered through the rooms, unable to sit or focus. She felt torn in two, as if the old Molly was starting to rip away from the person who now lived inside her skin, while bits and pieces of the scene at the party replayed in her head.

Jesus, she thought. The things we hurled at each other.

I am *not* a frigid bitch. I did not deserve any of this.

But Austin's words had burrowed inside like poisonous worms, causing tissue damage in all her most vulnerable places, and as she looked out the window at the impenetrable night, the doubtful thoughts wouldn't stop.

Did I really make him feel like he had to earn affection from me? she wondered. Did I really portion it out and make my love conditional, like my mom did with me? Or did he fire that salvo because he knew it was the one thing that would hurt the most?

Her breathing roughened, and tears burned at the back of her eyes until her attention snagged on the one anomaly from the whole debacle.

The vase. How had it broken? No one had been standing anywhere near it.

Why do I feel like... maybe I did that?

I'm not crazy. I'm not. Something came out of me. What was that *indefinable, invisible thing*?

And why did that man look at me with such a knowing expression? Russell called him Josiah. He must be the new DA. Why did he tip an imaginary hat to me? It's almost as if he also knew I broke the vase. Which is patently impossible. Isn't it?

She pressed her hands over her eyes, remembering the sparks of light at the edges of her sight and the burst of energy that had shot out of her body just before the vase crashed into a million irreparable pieces. Was she quite sure she wasn't going crazy?

The angry hornet of her phone wouldn't stop buzzing. Grabbing it, she checked the screen. There were many more texts and calls than before, and a low-battery warning that said she had less than ten percent power.

A power cord was another thing she hadn't thought to grab. She made another call to the concierge desk. Then she sat, cupping the phone in her hands and staring into space until a knock sounded at her door and everything she had ordered arrived.

After eating a few bites of pasta and drinking most of the wine, she finally felt calm enough to shower and fall into bed. As soon as her head hit the pillow, she went out like a light.

After a formless darkness, she found herself in a

kitchen.

It was large and Victorian, decorated with yellow-patterned tiles and pale green paint. Warm sunlight streamed through tall windows while, outside, someone was gardening. A man with shaggy blond hair walked by, carrying a rake over one broad shoulder.

A woman stood cooking at a clunky, ancient gas stove, her back turned to Molly. Graying hair tumbled down her back. She had a round, comfortable figure, and she wore an old flowered housecoat.

"You're a noisy one," the woman said. Her rich, warm voice washed over Molly's shattered nerves like a soothing balm. "Woke me out of a sound sleep, you did. I thought since I was awake, I might as well scramble a few eggs."

"I'm sorry if I woke you," Molly said. "I don't know how I got here."

"No? Well, don't fret about it," said the woman. "When are you coming to see me?"

"I don't know that either. I don't know who you are or where this is. Or, for that matter, what I'm doing here."

As Molly looked around, she realized she was sitting on a tall stool at a large butcher-block table in the middle of the kitchen. She was wearing the T-shirt she had worn to bed, and her legs were bare. Embarrassed, feeling exposed, she hooked her heels on the edge of her chair and tucked her knees under the shirt.

"Don't fret about that either," the woman said. She

turned off the stove, stepped away from an iron skillet, and bent over an old stone bowl. "It will come clear with time. Ah yes, I think this spell is about ready now."

"Excuse me, you didn't just say *spell*, did you?"

"As a matter of fact, I did."

"Now I know I'm dreaming," Molly muttered. She didn't know anybody who could cast spells. She had met a few nonhumans over the years, but for the most part the worlds of the Elder Races and their demesnes were a reality that existed far away from her life.

The woman took something out of the bowl. Molly could smell a mixture of lavender and lemon along with a sharp, spicier scent she couldn't identify. Then, as the woman turned to face Molly, she brought her open palm up to her mouth and blew.

Molly caught a glimpse of dark, powerful eyes. Before she could get a good look at the woman's face, a cloud of spice and energy enveloped her.

The woman said, "*Find me.*"

Then the woman, along with the kitchen, faded away, and she slept deep and dreamlessly for the rest of the night.

✧ ✧ ✧

"MOLLY! WHAT ON earth are you doing?"

On Saturday, a swirl of Dior perfume wafted over the table as Julia Oliver threw herself into the seat opposite Molly. She was shorter than Molly, and petite, delicately rounded at breast and hip, with dark, curly hair tumbling down her back. Outside the restaurant, bright spring sunlight danced along the sidewalks.

"I'm reading the list of today's lunch specials," she said with a quick glance up and a brief, preoccupied smile. "What on earth are *you* doing?"

"That's not what I meant, and you know it." Julia looked up as the waitress came to the table. "I'll have a lemon drop martini."

Molly raised her eyebrows. So it was going to be that kind of lunch, was it? Why the hell not? She shut her menu with a snap. "I'll have the same."

Their waitress came back quickly with their drinks and took their lunch orders. When she had left, Julia leaned forward. "Everybody's talking about what happened at your place on Thursday evening."

"I'm sure they are." She stretched her neck from side to side to ease the tension in her muscles. She didn't want to be having lunch with Julia, but the woman had been her best friend for the past five years, and Molly didn't feel right *not* talking to her.

Julia's gaze was lit with scandalized horror. "Did you really drop some other woman's panties into Austin's drink?"

"Yes."

Julia looked down at her drink, touched the sugared rim, and delicately licked the tip of her finger. "Do you know who the other woman is?"

Molly shook her head. "No, although I'm guessing I've met her at some point. You know how actively we've been entertaining."

"And after you confronted him, you just walked out?"

"Yes," she said again. She took a gulp of her drink. Ah, alcohol.

"I wish Drew hadn't been so sick. If I could have, I would have been there for you."

"You couldn't very well leave your five-year-old with a babysitter when he was running a 102-degree temperature," she pointed out. "And besides, it's not like I planned any of it. It just happened."

"Well, I still wish I could have been there for you." Julia considered her. "But why didn't you call to tell me?" A hint of hurt crept into the other woman's voice.

Molly shrugged and looked around the restaurant. What could she say that would make any sense? That bizarre things kept happening around her and sometimes she thought she was going crazy while at other times she felt certain she was causing them? She had been working hard to hold everything together for the past few months, but Austin and his infidelity had sent her over some kind of edge.

Finally she replied, "I know you would have been there for me, but I was so exhausted, all I did was check into a hotel, order room service, and fall into bed. And yesterday I was busy. I had to go to the bank and look for a lawyer. In fact, I have an appointment with one on Monday. After that, I just slept."

She had been so tired. She had lain in bed watching

the reflected sunlight on the wall until the room slowly fell into darkness.

She was still so tired. She felt like she could sleep for weeks.

"So you're doing it." Julia watched her face closely. "You're really leaving him."

She nodded. "I've already left. Now I'm going to divorce him."

Julia's expression twisted, a brief response, and then it smoothed over. "Good riddance then. I always said you deserve worlds better than Austin. But where are you staying?"

"Like I said." She shrugged. "At a hotel."

"Would you please come stay with us, so I can make you home-cooked meals and hopefully put a little meat on those bird bones of yours? Austin and Philip might be partners in the same firm, but you know how men are. They compartmentalize. They'll keep the private stuff separate from work."

"That means a lot." Feeling warmed, Molly smiled. "But I'm quite comfortable at the hotel. I've got one of their executive suites with a kitchenette."

Julia's hazel gaze was serious. "You're still welcome anytime. I want you to know that."

"I do." Molly looked down at her napkin, smoothing the edges with her fingers. "You might as well know I'm thinking about leaving Atlanta too."

"Noooo." Julia's pretty mouth turned down at the corners. "You're just reacting, that's all. And it's understandable. Austin acted like a pig, but this is your home. Your friends are here. Your *life* is here. Your mother's only forty-five-minutes away!"

Biting her lip, Molly waited until Julia sputtered into silence. Then she said, "My life as I knew it is over. It was slowly smothering me anyway, and I *want* it to be over. I'm not flying off the handle or doing anything impulsive. I just can't imagine staying."

With a tiny lunge forward, Julia grabbed her hand again. Julia touched people. Molly had seen her do the same thing a dozen times before.

"That's just how you feel today," Julia insisted. "Everything has got to be feeling off right now."

Not wanting to argue further, Molly nodded. "You have a point. In my mind, Atlanta has this huge cloud of unhappiness hanging over it. Eventually I'll figure out what I need to do. It just may not be here, that's all."

"I find this totally unacceptable," Julia declared while tears sprang to her eyes.

Molly caught their waitress's eye and tapped the rim of her glass. The waitress smiled and nodded.

Halfway through their second lemon drop, Julia said bitterly, "You're going to go off and find yourself and leave me here to be a corporate law partner's wife without you. I'll bet you're going to eat all the calories you want and stop shaving your legs and wearing a bra, and you're probably going to have one-night stands with sweaty mechanics in small towns."

Despite herself, Molly burst out laughing. "You

never know, I might."

She had a doctor's appointment after lunch, so she said goodbye to Julia and went in for her checkup. And since she had no idea how often Austin had cheated on her or with whom, she had her doctor run tests for HIV and STDs. Again.

Then she spent the afternoon shopping for the various items she needed. She could have gone back to the house to pick up her own things, but the thought of possibly running into Austin made her feel nauseated and furious. Tiny sparks appeared again at the corner of her vision, and she thought she might stroke out.

Eventually she would have to go back to the house. Probably.

She could technically survive without ever going back, but later on she would regret not picking up the box of childhood mementos and the photos of her late father.

Maybe Julia would go with her and help run interference, or even go in her stead to gather up everything Molly wanted to keep. She hated to involve someone else in her personal drama, but she didn't think the other woman would mind.

As the afternoon went on, the pleasant buzz from the lunchtime martinis wore off, leaving her feeling headachy and dull.

She headed back to the hotel and stopped at the bellhop desk in the spacious hotel lobby to have her shopping bags delivered to her room. When she turned away, she noticed the doorway that led to the hotel bar.

The open space seemed to beckon invitingly, and she gave in to the impulse to go inside. Maybe the sugar and caffeine from a Coke would banish her hangover.

As she stepped across the threshold from the lobby into the bar, a change occurred that was hard to define. The air felt different—cooler and sharper, full of energy. Her headache vaporized.

If the bar manager could bottle whatever was in the air, he would make a fortune. Inhaling deeply, she straightened her shoulders and looked around.

Dark cherry tables lay scattered over a patterned tile floor. Several of the tables were occupied. The bar itself was made of the same wood as the tables, and light reflected off shelves of colored bottles of liquor and the mirrored wall behind them, making everything seem hard and bright.

A solitary, dark-haired man sat at the bar, his long, folded figure indicating height and broad shoulders. As she glanced at him, he looked up from his drink and into the mirror.

His eyes, yellow like a cat's in a lean, suntanned face, met hers.

Surprise throbbed a single pulse beat throughout her body. Josiah Mason, Atlanta's new DA, lounged at the bar as if he owned it. As if he were waiting for something or someone.

Seeing him here, in a place she had unconsciously claimed as her own, brought back the sickened adrenaline from Thursday night. She fought an instinctive urge to bolt.

Leveling a long look at him, she thought, I'll be damned if I run. She gave him a civil nod and walked to the bar several seats away to settle on a stool and set her purse beside her.

When the bartender came to take her order, all her good intentions to avoid more alcohol vaporized. "I'll take a single malt scotch. Your best one."

"We have a twenty-one-year-old Balvenie, will that do?"

She raised her eyebrows. "Yes."

"You got it." He slouched away.

While she waited for her drink, she spread her hands flat on the smooth, gleaming wood surface of the bar.

Coincidences happen, she told herself. Don't look at him again. Look at your hands. People wig out and scream at their husbands at dinner parties all the time. You have nothing to be ashamed of. Austin is the one at fault, not you.

Besides, maybe he won't recognize you. You look completely different than you did at the party. This is no big deal.

Movement in the mirror caught her attention. Out of the corner of her eye, she watched as Josiah Mason slid out of his seat with casual grace. He wore jeans and a thin cream sweater that looked like it was cashmere and highlighted his healthy tan. Dark hair swept back from his strong forehead in a long, unruly wave.

He approached. Of course he approached. Her hands clenched. Damn it to hell, why was he ignoring the *go away* vibes she threw so strenuously into the air? Anybody with discretion or good sense would avoid her like the plague after witnessing her meltdown.

He was a powerfully built man, and he moved with the sinuous grace of a jaguar. He looked like he could take down any opponent in a championship boxing match. Like he could kill someone if he wanted.

As he neared, she felt the same thing she had sensed on Thursday, that he emitted some kind of dark, intense frequency that made everybody else in the bar appear pale and flat, like paper dolls. This man would re-form reality wherever he went.

Without asking permission, he slid into the empty stool beside her. When the bartender set her drink down, she signed for it, then wrapped both hands around the glass and clutched it as if it were her lifeline. Just stay calm and breathe normally, she thought.

In a low voice, she said, "I am intensely uncomfortable with you coming to join me."

"And I am positive you will survive it." His voice was deeper than she had expected. With a small jolt, she realized this was the first time she had heard him speak. "We haven't been properly introduced."

"I know who you are." She took a big gulp of the Balvenie. Fruity and smoky, the scotch glided down her throat as smoothly as a hunting knife sliding into a sheath. Warmth suffused her middle, spreading outward like a fresh pool of blood. She had turned unexpectedly morbid. "People call you hot shit, or so I've heard."

That probably shouldn't have slipped out of her mouth. Day drinking wreaked havoc on impulse control.

As she watched in the mirror, one corner of his long mouth tilted up. He didn't have yellow eyes so much as amber. They seemed brighter when the light hit them just right.

"I prefer Josiah." His strong throat muscles worked as he took a swallow of his own drink. It was something clear and bubbly on ice with a slice of lime, probably a gin and tonic, or vodka. Or maybe it was soda water. He didn't look like the kind of man who would enjoy losing control to outside influences.

"When I walked in here, it looked like you were waiting for someone." She took another swallow of her scotch. "Josiah."

His voice turned cold. "Don't be coy, Molly. It doesn't suit you."

Wait, *what?*

Sudden caution caused her to tense. He couldn't mean that he had been waiting for her. Could he? If so, that was insane, ridiculous. How could he have known that she was going to walk into the bar on impulse?

A chill ran over her skin. Had he been looking for her? If so, *how had he found her? And why?*

She realized she knew next to nothing about the man sitting beside her. Matching his tone with her own coldness, she replied, "How can you possibly know what does or does not suit me?"

"I came to apologize." He leaned his elbows on the bar. "When I cast a spell of finding, I didn't sense any witches of significant Power in Atlanta, which was one of the reasons why I moved here. If I had known you were here, I would never have intruded into your territory. Now that I'm here, I'm hoping you and I can come to some agreement about coexisting in the same city."

Spell of finding… What the fuck?

Witch.

The word reverberated in her head, drowning out the music and the sounds of nearby conversation. Carefully, she set her glass of scotch on the bar, reached for her purse, and began to slide off her stool.

"I have no earthly idea what you're talking about," she enunciated to the calm, sane-looking lunatic who sat beside her. "You have me confused with someone else. Please excuse me."

Swiveling with a speed that took her by surprise, he stared at her as if she were the lunatic. The dark slants of his eyebrows rose, and he began to smile, making him look more dangerous than ever.

"You have no idea?" he repeated. "*You. Have. No. Idea.*"

"Okay, nice talking to you." She backed away. "You have a good night now."

He said something swift and unintelligible. The words were strange, perhaps in some foreign language, and the sound sizzled through the air like broiling steak.

A shimmering, transparent barrier sprang up around her and Josiah, separating them from the rest of the bar. All other sounds cut off, and suddenly it was so silent she could hear her own quickened breathing. She stared around her, wild-eyed.

He had created it. She knew he had. She could sense the connection between the strange words and the barrier, and how it had all originated from him.

How could she feel that? How had he created it? Would it hurt her if she touched it? Was she trapped here, unable to leave?

With a smile, Josiah walked up until he stood very close, inside her personal space. The light hit his eyes just right, making them flare with lambent color. Shaking, she stared up at him. His body heat warmed her chilled skin.

Watching her intently, he put his hand on her forearm and slid long fingers down to her hand. Calluses rasped her skin. He closed his hand carefully around hers and lifted it. She tensed to resist yet didn't.

He took their combined hands and pushed them gently through the barrier. She flinched as her skin came into contact with it. It felt slightly cold, almost like a soap bubble. She stared as their hands passed through harmlessly.

"There's no reason to be afraid. It won't hurt you." His tone had lowered, to either accommodate their proximity or the intense silence that enfolded them. "It's a privacy spell. You're the only one here with the ability to see or sense it. Nobody else is paying any attention to us, and now they can't hear a word we say to each other."

"How did you do that?" But she already knew. He had cast the spell with those strange-sounding words.

"I can show you, if you like, but not if you run away."

She only realized he was still touching her when he slid his hand back up her arm, grasped her elbow, and urged her back to the bar.

"Sit and drink your scotch, although we should be opening a bottle of champagne. It's not every day one runs into an awakening witch."

Chapter Three

JOSIAH WATCHED MOLLY Sullivan's beautiful, dazed face in fascination. She really hadn't had any idea about what was happening to her or what she was capable of.

"You mean *me*." Molly seemed barely able to articulate as she slid back onto the barstool. "You can't be serious. This can't be happening."

"I'm deadly serious, and of course it's happening." He sat on the stool beside her again and swiveled to face her. "Some part of you has to know I'm telling the truth."

Casting another glance at the shimmering barrier, she held herself rigid. Her expression was unpredictable, as if she might bolt at any minute. He couldn't tell if she was panicking, but she probably was.

An unpleasant thought occurred to him. Those with magic abilities tended to congregate in magic-tolerant areas, such as close to the heart of the Elder Races demesnes, which existed overlaid with human geography. There were seven demesnes in the United States alone and many others scattered across the globe.

If they didn't live close to an Elder Races demesne, they often chose to live close to the crossover passageways that had been created when time and space buckled during the earth's formation. The crossover passageways led to magic-intense Other lands, where time moved differently, modern combustible technologies didn't work, and the sun shone with a different light.

But the magic-intolerant, or those who had xenophobic tendencies, tended to congregate in other areas, away from the demesnes and crossover passageways. The United States had seen a backlash of opinion against the Elder Races or anyone with magical talent, and Atlanta wasn't an area known for tolerance.

By far, most of the city's demographic was made up of plain old nonmagical humanity, and the area's voting majority was not pro-magic. Molly was going to live a miserable life if she couldn't come to terms with what she was experiencing.

"Look at me," he commanded.

Her widened gaze flew back to his.

"Something is happening to you." He leaned forward. "Maybe it was started by the trauma from your husband's betrayal, or maybe it's been happening over the past several months. Inexplicable occurrences… things like car breakdowns or power outages. You might be having strange dreams or seeing visions of things that can't possibly exist. Am I right?"

Her blank expression fractured, and her lips

trembled. She whispered, "It's been a couple of months now."

He pinched the bridge of his nose. She was turning out to be surprise upon surprise, all of it entirely unwelcome.

After a moment, he told her, "When you broke that vase on Thursday, I thought you were venting your rage in a way that wouldn't hurt anybody. It never occurred to me that you had no idea what you were capable of or what you'd done." He couldn't stand to look at her devastated face any longer, so he pressed the tumbler of scotch into her hands.

She blew out an unsteady breath and accepted it. In a quick move, she tossed back the rest of the drink. "I felt it," she confessed hoarsely. "I saw sparks at the edges of my vision, and I *knew* something had shot out of my body. And then the vase shattered."

"Yes." He nodded. Obeying an impulse he didn't stop to define, he touched her warm, soft skin, rubbing the sensitive spot at her inner elbow with his thumb. "That was you. There isn't one in a hundred thousand people like you. Not one in a million, possibly ten million. You hold an incredibly rare Power, and you're just now coming into it."

Carefully, she pulled away to run her fingers through her hair. "But this doesn't make any sense," she muttered. "We don't have witches in my family history, or any mention of magic whatsoever. We're just your ordinary, garden-variety humans."

"You may not have witches *that you know of*," he replied drily. "That doesn't mean you didn't have any. Witches have been known to conceal their true natures so they can coexist peacefully with magic-intolerant families and communities."

He watched his last statement slam home, and her expression filled with dismay. "But why me? Why now?"

He shrugged. "I don't think anybody knows. Everyone's different. Sometimes witches manifest early, from the time they're toddlers. Some come into their Power when they hit puberty. Others come into it later in life through personal trauma, like the death of a spouse or child, or a strong life shift like menopause."

"But what about the old family dynasties in the witches demesne—in Louisville, right?" she asked. "They seem to have witches in every generation, or at least that's what I've read."

"Those families have carefully married and bred to strengthen their magical aptitude, but that isn't any guarantee. Sometimes even the most Powerful families in the witches demesne can produce null offspring." After pausing, he continued more slowly, "I didn't have any history of known witches in my family either, but many years ago I was in an accident that put me into a coma for two weeks. When I came out of it, I was permanently changed."

She dug the heels of her hands into her eyes. "Is there any way to stop this?" she asked. "Any way to turn it off?"

He laughed, genuinely amused. "Of course not. Why on earth would you want to?"

"Maybe because it's scary as hell?" she retorted. "I don't want to blow fuses or have my car break down randomly, or possibly hurt someone without meaning to."

He sobered. "No, definitely not. You don't want to hurt someone by accident. Everything you do, you want to do with intention."

She looked more spooked than ever. "But I don't understand what's really happening or how to control it." Her voice rose. "I know nothing. This is the first time anyone has said anything to me about any of this!"

"In some ways you're a blank slate," he murmured as he studied her with an assessing gaze. While discovering her had been a massive inconvenience, maybe he could make it work to his advantage. "You're coming into so much magic it radiates out of you. You're going to be a very Powerful witch. The only way you can hope to control it is through training."

"Training." She leaned forward. "What kind of training?"

The intense kind that reshapes your life. He thought it, but he didn't say it.

Instead, he replied, "Practice, technique, and spellwork will help you gain control over your own Power. How long that takes is up to you. If you're dedicated and focused, it will happen quicker." His gaze narrowed as he considered the idea that had occurred to him. Unlike the other surprises, this one was not entirely unwelcome. "I could teach you."

"You could?" She looked even more astonished.

He poked harder at the idea. He hadn't planned on taking a student, and in many ways, it would be a hindrance to his goals, but with the kind of uncontrolled Power she was radiating right now, she was like a human Chernobyl. Unless she gained control over herself, she was going to draw unwanted attention to the area—attention he wasn't yet ready to face.

"Think of everything we could do." He studied her as he calculated this new turn of events. "Together, we could become a major force on the Eastern Seaboard if we wanted to—we'd be right up there with the Lord of the Wyr or the Elven High Lord."

She coughed out a disbelieving laugh. "Become a major force on the Eastern Seaboard? Where the hell did that come from?"

His eyelids lowered to hide his expression. "I have ambitions."

She shook her head. "My life is in shambles right now. This is too much to take in all at once. I didn't ask for any of it."

"You may not have asked for it, but you've got it." He took hold of her hand and gripped her fingers. "With my training and guidance, there's no limit to what you can do. Doesn't that appeal to you on some level? Think of it—really take a moment and think."

She hesitated, clearly snared by his words, and her

gaze focused on their hands again.

Turning his voice deep and seductive, he said softly, "You want revenge against your husband for what he did to you? With some discipline, training, and a little work, it's all yours. You want to be wealthy and powerful? You can achieve it, and it's easier than you might think." Obeying the impulse to touch her again, he lifted one hand to brush his fingers against her petal-soft cheek. "Wouldn't you like to stay as youthful-looking and beautiful as you are now, for as long as possible? Powerful witches can live much longer than the normal human life span. I can show you how."

Moving as slowly as he had, she pulled her face away from his touch while her gaze never left his.

Giving her a crooked smile, he let his hand fall to his thigh. "I can show you how to get anything your heart desires. *Anything.* Working together, we can create a new future, the likes of which you can't even imagine."

But he had pushed too hard—he knew it the moment the words came out of his mouth. She jerked her hand out of his grip and slid off the barstool.

"This is too much to take in all at once," she said abruptly. "Thank you for coming to find me and explaining everything. At least I'm not going crazy. I think."

Josiah straightened to his full height. "You're welcome, but don't go just yet. We've barely scratched the surface of what you're going through. You're bound to have a thousand questions."

She laughed as she backed away. "That's a massive understatement. I have no doubt I will."

"Have dinner with me, and we can talk over everything in more depth." He advanced close enough to smell the faint, sexy perfume that she wore. By the flickering of her expression, he could tell that she wavered.

She even leaned toward him again, and a slow, triumphant smile widened his lips.

But letting his triumph show was another misstep. Her gaze dropped to his mouth, and she jerked back. "Not tonight. I have too much going on." She waved the fingers of one hand in a circle beside her temple. "It's a mess in here. I need to think."

He cursed inwardly. "You're making a mistake. You'll think better if you talk things out. I can explain anything you don't understand."

Just when he thought she was going to bolt, she did the exact opposite. She took a step toward him and gave him another level look while her Power flared. "I said no."

Immediately he backed off and gave her a slight smile. "So you did. Here." As she watched warily, he reached into his back pocket, pulled out a heavy white card, and handed it to her. "My personal cell phone number. Feel free to call anytime, day or night."

She hesitated to take it, her reluctance obvious.

An edge entered his voice. "It's an offer I don't make to very many people, Molly."

"No, I'm sure you don't," she replied. "Just one thing. Is there a spell on that card?"

Surprise jolted him. He narrowed his eyes. "Why do you ask?"

Her expression turned fierce. "Because you put a spell on this bar to draw me in, didn't you?"

Another surprise jolted him. "Good question, and a very good observation. Yes, I threw a spell to lure you into the bar, but if you had been strongly inclined to do otherwise, it wouldn't have worked. It was more like an invitation." He passed a hand over the card and erased the small spell he had cast on it. "Now this one is gone too."

Her hand rose and hovered in midair. "What was it?"

"Same type of thing. A small encouragement," he told her. "A welcome, if you will."

She studied his expression, clearly questioning the veracity of that, but it didn't stop her from snatching the card. "Thank you."

"You're welcome." He waved his fingers, and the privacy bubble that had surrounded them vanished. "Talk to you soon."

Giving him a jerky nod, she walked away. Her relief at leaving was so palpable his expression turned wry. Most women didn't try so hard to get away from him. In fact, most women looked for ways to get closer. Talking to Molly had been a reality check for his ego.

His phone buzzed. Pulling it out of his pocket, he checked the screen. There was a text from Anson. `Did` `you get a chance to talk to the Sullivan woman yet?`

Fingers moving rapidly, he replied, `Yes.`

`How'd it go?`

Pursing his lips, he considered how to answer, and his mood turned grim. `We might be facing trouble before we had expected. You'd better warn the others.`

And they weren't ready for trouble if it decided to show up soon.

Lost in thought, he drove to his apartment in the city. The DA needed to spend some time in his fashionable apartment before anyone noticed his absence and began to ask questions he didn't want to answer.

BACK IN HER hotel room, Molly threw the card on the table and spent the rest of the evening taking tags off her new purchases and putting them away.

Josiah claimed to have removed the spell on the card, and she couldn't sense anything, but it gleamed against the dark wood as if enticing her to pick it up again.

She had felt overwhelmed before and talking to him was the equivalent of having *another* tidal wave wash over her head, only this one was bigger than the first. Now she felt so far underwater she had no idea how to swim to the surface.

As he had painted the picture of a possible future in his compelling, rich voice, she could see everything play out like a movie.

A life with no limits. Hadn't part of her always yearned for that? She had made her choices and she had tried to stick to them. God, she had tried.

Austin had been her career. She had done everything from picking up dry cleaning to helping him make and foster the right connections. She had poured everything into his law practice, into building their life together.

In an age filled with takeout and professional catering, people had relished her sophisticated, home-cooked cuisine. She knew how to talk to legal professionals, and she had prided herself on being warm and welcoming to everyone.

But she hadn't been loved or valued. She had been someone to *get under control.* With a fierceness that made her shake, she wanted to hurt Austin the way he had hurt her over the years. She wanted to make him cry like a baby. And wouldn't it serve him right to see her thrive while he suffered?

Josiah had said she could be powerful in her own right. Buy her own fashionable house in an upscale neighborhood. Buy multiple houses in different parts of the world. She could have all the lovers she wanted and more money than she could ever need.

And while she'd been blessed with good genes and still looked youthful, over the past few years a couple of delicate lines had appeared at the corners of her mouth and eyes, and her blond hair had lightened at the temples. She hadn't gone gray, not yet, but she would if she didn't do something to hide it. Or maybe she could do something to stop it from happening entirely?

But something felt off. She had to pick through her reactions to figure out what it was.

For one thing, she didn't trust herself right now. Normally she wasn't vengeful, but she was too angry and hurt, and what sounded good in this moment might turn out to be just as toxic as what she was escaping.

And Josiah was sexy. Very sexy. She felt too raw to be comfortable with how part of her had liked it when he'd touched her. The gentle rasp of his callused fingers against her skin had been distinctly pleasurable. It had been a very long time since she had felt simple desire.

Something else made her uneasy. He had been too calculating, too pushy. At some point during their talk, he had come to a decision and had zeroed in on it like a heat-seeking missile. Powerful men did that. She had watched it happen before, and he had already said he had ambitions.

And even if everything he had told her had been the truth, she wasn't willing to become the consequence of another powerful man's decisions.

After settling that in her mind, she deleted all the texts, emails and phone messages clogging her phone.

Some were from her mother, and she bit back a sigh. Molly couldn't put off going to see her any longer. She would far rather communicate everything in an email, but she should tell her mother what had happened in person.

Or at least they needed to talk about how she had left Austin. Her mother was the quintessential conservative and had consistently voted against any political platform that promoted the interests of the Elder Races or magic users. It would be beyond disastrous to talk about witches, spells, and suddenly acquiring Power.

Ugh, ugh, ugh. Tomorrow was going to suck. Grimly, she got ready for bed, and later that night she dreamed again.

When she came to awareness, she was sitting at the butcher-block table again while the woman stood at the counter, chopping herbs. This time the woman wore jeans and a black T-shirt, and her graying hair had been piled into a knot on top of her head. Molly glanced out the window. There was no sign of the shaggy blond man. Instead, rain lashed against the glass panes. A storm was rolling in.

"You're a metaphor, aren't you?" She huddled into herself. "Something I've created. You, this kitchen, and everything in it—it's some kind of message I'm trying to tell myself."

The woman's voice was gentle. "Because everything is all about you?"

"No, of course not! But I'm making this dream up. Right?"

The woman shrugged. "If you say so."

Uneasily, she shifted and rubbed her bare arms. "If I'm not making it up… You put a spell on me to find you. Why?"

"Seemed like a good idea at the time." *Chop-chop-chop.* The herbs smelled good and fresh. Molly recognized the pungent, distinct scent of sage.

"What if something happens?" she persisted. "What if the spell breaks? What if I don't want to come? What if I don't want to be controlled?"

"The spell will work if you want it to." The woman gave her a reassuring smile. "And it won't if you don't. It's as simple as that. You'll find me when you're ready. Or not. It's entirely up to you."

Molly muttered, "I don't find that at all reassuring."

Throwing back her head, the woman laughed while outside the window lightning flashed. Then the scene fell away, leaving her even more in the dark than before.

She woke with another headache, and Sunday went from bad to worse.

Early in the morning, she set up the new laptop and portable printer she had purchased. Then she organized the contents of the satchel that contained everything from their safe and started scanning files.

As she worked, she found a set of papers in a folder she'd never seen before. They looked like copies of bank statements, but they were from no bank she knew. And the numbers listed were astronomical—in the millions.

Millions she'd had no idea existed.

A cold chill raised goose bumps along her skin. As a partner, Austin made mid-six figures annually, which was quite a fine income. They owned their house and hadn't worried about money for a long time.

She could afford to stay in a comfortable hotel, buy nice clothes, and eat good food. She could also afford to take time as she figured out her next steps, and she felt extremely grateful to have her needs met while dealing with the emotional fallout from the end of her marriage.

But those numbers… She couldn't imagine how he might have gained access to so much money.

She didn't have time to obsess over it. Quickly, she organized everything else, finished an Excel spreadsheet listing all the assets that had been in the safe, and emailed the spreadsheet to herself along with a zip file of the scanned documents.

Afterward, she showered and braced to face her mother.

Visiting her mother was always like taking a trip into the past. Gloria Addison still lived where she had when her husband Samuel had been alive. The old, spacious house was on the National Register of Historic Places and had been in the family for several generations.

As Molly parked, the front door opened. Gloria's silver hair had been meticulously arranged, and she wore a stylish gray-and-pink dress with matching low-heeled shoes.

"I wondered when you might finally show up." Gloria's voice was chilly, her back ramrod straight. Both were indicators of how the visit would go.

Molly bit back a sigh and walked into the house. "Hello, Mother."

Gloria led the way to the kitchen, and Molly followed. She slid into a seat at the table while Gloria put together two salads.

While she worked, Gloria said, "Austin called me yesterday."

Trying to remain calm, Molly rubbed her temples. Gloria had always approved of Austin. The fact that he had gotten in touch with her first put Molly even farther into the doghouse. "What did he say?"

"He was looking for you." Gloria pulled salad dressing out of the fridge. "He thought you might be staying here. He said you'd had a fight, but I already knew that. Melinda found out. Her son Graham is dating one of the Johnson girls that works at Austin's firm."

"I wondered if you'd heard something." Again, she lied. She had to find a way to stop that. Where was her authentic self when Molly needed her the most?

Her mother brought the salads over along with silverware and the dressings, then sat to eat. "So, have *you* talked to Austin?"

"No." She pushed the plate away.

"Well, don't you think it's time you did? You've had your fight, but it's over. Now it's time to move on. He's worried about you, and he's hurt."

No mention of Molly's feelings. No question about whether or not she might be hurt.

She asked, "Did Melinda tell you what the fight was about?"

Gloria speared a small, bite-sized piece of ham. "It

doesn't matter. It's all in the past. The important thing is that you work on fixing your marriage and look to the future."

Her blood pressure was rising with every passing minute. "I'm not going back to Austin. I'm filing for divorce."

Gloria's eyes flashed up. She set down her fork and knife. "Impossible. You can't. He's the breadwinner, and he has been for the past fifteen years. You haven't done anything in your life except support him."

"Yes, by all means." Her jaw angled out. "Let's ignore the fact that being a successful law partner's wife can be a full-time job in itself, or that I fundraised almost three hundred thousand dollars last year for a charity just by working as a part-time volunteer."

"None of that paid you a living wage." Gloria pointed at her. "You'll take him back if you know what's good for you. You'll never be able to get a job that will give you the lifestyle you've grown accustomed to."

Her temper started to bubble over. "I can't stand the thought of being in the same zip code with Austin, let alone trying to live in the same house or, my God, sleeping in the same bed again. The marriage has been over for a long, long time. I'm meeting with an attorney tomorrow. The money will work out somehow."

Gloria's gaze fired with an angry light. "I did not raise you to quit on your marriage just when things get tough."

"When things get tough?" she repeated

incredulously. "Mom, he *cheated* on me. *In my own bed.* He cheated on me *repeatedly*—and then he was verbally abusive about it. The only thing I regret is staying with him as long as I did when, deep down, I knew better."

"So he cheated on you," Gloria said bitterly. "Men cheat. It's what they do. You can't expect to find another man who will treat you any differently, and you're too old to start over. You have no real job experience, and your degree is eighteen years old. If you leave him, you're throwing your life away with both hands."

Halfway through Gloria's speech, Molly realized that once again her mother wasn't talking about her. Gloria was talking about herself.

"Mom, what are you saying? Did Dad cheat on you?"

Gloria looked down at her napkin as she folded it precisely. "Your father and I had our share of problems, but that's none of your business. He loved you, and he wanted the best for you, as do I. You're making a huge mistake, Molly Ann. Go back to Austin while you can."

Talking to her mother was as draining as she'd known it would be. "We're not going to see eye to eye on this. You'll just have to trust that I know how to look out for myself."

But Gloria remained unconvinced, and eventually Molly gave up and made her escape. In the car, she checked her phone. There were more messages, several from Austin. She deleted them and started her car.

As she approached the city, the Atlanta skyline came into view. The tops of two of the buildings were tipped with gold, and as she drew nearer, lights illuminated the floors of several of the towers, sparkling like diamonds.

In the rosy gentle light of the deepening spring evening, the skyline looked like a fabled city in a fairy tale, a place that someone might fight with everything they had to reach, where one might hope to find brains, a heart, some courage, or to discover the way to go home.

As for the wizard… There was only one person that could be. Josiah. But he was too magnetic and powerful in a way she had never known before, both personally and magically. His dark, polished essence frightened as much as it enticed her.

She could feel the urge to go to him, and it disturbed her. He tugged at the weakest, most vulnerable part in her right when she needed to find her strength, not collapse into old, negative patterns of behavior.

Consumed by her thoughts, she parked the Escalade in the hotel parking garage and made her way to the lobby's bank of elevators. All she wanted to do was take a shower and put her feet up, maybe watch some mindless television and then go to bed.

"Molly!"

She had been watching the floor as she walked. At the sound of Austin's voice, she jerked her head up.

He strode across the lobby toward her, handsome face hard and eyes glittering.

Her mind launched into frantic speculation. How had he found her? Had he used the firm's private investigator? Or—damn it, she had used her credit card. All he'd had to do was check their bank's website.

Whatever. It didn't matter. The expression on his face, along with the tight, fast way that he moved, told her everything she needed to know. He was the angriest, iciest she had ever seen.

Another quick glance told her that nobody was around to witness what happened next. Earlier the hotel had been busy, but by an odd trick of circumstance, now traffic was at a minimum. And nobody stood at the concierge desk or the check-in desk.

She didn't pause to question her instincts. Instead, she bolted.

Chapter Four

AUSTIN CALLED OUT again sharply. She knew without looking that he was racing after her.

Bursting out of the nearest exit, she darted west and immediately ducked behind a six-foot-tall potted plant by the hotel entrance. A moment later, Austin raced past.

She slipped back into the hotel, ran to the elevators, and jabbed the Up button repeatedly. Her feint wouldn't confuse Austin for long. As soon as he looked around and realized she wasn't anywhere to be seen, he would head back inside.

It didn't matter. All she wanted was to get to her suite and slam the door on the world.

The elevator doors opened. She darted in, punched the button for her floor, then held her finger on the Close button. As the elevator doors slowly closed, she saw Austin race into her line of sight. Their eyes met for an instant before the doors shut.

Damn it! Now he would be able to trace what floor she got off on.

Quickly she punched several other buttons. Then, with a shaking hand, she pinched the back of her neck.

Even if he managed to narrow down which floor she was on, there were a lot of suites and rooms on each level. He couldn't know which room she was in. He could knock on every door, but if he did, she didn't have to answer. And the suite had a strong security door. He wouldn't get into her space unless she let him. And she wasn't going to let him.

When she reached her floor, she jogged to her suite and let herself in. Then she threw the latch and double-checked to make sure the door was locked.

Triple-checked.

Unable to help herself, she went over the same motions again and again. *Latch, door, lock. Latch, door, lock. Latch, door, lock.* I have to stop this, she thought, watching her hands as though they belonged to a stranger.

Her phone rang.

The phone that she had turned off.

Feeling hot and numb at once, she reached into her purse and pulled out her cell phone. She remembered turning it off. She distinctly remembered it.

Josiah's name appeared on the screen.

She hadn't entered his contact information into her phone. It should have shown up as an unknown number.

Moving on unsteady legs, she walked into the kitchenette, opened the microwave, and threw the phone inside. After slamming the door shut, she walked into the bathroom, braced her hands on the sink. Then she looked in the mirror.

She couldn't see herself clearly. Tears were streaming down her face, and the lightning flashes had appeared at the edge of her vision again. She didn't trust herself, and she really didn't want to hurt anybody.

Wiping her cheeks, she told the woman in the mirror, "You're going to be all right. I don't know how, but you are. It's going to be okay."

Because someone needed to say that to her even if she couldn't feel it.

Somehow everything was going to be okay.

✧ ✧ ✧

JOSIAH'S PHONE RANG as he sped toward Molly's hotel. Glancing at the dashboard of his Audi TT coupe, he saw the caller was Anson, so he punched the button to answer.

Anson's voice came over the speaker system. "Do you feel that?"

"Of course I do," he said grimly as he gunned around a street corner at a yellow light.

"Maria's picking up on it all the way from Birmingham, which is over two hours away. Is that *Molly Sullivan*?"

"Yes. I want you, Richard, and Henry to leave Atlanta. Meet up with Maria in Birmingham."

Anson swore. "Fine. For how long?"

"Let's play it by ear. Steven's still in New York, so he should be all right."

"We can't sit in limbo forever."

"I know, but we also can't afford to take unnecessary chances, and we're not ready for a confrontation. Just leave for now and hold tight. I'll get back to you soon with further instructions." He punched the button that ended the call.

She was spewing chaotic Power again, and this time it wasn't a brief spurt. Chernobyl was having another meltdown. And he didn't have her cell number, so he cast a spell to make a phone call go through to her, but she didn't pick up.

When he'd felt her Power surge, he had just finished putting in an appearance at his official apartment and was en route to the safe house. As luck would have it, he was only a mile away from the hotel. The chaotic Power lay in that direction.

He arrived a few minutes later. Whipping into a parking space on the street, he cast a cloaking spell over himself, put his phone on vibrate, and raced into the hotel.

Finding Molly's floor ended up being easy. He made his best guess, and when he exited the elevator on the eleventh floor, he could tell he'd gone too far up, so he loped down the stairs until he stopped on the landing of the ninth floor.

This was definitely the floor. He pushed through the stairwell door.

There were dozens of rooms and suites on each floor, but her energy signature shone like a beacon in his mind's eye. Unerringly, he turned right.

Down the hall, Austin Sullivan stood, talking to one of the hotel guests. Josiah felt an urge to violence as he came to a standstill. At the party, Molly and Sullivan had hurled nasty things at each other, but Molly's words had come from a place of truth and deep hurt while Sullivan had deliberately chosen to be cruel.

He was a snake, and Josiah would have no problem crushing him under his heel. But violence wouldn't solve Josiah's bigger issue, so he checked the impulse and coldly watched the exchange between Sullivan and a middle-aged woman.

Sullivan said, "I'm sorry again for bothering you."

"No problem." The woman in the doorway smiled. "I hope you find your wife."

"Thank you, so do I. This whole thing has been a misunderstanding." The snake gave the woman a charming smile.

Sullivan's presence had to be the cause of Molly's meltdown. She must know he was here. Josiah tossed around ideas for how to get rid of the other man without revealing his presence. Perhaps a panic spell would work.

General panic spells were interesting in how they affected the unwary and unaware. They caused the victim's mind to supply the reason for the panic by elevating their own phobias and fears.

Yes, that would do. After the woman had shut her door, Josiah tossed out the casting.

Sullivan had started walking to the next door, toward Josiah. When the spell hit, he slowed to a stop and glanced around. One corner of Josiah's mouth tilted up in a hard smile as the other man frowned and the conscious charm in his handsome expression transformed into anxiety.

Maybe Sullivan was recalculating the risk of drawing attention to himself by knocking on doors. Maybe he would think about what trouble he might get in if a guest complained. Or maybe he had an irrational fear of carpet. Josiah didn't fucking care as long as the spell drove him to leave the hotel as quickly as possible.

Sullivan paused, clearly struggling with himself. Then one of the hotel doors opened and a couple stepped out, giving him a curious glance as they walked past, and he broke. He pushed past them and headed for the elevators.

Leisurely, Josiah stepped out of his way and remained flattened against the wall until the couple had left. Then he thrust the other people out of his mind and headed toward Molly's room.

He located her chaotic Power at the third door from the end of the hallway, opposite where Sullivan had talked with the woman. Logic said Sullivan wouldn't have been heading back toward the bank of elevators if he hadn't already gone down the other side of the hall first.

So he had to have already knocked on Molly's door. Josiah imagined her looking out the peephole to find her ex-husband standing outside. No wonder she was stressed.

She hadn't picked up when he had called, so he knew she wouldn't welcome him standing at her door either. He placed a hand on the door's smooth surface and scanned the interior. Her distress beat at his senses.

Okay. He didn't dare cast a calming spell in her direction. As subtle as they could be, she had already picked up on the other subtle influence spells he had cast, and she wouldn't welcome another one right now.

He only had one real option. Digging deep for his own Power, he cast a wider cloaking spell—one big enough to encompass Molly's space on the other side of the door and also conceal him from other guests. Carefully, he built the spell around them so that none of his magic brushed against Molly's.

As the giant bubble formed, he held his breath.

Nothing happened. She didn't charge out spewing accusations. The hallway remained empty. Breathing a sigh of relief, he slid into a sitting position in front of her door. Then he pulled out his phone and sent a group text to Anson and the others.

`How is that? Better?`

Their replies came back in the affirmative.

Anson asked in the group conversation: `Do you still want us to evacuate?`

`Yes`, he replied. They had invested too much time and care in entering Atlanta under the radar of their dangerous prey, and he didn't want to blow it by being careless now. **`I'll keep watch here. If nothing happens over the next two days, it should`** `be safe enough for you to return.`

`Roger that.`

After the exchange, silence settled in. Molly believed she was alone, and her internal crisis continued. This could be a long damn night, but at least maintaining the cloaking spell would cost less strength than the initial casting. He relaxed against the door, forearms braced on upraised knees and phone clasped in one hand, but he didn't receive any further texts.

As it turned out, her upheaval didn't last all night. She didn't have the training or experience to sustain a large output of energy. After another hour her chaotic Power began to subside. As soon as it had lowered to a level that he deemed safe enough, he released the cloaking spell and stood.

Molly, Molly, he thought. What a spectacular inconvenience you've turned out to be.

He shook his head, then wryly headed for the exit. At least he should be able to get some sleep at the safe house tonight, which was good because his new job hadn't shown any signs of slowing down.

And Atlanta's new DA had a big agenda and a lot to do.

The next day began as hectically as he'd suspected it would, but he had practiced law for a very long time, and nothing out of the ordinary occurred that was beyond his capacity to handle.

Midmorning, his cell phone rang. He glanced at the screen and surged out of his chair to close the door to his office. He recognized that number. It was the same one that had shown up when he spelled the phone call to Molly.

Hitting Accept, he held the phone to his ear. "Hello?"

He heard traffic in the background. She was slow to speak, but he could muster a wealth of patience when it mattered.

"Josiah."

Take it easy, son, he told himself as he relaxed back in his chair. Don't scare her away again. "Molly. Good to hear from you. What can I do for you?"

She demanded, "How did you spell my phone last night?"

He found his lips curving in an amused smile. She was obviously still mad about it. "Have lunch with me, and I'll tell you. Better yet, I'll show you. It's easy."

"I can't have lunch. I'm across town from your office."

"Then have dinner with me. I have plans, but I'm happy to cancel them."

"Maybe." Her reluctance came through loud and clear.

His smile widened. "Such enthusiasm. It's a good thing I have a healthy ego, otherwise my feelings might be hurt."

She snorted. "Listen, you've done too many things to try to influence me, and I don't trust you."

"Ouch," he said, his amusement turning rueful. Over

the years, he had grown so used to using small influencing spells in order to get his way he often cast them without giving it a second thought. But she was too intelligent and sensitive, and he had been too heavy-handed. "I deserve that. Does it help to know I only cast spells that would give you an encouraging nudge in the right direction?"

"Because you're the one who gets to decide what the right direction is?" Her voice turned hard. "Anyway, I don't care. It's manipulative, and if you do it again, I'll find some way to retaliate."

Abruptly his amusement returned, along with curiosity. Spinning his chair in a slow circle, he asked, "What would you do?"

"I would..." Her voice trailed away. "Well, I don't know what I would do. But I would figure something out."

He had no doubt. If she knew a fraction of the things he knew, Molly could do an incredible amount of damage to an opponent. "I believe you, but that's beside the point. I apologize, and I promise to never cast an influence spell on you again. Will that do?"

She blew out a slow breath. "Maybe. But what if I decide to trust you and you go back on that?"

"I won't," he said flatly. "For one thing, I respect your awakening Power too much. I don't want us to become enemies. For another, I just gave my word, and that means something to me."

She went silent again, and a car horn honked in the

background. This time he knew better than to push too hard, and she had been the one to call him, so he waited.

Finally she sighed. "Okay. I accept your apology. Unless you prove me wrong, I'll take you at your word."

As entertaining as this conversation had been, he had a mountain of work to do, so he turned brisk. "Great. I'll ask again—what can I do for you?"

She lowered her voice. "What if I knew someone who might want to give the DA an anonymous tip?"

More surprises. She was turning out to be a wealth of interesting experiences. He straightened. "I would say the DA is intrigued. Tell me more."

"It might lead somewhere, but then again it might not."

"It happens," he drawled. "Anonymous tips are notorious for that."

"Also, it would be very good for your source if no action was taken until after her divorce was finalized." She hesitated again. "You know, just in case the tip actually did lead to something."

"Well, I don't know what the information is. Nor do I know how long the divorce will take, but if it's possible to wait, I think I could agree to that."

"I met with a divorce attorney this morning," she confessed. "Austin figured out where I was staying and showed up at the hotel last night, so she's going to file papers and a restraining order right away. She'll also be sending Austin a settlement offer I don't think he can afford to refuse. Anyway, hopefully the divorce won't take too long."

"It must have been very unpleasant when Sullivan showed up," he said quietly. "I'm sorry you had to go through that. What have you got?"

"A proposition," she replied. "I'll tell you what I know—and I have to warn you, it isn't a lot to go on—and in return I want you to teach me how to defend myself."

He straightened from his slouched position. "Do you feel like you're in danger?"

"Honestly, I don't know." Tension like a finely spun wire ran through her reply. "Maybe not. But I do feel uneasy, and I would like some insurance. Something up my sleeve, just in case. I'm not talking about a long-term commitment. One spell would do it, or even a way to somehow channel the ability I've already got. I would rather do that than buy a gun. Guns can be taken away from their owners, but nobody can wrestle this Power away from me."

Ah, such naïveté.

Still, given her current level of knowledge, she wasn't wrong, and respect stirred. "Is this connected to your tip?"

"Yes. I think Austin's dirty. I found something in the contents of our safe."

He raised his eyebrows. "I accept your proposition. Now you have to have dinner with me and explain what's going on. After I cancel my other plans, I'll be all yours for the evening, but we shouldn't meet in public."

Her relief was palpable. "No, I don't think we should meet in public either. We shouldn't be seen together. Where do you want to meet?"

He considered various options. "Somewhere outside the city. Do you know the Sweetwater Creek State Park? I haven't been there yet, but from what I've read, the park is huge. That should offer enough privacy."

"Of course. It's a beautiful place. I've been many times, and it's only about thirty minutes out. Yes, I'll meet you there. The park has a visitor center. Once you locate that, there's a picnic area not too far away." She rattled off directions, and he grabbed a pen to jot them down.

"Got it," he told her. "I'll leave right after work and meet you at six."

"Thank you." She paused, and when she spoke again, the reluctance had returned. "If you're coming right after work, you'll be hungry. I'll bring something to eat."

An inexplicable reaction warmed him. They weren't friends, and he had given her good cause to be wary of him. He couldn't think of a single reason she would make such an offer unless she was just… nice.

"Thank you. I appreciate that."

"See you then," she said.

Before she could disconnect, he added, "Oh, and Molly? If someone is really intent on doing you harm, a restraining order isn't anything more than a piece of paper. You should relocate, and this time don't use your credit card."

She blew out a breath. "That's next on my list of things to do. I checked out this morning, and as soon as the bank opened, I bought some prepaid Visa cards. After I finish talking with you, I'm going to find somewhere else to stay."

Relaxing, he smiled and purred, "I knew you weren't just a pretty face."

"You think I'm pretty?" She sounded astonished but then added quickly, "I'm hanging up now."

He laughed. "I think you're beautiful, and I'm hanging up now too. Be careful, and make sure you don't have somebody following you. See you soon."

After the call ended, he fired off an email to cancel his dinner date and then sat back in his chair.

So, Molly thought Sullivan was dirty. How about that.

Her information might or might not be relevant to Josiah's interests, but that didn't matter. The main thing was, he should be able to gain more of her trust, at least enough so he could give her some training.

That could be enough for her to exercise control so she would stop being so damn visible to those who had magic sensitivity and enough interest in the Atlanta area to check out new anomalies. Helping Molly helped him.

He found himself smiling again. They hadn't talked that long, but she had still managed to evoke a surprising number of emotions. And with every change in her inflection, he could imagine her expressions.

She was busy and preoccupied with her own

problems, but she wasn't letting any of that dull her sharp mind. Yes, she was beautiful, but beauty was overrated in these modern times. A woman with her kind of intelligence was sexy as hell, and he liked that. He liked her very much.

But that was irrelevant. He had no place in his life for nice people—not with the kind of damage he intended to inflict and the danger that came along with it.

It took some effort, but eventually he put her out of his mind and got back to work.

Chapter Five

MOLLY SLIPPED HER phone back into her purse and climbed into her SUV. Only time would tell whether Josiah was as good at keeping his word as he claimed. She had set her course of action. That had to be good enough for now.

The early-morning meeting with her new attorney, Nina Rodriguez, had highlighted everything that had been bothering her, and not in a good way. Nina was an attractive fifty-year-old Hispanic woman with sharp dark eyes and a warm smile who, she said, loved to take cheating assholes of either sex to the cleaners.

Molly had emailed the zip file of documents to Nina the night before, and they went over everything in person. As soon as Nina had laid eyes on the mysterious bank account, she'd recognized the format from a bank in the Seychelles islands.

"Is your husband laundering money?" Nina asked, one eyebrow raised.

"I-I don't know," Molly replied. When she'd found the violet panties, she had thought Austin couldn't do anything more to rattle her. She'd been wrong.

Now, indulging in a newfound sense of paranoia, she drove around in circles while she kept an eye on the surrounding traffic. She was more shaken than she liked to admit, and she'd grown uncomfortable driving the Escalade. It was too distinctive, and the license plate a matter of record.

So she drove to the nearest Cadillac dealership and sold it. While she waited for the dealer to cut her a check, she called a car rental—not the one conveniently located across the street from the dealership, but one from a few miles away—and reserved a sedan. The rental company offered a pickup service, so she was able to complete both transactions within a couple of hours.

After that, she searched on her phone until she located an available Airbnb apartment in a trendy neighborhood near Clark Atlanta University. She chatted with the owner for ten minutes, then bought a week's stay with one of her prepaid Visa cards and drove to the new place.

The owner lived in a midcentury house, and the one-bedroom rental was over a detached garage. She had invited Molly to use the driveway, so she parked on one side of the garage, near the outside set of stairs that led up to the rental. The door was locked with a lockbox, and the owner had given her the code, so she was able to let herself in.

After a quick walk-through, she discovered the other woman hadn't been exaggerating when she'd said the apartment was utilitarian. There were basic furnishings—

a couch, a chair, a coffee table, and a forty-inch LED TV in the living room, along with a dinette set in the kitchen, adequate bedroom furniture with a double bed, and minimal wall decor.

But it was clean, and the large windows looked out at plenty of trees, giving the space an airy, peaceful feeling. And it was another place that felt fresh and new, a place where Austin had never been.

Most importantly, it was a place where now, hopefully, nobody could find her.

She hauled her luggage up the stairs, unpacked, and then went grocery shopping. By the end of the afternoon, she felt better than she had in days. She had a couple of bottles of wine, she could cook comfort meals, and she didn't have to go out unless she wanted to.

Other things nagged to be added to her to-do list. Things like finding a permanent place to settle down. Trying to find the woman from her dreams, or some other teacher, someone she could trust who was not Josiah.

But thinking about the rest of her life was overwhelming. She wasn't ready to make any more decisions that would have long-term consequences, and she backed away quickly. That wasn't what she needed to concentrate on this evening.

She still wore the two-piece suit from the meeting with Nina. Stripping out of her clothes, she had a long, luxurious shower, dried her hair, and dressed in jeans, a sweater, and a new leather jacket. It would get chilly in the park as the sun set.

No makeup. She pulled her hair back into a plain ponytail at the nape of her neck and gave herself a long, level look in the mirror. The woman staring back looked strong, no-nonsense, capable. You couldn't tell her life was in ruins and she was a stranger to herself.

After shoving cash and identification into her jeans pocket, she folded a photocopy of one of the foreign bank statements and shoved that into another pocket, scooped up her keys, and left to pick up dinner.

When six o'clock came, she sat on one of the picnic tables underneath a shelter, feet planted on the bench seat and dinner sitting in two paper bags beside her.

Something brushed along her awareness. A car sped into view and parked beside her rental. From where she sat, she couldn't tell what model it was, but it looked dark, low-slung, and powerful. While she waited for Josiah to emerge, she ran her gaze over the area.

A woman with a Great Dane jogged along the side of the park road a couple hundred yards away, but Molly's and Josiah's vehicles were the only two in sight. In the summer this picnic spot would be crowded until sunset, but now, as the evening chilled, they should have the clearing to themselves.

Josiah climbed out and strode across the open area like he was conquering it, his body loose-limbed and comfortable. Like her, he wasn't young. He looked to be early- to midforties, but for all his maturity, his long, athletic body didn't carry an ounce of spare fat. There was a tight, whipcord element to the breadth of his muscles. He looked nothing like Austin's pampered, gym-built physique.

Okay, she had to be honest. The man was sex on a stick.

He wore a similar outfit, jeans, a black shirt and leather jacket, and the slanting evening sun gave his dark hair chestnut highlights. Look at that, he wasn't quite as dark and dangerous as she'd first thought.

Then she met his hard, catlike amber eyes. A sense of his magic, dark, polished and well-honed, shimmered against her mind's eye. It felt as sleek as his car looked and infinitely more powerful.

She threw everything into full reverse. He was every bit as dangerous as she had first thought. Every bit and more.

Maybe it hadn't been the smartest idea to meet him in such a secluded spot. But he was a district attorney, she reminded herself, not a serial killer. By the time Josiah reached the picnic shelter, she had wrestled her reactions under control.

He climbed up to sit beside her, moving his long-limbed body with fluid ease. "Good venue for dinner."

"I thought so too." Digging into the first of the two bags beside her, she pulled out a six-pack of craft beer and offered it to him.

He accepted a bottle. Setting the six-pack between them, she handed him the second bag. He peered into it and then at the logo on the outside of the bag. "I'd hoped I was smelling fried chicken. Is this from a chain?"

"Nope. You will want to remember the name of this place. Best fried chicken in Atlanta." She used the opener she'd bought to pry off the bottle cap, handed the opener to him, and took a pull from her bottle.

"Excellent. I was too busy to have a real lunch." He selected a large piece and handed the bag back.

"How's your job going? No nasty surprises, I hope?"

He replied lazily, "Nothing I can't handle."

I bet. She avoided saying that out loud.

Searching through the bag, she pulled out a foil-wrapped biscuit. The food was still hot, and she rolled the top of the bag down over the rest to hold in the warmth.

Then she crumbled her biscuit and sipped at her beer while Josiah ate in silence. When he finished his first piece, he fished out another. He seemed to be in no hurry to break the silence, but she had an agenda.

"What do people call you?" she asked. "Are you a witch or a warlock?"

He shrugged, finished his beer, and took a second bottle. "Either or both. Sometimes *sorcerer*. Occasionally *asshole*. Personally, I'm not in love with labels."

Lingering warmth from the sunlight touched her face and hands, but the evening chill was setting in. "I don't want to become a major force on the Eastern Seaboard. The thought never occurred to me, not even in my wildest daydreams."

He grinned. "That was where I lost you, wasn't it?"

She nodded. "One of the places. I could tell you want it though."

"Oh yes," he said, his voice deepening. "I'm going to be governor of Georgia within the next two election cycles."

Looking at his hard, determined profile, she believed him. "But when you say *become a major force,* you don't really mean by using the human political system. Do you?"

"No, although it will help to gain political power as well." He glanced at her, a quick, calculating look, and then back over the clearing. "Most witches are territorial, especially in the witches demesne, which is run by a very old, well-established council. Outside Louisville, you might find areas held by either solitary witches or full covens. They don't much like other people of significant Power moving in on their turf. Wars have been fought over who gets to hold which city. You might as well know I intend to claim Atlanta for my own."

Wars.

Abruptly certain she shouldn't be drinking alcohol while talking to him, she set aside her beer. "The Atlanta area isn't pro-magic."

"Give me enough time and I can flip it."

His confidence was so rock-solid she believed him. "Why don't you make your move? If there isn't any other mature, practicing witch here, the city is wide open for the taking, right?"

He shook his head. "That's not a yes-or-no answer. Atlanta may not be claimed by a resident witch, but it's a place of special interest to a certain dangerous Power, which brings me to an important point. This Power likes to operate under the radar, out of public sight. I know you think I spelled your cell phone when we talked in the bar, but I didn't. I could tell you were under some distress last night, and that's why I cast a spell to contact you. The communication spell uses the nearest and best available way to reach out. At the time, that happened to be your cell phone, but it could also have been your television screen or computer monitor."

"I see." She took a slow breath. Looking at him sidelong, she asked, "How did you know I was distressed?"

"I could feel it. You were spewing Power like a geyser." He tilted back his head and finished his beer. "More importantly, any creature with sensitivity and Power would have been able to feel it, and Molly—if you don't trust me on anything else, trust me on this one thing—you don't want to come to anyone else's attention like that. It shows you're out of control and makes you a mark to predators. There are creatures in this world that would love to sink their teeth into you and suck all the magic out of your bones like sucking the juice from a ripe peach."

She could feel the blood drain from her face. "That's a pretty grim image."

"It's pretty grim when it happens." His narrowed

gaze met hers. "But here's the good news. You can avoid that, and you can avoid hurting anyone by accident, with a few simple techniques."

"Such as?"

"Meditation, for one. Start for ten minutes at a time, three times a day, and build up from there. That will help to keep your Power under better control until you acquire the training you need. A daily yoga practice also helps. And you need to develop a technique for stressful situations. Practice that one like your life depends upon it, because it might." He wiped his mouth and hands with a paper napkin, then helped himself to another beer.

She'd never been drawn to meditation, but ten minutes at a time sounded doable, and she would gladly take up yoga again. "What kind of technique?"

"It can be anything that calms you down in a stressful situation and allows you to maintain self-control. You could try the four-seven-eight breathing technique. Breathe in to the count of four, hold it and count to seven, and breathe out to the count of eight." One corner of his mouth notched up. "If nothing else, all that counting should ground you. And if a situation is too stressful to count in, you have worse things to worry about than fluctuating Power."

Reluctantly, she smiled back. "That's the worst attempt at reassurance I've ever heard."

"You should see my bedside manner."

Ha. She eyed her beer. If she was going to be

cautious, she should never have contacted Josiah to begin with. Screw it. She reached for the bottle.

"Molly," he said. She looked up from her drink and met his intent amber gaze. "Meditation, yoga, and breathing techniques—those are all Band-Aids. You have far too much Power." He paused, and then for the first time in her life, someone else's voice entered her head. <We're not talking a sparkle of a little magic that gives you the ability to telepathize or see shiny spells. You're capable of doing incredible damage. Ignore your own Power at your peril—and at the peril of everyone around you.>

The meaning of his message slid away as she realized he was…

In. Side. Her. Head.

The beer bottle fell out of her lax fingers. She launched off the picnic table and didn't stop until she had put fifty yards between them. Then she turned in a circle, hands clapped to her temples.

"You could have given me some warning!" she yelled when she faced him again.

He laughed so hard he nearly fell off the table. "How could I know you hadn't tried telepathy before now? It was the first thing I reached for when my Power awakened."

"I've been a little preoccupied with other things!" She stomped toward him. "Don't talk to me that way again!"

He waited until she had almost reached him. <Why?

Other people are going to try telepathizing with you, so you might as well get used to it.>

"Agh!" She clapped her hands to her head again. "I don't have to get used to anything right now! Seriously, *stop*!"

His face was still creased with amusement. "When I offered to take you on as a student, I didn't realize how entertaining it could be."

"I'm not your student," she told him irritably. "This is a onetime lesson, remember?"

His laughter faded, and he eyed her with a leisurely, almost sensual glance. "It doesn't have to be. Nobody else can teach you what I can teach you. Nobody else will encourage you to be whoever you want the way I would. To shed your inhibitions and explore everything you're capable of being."

She let herself be ensnared by the allure in his words, by his sexy voice. Just for a moment. It was such a dangerous, pretty fantasy to run to someone who claimed to have all the answers.

Then she looked away, and the fantasy burst. "I still don't trust you," she heard herself saying. "You're too ambitious, too manipulative. I can see you calculating every move as you weigh what's in it for you."

He didn't try to deny it, nor did he sound angry, just matter-of-fact. "Doesn't everybody? You're lying to yourself if you try to claim otherwise."

Her lips tightened. "And you threw spells on and around me as though they were confetti."

The last of his amusement vanished, and he pushed from his sitting position on the picnic table. He looked like a tiger about to pounce on its prey. "I already said I would stop. If you don't believe me, why are you here?"

"Because in spite of all that, I think I like you." She surprised herself, and she could see from his expression that she had surprised him too. "At least, I don't dislike you enough to want to avoid you. Besides, I don't have anybody else I can call right now."

As that last left her mouth, she marveled at her own tactlessness. Go ahead, genius, piss off your only teacher for miles around. But thankfully he looked amused again.

He studied her. She wanted to squirm under his scrutiny and tightened her muscles against the impulse. Backing down or flinching away from the tiger sounded like a very bad thing to do.

"Fair enough," he said at last. "Now, why don't you tell me more about that tip? You said earlier you were filing for divorce and getting a restraining order."

She hesitated. The lone female jogger and her dog had long since vanished, and the solitude made everything feel riskier, the approaching night full of shadows and unseen peril.

But she was the one who had started this, so she gestured to her upper arm. "I still have bruises where Austin grabbed me, and he showed up at the hotel last night. He's very angry, and when he gets the divorce papers and settlement offer, he's going to get angrier. You see, when I left on Thursday, I cleaned out our house safe and took everything."

A small smile touched the corners of his hard mouth. "You were very upset that night, but you didn't let that stop your thinking."

"No, I didn't. Since then, I've discovered something that doesn't add up in a—well, in a pretty major way." She dug into her pocket, pulled out the folded paper, and handed it to him. "This was in one of the files from the safe. Nina Rodriguez is my lawyer." The legal community could be a tight-knit one, and she paused to ask curiously, "Ever heard of her?"

Silently, he shook his head.

"Well, she's very sharp. Nina and I constructed my settlement offer so Austin gets to keep what's in this bank account while I keep everything else. At first glance, it looks like he gets the better end of the deal, because… just look at those totals."

He unfolded the paper, and his lips pursed in a soundless whistle. "That's a shockingly healthy bottom line."

Now that she had taken action, the tension left her body. Walking back to the table, she picked up her beer bottle. "Like I said, the numbers don't add up. Everything else looks fine. Our assets and retirement and savings accounts are what I'd expected from what we've accrued. But I didn't even know this was from a bank account in the Seychelles until my lawyer recognized the format. Austin has be dirty. I don't know how else he could have accumulated that much money in a hidden account."

He looked over the paper and met her gaze. "In your settlement offer, you're keeping all the legitimate assets and leaving him with only this. And you just informed the DA about it."

She lifted a shoulder. "If it's legitimate and he was just hiding it from me, he gets to keep a lot of money. If it isn't, he deserves whatever he gets."

"And he loses everything." He smiled. "I like the way you think."

She nodded and looked away. "Either way, I'll get more than enough from the settlement to meet my needs, and I'll be free of him. But this only works for me if you don't do anything until after the divorce is finalized."

"You think it will be uncontested?"

"Oh yes. I don't think he wants the court to get this information." She shrugged. "It's possible he made that money legally. I don't know how, but he didn't keep me current on everything he was doing, so…"

"Did you file taxes jointly?"

"Yes."

"So you've seen your tax returns for the past several years? You must have, in order to have signed them."

"Yes."

"And none of your tax returns declared this income?"

She made a face. "No. Of course not."

"Then you're not wrong. If nothing else, he's guilty

of tax evasion and liable for quite a lot of money. Since he hid the income, he probably didn't get it legitimately, although it's possible he was only hiding it from you and the US government."

She could feel her teeth grinding. "I thought of that too. He might have wanted to hide some of his assets if he was getting ready to leave me."

Josiah folded the paper and tucked it into his jacket. "If your divorce is uncontested, it should be finalized in sixty days or so, and careful investigations aren't like hour-long TV shows—they take time. Even if this does lead to something, my office wouldn't be ready to make a move for several months anyway."

She blew out a breath. "So you *are* going to investigate?"

"Oh, yes. I can't wait to follow the threads and see what's behind them." He paused, and his expression turned calculating. "And Sullivan didn't acquire that money in a vacuum."

Briefly, her mind opened up to just how big Josiah's investigation might get. Other people had to be involved, powerful people. Probably even people she had met at their many dinner parties. The amount of money involved all but guaranteed it.

With an effort she pulled out of conjecture. "I've been wrapped up in my own concerns. I didn't consider how big this could get. And you know what? I don't care. All I want is to decouple from him legally and financially so I can move on with my life."

Josiah leaned forward. "This all ties back to that defensive spell you want to learn."

"Yes. I switched to a new location, but I want to be prepared just in case." She gave him a level look. "I *will* buy a gun if I have to, but is there a protective incantation or potion that would be better?"

His keen gaze probably saw more than she wanted. "I'm not against guns. I own several myself, but you're right. You don't need one to protect yourself. There are more elaborate incantations, potions, and spells you can learn over time, but you've already demonstrated you can call up everything you need for now."

She blew out a breath, feeling both exasperated and intimidated at once. "What does that mean?"

"Come on." He scooped up the six-pack from the table.

Grabbing the empty dinner bag, she tossed it into a nearby trash can as she followed.

Halogen streetlights had switched on, casting white light over their cars. Josiah strode to the middle of the parking lot. Pulling out an empty beer bottle, he set it on the asphalt. Then he walked back to where she had stopped, several feet away.

"Everything you need is inside you." He looked down into her eyes. "You don't need a spell for this."

She thought she knew where this was going. "You want me to knock that over like I broke the vase at my house."

"Yep." He set the six-pack beside his feet and

crossed his arms. "Go ahead. Do it."

She threw up her hands. "I can't."

He lifted one broad shoulder. "If you think you can't, then you can't. But the Powerful woman I saw at the party didn't say she couldn't do things. She just did them."

"That's overly simplistic."

"Is it?" he replied. "Watch this."

He turned to look at the bottle. An invisible force shot out of him, blazed across the intervening feet, and the bottle exploded.

"Holy crap," she whispered. Turning her back, she scrubbed her face with both hands.

Like darkness eclipsing the day, he came up behind her and whispered in her ear, "I would never have been able to learn that if I had said *I can't.*"

She spun around again. "Okay, I take your point. But the last time I did this, there were sparks of lightning at the edges of my vision. A huge emotion had built up in my body and it didn't have anywhere to go, at least not until it shot out of me. I don't know how to access that. I can't..." At his expression, she swallowed down the rest and made a frustrated noise at the back of her throat.

He snatched up another beer bottle, stalked to the center of the parking lot, and set it into place. As he returned, he pointed at it. "Go."

She glared at the bottle and tried to push out mentally. It remained upright. She tried again. And again.

And again, until her head started to pound with a dull ache. Josiah stood watching, arms crossed. He looked unimpressed, impatient.

"Stop staring at me," she snapped.

One dark, sardonic eyebrow rose. "Certainly. That should fix everything."

"Oh, shut up. I can't—" His face darkened, and the words hitched in her throat. She growled and started again, this time reaching for better words. "I don't know how to access that part of me. It's… it's…"

"Tied into your emotions, you said." He sounded bored, his voice cutting. "So access your emotions."

"Agh!" She pressed her fists against her thighs and tried to remember just exactly how it had happened. She had felt so full of pain and rage she could barely see straight, let alone talk coherently.

The *memory* was easy enough to access. But pulling up the emotion itself was another matter. Violent, powerful emotions didn't just lie around waiting for someone to trip over them.

Maybe she was defective. Maybe she wasn't going to be as Powerful as he thought she was. Maybe she didn't have the full range of capability other awakening witches did…

Josiah hauled her into his arms. Her lips parted on a shocked gasp. He clamped a hard hand at the back of her neck, and his head plummeted down.

What. The. Hell.

That was as far as she got. Then her spinning

thoughts blew to smithereens as his mouth came over hers. He kissed her hard, clamping her against his long, muscled body.

It had been years since anyone other than Austin had kissed her. Years and years. The shock of contact jolted everywhere, followed swiftly by astonished pleasure and outrage.

No, she was pretty sure that was pleasure. Wait, outrage.

Pleasure. Outrage?

She forgot to breathe as her lips moved tentatively under his. Somewhere in her head, a siren began to blare in a klaxon warning.

Austin might have cheated, but she never had. Even though she was getting divorced and no longer owed him a damn thing, she was deeply faithful by nature. This felt like crossing a line she wasn't supposed to cross. It felt good, but it also felt wrong.

Then Josiah's tongue plunged into her mouth. *His tongue.*

Inside her mouth.

A muffled, wordless *hnnnf* came out of her. Her body caught up with what had happened, and she started to struggle. For a moment his arms remained around her, as unbreakable as iron bands.

Then he let her go. Panting, she fell back and glared at him. He glared back, his amber gaze lambent. She couldn't tell if he was close to laughter, anger, or arousal—or if it was a combination of all three.

She needed to slap him. Lightning sparked at the edge of her vision.

His eyebrows rose. He pivoted to point at the beer bottle in the middle of the parking lot.

She swiveled to stare where he pointed, and there it was. Power rose up inside, and as she focused her attention on the bottle, the Power shot out of her like a lightning bolt.

Fifteen feet away, the bottle wobbled and fell over.

The bottle fell over.

She whispered, "I did that?"

"You did that," Josiah said. Fierce satisfaction filled his voice.

She remembered what had just happened and rounded on him. *"What the hell!"*

He gave her an insolent, unrepentant look. "Now do that five hundred times. Don't overthink it, don't doubt yourself, and don't split your energy by worrying about things." He stuck his face into hers and snapped out, "Don't make me kiss you again unless you really mean it. You reach that part of yourself and pull it out on your own. Make it happen."

Don't make me kiss you again unless…

He hadn't meant the kiss. She had tied herself up in knots and felt like she had crossed an ethical line *when she hadn't*—and he hadn't even meant it.

She scrubbed her mouth with the back of one hand. "You manipulative son of a bitch!"

He pointed at the fallen beer bottle. Turning, she

glared at it.

There it was, inside her, just as Josiah said it would be. She knew how to find it now. Her magic flared, bright and deadly like a supernova. She focused it on the target.

This time when the bolt left her, the bottle shattered.

"There you go," Josiah said. He gave her a nod. "You're welcome."

She was so furious she didn't know what to do. She spat out, "Try to manhandle me like that again, and you'll regret it."

His eyes glittered. "I tolerated the first threat you made. Be careful. I won't be tolerant very much longer."

The tiger was no longer amused. She forced herself to take in a deep, shaking breath. "You're such an asshole."

"That must make you Captain Obvious." He shook his head with a snort. "It was a kiss. Get over it. I manhandled you *a little*, and I let you go as soon as you started to struggle. More importantly, it gave you the shock you needed to get the job done. Now, I have a breakfast meeting with the mayor in the morning and a major new investigation to start. Do you have any more tips for me?"

Still breathing hard, she shook her head. She didn't trust herself to speak. She wanted to plant her fist in his arrogant, unrepentant face.

"All right," he said. "Remember, do it at least five hundred more times. Do it until it becomes second nature and you don't have to struggle to access that part of you. Practice it on different targets—on moving targets, if you can find any. Practice it when you're exhausted and when you first wake up. Good night."

With that, he turned and strode to his car, leaving her standing alone in the parking lot, staring after him. Her lips still throbbed from the hard pressure of his mouth, and adrenaline pounded through her body.

Just a kiss, he said. *Get over it.*

But it had been more than just a kiss. It had been her first delicate exploration beyond her dead marriage. Her first hint of pleasure with someone other than her husband.

But he hadn't meant it.

And for the space of a moment when she had struggled against his strength, she had been very aware that he could overpower her with little effort. And that she couldn't get free of him unless he chose to let her go.

As her blood cooled in the evening chill, she calmed enough to think. Maybe that wasn't what he had intended. Like he said, he had let her go as soon as he felt her struggle.

Yet for that one moment she had felt what it was like to be overpowered by someone larger and physically stronger than she was.

She took another beer bottle, set it on the asphalt, and walked several yards away.

As she eyed her target, she whispered, "I'm not going to get over it."

Then she concentrated on pulling up her magic and focusing it like a weapon.

Another beer bottle shattered.

Four hundred and ninety-nine more to go.

Chapter Six

HE SHOULDN'T HAVE kissed her.

That thought dominated as Josiah pulled onto the interstate to Birmingham. He sped through the deepening night, his mood turning savage.

What the fuck had he been thinking? He'd meant to get her riled, but there were a thousand other ways he could have done it, and the desire to explore her beautiful lips had mingled disastrously with the urge to knock her out of her shackles of self-doubt.

And as he had so many times already, he had miscalculated. Badly. But that wasn't what had seared his brain.

She had responded to his kiss. Her spectacular mouth had moved so gently and hesitantly under his it had made some long-dead thing in his chest squeeze tight.

Even now as he thought of it, his skin grew hot and his groin hardened in the first involuntary response he'd had in…

Gods, he couldn't remember how long it had been.

Abruptly, he did a mental one-eighty. Hell, it was a

good thing he had burned down the new, tentative bridge they had begun to build between them. Just as well that she ended up looking at him like he was Satan personified and the embodiment of every male asshole on the continent.

He'd already squandered far more thought, time, and effort on her than he'd ever intended. As he already knew, *quite well goddammit*, there was no room for nice people in his life. And there was absolutely no room for beautiful, vulnerable women no matter how intelligent they were or how promising their future looked.

Or how soft and inviting their lips looked. Felt.

As he drew close to his destination, he pulled out his phone and punched Maria's number. When she picked up, he said, "I'm calling a coven meeting."

Her lightly accented, low contralto sounded in his ear. "When?"

"In fifteen minutes. I'm almost there." Gathering in person was rare, but the others had already evacuated to Maria's safe house, and there was no time like the present. "Tell the others. We'll have Steven FaceTime from New York."

One thing he appreciated about Maria—she didn't waste time on unnecessary conversation. "Okay. We'll be ready when you get here."

He signed off. Then, even though he had been watchful from the moment he had left the office, he drove through a series of maneuvers designed to lose a tail.

While his Audi purred along neighborhood streets, he whispered spells to prevent farseers from gaining accurate visions of his actions. It was all standard procedure that he insisted his coven employ whenever they gathered. His insistence was why they had all survived as long as they had.

He was confident he had garnered no more than the usual mundane interest from starting the new job, but he never, ever left things to chance. Sloppiness could get you killed.

Or worse. There were much worse things than death.

Finally he reached the address at the southern outskirts of the city, another country house as unprepossessing as the one outside Atlanta. He followed the gravel drive around to the back and parked beside two pickups, a Subaru Outback, and a Honda CRV.

As he climbed out, Maria appeared by the car door. She was a short Hispanic woman with long black hair pulled back in a braid and large, luminous eyes. She looked like a human Bambi, and her aura of harmless vulnerability was one of the most lethal illusions he'd ever seen.

She hugged him. "What's wrong?"

"Wrong question," he told her, returning the hug. "If my intuition is right, we may have been presented with an unexpected opportunity."

"Oh good!" She relaxed visibly. "You had us worried, especially after last night."

He glanced around. With four members of his coven

present, he had no doubt the area was clear of potential threats, but some habits never died. "Let's get inside before I say more."

"You bet. Do you need some supper?"

"I've already eaten, thanks. The sooner we get to business, the sooner I can get back to town. I've got to be in the office at eight in the morning."

She gave him a quick, rueful glance. "Have you ever had to punch someone else's time clock before?"

"No," he said drily.

"It's quite different from working for yourself. And you've been burning the candle at both ends these days, haven't you?"

"Story of my life until this is over."

"Maybe so, but the rest of us will do what we can to share the load."

Shc led him in the back door and directly into the basement where Anson, Henry, and Richard waited. Some part of Josiah that remained on perpetual high alert relaxed when he felt surrounded by the protective spells on the basement's ceiling, floor, and walls.

The group kept their greetings brief. While Anson drew a pentagram on the floor, Maria established a FaceTime connection with Steven, setting the phone where he would stand in person, and everyone stood in a circle.

Josiah took a moment to look around. Richard had been in the armed forces and still carried the demeanor of a soldier in his long, straight body. Henry was a numbers guy and Harvard educated, while their designated geek Steven was a graduate from MIT who specialized in the intersection of technology and magic.

Maria, the strongest seer of the group, appeared to be an attractive thirty-year-old, but in reality she was closer to sixty, and at two hundred years of age—twenty-six years older than Josiah himself—Anson was the oldest. He looked exactly like what he had been when his Power had awakened, a kindly grandfather with graying hair.

Covens were created for any number of social, political, and financial reasons, and some lasted for generations. Josiah had created his to fulfill a single purpose. He had painstakingly researched each member before recruiting them in a careful process that could take months. In Anson's case, it had taken two years.

The coven members weren't friends. He and Richard could barely stand one another, but in some ways they were closer than family. As he considered Henry's whip-smart, icy gaze, Josiah wondered what would happen once the coven had finally accomplished what they had set out to do.

He could see some taking off, never to be heard from again, but other connections, like possibly his relationships with Maria and Anson, might last longer.

In any case, none of that mattered. They were united now, had been for decades, for the sole purpose of destroying one man.

After Richard lit the candles positioned at each point

of the pentagram, Josiah raised his Power and extended it out to Maria on his left and to Richard on his right. The others did the same until their Powers merged with a *snap* and the circle was completed.

It was weaker than it would be if Steven were physically present. Even so, he could extend some energy through the FaceTime connection. As Josiah eyed their handiwork with a critical eye, he was satisfied that the merging was strong and solid.

As disparate as they were in personality and talent, his coven had learned to work well together. As long as they held their circle, no outside creature could see what they did, nor could anyone hear what they discussed, not even the world's rare, dangerous Djinn.

In the unlikely event something had slipped past the electronic security systems, the driving maneuvers, the spells of aversion, and the spells cast on the ceiling, floor, and walls of the basement, this circle was their last, strongest layer of protection.

He pulled out the folded photocopy Molly had given him and tossed it into the middle of the pentagram. "Tell me what you see when you look at this," he said to Maria. "Does it connect to our mission?"

"What is it?" Richard asked, eyeing the folded paper curiously.

Quietly, Josiah replied, "Hold on. I want to know if Maria gets any hits off it first."

Maria's sight tended to yield purer results when she didn't hold preconceived ideas. Beside him, she tilted her head. Her large, lustrous eyes had taken on an extra sheen. They glittered like black diamonds, reflecting light.

She murmured, "What is the subterfuge that lies around this?"

She was that damn good. Smiling, he said, "There are a couple of layers of subterfuge. The person who gave it to me did so in secret."

"And it contains a secret."

"Yes."

"A dangerous secret." In that moment, she looked quite alien. Breathing deeply, she nodded. "This does connect to our mission, but it's a winding thread that doubles back on itself. I can't see the twists and turns. Some of it is technological, and some financial. All I can see for certain is that someone doesn't want this found."

Josiah rubbed his jaw. "No, I don't think they do."

"Be careful, Josiah." Her unblinking, glittering gaze fixed on him. "I see violence surrounding this."

He was always careful. "We knew the closer we got, the more dangerous things would become." They never mentioned their adversary by name in case it triggered his attention. "You said this connects. Does this lead to our target?"

"I think it might. A lot depends on the choices we make and if we can follow the twists and turns of the thread." Her blank expression fractured into frustration. "Our circle may be protective, but it also limits my sight. I need to step out to see more."

"Stop," he said immediately. "It's not worth the risk. You've confirmed there's a connection to our prey, and that's enough for now."

The glitter left her eyes, and she began to shudder. "I also heard a lot of spirit whispers down that winding thread. Souls that have been killed or maimed."

A pained silence greeted that.

Anson asked softly, "Were any of them ours?"

They had all lost something to the one they hunted. Family members, former lives they had lived. Josiah had lost years of his life. Their loss was what united them. Still, he thought as he saw the stark grief flash over Maria's expression, it wasn't fair to ask her.

In spite of that, her reply was gentle. "I don't know, Anson. I didn't catch a glimpse of specific faces or hear names. But it's possible."

"I apologize." Anson rubbed his face. "I shouldn't have asked."

"It's all right," she told him. "Believe me, I understand."

Josiah stepped to the center to retrieve the paper. Unfolding it, he held it out to Richard, who studied the contents closely before handing it to Anson.

The paper reached Henry, who came to attention like a hound scenting blood. "This looks interesting."

"Yes," Josiah said. "It's also significant enough that we can't afford to mishandle it. I want to start with some forensic accounting. Henry, see what you can trace using mundane techniques. Work with Steven to make sure you don't trigger any magical snares and remember—we need to be accurate and safe more than we need to rush. We haven't come this far to get sloppy now."

Steven spoke over the FaceTime connection. "Henry should stay away from Atlanta while he works on this. Like I said the last time we convened, there are spells layered over the internet hubs in Atlanta. I'm pretty sure they're alarms. They might be triggered by using certain search terms and databases. He needs to use a different IP address."

"Is Birmingham far enough out?" Henry asked.

Steven paused. "I think so."

Henry grinned at Maria. "Guess I'm bunking on the couch for now."

She snorted. "I'll do even better than that and pick up an air bed for you." Her dark gaze shifted to Josiah. "Want me to stay on task?"

Maria's job was monitoring the various bugs he had planted throughout the district attorney's offices, his city apartment, and around the exterior of the Atlanta safe house.

"Yes," he replied. "Chances are Sullivan's Seychelles funds are somehow connected to Sherman & Associates. Richard, I want you to start digging into Russell Sherman's background. Again, use only mundane techniques. No magic."

"What about me?" Anson asked.

Anson was Josiah's man on the ground while his time was eaten up by working the DA job. "If things remain quiet, you can return on Wednesday and resume providing backup."

The older man nodded. "Sounds like a plan."

A short time later, Josiah said his goodbyes. As he drove back to the city, he began to smile. The years of careful preparation were beginning to pay off. He had no doubt they would soon have their quarry in their sights.

Then the endgame would begin.

FOR THE REST of that week, Molly practiced diligently until she could hit both stationary and moving targets and she no longer had to struggle to reach the Power that resided deep within her core like a golden well of light.

The results of her blood tests came back. She was relieved to hear they were all negative, though she'd have to have follow-up HIV tests in six months to be certain. She also found a broker to sell her jewelry, including her diamond engagement ring.

It had appreciated dramatically over the past twenty years, and everything sold within a couple of days. After paying the broker's fees, she added another significant amount to her expanding bank account.

On Wednesday, Nina had a draft of the divorce settlement ready for her approval. After discussion and a few alterations, Nina had the papers served to Austin first thing Friday morning.

Austin might take days or even weeks to consider the

papers and respond, but Molly knew he would read them that morning. She could almost sense him flipping through the package, his fury ratcheting higher with every page.

That thought put her in such a celebratory mood she went car shopping and decided to buy a new Jeep Cherokee. Since she paid in cash, the process took less time than it would if she had taken out a car loan.

By midafternoon, she was free to drive her new car off the lot. As she started the ignition, her cell phone rang. After making sure the car was in park, she checked the phone. Nina's name lit the screen.

Molly's heart pounded. She punched Accept. "Nina, what's up?"

"Excellent news," Nina said. "Austin accepted the settlement and signed the papers."

"Wow, that was fast." Vindication, triumph, and relief rioted through her veins along with a healthy dose of shock. "He accepted *all* our terms?"

"All of them. He signed over the deed to the house, the retirement accounts, everything."

She coughed out an incredulous laugh, then swiped at her face. "I don't know why I'm crying."

Nina said gently, "It's because you know there's no miracle that will fix your broken marriage."

"I guess. I already knew it, but this makes it more real." She leaned back in her seat and stared sightlessly out the window. "Mostly I feel relieved, and I'm still really angry."

"That might take some time to process. For now, try to celebrate. You've got him by the balls, and he knows it. And you know what's worse for him? He knows *we* know it. He'll be out of the house by the end of next week, and you can take possession next Saturday. I'm headed to the courthouse, so I'll get this filed this afternoon. You're on your way, Molly."

"Thank you for everything."

After they disconnected, she sat for several more minutes with her phone in one hand. Then she called Josiah.

He picked up on the third ring. "Molly."

"You're still an asshole."

"You're still Captain Obvious," he replied. He sounded busy and annoyed. "Still angry over that stupid kiss?"

She clenched her free hand on the steering wheel. It still stung that it had meant nothing to him.

What the hell, she thought. I put one man on a hook today. Might as well try for another one. In a steady, cold voice, she said, "So you think kissing me is stupid?"

The change in atmosphere was almost electric. "That's not what I meant."

"Isn't it?" She imagined each syllable like an ice pick driving into his skin. "You made it abundantly clear on Monday how you only kissed me to get me riled."

The intensity on the other end increased until she felt like her ear might start to sizzle. He bit out, "That is not what I said."

"It's exactly what you said," she snapped. "You kissed me to rile me up. You wanted to make me do what *you* wanted me to do. You manipulated me—again. And maybe you only manhandled me *a little*, but what makes you think *a little* is acceptable? Then you got condescending when you talked about *tolerating* me because I dared to respond with outrage. So yeah, I'm still angry, and I don't know when or if I'm going to forgive you. And I certainly don't know if I'm going to trust you again."

Silence pulsed. When he spoke again, the impatient annoyance had left his voice and he sounded serious. "Okay. You're right about all of it. I behaved badly, and I'm sorry. You didn't deserve it, and I shouldn't have done it."

She told him, "That's what you should have said on Monday."

She could hear his slow, staggered breathing and began to count. Four. Seven… One side of her mouth lifted. He was using the four-seven-eight breathing technique.

She'd gotten under his skin.

Good. He deserved it.

When he finally spoke, he sounded brisk and calm. "Is that why you called?"

"No, but I'm glad I got it off my chest." She ran her gaze over the dealership's busy parking lot. "Austin accepted the divorce settlement approximately ninety minutes after he received the papers. My lawyer is filing the papers this afternoon. I'll let you know when the divorce is finalized. That's all."

"Wait. I'd like to…"

A younger, softer Molly might have listened. She would have been eager to please and anxious to smooth things over. But she wasn't that younger, softer Molly anymore. She felt no need to contort herself into another shape just to fit other people's desires or expectations.

So she interrupted. "I don't care what you would like. I don't want to hear from you. I don't want to think about you. I don't want to be manipulated by you anymore. If I have something to say to you, I'll call. Otherwise, leave me the hell alone."

She hung up, glared at the phone, and held her breath.

It remained silent, as well it should.

After a few moments, she started the Cherokee again. She felt strange and hollow, as if all her purpose had been cut out. Back at her apartment, she played desultorily with cooking a bolognese sauce, but her heart wasn't in it.

She felt like she was waiting for something else to happen. Things felt incomplete, like a lump of half-molded clay on a sculptor's table. The true face of her new reality had yet to emerge. There had been no real resolution between her and Austin, just a phone call from Nina to say her marriage was over. While that was a victory of sorts, it felt odd to not speak with him.

Not that she *wanted* to speak with him—in fact, the

opposite was true. She didn't miss him, not in the slightest.

The more time passed, the more she realized how much of a habit living with him had become. Austin had been part of the list of "shoulds" that had dictated her life. She *should* be married to him, or so she had thought, just as she *should* be a dutiful daughter, despite the fact that her mother treated her with a lack of loving warmth and a wealth of judgment.

Still, a few weeks ago she and Austin had been talking about putting in a new sprinkler system in the front lawn. The meandering years of conversation that had made up their marriage had been chopped off midsentence.

Now the shackle of their home and all their possessions settled around her neck, and she felt too empty to celebrate. She had begun on her path to freedom, but she wasn't free yet.

After a while, she turned off the stove, searched for local real estate agents on her phone, and began calling down the list until she connected with a live person instead of voice mail. The agent, Tanya Martin, was smart and charming. Molly arranged to meet Tanya at the house on the following Saturday when they could go over the property and sign Tanya's contract.

After that, she spent the weekend at the public library, researching witches and witchcraft. She also meditated religiously and started taking yoga classes again. It felt good to practice the simple disciplines, and she could sense the deep, interior golden well settling into a pool of calm.

Julia called on Monday. Molly felt a huge emotional disconnect from the conversation, but she stuck with the phone call for Julia's sake.

Still, she had little to say. What could she offer? "Hey, I discovered I can break bottles with my mind, and I really want to learn that privacy spell the new DA cast last week."

Yeah, that would go over well. So she mostly listened. When Julia complained about the long hours her husband worked, Molly realized that Julia complained about her husband all the time.

"You know you don't have to live that way if you don't want to," she said.

"That's easy for you to say now that you've taken the plunge and left your own asshole husband. You don't have a child to think about, or daycare expenses, or how you would manage being a single mother on child support."

Molly marveled at the depth of her friend's discontent. Had Julia always sounded so negative, or was this something new? Or maybe now that the blinders had fallen from Molly's eyes, she was seeing everything more clearly?

"All of that is true," Molly replied dryly. "But it still wasn't easy. And if you really need to leave, you know the child support would be enough. You might have to cut some corners and get a job, but you could make it work."

Julia's exhalation of laughter sounded bitter. "You know, it's funny. I used to envy your and Austin's lifestyle. Everything seemed so easy for you, but then you left him and altered almost everything about your life, and you know what? Nothing's changed. I still envy you."

Soon after, Molly ended the call on the pretext of needing to leave for an appointment. As she hung up, she realized she and Julia didn't have anything in common anymore.

She was supposed to see her mother that week, but when Wednesday arrived, she decided to call instead. As Gloria answered, she said, "Hi, Mom, Just wanted to let you know I won't be coming to see you today."

"Austin said you filed for divorce." Gloria's voice sounded cold and flat, the way she did when she was disappointed in Molly. "In spite of my best efforts, you're intent on ruining the best thing that ever happened to you."

Just a couple of months ago, Molly would have clenched from the stress of confronting her mother. She had heard that divorces divided friends and family, and Gloria always had liked Austin better.

Now she put her feet up on the coffee table and watched a sparrow nesting in a maple tree outside the rental's window. The sun was shining through the leaves, and she felt like she was immersed in a sea of gold-dappled green.

It was a damn beautiful day.

"You're wrong, you know," she told Gloria cheerfully. "Filing for divorce is the best thing that ever happened to me. I'm going to change my name too, but not back to my maiden name. I'm going to pick an entirely new name, just for me. You will hate it, of course, and I don't see why I need to drive forty-five minutes for us to have this talk in person. In fact, I don't see a reason for us to have any further conversations at all."

"You're an embarrassment," her mother snapped. "I don't have any idea what to say when my friends ask about you. I tell them you're having a midlife crisis and you've lost your damn mind. When you come to your senses, Austin will be long gone, and you'll be sorry, aging, and alone."

"Thank you, Mom. Thanks for making it clear that I'm making the right choices."

"What are you talking about? I don't support anything you're doing!"

"I know. And that's okay. You get to be you. But you know what? I get to choose to not be around that—and I get to be me."

"What are you saying, that my only daughter is going to abandon me?"

"I'm not abandoning you. In spite of everything, I love you. But you've been verbally abusive and controlling my whole life. In fact, you set my expectations so low it's no wonder I got entangled with someone like Austin. And I'm no longer going to put up with someone who treats me like that."

"How dare you." Gloria's words turned low and venomous. "Don't think I'm going to leave you anything in my will. I'd rather give my money to charity. At least then I know it will go to someone who is grateful to get it."

Ah, the ungrateful daughter card.

"Go right ahead. Give it all to charity." She sighed. "I don't know why you are the way you are. I know your mother wasn't very nice to you, so maybe you're just passing down the way you were treated. But I've finally had enough. The only regret I have is that I didn't get to this point sooner."

"The way you're acting would break your father's heart."

She nodded to herself. Breaking her father's heart was another one of her mother's favorite admonishments. "If you ever want to talk to me in a way that is loving and supportive, please give me a call. I would love to hear that from you. Until then, I don't want to talk to you."

"I mean it, Molly Ann. I'll cut you off without a cent."

Feeling twenty pounds lighter, she said softly, "Bye, Mom."

So, Austin got the friends and the mother. Molly got the house and all their money.

She smiled. That was okay with her.

Chapter Seven

THE REST OF the week passed peacefully. According to the agreement, Austin was supposed to be out of the house before Saturday. Once Molly received the go-ahead from Nina, she confirmed the meeting with the real estate agent for six o'clock Saturday evening.

The timing was somewhat unusual, but Tanya was amenable, and going back to the house at suppertime gave them the best chance of avoiding curious, nosy neighbors dropping by.

When midafternoon on Saturday came, she reluctantly decided she should go over an hour early. Tanya knew a company that would sell the contents of the house at a flea market for a commission, but Molly wanted to collect photographs of her father and make sure there wasn't anything else she wanted to keep.

When she pulled into the long, familiar driveway, a sour feeling like heartburn settled at the back of her throat. She parked and studied the scene.

It really was a beautiful house, spacious and well-positioned on a large corner lot. The backyard faced a large park with lots of trees that offered a nice sense of privacy. She hated the sight of it.

When she let herself in the front door, a rotting smell assaulted her.

What the hell? Quickly, she walked through the silent downstairs.

The kitchen was exactly as it had been when she had left the house a few weeks ago. Everything single thing.

The un-iced cake still lay on its plate. Browned wedges of lemons and limes filled serving bowls and dirty drink glasses. Uneaten hors d'oeuvres lay scattered on serving trays. Curling veggies and congealed dip sat on a party tray, and in one side of the sink, a large ceramic pot was filled with the rotting, marinated chicken that had never been cooked.

He hadn't touched any of it. If anything, he had added to the mess by throwing dirty, food-crusted plates into the other side of the sink.

He could have done nothing, and the cleaning service would have come on Wednesday and taken care of everything. Instead, he must have canceled the service and left the mess for her to face.

"You petty son of a bitch," she muttered.

Anger clenched her muscles. Moving quickly, she walked through the rest of the house. His office was bare, all the furniture gone.

There were other spots of nastiness. The master suite was a mess. He had left drawers pulled out and hangers strewn on the floor. A sour smell rose from the dirty, unmade bed. In the bathroom, bottles of her shampoo and conditioner were opened and dumped upside down in the sink where the liquids had hardened and congealed.

She jogged downstairs again to check the area where they had hung a collage of family photos.

The wall was empty. Every good photo she'd had of her father. They were all gone.

Furious and hurting, she rushed outside. The garbage was picked up on Thursdays. He might have just thrown the photos away. They might still be in the trash bins in the nook by the side of the garage.

When she reached the big, black bins, she threw back the hinged lids on both the recycling and the garbage bins. They were empty.

A sob tried to bubble up. Wiping at her face with the back of one hand, she bit it back.

She had hung the best photos, but there was still one last chance to find something from her father. Otherwise, she would have to go back to her mother and endure more recriminations and emotional blackmail.

She kept mementos in large plastic tubs in the basement. If Austin's spite hadn't driven him to destroy things down there, there were a few photos, things that were too damaged or deemed too goofy to hang on the wall. Slamming the lids down, she jogged back through the house and down the basement stairs.

She had tucked the storage containers high on a shelf underneath the stairs to protect them from potential flooding. As she looked into the shadowed niche, the bins were still in place. Hardly daring to hope, she pulled them out and opened them.

Everything was still neatly packed as she had originally left them. Her high school and college diplomas. Childhood drawings and holiday cards and family snapshots, many of them faded. Some were torn and bent. One was of her father standing by another man at a barbeque. He wore a plaid, short-sleeved shirt and held a martini glass.

Molly couldn't remember who the other man was. In the photo, both men were laughing. She touched it gently. This would be enough.

After she put the bins in the back of her Jeep, she got to work. When the doorbell sounded a few minutes after six, she had cleared out the rotting food, thrown away everything in the fridge, and the dishwasher was running with a full load while the worst of the crusted dishes soaked in the sink. She had left the back door wide open to air out the smell, and a cool breeze swept through the house.

Wiping off her hands, she went to answer the door.

Tanya Martin was a young, attractive woman, perhaps thirty years old, with improbably red hair, immaculate makeup, and a wide smile. They talked for forty-five minutes and went over the comps Tanya had pulled for house prices in the neighborhood.

Then Molly signed the contract and Tanya took her leave. As Molly closed the front door, she smiled with relief. The house was well maintained, stylishly decorated, and located in a "blue chip" neighborhood that never went out of demand. After the first weekend of showings, they would probably see several offers. Maybe even a bidding war.

If Molly stuck to her intention of only accepting a cash offer, she could be rid of the property within a few weeks. This was going to go quickly.

Alone once more, she turned her attention back to cleaning. By the time she was nearly finished, darkness had fallen.

The last thing to do was change the bed. Quickly, she tore off the bedding and made the bed with a coverlet in a classic faded paisley pattern.

After patting the pillows into place, she turned to confront the pile of dirty bedding she had dumped in the hall. The last thing she wanted was to stick around and do laundry.

Too bad she didn't know any housework spells. (Yet?)

"Screw it," she muttered. "I'm done cleaning up after that bastard."

Gathering the pile into her arms, she carried it downstairs and out the back door to the garbage bins. Letting it fall to the ground, she threw open the trash bin and went down on one knee to gather it up again.

As she did, a pair of familiar shoes and long, jeans-clad legs came into view.

Austin.

She leaped to her feet.

She wasn't fast enough.

Something hard came down on the back of her head. Pain exploded, and the world disappeared in a gray haze.

She didn't pass out, not quite. As if from a long distance away, she felt her body collapse where the gravel met grass. Something hard hit her again and again. Maybe a golf club or a baseball bat. She hadn't known she could feel so much pain.

Coughing, she tried to curl into a fetal position and cover her head with one arm. Austin kicked her in the abdomen. The blow knocked her over. She rolled with it and landed flat on her stomach, working desperately to suck air into her cramped lungs.

Agony stabbed her through the chest. She had no breath. She couldn't shout or scream for help.

As she fought to get upright, he landed with his full weight on both knees at the small of her back, knocking the air out of her again as he drove her flat.

Gravel ground into her cheek, and red pulsed in her gaze. Something wet ran down the side of her face. Vaguely she felt her fingers scrabble at the rocks and grass.

Somewhere inside she had a new, burgeoning Power just waiting to be deployed, if only she could figure out how to use it.

Funny, she thought. It never occurred to me to practice throwing Power behind my back. I always had to look at whatever I was hitting. Joke's on me. Ha ha.

Hard fingers tangled in her hair. New pain flared as

Austin yanked her head back and whispered in her ear, "You had to take *everything*, didn't you? It wasn't enough to serve me with divorce papers. You had to take the whole goddamn thing. Everything I worked for all these years. All the investments. Did you think I was just going to let it go and walk away, you stupid cunt?"

He knew how much she hated that word. It must have given him a lot of satisfaction to finally call her that.

She coughed, "You know, I kinda did."

Her scalp was on fire. Everything was on fire. She tried to twist around so she could see him. If she could lay eyes on him, she could hit him, but his knees drilled into her back and kept her pinned in place.

"Maybe I will let it go and walk away," he whispered. "But first I want that file back. You know the one."

Oh yeah. No doubt about it. He was so dirty.

She tried to laugh, but her bruised rib cage wouldn't let her. As she closed her fingers around a handful of gravel, she gasped out a laugh. "You really think I didn't make a copy? Several copies?"

"We're going to clear out your email," he growled, yanking cruelly at her hair. "You're going to give me back the original and any copies you made, and then I'm going to let you go. It's as simple as that. All you have to do is cooperate, and this will all be over with."

All except for Josiah and his investigation.

Ha ha.

"And if I don't?" Just as she couldn't hit him with her magic, she couldn't throw the damn gravel in his face while he had her pinned on her stomach. The angle was wrong.

"If you don't, I'm going to hurt you a lot more than I have already. Believe it or not, I don't want to do this." He grabbed her wrist and shook it. "Drop what's in your fucking hand or I'll tear out your fucking hair."

She opened her hand and let the rocks drop to the ground.

When she was done, he twisted her arm behind her back, and his weight lifted from the base of her spine.

She had no time to feel relief. The world tilted and agony screamed when he used her twisted arm to haul her upright. Staggering, she fought to get her balance and turn so she could face him, but he kept her arm twisted behind her back and hooked an arm around her neck, bending her backward and keeping her off-balance. Keeping her under control.

"We're going to walk to my car." His breath touched her cheek, and she caught a whiff of alcohol and garlic. Apparently he had enjoyed a nice meal before he came out to the house to kick the shit out of her. "Then we'll drive to wherever you're staying. You're going to give me everything, and we'll wipe your email account and your computer, and I'll leave. We'll be done, and we'll never have to see each other again. You understand?"

"Got it," she croaked.

He frog-marched her through the backyard to the side street that bordered the property. A grinding red agony flared with every step. He had cracked a few of her ribs. As they went, she tried to look around, squinting through a stinging wetness in one eye.

Half the neighboring houses were dark. It was Saturday night, and many people would have gone out. He was abducting her, and there wasn't anybody around to witness it.

Austin had tucked his BMW unobtrusively in the shadow of a large maple, around the corner from the house. When she saw the shadowed car, something happened to her blurred vision.

The outline of the car faded. She distinctly saw red plastic gasoline containers and coils of rope in the trunk.

Gasoline and rope.

What a shock. He had no intention of letting her go after destroying all the copies of the bank statement and wiping her email.

Well, fair enough. She had no intention of meekly climbing into his car.

It wasn't hard to pretend to stumble. She went down, biting back a groan as her throat and her twisted arm took the full weight of her body where Austin restrained her.

For a moment she choked at the tight band of his arm around her windpipe while the socket in her shoulder popped. Then with a muffled curse, he released her. She dropped to the ground and rolled onto her back.

He was already moving to restrain her again, kneeling on one of her arms while he leaned hard on one elbow at the base of her throat.

She barely paid attention. The moon cast his features and the bulk of his shoulders in shadow, but she could see him well enough.

This time the lightning did not just flicker at the edges of her gaze. Instead, it filled her vision entirely. Power illuminated her body from within. Tucking in her chin, she focused on his chest and released.

Power blew out of every pore in her skin. When it punched into him point-blank, it lifted him into the air and threw him several feet away. He landed heavily, with an audible *thump*.

For a moment neither one of them moved.

Get up, she told her body fiercely. *Move.*

Easier said than done. She rocked onto her side, letting the spike of renewed pain out in a hiss as she dragged first one knee underneath her torso, then the other, balancing her weight on one hand while the arm that Austin had twisted hung uselessly at her side.

Austin groaned from where he had landed. He was stirring too.

She beat him upright, just barely. Fighting to stay on her feet, she waited until he straightened. He stared, his expression full of uncomprehending shock.

"What the fuck was that—"

There was so much lightning she could barely see through it. Her body couldn't contain it all. It blew out of her, and she hit him again.

This time the blow spun him around. He twisted and

fell as hard and gracelessly as he had before.

That gave her the chance to secure her balance. Sucking air, she took her first real breath since he had hit her. Something ground in her chest as her lungs expanded, but the oxygen helped to clear her head.

She swiped at the wetness obscuring her left eye, watching warily as Austin coughed and moaned. Her phone was in the house, resting on the kitchen counter. She couldn't call for help until she got inside. She couldn't run to get to it, nor could she run away.

She might be able to hobble. And it seemed like too much damn effort to suck in a deep enough breath to scream for help—if any of her neighbors were around to hear it. Her ribs were giving her hell.

Meanwhile Austin struggled to get up again.

Sometimes you have to go with what you've got.

"Earlier I was feeling like there was something lacking from this divorce," she croaked as she limped toward him. "Some kind of final conversation, a mutual acknowledgment that this is the end."

As he lifted his head, he gave her a look filled with wide-eyed dread. She hit him again with magic, hard.

She told him, "I'm not some piece of property to *get under control.* I'm not obligated to spread my legs just because you happen to want sex. So you had to earn every fuck you got out of me. Cry me a river, asshole."

The Power was so lovely and light. Wielding it was like wrapping her fingers around the sun. She poured it down her arm and held it in one hand, relishing its warm, radiant glow. When she flung it at his face, it struck him with an audible slap that knocked his head back.

"I'm not someone you can cheat on whenever it suits you while you ignore every promise and vow you ever made to me."

She struck him again. This time she knocked him onto the street, and as he stumbled and went down, he cried out, a high, thin sound that barely caused a ripple in the air. Collapsing, he lay sprawled on the pavement and didn't move.

Had she killed him? She hadn't meant to, but she wasn't sure.

You don't want to hurt someone by accident. Everything you do, you want to do with intention.

She should probably stop pounding on him, but she still had so much rage left. The Power told her Austin had tucked a cigarette lighter in his front pocket. Carefully, she bent over to fish it out. Then she turned to regard his beloved BMW. He had always taken take care of that car like it was his own baby.

This time the blast that blew out of her was like a ground-to-air missile, taking with it the last of her strength. The car flipped into the air. With a booming crash that splintered the peaceful night, the BMW landed on its roof and rolled three times before it came to a halt. The smell of spilled gasoline wafted over to her.

She told Austin's immobile form, "I'm not some possession you can destroy just because I'm no longer convenient."

In the distance, she heard a shout. Then another. People would be arriving on the scene very soon, but she had one final thing left to do.

Limping over to a wet, spreading stain on the pavement, she squatted, flicked the cigarette lighter, and held the small flame to the liquid. It caught, and a blue flame streaked along the path the liquid had taken, back to the car. Within moments, the BMW was engulfed in flames.

Straightening, she walked away. She made it halfway back across the lawn before the car exploded. The concussion slapped her in the back, followed by a warmth like a spread of fiery wings, and boiling heat and light turned the night into day.

She glanced over her shoulder. Austin hadn't been caught in the explosion, not that she had stopped to calculate one way or another. He lay prone and unmoving while, several yards away, his car burned in the fireball from the ignited gasoline.

She nodded. There was the closure she'd been looking for.

✧ ✧ ✧

SHE MADE IT back to the house, locked the back door, and turned off the lights. Then she scooped up her phone. Leaning against the counter for support, she punched Josiah's name with a shaking finger. She listened to it ring. And ring.

Well, shit. Her knees wobbled, and she sank to a

sitting position on the floor.

Just when she was about to tap Off, he picked up. "Molly." His voice was cool and guarded. "I'm surprised to hear from you. What do you want?"

"I might have killed Austin," she croaked. "Oopsie?"

His coolness vaporized. "What happened," he demanded. "Did he hurt you? Where are you?"

"At the house. His car's on fire. The neighbors are disturbed." Leaning her head back against the cabinet, she said tiredly, "I might know only one magic trick, but it turns out I can do a lot with it. I can't stay here."

"You didn't answer my question. Did he hurt you?"

"Yeah."

"How bad is it?"

"Do doctors still tape broken ribs?"

He swore, and her thoughts scattered like buckshot. If she went to the hospital, they would ask her questions she didn't want to answer. Meanwhile, when Austin's car stopped burning, some bright expert would inspect it.

There were no skid marks on the road, no other signs of impact. What about the extra gasoline? Cars carried a lot of gasoline anyway, so maybe that wouldn't matter, but the BMW was in park, and that was decidedly incongruent with an accident.

It was going to look exactly like what it was—arson.

"I can hear the approaching sirens." Josiah's voice brought her from her mental wandering.

How could he hear the sirens from where he was? Belatedly, she realized she could hear approaching sirens too. He must have caught the sound over the phone. Shock was turning her stupid.

"I could come pick you up, but it would take time for me to get there. It would be better if you could leave before they get organized at the scene. Can you drive?"

She sighed. "Only way to know is if I try."

His voice gentled. "All you need to do is get a quarter mile away and you'll be out of the activity. Do that, and I'll meet you wherever you are."

"Got it."

"Stay on the line."

"Can't," she grunted. "Need both hands to get up."

He swore again, a quiet whiplash of profanity. "Call me back as soon you can."

"I'm not going to call you back right away. I'm going to try to make it back to my apartment."

"Fine, dammit. Give me the address and I'll meet you there."

She told him, hung up, and concentrated on getting upright, finding her purse and keys, and slipping out the back door.

To her left, the edge of the scene was barely visible. She couldn't see the car itself, which was around the corner, but she could see the glow from the fire along with a few people who had gathered. Their attention was on the unfolding drama.

She didn't think anybody noticed as she slipped around the garage to where her car was parked in the driveway.

Climbing in made every injury flare with such intense pain she almost passed out. Hunched over and panting shallowly, she started the ignition, reversed, and eased down the street in the opposite direction from the fire.

Once she was stationary and had the Jeep in motion, driving became easier. Her body decided it was a good time to start shaking, so she took her time. When she finally turned into the driveway by her apartment, a dark, powerful, low-slung car waited down the street, lit by a nearby streetlight.

She put the Jeep in park. Her door was yanked open, and Josiah's big body filled the open space. When he saw her, he hesitated, and his face tightened.

"Okay," he said carefully while a muscle bunched in his lean jaw. "You're going to be okay."

She gave him a thumbs-up. "Piece of cake."

Something happened to his tight features. She was too preoccupied with her own problems to figure out what it was.

Gently, he cupped long fingers around her hand, upraised thumb and all. "Can you swing your legs out?"

She thought that over. It was a surprisingly complicated maneuver that would mean shifting her ribs and using abdominal muscles. "Sure. Give me a few minutes."

"You don't have to," he told her. "I can move you, but that's going to hurt too. Are you ready?"

She nodded. He slipped a hard, muscled arm underneath her knees. When he eased her legs out, the broken ribs ground together. A cry tore out of her, and stars flashed against her eyelids.

Then a black hole swallowed her whole, pain and all.

Chapter Eight

JOSIAH HAD BEEN spending the weekend reviewing the last of the open case files his office inherited from the previous DA. Working extra hours didn't bother him in the slightest. The sooner he got through the backlog, the sooner he could concentrate more on his own agenda.

He had taken two portable office files "home" with him. With ample food-delivery options, he'd had no plans for leaving the city apartment. That way he could kill two birds with one stone—he could process old case files while putting in an appearance at the address of his official life.

At least that was the plan until he received Molly's phone call.

When his phone rang and her name appeared, he had to wrestle with an unruly surge of pride as he considered whether he would answer.

She'd ripped him a new one in their previous conversation, and he was honest enough to admit he had deserved it. But when he'd tried to extend a new olive branch, she had shut him down so hard he still heard the ice in her voice when he looked at her name on the screen.

He refused to be at the beck and call of *any woman*, no matter how intriguing, gifted—or right—she might be. But then curiosity got the better of him. It had been blazingly clear Molly had meant their previous conversation to be their last, so why was she reaching out again?

He picked up… and her first words galvanized him into action. He was already racing out to the parking garage and leaping into his car before they had even hung up. Casting a cloaking spell over his vehicle, he broke speed limits to reach her rental, only to be forced to sit in place until she arrived.

While he waited, he called Anson. "Austin Sullivan attacked Molly at their house, and she put him down hard. She doesn't know if she killed him. I need you to monitor police channels and go to their house to check things out."

"I'm on it. What am I looking for specifically?"

"For one thing, I want to know if he's alive or dead, because that will impact her legal situation." He fell silent, his thoughts racing as he kept a sharp eye on the quiet street.

Maria had sensed violence surrounding the Seychelles file, but they had assumed any violence would be connected to their investigation. Everyone in his coven had already accepted they walked a dangerous path as they stalked their quarry.

It had never occurred to them that Molly might

become the target of violence. Maybe it should have, but she'd been smart and sensible when she'd taken precautions and rented her new place.

Then she negated all of it when she went back to her old house.

"Josiah, you still there?"

Anson's voice snapped him back into focus. "Yes. Sorry. For another thing, we don't know if this is purely a domestic dispute or if it's related to the intel she gave me. Be careful, Anson. We don't know who's involved."

"Understood. I'll be in touch when I know something." The other man disconnected.

A few minutes later, an unfamiliar Jeep Cherokee turned into the neighborhood street and approached too slowly. Josiah readied for possible battle until the SUV turned into the driveway for the rental and light from a nearby streetlamp fell on the driver.

It was Molly.

He didn't remember leaving his car. The next thing he knew, he had muscled into the open space left by her open car door and was staring down at her.

He'd seen dead bodies and victims of violence before, both in crime photos and in real life. He was no stranger to the pallid complexions, the bruising and contusions, the lurid appearance of blood. He'd witnessed dismemberments and the gruesome results of what happened when coyotes and other wildlife feasted on a body.

But there was always an extra punch when violence

hit someone he knew. His gut tightened as he looked at what Sullivan had done to his beautiful wife.

She looked dead pale, with dark hollows like bruises ringing her eyes. Blood had dripped from a scalp wound into one eye, and the opposite cheekbone was swollen and discolored. She held herself like every movement, every breath, was an agony. He'd had broken ribs before and knew just how bad she felt. God only knew what other damage she had sustained.

But he was jolted to see that somehow none of the visible wounds detracted from her beauty. She held herself with such fierce stoicism that, if anything, she looked even more beautiful than ever.

She looked like a warrior. Like a survivor.

Something powerful and unrecognized welled up. He didn't understand it, and when his eyes dampened, that shocked him more than anything.

It was a relief when she passed out. His brain rebooted, and he could think again. Scooping her up, he carried her to his car and buckled her into the front passenger seat. Then he grabbed her purse, phone, and car keys and raced back to his Audi, climbed in, and drove to the safe house.

This time he followed more safety precautions than usual and drove a circuitous route. That meant the journey took twice as long, and all the while he whispered deflection spells until they were as safe as he knew how to make them. Only then did he pull behind the country house. Easing Molly's lax form back into his arms, he tucked her possessions on her abdomen and carried her down to the basement.

Once he'd laid her on the bed, he cast a spell of divination. The areas of damage lit in his mind like flares. She had a concussion, two broken ribs, and some hellish contusions. Her left shoulder was strained badly, but there was no real damage to the joint.

She also had some internal bleeding, but it wasn't life threatening and had almost stopped. And she should probably get stitches for her head wound.

Sullivan had used some kind of club, because the bruising and contusions striped her body in livid bars. The beating spoke of rage and cruelty. If Sullivan's goal had been to knock her senseless, a simple blow to the head would have sufficed. He had wanted to inflict maximum pain and damage.

Josiah balled his hands into fists. He despised men who beat those who were not as physically strong as they were. "If she didn't already kill you, I will," he whispered to the absent man. "And I won't just murder you—I'll crucify you."

He could be patient. If there was one thing he knew how to do, it was how to wait for the right opportunity.

But right now he needed to focus on more urgent matters. His magical talent didn't lie in healing, but he knew basic spells to mend damage, and that was really all she needed. It would also be a kindness to cast them while she was still unconscious.

He took several photos quickly in case she decided to

press charges, and then he started with the head wound since that injury concerned him the most. It was still seeping blood, so he carefully pinched the torn skin together and held it with his fingers while he cast spells, pausing only long enough to verify that her body had absorbed one before moving on to the next.

She began to stir, and he muttered a mental curse. Healing damage was a painful business as the magic forced the body to knit together. They weren't going to get lucky tonight. The discomfort was bringing her around.

Gingerly, he lifted his hand away from the head wound and inspected the area. The edges held, at least for the moment, but she needed more healing before she was out of danger.

She pushed his hand away and curled on her side. "What arc you doing?"

"I'm healing you, or at least I was." He squatted by the edge of the bed so that he was in her line of sight.

"My head is splitting." She licked her lips. "And I'm thirsty."

"You have a concussion. I'll get you a drink of water in a minute." He looked her over. Then, even though it didn't matter, he found himself asking, "What did he hit you with?"

"I don't know. He came at me from behind when I was taking out some trash." Her good eye was cloudy and hazed. "I did everything you told me to do, but it never occurred to me to practice hitting something behind me. That's why he was able to get so many strikes in."

"You did well." He touched her shoulder with light fingers.

Her gaze traveled away from his expression and she frowned. "This doesn't look like my rental. Where are we?"

"I brought you to a safe house outside the city limits." He wanted to touch her again. The compulsion confounded him, so he didn't. Instead, he pressed a fist against the cool bedspread. "We're in the basement."

She frowned. "Why?"

"Why are you in the safe house?" He was prepared to be patient. Sometimes concussion victims struggled with confusion.

"No." Her frown deepened, and she focused on him again. "Why are we in the basement?"

She stared as if *he* were the one who struggled with confusion, and he bit back a smile. "Mostly because there isn't any furniture in the house, but also there are protection spells down here. Can't you feel them?"

Sudden panic and grief cracked her ravaged face. She clamped a hand on his wrist. "I can't feel anything. My Power was like a deep golden well at my core, but now it's gone. What's wrong?"

Her panic jolted him. He had been so preoccupied with checking her over for physical damage, he hadn't checked for magical injuries.

"Calm down. I'll check you over."

Swallowing hard, she curled tighter as he scanned her again. Her taut grip cut off the blood supply to his hand, but he didn't dislodge her fingers.

Almost immediately he understood what she had meant. Where he had once sensed her Power now felt raw and dark. Carefully he probed, but he didn't sense any permanent damage.

Once he was sure, he said, "You're all right. You just overextended yourself and burned out your source."

"My source," she repeated softly. Her death grip never eased.

He put his free hand over hers. "Imagine if you tried to sing a two-hour-long opera without conditioning your vocal cords. You would experience throat strain, and you might even lose your voice for three or four days until you recovered. That's what you did to your magic. It may take up to a week or so, but it will come back."

Midway through his explanation, she closed her eyes and sighed. Only then did her grip ease.

Most victims of violence acted like victims. They were hurt and traumatized, at least until they recovered their emotional bearings again. But her emotional bearings hadn't been rocked one iota until she thought she might have lost her magic.

He had wondered how she would handle having magic ability. It appeared she had come to terms with it very well.

The blood that had poured down half her face bothered him. He said abruptly, "Hold on a sec. I'll be right back."

Straightening, he went into the utilitarian bathroom and checked his phone. No word yet from Anson. He kept a glass at the bathroom sink. He filled it with water, and then he dampened a clean washcloth and took both to her.

With his assistance, she swallowed a few sips of water and wiped away the worst of the blood. When she eased back down on his pillow, she was paler than ever. Dropping the soiled cloth on the bare floor by the doorway, he sat on the edge of the bed beside her knees.

"I'm worried about that head wound. I want to cast more healing spells on you, but fair warning—my healing skills aren't fancy. They're going to hurt, but they're also the quickest way to shore up that concussion and strengthen your ribs. Are you game?"

She closed her eyes again. "Do you have to?"

For the first time she sounded as miserable as she looked, but he hardened his heart against it. He replied flatly, "It's either that or I take you to the nearest hospital. I don't have time to babysit someone with a concussion."

"Okay." Her lips tightened. "Do it."

He rested one hand on her shoulder. In spite of his hard words, he hesitated, but he had spoken the truth. He didn't have time to babysit someone with a concussion, and right now she couldn't afford to answer any questions that health practitioners at an ER would ask.

So he cast spell after spell, watching as each hammered into her body. At the first one, she flinched and hid her face in the crook of her arm. Then she didn't move again or make a sound until he stopped.

Was she breathing or holding her breath? He stroked bloody, tangled hair back from her forehead as he scanned her head. Quietly he murmured, "You need more healing, but we've hit your limit. Your body won't absorb any more right now."

She shifted cautiously. "Thank you. Seriously, Josiah. Thank you for everything."

The gracious thing to do would be to accept her thanks, but he had never been a gracious man. He set his teeth. "You're a fucking disaster."

One corner of her mouth notched up, astonishing him. "I thought I had promise. I thought if I hitched myself to your little red wagon, the sky would be our limit. What happened to us ruling the Eastern Seaboard together?"

He coughed out an angry laugh. "That was before I discovered how high maintenance you are. You had balls, calling me after our last conversation. What makes you think you can hang up on a man and still call him for help? Why was my number the one you dialed?"

"I didn't have anybody else," she whispered. "You were the only one I could call."

Silence fell inside him, deep like a snowfall, as he absorbed that. Then he thought of how crowded her house had been the night of Hell Party.

"Bullshit," he snapped. "You must have a list of friends as long as my arm."

"Maybe I have a list of people I could ask out to a martini lunch." Her cloudy gaze had cleared, and she gave him a steady look. "But you were the only person I could call tonight. You're the only one who understands what I'm going through. I didn't even know if you would pick up, but then you did, and that was when I knew you would help me."

"I almost didn't, and it would have served you right." He glared at her, then stood to pace.

"Maybe," she admitted. "But I'm not going to apologize for losing my temper. In some ways you've helped me, but in others… Josiah, you've not treated me very well."

The room felt too small and confined. He stood in the open doorway and looked out at the rest of the unfinished basement while resting hands on his hips and tilting his head back and forth to ease the tense muscles in his neck and shoulders.

She was right. He hadn't treated her very well. Meeting Molly, and interacting with her, was like confronting himself in a fucking mirror after decades of avoiding his reflection.

And he didn't particularly like the man he saw. He had fallen into the habit of seeing people and things as potential tools he could use to achieve his objectives. The long years of focusing single-mindedly on his mission had changed him, and not for the better.

"Guilty as charged," he muttered. More quietly, he added, "I'll do better."

"Well," she said after a moment. "Helping me tonight has also gone a long way toward erasing the rest, and I won't forget that." The bedsprings creaked. "I'd kill for a hot shower."

Turning, he found her sitting up, sore arm cradled against her torso. "There's a bathroom down here. Think you're steady enough to keep from falling in the shower?"

"Only one way to find out." She pushed to her feet and her complexion whitened further, but she didn't sway or stumble. Frustration twisted her features. "I can't lift my arm over my head."

"Hold on." Pulling out his pocketknife, he urged her to turn her back to him. When she complied, he cut the soft material of her T-shirt from neck to waist and sawed through the armhole of her bad arm. After stripping the ruined material off, he tossed it on top of the soiled washcloth. "Can you take off your pants on your own?"

"I think so." Her head bent as she unfastened her jeans.

As she kicked out of them, he walked to the battered dresser and pulled out one of his old T-shirts. The cotton material had been washed so many times that the material felt butter-soft to his callused fingers. He was big enough that the bottom of the shirt should hit her thighs. He pulled out a pair of gray sweats and athletic socks.

"I have some clothing essentials here, but none of it's fancy."

"Trust me." She gave him a dry look. "Fancy is overrated."

"You're going to have to do without underwear until we wash what you're wearing or get you something new." When he turned back to her, the sight of her nearly nude body stopped him in his tracks. Still clad in a lacy gray bra and panties, she was as covered as any modem woman on a beach.

But they weren't on a beach. She stood in a private place where he often slept, and she was beautiful everywhere, with a racy-looking body, long, delicately muscled legs, and high breasts that he immediately wanted to cup in his hands.

But if he'd thought her face had looked bad, the marks of damage on her body looked worse. He had targeted her concussion with most of the healing spells, but some of the magic had filtered down to other injuries. It was enough to advance the bruises and contusions to what would have been the second or third day of the healing process—right about at the point when they looked and felt the worst.

"Brace yourself, babe," he said bluntly. "There's not much of a mirror in the bathroom down here, but you look like shit."

The edges of her full lips turned downward as she ran fingers over the blackened mottling over her narrow rib cage. Her voice was quiet. "It's nothing that won't heal."

"You were lucky." He handed her the clothes. He still wanted to touch her, only this time the desire was almost overwhelming. "There's soap and shampoo in the shower stall and towels in the cabinet. Call if you get dizzy or need help."

"Will do." She gave him an unfathomable look before turning away.

There were only three rooms in the big basement. They bordered a large open area that held a washer and dryer, the furnace, and the water heater. The bathroom was located right by the bedroom. She went around the corner and shut the door.

He waited until he heard the shower going. Then he pulled out his phone to text Anson. `Report.`

Anson responded swiftly. `I'm surveilling the house. They've put out the blaze. Police and fire crew are monitoring while the car cools. There's an ambulance and tow truck present. I haven't heard talk over the police scanner about finding a body or transporting someone to the hospital. I think Sullivan disappeared before they got here.`

Either Sullivan hadn't been as hurt as Molly had thought and had left on his own, or he'd had help.

Josiah's fingers moved rapidly over the screen as he replied. `Nobody would bother transporting a dead body. Sullivan isn't dead—or at least` he wasn't when he left the scene. Question is, did he have help?

Agreed. Any further instructions?

He tapped the corner of his phone against a front tooth as he thought. No point in hanging around and risking discovery. Keep monitoring police communications and let me know if you find out anything else.

Will do. What about Molly Sullivan?

I'm handling Molly, he responded.

The silence between Anson's texts stretched out. While Josiah waited, he listened to the shower running and imagined Molly's slow, pain-filled movements as she worked to get clean.

Then his screen lit up. Is she becoming a distraction?

His internal reaction was immediate and profound, but this time he was the one who hesitated before he answered. I'm protecting our only witness should we decide to pursue a legal case through official channels.

I didn't consider that as an option, Anson sent back. That would be provocative, and risky for you.

There may be value in drawing fire while the rest of the coven remains free to act. We need to keep all our options open. He lifted his head as the shower stopped. Gotta run. Touch base in the a.m.

Roger that. Be careful, Josiah.

You too.

After that, his phone remained silent. While he waited for Molly, he flipped back over the exchange.

I'm protecting our only witness, he had written. But that hadn't been his first response to Anson's question.

And he had intentionally avoided telling Anson he had brought Molly to the safe house, because in all the decades his coven had worked together, never once had anyone brought an outsider to one of their safe houses. Doing so heightened the risk of discovery for everyone.

The bathroom door opened, and she stood shivering and clinging to the knob. She had managed to wiggle into his T-shirt, but her long legs remained bare, and her wet hair hung in ropes down her back.

He shoved his phone in his pocket and sprang forward to catch her by the elbows. As she swayed against him, the scent of his soap reached his nostrils.

"Let's sit you on the bed and I'll get the hair dryer," he said, putting an arm around her shoulders and leading her into the other room.

"You don't have to do that. I don't care if I go to bed with a wet head." She sounded utterly spent.

"I've done that before. It's cold down here in the basement, and my hair is much shorter than yours. We can at least get you a little drier. Right now you're dripping."

"Okay, if you don't mind."

He tightened his arm. "I don't mind."

Is Molly Sullivan becoming a distraction? Anson had asked.

And his first, most honest response had been, hell yes. Yes, she was. It was unplanned, unwanted, but it was also more powerful than he knew how to resist.

✧ ✧ ✧

SHOWERING WAS ROUGH.

Josiah had warned her, so she'd been braced when she'd checked her appearance in the small mirror. And it wasn't as bad as she had imagined.

It was a lot worse. Half her head was soaked in blood. Her cheek was swelling, and it looked like it had been abraded with a cheese grater.

She whispered to her image, "No jury in the world would have convicted you. You should have gotten whatever he had beaten you with and thrown it beside his body."

Then, possibly, it might have looked like she had used Austin's own weapon to fight back, especially since nobody from her old life knew about her burgeoning Power. Except there was no good way to explain what had happened to his BMW.

At least now if anybody questioned her, she could claim she had no idea what had happened, as long as nobody laid eyes on her until she healed.

She turned on the faucets. Pain flared again when she stepped under the warm flow of water. Injuries throbbed, and her torn skin stung like a bitch. But avoiding discomfort wasn't an option, so she sucked it up and washed herself as best she could.

By the time she'd finished, she was so exhausted she gladly leaned against Josiah as he helped her into the bedroom. Then she sat forward, elbows braced on knees with her head bent while he plugged in a hair dryer and turned it on her, running long fingers gently through the wet strands.

He had to use his hand because he didn't have a hairbrush, or at least she hadn't found one in the bathroom. The repetitive motion was incredibly soothing. Soon her eyes closed. Against the blackness of her inner lids, she thought of what he had looked like when he had cast the healing spells.

He had started speaking in the foreign-sounding language again. It sounded elegant in his dark, low voice, imbued with Power and tense with a meaning that escaped her. Was it Russian?

No matter how she'd tried to concentrate, the words shot away like sparks flying out from the strike of a blacksmith's hammer, and the spells took shape in the forge of his magic.

She had never seen or heard anything so compelling in her life. Then the pain from the healing spells had driven everything else out.

He ran his hand through her hair one last time before turning the hair dryer off. "That should do."

"Thank you." She tested the hair at the back of her head. It was perfectly dry, and she felt warm all over.

"You're welcome." He took the dryer away and returned with another glass of water and an ibuprofen bottle. Shaking out some pills, he offered them to her.

Wordlessly she swallowed them down and drained the glass. When she had finished, she said, "He wanted me to give him all the copies I'd made of the Seychelles file. He was going to kill me. I don't know how I could see it, but I could tell he had containers of gas in the trunk of his car along with some rope that I think he meant to use to tie me up."

"Sometimes visions come when a witch is in crisis even if they're not normally a seer." He sat beside her.

"I keep running over everything in my head." She rubbed her face. "I have a restraining order on him, and he signed the house over to me. A jury would take one look at the damage he caused, and whether I killed him or not, I'd get off on a verdict of self-defense. But then I remember his damn car was in park, and that swings everything back around to arson."

He put a hand on her arm. Obeying the slight pressure from his fingers, she turned to face him.

His amber gaze was intent. "I had one of my people check things out. Molly, Austin wasn't at the scene when the emergency responders arrived."

She had thought she had used up her body's store of adrenaline, but there was enough left for one tired pulse. "Are you saying he's alive?"

"It looks that way. At least it appears he was alive when he left the scene."

"Dammit." She started shivering. "I don't know if I'm disappointed or relieved. He deserved everything he got and I'm not sorry, but..."

He pulled up a section of the bedspread and tucked it around her shoulders. "But it's a hell of a thing to kill somebody," he said quietly. "Especially if you've never killed before."

Did he know that from experience? She darted a quick glance at his unrevealing expression and decided to let that go. "This means Austin has to explain things, not me. What he was doing in the neighborhood. How he got hurt. Why his car was parked so close to the house. How it caught on fire. I can claim to know nothing about any of it. I met with the real estate agent at the house, left shortly afterward, and I didn't see a thing."

"If he survives the night, yes."

She narrowed her gaze. "What do you mean?"

"The way I see it, there are two possibilities. He may have gotten up and left on his own, or somebody moved him. If that happened, we still don't know if he's alive or dead." He hooked one bent leg on the bed so that he could turn to face her directly. "Think back. Did you notice anything different or see anything that might have indicated someone else was there?"

Josiah was a strong personality at the best of times, and now, sitting this close to her when she felt so low and vulnerable, he was almost overwhelming.

Fighting the urge to retreat, she said drily, "I was pretty busy at the time. You know, getting the shit kicked out of me and fighting for my life and all."

One corner of his mouth lifted at her sarcasm, but he was dead serious when he replied. "We take in a lot more than we realize. Think about what was to the left of you and to the right."

Blowing out a breath, she tried. "The copse of trees bordering the back lawn was to my left. I didn't sense any presence or movement over there. To my right was the back of the house, until we walked toward the side street where he had parked his car. Then there was the intersection of the two roads at the front of the property. Nobody was there. The house across the street was dark. I remember looking that way after the car exploded."

"What lay straight ahead?" he pressed. "Did you hear anything behind you?"

"I told you already," she said impatiently. "The side street lay ahead, where Austin parked the car. He put it under the shadow of a maple tree, probably so it wouldn't be very noticeable. And no, I didn't hear anything behind me other than Austin before I got free."

Austin's voice in her ear. His body pressing against her shoulders while his arm pressed against her windpipe, forcing her to arch back. She shuddered, and Josiah's sharp gaze caught it.

"What did you remember?"

She pressed shaking fingers against her mouth. When she forced out the words, her voice sounded scraped thin. "He had his arm around my neck when he was forcing me to the car. Do we need to do this right now?

Why do you think someone else might have been there?"

"Yes, we need to do this now. I need every detail I can get while the experience is still fresh. As for why I think someone else might have been there…" He rolled one wide shoulder in a shrug. "You thought you might have killed him, but he wasn't there when the police showed up. I'm just pursuing every angle."

She glowered. He sounded like a cop, one that knew the whole story and knew what to ask. "You think someone else is involved, don't you?"

"It's possible, even probable. The money in the Seychelles account came from somewhere. He didn't conjure it up on his own." He studied her. "Did Austin give you any indication before now that he might be capable of committing murder?"

Shifting to try to ease the ache in her ribs, she snapped, "If I had ever once seriously entertained that possibility, I would have left him a long time ago. At worst, I expected unpleasantness. An inappropriate confrontation. Maybe a slap, or he might have grabbed me again and left more bruises."

"You've known him a long time. You also have good instincts, possibly even a touch of precognition. Now that he's attacked you, what do you think? Is this a part of his personality that he's been hiding, or is this outside his norm?"

The way he asked the questions made her consider things in a way she hadn't before. "While you wouldn't know it from what happened at the party, Austin's a charmer. He likes things to go his way as easily as possible. It's only when you cross him that his uglier side comes out, but even so, this is something far outside what I would have predicted he might do." She shook her head. "I've been feeling so stupid this evening, like I should have seen it coming, but I didn't."

"So it's outside his norm."

"Yeah. I'm surprised he was capable of it." Her mouth tilted in an ironic slant. "But you're giving me too much credit. I lived with him for a long time, and I never really knew him. We were both playing the roles that were expected of us."

"How long were you married?"

She blew out a breath. "Twenty damn years."

His eyes narrowed. "He liked playing the married role."

"I think we both did. He likes the trappings of a successful life and the reputation that comes with it. He likes being a partner in a successful law firm…" Her voice trailed away as she remembered the night of the party.

And Russell as he turned away, telling Austin, *Get her under control.*

Then Austin, moving to obey. Austin always moved to obey Russell. Holding parties when Russell told him to, going to the right dinners, taking on the right clients.

Austin was smart and cunning, but he didn't have the power of personality that Russell did, nor did he have the same kind of power politically or financially. Russell was the undisputed alpha at Sherman & Associates. Where he led, Austin would follow.

And Russell Sherman wasn't just the firm's managing partner. He was the founder, and he had built his firm from the ground up. Now Sherman & Associates was the largest, most powerful corporate law firm in the state.

Josiah watched her with the patience of a predator. He looked like he could wait all night if he had to.

She said softly, "Austin takes orders. He's not a maverick. He's a team player."

"That would have been my assessment," Josiah replied. "But I don't know him like you do."

She felt it then, a click of certainty, the way she had known Austin would think like a lawyer when she left him. Only instead of telling Austin to get her under control, this time Russell had said, *Shut her the hell up.*

And Austin had tried.

She was so *sure* it had happened. She could see it as clearly as she could see what had happened the night of the party. As clearly as she had seen the gas cans and rope in the back of the BMW. Was this what Josiah had meant by precognition?

Rage flared, as hot and fiery as the car's explosion. How dare they—*how dare they* think they could just end her life as if she were a disposable commodity? She wanted to hurt them. She needed so badly to make them pay it left her shaking. She didn't have the physical reserves to sustain that kind of powerful emotion.

She met Josiah's waiting, calculating gaze. "Austin might have been the one who tried to kidnap and kill me, but Russell was the one who ordered him to do it."

His expression turned fierce. "Are you sure?"

"I'd bet my entire divorce settlement on it," she said grimly. "And I'm going to get a lot of money."

Chapter Nine

AFTER SHE SAID that, exhaustion slammed home. Her mind ground to a halt and blackness hovered near. Even though she fought to stay upright, she couldn't and sank down on the bed.

Josiah took note. Standing, he tucked one arm underneath her legs and lifted her up while he yanked the covers down. Then he let her back down and pulled the covers over her supine body. He sat beside her again, bracing one hand beside her head as he leaned over and looked into her gaze.

"I can't stay," he told her. "I have too much to do. In the open area, there's a microwave on a cabinet. If you get hungry, there are cans of soup and packets of popcorn in the cabinet, along with some instant coffee, bowls, and mugs. It's pretty basic, but it will have to do until I return."

"I don't care." The thought of trying to eat something made her feel queasy.

The mattress bowed under his weight, shifting her against his hip. Light from the bedside lamp gleamed in his dark hair, along the tanned skin of one lean cheek, and sparked in amber eyes.

He had a knowledgeable gaze, like a man who had seen too much of the world and had not thought highly of it. Something rough had weathered him. She wondered if she would ever learn what it was. Yet despite that, he had probably saved her life tonight.

For the second time, she touched him voluntarily, resting the fingers of one hand on his hard, muscled forearm. His skin was warm and sprinkled with dark hair. He looked down at her hand and took in a quiet breath as if he might say something.

Her eyelids drifted closed as she waited for him to say what was on his mind.

The bedsprings creaked as he eased away. She hurt too much to lay flat on her back, so she curled on one side.

He must have thought she had fallen asleep, and she very nearly had. She watched him through her eyelashes as he began to walk out, but then he paused, his head angled to one side. She followed the direction of his gaze. For the first time she realized her purse sat on the floor, her phone and keys thrown on top of it.

Bending, he took her phone and pocketed it. Then he continued out the door.

He took her phone.

A cold knot settled in the pit of her stomach, but it was a problem that had to get in line, because meeting the imperative demands of her abused body had to come first. Closing her eyes for real, she let the darkness take her.

✧ ✧ ✧

HE'D FUCKED UP. Molly was a distraction, and now he was going to pay for it.

Grimly, he stepped into the tech room to check his email and scan the security monitors. Everything looked quiet and normal. The protection spells that surrounded the basement felt solid, unbreached. Maybe they would block anyone who might try to trace her whereabouts by using the GPS on her phone.

But *maybe* wasn't something he relied on, ever. Checking Molly's phone, he found that she hadn't bothered to lock it with a password. He wasn't surprised. Most people didn't.

That meant her texts, phone calls, contacts, and settings were easily accessible. She had the location settings turned off, but that wouldn't disable the phone's GPS.

Quickly he exported her contacts to his email address. After the transfer had completed, he took out the phone card, dropped it on the floor, and crushed it under his heel.

Then he sat to compose an email to his coven.

"The integrity of the safe house here has been compromised. Do not approach. Seek other options if necessary."

If someone searched Molly's phone records, they

would find several calls connecting to his number, but that didn't concern him. The number was registered to a local laundry service, and he had another phone specifically for the DA's use.

His main concern was how likely it was that someone might have tried to find Molly over the past several hours. For decades he had felt like he was playing chess with the unknown. This was another move on the board.

If Sullivan had left the scene on his own, he might not have had a chance to confess to Russell Sherman or to anyone else that he had failed to take care of the Molly problem. But if he'd had help—if he was dead—then interest in Molly would have spiked.

So it was possible.

His computer pinged. He had a response from Steven, who was a night owl. He clicked on the email, which said: "What's up? Need help?"

He replied rapidly. "Unclear. I brought subject back to the safe house. I didn't consider her phone's GPS until too late. Would the protection spells block traces?" When he finished composing, he hit Send.

His email pinged again. Steven had written: "Let me think. I'll get back to you in a sec."

He sat back, arms crossed, and waited while he watched the screens. In the far corner of the property, a possum trundled past the security camera.

Another email came through. He clicked Open. Steven had written: "You should be good while you're in the basement. But you'd be vulnerable before and after. My best advice—destroy the phone card ASAP."

"Already done," he typed. And he hadn't wasted any time when he had brought Molly here. He thought of the speed with which he had gotten her under cover and relaxed slightly. "Thanks and have a good night."

The risk was minimal enough that it wasn't worth moving her again. She was as safe as he could make her tonight.

He pushed to his feet and locked the door of the room as he stepped out. When he checked the bedroom, Molly lay still and quiet. It was time to head back into the city.

He paused just before climbing into the car and looked at the quiet country scene. Moonlight illuminated the back of the dark house. It was a creepy, isolated setting, and he didn't like leaving her like this, but that was no reason to stay. She was hidden, and she had all her essential needs met. She wasn't going to die.

She messed with his head too much.

Swearing under his breath, he drove away. First item on the agenda was to drive through the neighborhood of her rental. He did so with disciplined patience, all his senses wide open. It was close to three in the morning, and there were a few houses still lit where people were active, but most were dark and peaceful. The last thing he did was park the car and walk over a few blocks to the rental itself.

Everything looked as it had when he had last seen it.

The Jeep still sat where Molly had parked it. He scanned the vehicle for magic but didn't find anything. He eased up the stairs to the rental to test the door. It was locked, the interior dark and silent. The location appeared to be secure.

Maybe Sullivan's attack on Molly was all of it, at least for the time being. Finally satisfied, he drove to the apartment. As he pulled into his parking space, his phone rang. It was Anson.

Instantly, tension came roaring back. Throwing the Audi in park, he answered. "Anson."

"You took her to the safe house, didn't you? That's why the location is compromised."

"Yes."

Anson's sigh was audible over their connection. He said somberly, "It's probably just as well."

He had expected friction from Anson, especially after their earlier text conversation, but that surprised him. He narrowed his eyes. "Something happen?"

"There's another fire. This time it's a house near the university. One body has been discovered, a female. There's no official ID on her yet, but tax records list a woman named Nina Rodriguez as the property owner. I've been doing some searching. Apparently she's a divorce attorney."

Josiah's thoughts winged back to the conversation he'd had with Molly in the park. She'd said, *Nina Rodriguez is my lawyer. Ever heard of her?* He swore.

Anson asked, "Do you know who she is?"

"Unless there's another divorce lawyer in the area named Nina Rodriguez, she's Molly's attorney."

"So the two incidents are connected," Anson said heavily.

"Looks like it." He tapped his fingers on the steering wheel. "Text me the address, will you?"

"Sure. Are you going to check out the site?"

"You bet your ass I am." He started the car again.

The district attorney's office in Fulton County had a hundred assistant district attorneys statewide and close to a hundred and fifty other staff that included administrative personnel and investigators.

It might be quirky for the DA himself to show up at a house fire in the early hours of the morning on a weekend, but it wasn't beyond the realm of possibility. Besides, it might be useful for him to develop a reputation for being a quirky, hands-on kind of guy, and two suspicious fires in one night warranted some attention.

Once he received the address, he plugged it into his GPS, and twenty minutes later, he parked half a block away from a house fire that turned the night sky red. Despite the odd hour, the scene had drawn several onlookers who clustered across the street, clad in pajamas, bath robes, and other random, casual outfits.

Patrol cars, fire trucks, and an ambulance were parked nearby, along with a black van with white lettering that identified it as a medical examiner's vehicle. All standard operating procedure. He scanned the area for any present or residual magic but didn't sense anything.

His phone buzzed, but he ignored it as he breached a simple police barrier constructed with tape run between two parked squad cars. When a uniformed policeman strode over to turn him back, he introduced himself and showed his ID.

Within a short amount of time, he had located the fire chief on site and introduced himself again. Together they stood watching the firefighters work. "It always saddens me when a house goes down, and this one was a beauty." The chief gave him a sidelong look. "Kinda late for most people to be out and about."

"I couldn't sleep," Josiah said. "When I heard there've been two fires in one night, I thought I'd drive over and take a look."

"You don't know? There's three now." The chief was a fit man in his fifties with short gray hair, sharp eyes, and a hangdog expression. "You must have been on your way here. I got word less than ten minutes ago that a law office in a strip mall was firebombed."

Josiah held himself still. "Where?"

"Over in Piedmont Heights. Still no word on if there are any casualties, but it's three fucking thirty on a Sunday morning, so we can hope not." The chief gave him a sympathetic look. "You've only been at your new job for a few months, and the city's going up in flames tonight."

"Yeah, it's going to be a busy week." His phone

buzzed again. Pulling it out, he glanced at several texts from Anson and took in the phrase: `Office of Nina Rodriguez Atty at Law has been firebombed.`

Gently he tucked the phone back in his pocket. "Do we know what caused this fire?"

The chief shook his head. "We won't get a good look inside until everything has had a chance to cool down."

"Give me your best guess."

"Unofficially?" The other man snorted. "Your ordinary, garden-variety house fire doesn't burn in such a thorough, even pattern as this one has. When we got here, it was engulfed from end to end. I'd say somebody really wanted this house destroyed."

"That would be my take too, but I wanted to get your thoughts. How soon can we get an arson investigator in there?"

"Tomorrow's Monday. The house should be cool enough to get someone in first thing."

He handed the chief one of his cards. "Keep me updated."

"You bet." The chief pocketed his card. "And congrats on winning the election."

"Thanks."

He spent ten more minutes at the scene, introducing himself to the other responders on site and taking a quick look at the victim in the body bag awaiting transport in the medical examiner's van. The woman was burned badly, but her features were still recognizable. Tightening his jaw at the scent, he snapped a few photos, then exited to inhale a deep lungful of the fresh air outside.

His phone buzzed again.

Anson: `Responders just pulled a body out of the law office. An unidentified male, Caucasian, tall, dark hair, midthirties to fifty. I'm at the scene now.`

Reeaally. He asked, `Any magic involved?`

`I don't think so, but I can't get close enough to tell for sure. If you're at the house, you're less than ten minutes away.` Anson sent him the address.

Josiah replied, `On my way.`

The sky had started to lighten with predawn when he arrived at the strip mall. This time there were far fewer gawkers, just a few cars pulled to the opposite side of the road. He caught a glimpse of Anson's rugged profile in one of the cars, but he didn't greet him or acknowledge his presence.

There was no sign of magic here either, and the fire had been smaller. It was already out but still smoldering. He went through the same round of introductions as he had at the previous scene, spending a few minutes talking with each professional before handing over his card.

This scene didn't have an ME van, so he climbed into the ambulance to get a look at the unidentified male. He uncovered the head and gazed down at Austin Sullivan's handsome, still features.

By that point he wasn't surprised, but for the benefit of the EMT and a uniformed policeman looking on, he said, "Well, damn. I know this man."

"You do?" The uniform pulled out a notepad. "Who is it?"

"Another lawyer. Austin Sullivan. He was a partner at Sherman & Associates. I went to a dinner party at his house last month." He let the sheet fall back over Sullivan's lifeless face and asked the EMT, "Any idea about the cause of death?"

"You need an autopsy to be sure, but the back of his mouth looks reddened like he might have suffered some airway burns," the EMT told him. "He's pretty banged up, but they found him under some rubble in a collapsed doorway, so that might explain it. It's possible he got knocked out and smoke inhalation killed him, but what he was doing in there in the middle of a Saturday night is anybody's guess."

Josiah thought he had a pretty good idea what had happened to Sullivan, but he kept to his role. "What a mess. I'll be reading the reports on this personally."

With that, he took his leave. The space where Anson had been parked was empty, so he texted the other man the news, then added, `I think we've learned everything we can for the night. Looks like we're going to have a long week. You should get some rest.`

`You too, if you can.`

But Josiah had no intention of resting. Instead, he

stopped at a twenty-four-hour grocery store to pick up various items—ready-made deli sandwiches, fruit, cheese, milk, peanut butter, bread, more coffee. A quart of milk. He was in and out in twenty minutes.

Still, it was well past dawn by the time he finally started back to the safe house.

With a little luck, the rest of Molly's night had been much more uneventful than his had been, and hopefully she would continue to sleep for several more hours. Her body needed to rest in order to recover, and he was feeling the effects of a tense, sleepless night.

And in any case, he wasn't looking forward to breaking the news to her that she was now a widow.

✧ ✧ ✧

FORMLESS BLACK.

Then the woman with the dark, powerful eyes stood in front of her, one eyebrow raised. "Taking your own sweet time, I see."

"I've had a lot to do," Molly told her. "It's complicated."

The woman snorted. "It's always complicated. Well, I'm too busy to look for you. Either you'll show up or you won't. But you should know time is running out."

Why was time running out? She wanted to ask, but the formless black swept her away again until Austin's familiar shoes and long, lean, jeans-clad legs came into view.

And she moved as fast as she could, but she wasn't

fast enough. Something hard came down on her head…

Surging awake to total blackness, she jerked to a sitting position. Bruises and contusions screamed in reaction, and a sharp headache spiked behind one eye. Disoriented and panicked, she flung out a hand to grab something to anchor herself. The back of her hand knocked into a cool, hard surface, and a heavy object crashed to the floor.

The air was cold and strange. Memory surged in. She was in the basement of a safe house. At least that was where Josiah had said she was. And she had just knocked the bedside lamp to the floor.

After the first gigantic throb of protest, her body settled into playing a symphony of pain. Maybe enough time had passed that she could take more pain medication. She slid out of bed and grunted at the effort of bending over to grope for the lamp. Her fingers collided with the round, broad base. Picking up the lamp, she felt her way to the switch.

Light blazed, causing more stabbing pain behind her eye. Her body shrieked that it needed to be horizontal again, but she forced herself to move. Screw it, she thought. I'm taking more ibuprofen whether it's time or not.

After dragging on the sweatpants and thick athletic socks, she limped to the bathroom, shook out more pills, and swallowed them down. Then she drank three more glasses of water until her nagging thirst had eased. Only then did she push her way out of the bathroom to take stock.

Gray light filtered down the basement stairs. Dawn must not be that far away. Like the T-shirt, the sweatpants and socks were too large. She hiked the pants up at the waist and took care not to stumble in the socks.

It was creepy as hell that he'd stuck her in a basement in the middle of the country. Drawing in slow, deep breaths, she counted until the racing panic eased enough for her to think.

The raw, empty place deep at her core was gone, and what had returned… Well, it wasn't the golden well of Power from before, but it wasn't nothing either. More than that, her senses had cleared, and she felt surrounded by a steady glow of magic.

It was everywhere. At her feet, overhead, on all sides. Josiah had said the basement had protection spells. Why the basement? Why not upstairs too?

The furnace kicked on, and she nearly jumped out of her skin. Coughing out an unamused laugh, she searched for more light switches until she stood in the middle of the unfinished section that blazed with illumination. There was the open door leading to the bedroom, the bathroom, the microwave sitting on an old cabinet, a minifridge, a washer and dryer, a furnace, water heater—and a closed door with a high-end electronic lock.

She frowned at the locked door. Then, leaning heavily on the railing, she climbed the stairs to a narrow landing and looked out the window at the back door. A large, unkempt lawn led to a tangle of trees. Three more stairs took her to a large kitchen that was badly in need of being updated.

She stared around. It was a *really* empty kitchen. There was no stove, fridge, or microwave. She opened a couple of cupboards at random. They were all bare.

Moving her stiff, protesting body as fast as she could, she inspected the upstairs. Aside from two chairs and a television on a simple stand in the living room, along with a few lamps on timers, the rest of the large house was as empty as the kitchen. The television wasn't even plugged in.

When she had finished, she sat thoughtfully in one of the armchairs and looked out the large picture window. This was the only house, and it sat at the end of a country lane. It would be easy to defend. Easy to isolate. Nobody would hear screams coming from this place. The thought made her shudder.

Still, she wasn't barred from leaving. She could put on her shoes and walk down that country lane if she wanted. While it had been terrifying to watch Josiah pocket her phone, he hadn't tried to imprison her in any way.

She tapped a thumbnail against her teeth. In fact, there were only two things he had barred her from doing. She couldn't make any phone calls, and there were any number of reasons he might have wanted to keep her from calling out. Some were more sinister than others.

And she couldn't open that locked basement door.

Or could she?

Pushing out of the chair, she went back into the basement, and the warm, steady glow of spells surrounded her again. Okay, she was still rattled, but she had to admit the magic felt good.

A deep shakiness had set in, and the hollow ache in her stomach reminded her that she hadn't eaten since early Saturday. Impatiently, she attended to her body's needs and nuked water in the microwave to make a mug of double-strength instant coffee while she ate soup straight from the can.

The cold soup felt slimy in her mouth, but it stopped her stomach from complaining. She glowered at the locked door as she drank the coffee. The medication had done its job, and her pain had eased to a bearable ache. While she didn't exactly get a burst of energy from the caffeine, at least she no longer felt like she was going to fall over.

Most importantly, she could feel a small trickle of returning Power. Would it be enough?

Setting aside the half-empty mug of coffee, she went to the door to lay a hand on the electronic lock. Even if she had enough juice, *should* she do this?

Whether or not she was successful, this was going to make Josiah angry. And while he had manipulated and offended her, he had also helped her tremendously. She thought back to Monday's kiss and discovered the memory had changed.

This time she remembered how he had held very still

as she had gently, tentatively moved her lips under his, and then he had shifted to deepen the kiss. She had been the one to push him away.

He had tightened his arms, not to overpower her but in protest before he let her go. And of all the ways he could have chosen to get her riled…

Her mouth widened in a wry smile. As tactless and manipulative as it had been, he *had* meant that kiss.

But he had still taken her phone, and whether it made him angry or not, she wanted it back. And she wasn't going to break through that door easily. Digging deep, she wrenched out as much Power as she could and used it to blast the door open.

Chapter Ten

THAT HAD BEEN imprudent.

Ripping out the small trickle of returning Power *hurt.* Inside, the raw darkness had returned, and she felt shaky again. Gasping, she leaned against the doorframe until the black spots dancing in front of her eyes disappeared.

She couldn't afford to do that again until she healed properly. For one thing, she might pass out, and for another, she might do permanent damage to an ability she was quickly coming to treasure.

But the door had creaked open. When she inspected it, she discovered she hadn't dented the electronic lock. The doorframe, where the bolt inserted, was what had splintered.

After registering that in a quick glance, the interior of the room caught her attention.

She had expected it to be dark. Instead, it was lit by several security monitors hanging on the wall over an L-shaped computer desk. Staring, she felt along the wall by the door until her fingers encountered a switch. She flipped it, and bright, overhead light flooded the room.

A large floor safe sat in a corner opposite the desk. The desktop held a coffee mug and a scattering of papers and files, and a computer was hooked up to two more monitors. Absently, she retrieved her coffee and took a sip of the dark, bitter brew as she approached the desk.

Her phone! Snatching at it, she tried to power it up, but it was dead. Upon closer inspection, she discovered the phone card was missing. Frustration gnawed, and she tossed it back on the desk. Then her name leaped out from the papers and files.

Slowly, she sank into the desk chair, set her mug down, picked up the manila file that bore her name, and began to flip through it. Childhood background. The name of her high school and a list of her friends. Information on her parents. Her father's date of death. Their address. Molly's college transcripts. The address of her house. The list of places where she had either volunteered or worked.

The file slipped out of her fingers, and she scrambled to look at the other papers and files. There was a file on Austin and another one on Sherman & Associates. And another file that looked like a list of employee records for the district attorney's office. Another one on local judges. That one had a sticky note on it that said GO DEEPER?

There were other files, but the information they contained had no meaning to her, nor any overall pattern that she could understand. Finally she sat back and drank the rest of her coffee while she stared at the images on the security monitors. After a moment she recognized the scenes as the property surrounding the house.

She was still sitting there when a dark Audi appeared. It jumped off one monitor and onto another as it swung around to the back of the house. When it stopped, Josiah's long, powerful body unfolded from the driver's seat. He carried several grocery bags to the back door.

She listened to the sound of the door opening and closing, then footsteps on the stairs. They paused, then continued more slowly.

The fiery, dark essence of his presence filled the doorway at her back.

"I see you've been busy," he said expressionlessly. "You shouldn't have done that."

"I wanted my phone back. Not that it did me any good." She swung the chair around to confront him. "Why did you destroy the phone card?"

Exhaustion and anger stamped his hard features. His gaze was sharp like knives carved from amber. "Even if you have your GPS turned off, the location of your phone can still be traced."

She took in a quick breath. Of all the crazy thoughts that had raced through her mind, the danger of being traced by her phone's GPS had never occurred to her. Then she snapped her attention back to what really mattered. "This is no normal safe house. In fact, this is far, far from normal. Who are you? What are you really doing?"

He shot her a furious, filthy look and walked away.

"Oh, no you don't." She launched out of the chair as fast as she could, which admittedly wasn't very fast. When she reached the doorway, he was crouching in front of the minifridge, shoving food from the grocery bags into the fridge. "You have a file on me. On my parents. You have a list of my high school friends. *Why?*"

"You know why." He glared at her again. "You became unusual."

"You had no right to dig into my past like that!" she snapped.

He snatched up a wrapped sandwich and stalked into the bedroom.

"Quit walking away from me!" Following him, she found that he had sat at one end of the bed.

He leaned forward, elbows on his knees while he tore the wrapper open. With his gaze fixed on the food in his hands, he said between his teeth, "You're rattled and spoiling for a fight. I get that. But I've been up all night casting spells, I didn't have supper, and I'm going to eat a fucking sandwich. So get out of my face for a few fucking minutes."

Gah! She wanted to strangle him. Her hands closed into fists, but after a moment she asked, more or less calmly, "Did you bring one for me?"

"What do you think?" He snapped off one end of his sandwich with strong, white teeth.

She thought maybe she needed a few fucking minutes too. Striding over to the fridge, she yanked open the door to stare at the food he had brought. There were three more wrapped sandwiches, two turkey and cheese, one beef and tomato. She snatched at one.

The only two places to sit in the basement were the bed or the desk chair. She wasn't about to join him, and she didn't feel like walking into Creepy Monitor Room again, so she ate her sandwich mechanically while standing in front of the microwave, forcing each mouthful down her throat. It tasted like sawdust and she could only manage to eat half, so she rewrapped the rest and put it into the fridge. Then she went back into the bedroom.

He had finished his sandwich and had lain back on the bed, one tanned forearm draped over his eyes. She took in details she had been too preoccupied to notice before. He wore a pair of faded jeans and well-used athletic shoes, and a gray T-shirt stretched tight over his wide chest and muscled arms.

And while the bedroom had only basic furnishings, there was an antique, faded rug that gave the room a sense of richness. The old dresser, the bedside table and lamp—they might be used, but they were all quality pieces.

She walked to the bed and sat beside him. "Who are you really?"

His arm obscured half his face and highlighted the sensuality of his firm mouth. "I've been Josiah Mason for the past forty years. I carefully targeted the DA position and constructed and executed a successful campaign strategy to win the election."

Did that really answer her question? A chill went down the back of her neck as she thought of how he had worded his reply and what he didn't say.

And very Powerful witches could live much longer than the normal human life span. He had told her that himself.

She asked quietly, "What was your original name?"

"That was a long time ago, and it belonged to a different man."

"Was it Russian?"

No answer. He lifted his forearm to frown at her. "What are you doing up, anyway? You should still be out."

"I dreamed about Austin's attack. It woke me up." She rested her folded hands in her lap. "I may not be an expert on what safe houses should look like, but even I can tell this place isn't normal."

"No, Molly. It is not." He let his forearm rest against his eyes again.

The food sat uneasily in her stomach, and she fought against the urge to lie down. She had too many questions she needed to have answered. "Why are there protection spells all over the basement? Why not the rest of the house?"

"The ground helps to absorb and hide the magic. The protection spells might be sensed if they were aboveground."

"And for some reason you need the protection, because… because Atlanta is a place of interest to a certain dangerous Power, isn't it?" She thought of all the security monitors in the other room, and for the first time she felt like she was starting to piece together the bits of what he had told her over the past several weeks. She asked, "Possibly something or someone that might love to sink its teeth into someone's bones and suck the magic out of them like sucking the juice out of a ripe peach?"

"I really wish you were asleep. You're too smart for your own fucking good." He sighed. "I have news."

Dread felt heavy on her overstressed body. "What's happened?"

He sat in a fluid motion and turned to face her. "Austin's dead."

It hit her like a punch. If she was so smart, why hadn't she seen that one coming? Through numb lips, she asked, "Did I kill him?"

"I don't know yet. The preliminary evidence suggests not, but it'll be a couple of days before my office gets the official autopsy report." He looked at her hands lying in her lap. She had twisted them together, gripping so tightly her knuckles had whitened. He covered them with one of his own. "There's more. I need you to identify another body. Can you do that right now?"

She managed to respond with a jerky nod.

"The photo will be difficult to look at," he said quietly. "Are you sure?"

"Yes."

He pulled out his phone, and this time when he

turned to her, he gripped her shoulder in a strong, bracing hold as he tilted the screen toward her. "Is this your divorce lawyer, Nina Rodriguez?"

It took a few moments for her frozen brain to process what she saw. Nausea surged, and she bolted for the bathroom. She slammed the door shut and locked it, then spun to heave over the toilet.

It was excruciating as her abused ribs protested. She struggled through it, and afterward she rinsed her mouth, splashed cold water on her face, and brushed her teeth.

Only when she was ready to face him again did she unlock and open the door.

He waited just outside. "I take it that's a yes."

✧ ✧ ✧

SHE NODDED.

Her expression was devastated. The color had leached out of her complexion, making the discolored bruises stand out, and there was a fragility in her gaze that he'd never seen before.

"This is about the Seychelles file." She looked sick. "I got her killed, didn't I?"

"You did not get her killed," he said carefully. "Austin did. But yes, this is about the Seychelles file. At least that's how I'm piecing together the information right now. Austin was desperate to get all the copies back from you—desperate enough to kill you to make sure you couldn't talk. And Nina Rodriguez was the other one who knew about it, because she wrote it into your divorce settlement." He paused. "How specific did she get in the wording of the settlement?"

"She was very careful. We didn't want the documents to trigger extra scrutiny in the court system. We wanted the divorce to go through, so she just called it foreign investments." She wiped her eyes. "Austin and I didn't have any foreign investments. He knew what we meant."

She looked like a feather could knock her down. Gripping her arm, he steered her back to the bedroom where she sank onto the mattress, lay down, and curled on her side.

He was too damn tired to resist the impulse that came next. Sliding onto the bed, he fit his longer, bigger frame along her slender, curved back and dragged the bedspread over them both. "I have to get a few hours' sleep. After that, I should be able to cast more healing spells for you."

"Fine, whatever." Her whispered reply was listless, but she didn't protest when he tucked an arm around her.

Hell, he didn't know why he did it. Maybe to comfort her. Maybe to get some comfort for himself. Letting his nose come to rest in the soft curtain of her hair, he closed his eyes, and despite the burning bedside lamp and the mountain of things he had to do, everything fell away and he slept.

When he opened his eyes again, he knew he had gotten enough sleep for survival, but it wasn't a true, deep rest.

From where he lay, he could see out the open bedroom door to the bottom of the stairs. The filtered light that shone down the stairs was stronger, more yellow. The day had advanced. Moving carefully so he wouldn't disturb Molly, he pulled out his phone to check the screen. It was almost noon. He had slept for over five hours.

Pushing himself on little rest had become a way of life, so five hours was actually a good amount for him. Easing away from Molly, he stood and paused to regard her slumbering form with a frown.

He didn't sleep with women. He hadn't even when he had lived with his wife, now long dead. But it had felt good to curl around Molly and hold her in his arms. Too good. Worse, he didn't want to leave her. He wanted to stroke his fingers along her pale cheek, to erase forever the marks that Sullivan had put on her body and replace those memories with pleasure.

He had veered dangerously off-track.

Moving quietly, he gathered a clean outfit from the dresser, turned off the bedside lamp and closed the door as he exited. Once outside, he showered, shaved, and fixed a strong cup of coffee. Taking it into the other room along with another sandwich, he sat at the desk and ate as he considered this current debacle.

Molly never should have been able to see the contents of this room, but she had recovered Power much faster than he'd anticipated. From the questions she had asked, he realized he had revealed far more in their previous conversations than he had ever meant to. How the hell had she known to ask if he was Russian?

As soon as he thought it, the answer came to him. He had cast spells in front of her. Of course she had paid close attention to everything he had said whether she understood it or not. He had been her only real source of information about something that was very important to her.

He could spellcast in English, but sometimes he fell back on casting spells as he had learned them in his native language. That had been a sloppy mistake. She might not know how to speak Russian, but she sure as hell knew how to make an educated guess.

His coven email had blown up while he'd slept. He skimmed through the various reactions to the news of the compromised safe house. Questions, speculation, arguments. Richard was pissed, and so was Henry. They wanted to know what had happened. Anson had jumped in later to give an update on Saturday night's deaths.

"Unless you're going to haul me in and charge me with something, I've decided I need to leave Atlanta," Molly said from behind him, her voice rusty. "I'd been thinking about it anyway, and what happened to Austin and Nina just solidified it. And whatever you're involved in that necessitates all these precautions… that's way beyond my coping skills."

He put his computer in sleep mode and sat back. "You're right. I was going to suggest it when you got up."

"You're so full of bullshit." She coughed out a laugh. "What happened to 'Let's rule the Eastern Seaboard together'?"

Because she had more raw Power than the rest of his coven put together. Instead of telling her that, he raised his eyebrows and spun around to face her. "Once you get ahold of something, you don't let go, do you?"

"Not usually, which is one of the reasons why I stayed in a dead-end marriage for so long." She grimaced. "It's one of my worst personality traits."

"Or one of your finest." A small silence fell. Then he shrugged and said, "Anyway, offering to teach you was a bad impulse, and I've since thought better of it. You're in danger here, and I don't have time to babysit a new witch." Or any time to indulge the dangerous distraction… obsession she had become. "As soon as you're on your feet, you need to relocate."

Licking her lips, she moved into the room and leaned against his desk. His clothes looked ridiculous on her. The T-shirt gaped at her slender neck and arms, and the sweatpants hung low on her hips. Even his thick white socks were somehow adorably oversized on her narrow feet. And the nipples of her small, firm breasts were visible against the old, thin material of the shirt.

He had to throttle down a surge of anger. Even beat up and badly dressed, she was gorgeous, and she was becoming more compelling by the minute. Sullivan had been a remarkably ugly, stupid man.

"Somebody killed Nina," she said in a low voice. She

glanced in his coffee mug, then picked it up to take a deep swallow. "And if I didn't kill Austin, somebody else did. They're going to want me dead too. I don't know how to live in hiding. How do I leave without getting caught?"

Wearing his clothes. Drinking his coffee. Leaning back against his desk while they talked.

For a blistering moment, he imagined it happening in another life where they were both safe and free from secrets and they chose to share such domestic, intimate moments with each other.

Either before sex or after. His whole body tightened. Now who was being stupid?

Rubbing his face, he fought to get his unruly body under control. "I can get you new identification, a new birth certificate, passport, driver's license, social security number—the works—by Wednesday or Thursday. Everything you need to start up somewhere else."

"You can do that?" She stared at him, then shook her head. "Even so, it's still not going to be easy. I need the money from my checking account… And I just bought a car, but I haven't had time to get it titled yet. Then there's my house. My real estate agent thinks she can get high six or low seven figures for it. And there's the retirement accounts. I won't be able to access those without either the finalized divorce papers or Austin's death certificate."

He took her hand and laced his fingers through hers. "Molly, you're about to become a person of interest in a murder investigation. You can't tie up those loose ends without running the risk of being found, either by the authorities or by whoever committed the murders. You've got to walk away from everything. I can have your estate held while an investigation is ongoing, and I'll order a detailed audit. That will buy you some time, but you need to come to terms with it now—you're not going to get out of this financially unscathed."

She calmed as she listened. "What if I get a cashier's check for what's in the checking account?"

He frowned. "How much is in there?"

"Over forty thousand. I took what we had in our savings and checking accounts, and then I sold my jewelry, and after I switched cars there was still some money left over from the sale of the Escalade. That should be enough to at least get me started."

He thought it over. "It's too much of a risk."

She jerked her hand away. "Maybe it's a risk I'm willing to take. The police won't be moving fast enough if I get to a bank branch first thing tomorrow."

He snapped, "This isn't about the police. I might know something about who could be hunting for you, and believe me—*that's* not a risk you should be willing to take."

Her eyes widened. "You *know* who's behind this?"

"There's evidence to suggest that my reason for being in Atlanta coincides with Austin and what has happened to you. The fact that you're an awakening witch just complicates things." He could no longer sit still and pushed to his feet.

She had drained his mug. He grabbed it and went to heat more water. This time he put two mugs in the microwave.

She followed him. "How do you know everything's connected?"

He might have compromised his safe house for her, but he wouldn't share anything about Maria without Maria's express permission. "I have sources." When she opened her mouth, he glared at her. "That's all I'm saying. If you get caught, you can't give away details you don't know."

She drew herself up. "I wouldn't betray your confidence."

He gave her a grim look. "I might trust your integrity and good intentions, but anyone will talk sooner or later if they're tortured long enough. You're going to have to trust me."

"Wow." She paled even further. "But you're asking me to walk away with nothing. How do I disappear without resources? I wouldn't even have a car. Even bus stations have security cameras these days."

He spooned instant coffee into one of the steaming mugs and shoved it in her direction. "I'm working on it."

Wrapping her hands around the mug, she took a sip, then said bitterly, "And why the hell you have this god-awful instant coffee boggles my mind. You spent thousands of dollars on the contents of that monitor room, and you couldn't even buy a Keurig?"

He rounded on her. "It's caffeine. It's fuel. Shut up for a few goddamn minutes and let me think."

She slid sideways, mouthing at him silently, *Fine. Just fine.*

He glared as she limped up the stairs carrying her mug. When the floorboards overhead creaked, he opened the fridge. She hadn't touched any of the food since she vomited, and that had been hours ago.

Stalking over to the foot of the stairs, he roared, "And eat something with that coffee! How can you expect to heal if you don't fucking eat?"

Blistering silence roared back. Great job, asshole, he told himself. She just learned she lost her husband and her lawyer. She's losing her entire life, and you had to bite her head off.

She was a time suck. A disaster. And now she was probably going to become a money pit. Women like Molly Sullivan were high-end luxury mammals. They cost a goddamn fortune to maintain. He happened to have a goddamn fortune, but a lot of his liquid assets were tied into fueling the coven's efforts.

He slammed a spoonful of coffee into his mug. Fresh brewed coffee *would* taste better. Goddamn it. Baring his mental teeth, he chased that thought out of his head, then he glared at his surroundings. He was sick to death of living in basements.

Grabbing his mug, he strode upstairs. Molly huddled in one of the chairs in front of the living room window, looking out as she cradled her mug underneath her chin.

Her eyes were reddened, but he didn't discern any extra splotchiness in her bruised face. He guessed she hadn't been crying. Probably hadn't.

He sat in the opposite chair. "I'll loan you forty thousand, interest free. And I'll get you a car."

She took in a quick breath. "That's very generous. Thank you, but it's a lot of money. What if I can't pay it back?"

Unless he was badly mistaken—and he rarely was about people anymore—she was the type who wouldn't rest until she found some way to repay him. "You might take some financial hits, like property taxes and other expenses, but eventually you'll get the bulk of your estate. You can pay me back then." A corner of his mouth lifted drily. "Either that or I'll be dead, and the loan won't matter."

Her gaze widened. "Why are you going after someone so dangerous? What did they do to you?"

He thought about deflecting that, but then suddenly he didn't even want to try. She had already guessed or discovered so many of his other secrets. What did it matter if she knew the whole truth?

"I was born to a life of wealth and privilege when the world still had empires and kings," he said. "And at the appropriate age, I married an appropriate woman and fathered two sons. I became interested in improving steam-locomotion technology. The ruler at that time placed some significance on expanding railways, so when my father died, I inherited a lot of money and then I made more."

Fascination overtook her expression. She swiveled to face him fully. "You had a marriage and family. Your wife… did you love her?"

He snorted. "No. In the circles we moved in, we thought of marriage differently. But she gave me two sons whom I loved, and for several years I had grown somewhat fond of her. Then I was badly injured in a carriage accident and lay in a coma for two weeks."

She winced. "That was when your Power awoke, right?"

"Yes. I could feel it inside, burning like a furnace." His expression hardened. "I couldn't move or speak, but I heard everything that everyone said around me. What the doctors said. Things my wife said. What my two sons said. How the three of them planned on disposing of the family assets, and how tired they grew of waiting for me to die."

"But it had only been two weeks?" Her gaze darkened with sympathy.

He didn't welcome her sympathy but acknowledged where it came from. They both had families who had betrayed them. "After a few days, my sons thought they should give nature a hand and help me to my eternal rest. We had a lot of servants, and my youngest son was afraid of getting caught. That was the only thing that gave them pause. Thankfully, that was enough for me to come out of the coma. I disinherited them, left my wife, and searched for someone who could explain what was happening to me."

"How horrible," she murmured. "I thought Austin was bad, but you must have felt so hurt when your family turned on you like that."

"I suppose I did, but it happened so long ago, my children's children have died of old age." He added softly, "And it was nothing compared to what came next. War was breaking out. I backed out of old business interests and moved the bulk of my capital to America. In the meantime, I grew desperate to understand how to handle my awakening Power, so I traveled to see the only man I knew who might be able to help. That was the worst decision I've ever made."

Chapter Eleven

MOLLY HAD BEEN so mired in the destruction of her life as she knew it, she would have said nothing could pull her out of her own misery.

Yet Josiah managed to do just that. Fascination and curiosity ran rampant as she listened to his story. He omitted place names and other identifiers, but there were a few clues, like his ties to the railroad industry, that gave her enough fuel for some conjecture.

If her guess was right about his language of origin, then he had lived in the Russian Empire in the late nineteenth or early twentieth century. She rifled through her history education. The war that broke out… could it have been World War I?

Her coffee had gone cold, but she sipped it anyway as she watched him. The spring sun threw shadows over his expression. There was a rough elegance to the strong bones of his face and frame, a sense of tough endurance that had enormous appeal. The more contact she had with him, the stronger that appeal grew.

She still wasn't sure she liked him. But she was beginning to understand how difficult events had shaped his nature, and when push came to shove, he had been there for her multiple times. Astonishingly so.

"If only we could talk to our younger selves," she muttered wryly. "Think of the pitfalls we could have avoided."

"I wouldn't skip one of them." His voice turned hard. "Each one taught me something. I survived, and I'll never be trapped by those mistakes again."

Respect stirred. She tilted her coffee mug at him. "Good attitude."

He gave her a cynical smile. "Having said that, the next several years of my life were a nightmare. The man I went to see was a court favorite and had powerful influence over the royal family. He was a very old witch—and there's something you should know about very old witches. If you choose, as some of us do, to extend your life, eventually our Power runs down and our human bodies rebel as the longevity spell fades. Then what you would have fallen prey to during your normal lifespan will still occur, and often it hits harder. Cancers, heart attacks, strokes, dementia, renal failure. The longevity spell only delays the inevitable. In my opinion, it's well worth it to live potentially hundreds of years, but eventually every witch faces a choice. Either they exit their lives with integrity, or they steal what is forbidden—someone else's Power."

"Oh no," she murmured. The ache in her fingers made her realize she was gripping her mug too hard. She made a deliberate choice to relax.

"Oh, yes. I had a lot of Power, and I didn't know what to do with it. As worldly as I had become about everything else, I was helpless as a baby about this one thing. And that old witch had made his choice long before me to feed off the Power in others. At his behest, the royal family threw me in prison on trumped-up charges, where I was held indefinitely. He had access to see me whenever he wanted. Every time my Power started to return, he sucked me dry until I'd forgotten what it was like to live without a raw, empty wound at my core. That went on for years."

She swallowed. "I can't imagine. It's been bad enough to lose mine for a few hours. How did you keep from going crazy?"

He raised one eyebrow. "You're assuming I haven't."

"You're hard and single-minded, and you can be thoughtless, but you're not crazy," she said with certainty. "How did you get free?"

"He disappeared for a while. I found out later someone had tried to assassinate him. Everyone thought he was dead. I believe he took the opportunity to reinvent himself. It's an old tactic many of us have used. Historically, long-lived witches have not been welcome in many communities. Sometimes they've been hunted and burned—and the royal court hadn't realized he was a witch."

"Nobody noticed anything odd about him?"

He gave a cynical shrug. "He'd been known as a holy man who performed miracles of healing on their prince, but they didn't call that magic. They called it religion." After a pause, he continued. "Then there was a revolution—well, two, actually—and the royal family was slaughtered. The world went to hell. I escaped in the chaos and eventually relocated here. I soaked up every scrap of magical knowledge I could find and studied law. I trained to become the best fighter I could and a crack shot, and when I got enough experience, I started a careful, patient search for him."

"You're sure he's still alive?"

"I'm positive." His expression turned thoughtful. "I wasn't his first victim, and I was far from his last. I've been able to build up a network of support from some of his survivors. We've been hunting him for a long time, and it led us here."

"That sounds crazy," she said. "Don't get me wrong. I believe you, but things like that don't happen here. What would you call him, a vampire witch?"

"Like I said before, I'm not into labels." He shrugged. "But that one fits well enough."

She waved a hand. "You get my point. Woo-woo stuff happens somewhere else. It's astonishing that what started so long ago in another part of the world might be coming to a head here, of all places."

"That may be precisely why it's coming to a head here. Think of this big, beautiful city filled with humans crowded together like so many sheep. It's not the seat of an Elder Races demesne, and it has no other major competing Power. Charleston is a bit close, but the

Elven High Lord is well known for being disinterested in matters that lie beyond his Wood. And there's a distaste for magic here that adds blinkers of denial to the public eye. You said it yourself—magical events happen elsewhere, not here in good old Atlanta. That kind of denial makes an excellent hunting ground for an old, rapacious wolf."

She shuddered. She was beginning to feel shaky again, so she pushed to her feet. "I think I'd better do as you said and eat something."

He unfolded from his chair. "As soon as you have, I'll cast more healing spells, but right now I'm going to start acquiring your documents, money, and a new vehicle."

"And a new phone," she added quickly. "Or at least a new phone card. It's only fair, since you destroyed my last one."

He sighed. "And a new phone."

She drew to a halt and looked up at him. "You've already done a lot, and you're continuing to do so much more. I won't forget this, Josiah."

His expression turned inscrutable. "My help doesn't come without strings. If it looks like a legal battle is the right way to go, I may call on you to testify. Will you agree to do that?"

She hesitated. "As long as you do everything in your power to make sure I'm safe while I'm testifying, then yes."

Satisfaction gleamed in his hooded gaze. "It's a deal."

She followed him back down to the basement, which no longer seemed quite as creepy. When he walked into the monitor room, she rummaged in the fridge, but nothing appealed.

"Would it have hurt you to pick up a few chocolate bars for the woman in distress?" she muttered.

His sigh was audible from the other room. "I'll try to remember to pick up chocolate tomorrow after work."

She paused. "You're going to work?"

"It's more important than ever that I'm seen to keep a normal schedule."

"That means I'll be stuck here by myself all day, and you don't even have cable." She pulled a face. "I know it shouldn't matter."

He appeared in the doorway and rounded the corner. She thought she heard him mutter, "High-maintenance, high-dollar mammal."

"I'm not ungrateful," she said warily as she straightened.

He clamped both hands onto her shoulders and looked into her gaze. After a moment, he said with severe patience, "There's a country store about two miles away. I'll see if they carry any magazines or books."

The heaviness she had been carrying ever since she woke up lightened just a little. "Would you be so kind? I'd appreciate that so much."

"I'm not kind," he said through his teeth.

She backpedaled quickly. "No, of course you're not. In fact, you're really quite horrible when you think about it."

He made a sound she had never heard him make before.

"What?" she asked. "Too much?"

Then he pulled her against him gently and kissed her.

Gently.

Gentleness was not a good thing for her right now. Her mouth shook under his. He made the sound again and pulled her into his arms. She was too tired to withstand him and too heartsick to pull away from the comfort of his touch. A tear slipped out from one of her eyelids, and then another. Reaching up to wrap her good arm around his neck, she leaned against his strength.

He jerked his mouth away and told her in a strangled voice, "I'm going to the store now."

The magnetic pull toward him had grown stronger than ever. It was hard to withdraw, but she made herself do it. Turning away, she wiped her eyes. "You do that."

He took the stairs two at a time. Clearly he couldn't get away fast enough from the situation. Big deal, she couldn't get away fast enough from it either. Snatching up a sandwich and an apple, she went upstairs to eat.

He was gone longer than she expected. She finished her meal, and then, tiredness dragging at her sore limbs, she went back downstairs to take more ibuprofen and lie down. She turned off the light in the bedroom but left the door open. The image of Nina's body haunted her and it hurt to breathe, but eventually she was able to drift into a doze.

The sound of the back door opening brought her to alertness. She listened to him descend the stairs. Then he moved around the unfinished area and bags rustled. When his footsteps came to the bedroom doorway, she said, “I’m awake.”

He walked to the side of the bed and dropped lightweight things onto the bed in front of her. Lifting her head, she looked at them. Six chocolate bars lay on the bedspread.

“Oh my God, you found chocolate.”

He set a stack of other things in front of her—three books and several magazines. Wonderingly, she picked up the first book. It was a used paperback, a romance. The second one was a Western, the third a thriller.

“I didn’t know what you like,” he said without expression.

“This is perfect. They’re wonderful.” She was thankful the room lay in such deep shadow, because the too-easy tears blurred her vision again.

“They’re not wonderful. They were seventy-five cents each.” He dropped one last item on the bedspread. It was a new prepaid phone, still in its packaging. “I figured you shouldn’t be out here alone without a way to get in touch with me, just in case. But if you use that to call anybody else you know, I will strangle you myself.”

“I won’t.”

He walked out as she pushed to a sitting position. She stared at everything. They were such simple items, just a few used books and magazines, some chocolate, and a phone. It was incredible how much better they made her feel.

She climbed out of bed to look for him. He knelt on one knee in front of the minifridge as he unboxed a cheap, off-brand coffee maker. A can of ground coffee and a packet of filters already sat on the fridge.

He was scowling, his expression irritable. "I bought more food. None of it is fancy, but there's enough to eat for a day. You can take the phone when you go, but this coffee maker is mine."

Who was this strange man, and what had he done with that bastard Josiah? She nodded, then realized he wouldn't see it because he wasn't looking at her. "Makes sense."

He set the coffee maker on the minifridge, then straightened. "The computer's off-limits. It's password protected, and not in English."

She held up both hands. "Not even going to try to decode it."

Finally he looked at her. A muscle flexed in his jaw. "Fine. I'm going to cast as many healing spells as your body can handle. Then I have to head back to town. I have an eight a.m. staff meeting to prepare for."

She didn't want him to go and tightened her hands into fists. Forget about wondering where that bastard Josiah had disappeared to—who was this strange woman inhabiting her body? "I would appreciate a few more healing spells, but don't tire yourself out. You've got a lot going on this week."

"I'm not going to give you anything I can't afford to give," he said grimly. "We'd better get to it."

Damn it, why didn't he have any proper furniture down here? She looked around, at a loss, and only started toward the bedroom when he put a hand at the small of her back and urged her in that direction.

He flipped on the light as they entered the room. When she sat on the edge of the bed, he sat beside her. "I'm going to concentrate on your broken ribs this time."

Terrific. This was going to suck, but it would be worth it to be able to breathe without the constant, nagging stab of pain. "Let's do it."

Twisting, he rested one hand on the mattress behind her and laid his other hand over the broken ribs until she felt surrounded, immersed in his presence. Then he began to speak in that foreign language, and sparks of his magic flew through the air.

She had enough time to notice the beauty and Power in it before pain slammed into her rib cage, squeezing her in a vise. She turned her face away.

After what felt like a hundred years, he paused, then said roughly, "Breathe."

"Sure thing," she wheezed.

He pulled her against his side, supporting her body until the vise around her lungs eased. Feeling lightheaded, she didn't bother to try to straighten. If he wanted to keep her sitting upright, let him.

He gently prodded her ribs. "Can you take any

more?"

"Of course. Wouldn't stop this much fun for the world."

He snorted. "Now who's full of bullshit? Let me know when you're ready."

Turning toward him, she knotted one fist in his shirt and tucked her face into his neck. "Ready."

"You're killing me," he muttered.

The edge of his jaw came down on the top of her head, and he wrapped his arms around her. Then the torture began again. She endured until he finally fell silent.

"That's it, I'm done." He sounded hoarse. "Jesus Christ."

Neither of them moved for a long time. She leaned against him. His arms remained locked around her. Finally she pushed at his chest, his arms loosened, and she straightened. When she met his gaze, she felt taken aback. He looked almost as if he hated her.

"What's my phone number?"

After their exchanges, the number was etched indelibly in her mind. She recited it.

"Fine. I'll be here sometime after work tomorrow. I don't know when." He stood. "Don't call unless it's an emergency."

Anger stirred. It had taken him a while, but the bastard Josiah had finally put in an appearance. "You think I'm going to call to discuss the stock market or the weather?" she snapped. "Thanks for the healing spells, but don't fucking patronize me."

"Right." A muscle bunched in his jaw. He walked out.

She stayed where she was. A moment later, the back door opened and shut, and the big house resettled around his absence.

The air felt strange and cold, and the basement had turned creepy again, but she could take a deep breath without pain. Pushing to her feet, she walked into the bathroom to inspect her reflection and torso.

She touched her cheekbone. It had not been twenty-four hours since Austin's attack, but the swelling had completely disappeared, and what remained of the bruises looked a good two weeks old. She could now hide the rest under makeup and pass for normal.

Damn it. She wanted to call Josiah.

Just to mess with him, she told herself. She would die before she admitted she wanted him to turn around and come back. Her skin still remembered the pressure from how he had held her.

She unboxed the phone and plugged it in so it could charge, just in case an emergency did arise. Then she brushed her teeth, crawled into bed, and slept like the dead for eighteen hours.

AFTER THE ENERGY in their last spat, Josiah knew the safe house would have to be burning down around Molly's ears before she dialed his number. Then he thought of the fiery outrage burning in her gaze.

Scratch that. She'd probably let the house burn.

Just as well. He needed a serious break from that woman. In fact, it would do him good to go a month without thinking about her. Then he might be able to yank himself back on track and stay there.

If only he could tear out the traitorous part of his brain that would not stop focusing on how beautiful she looked no matter how wrecked she was or how badly she was dressed.

On the nuances that shifted in her intelligent gaze like ripples over a deep, sky-blue lake. On how she took the agony from the healing spells without making so much as a goddamn peep—and he had known strong men who had cried under that kind of pain—or how the need to kiss her properly had begun to pulse in his blood like a fever.

He felt infected with her. It eroded the purity of purpose that had driven him through so many decades. Other thoughts crowded in, like wondering what it would be like to sleep late, tangled in the bedsheets with her long body resting against his. Or how luminous she would look if she were truly happy.

Maybe he hadn't liked the man he had seen when he had taken a good, hard look at himself. He had turned single-minded like a shark intent on the most important meal of its life. So what? Who fucking cared?

When he and his coven finally destroyed their quarry, they would be doing the world a goddamn service. Then he could go sleep on a beach in the Maldives for a year and decide if he cared about living the rest of his life.

But he wasn't finished yet. Taking an exit ramp at this late stage in their hunt Was. Not. An. Option.

He couldn't even be done for one goddamn evening. Halfway back to the apartment, he punched Steven's number. When Steven replied, he told him about the package of documents he needed for Molly's new identity.

"Send me photos for a new passport and driver's license," Steven said. "Digital is fine. I can print them up here, and I'll FedEx everything to you in forty-eight hours."

"That's fine. I'll take photos tomorrow after work. I also need Maria and Henry to deliver a reliable car to the safe house. I don't want Molly to see their faces. They can park it at the end of the lane and leave the title work in the glove compartment. Have them text me after they make the drop-off."

"Got it," Steven said. "I'll let them know. What else?"

"That's it." He would have to do the rest himself. Sometime in the next two days, he needed to stop at a bank to make a withdrawal.

They talked a few minutes more, then he ended the call. By that point he'd arrived back at the apartment where he spent the rest of his evening organizing the case files he had brought home and preparing for the staff meeting.

When he finally finished, it was midnight and he was facing another short night of sleep. He took a half hour, as he always did, to review everything that had happened and what he thought might come.

By Monday night, Tuesday at the latest, the police would figure out Molly was missing. By then they should have also made connections between Molly and Nina Rodriguez.

That week there should be two arson reports to review. The autopsies on Austin and Nina might be done by Wednesday. He was not convinced the verdict in the autopsies would matter to anybody except Molly. For her sake, he hoped the coroner could confirm she hadn't caused Austin's death.

Then there were those who would be searching for Molly in order to silence her. Molly had felt certain Russell had dictated Austin's actions, and Maria had seen a link between the Seychelles file and their quarry. So it was logical to see a potential connection between Russell Sherman, the Seychelles file, and their quarry as well.

Sherman had wanted so badly to make friends and begin exerting influence over Josiah on the night of Hell Party. Now Josiah was inclined to let Sherman catch his prey.

The next morning he rose at five. After meditating and an intense tai chi session that had sweat pouring down the hollow of his back, he showered and ate, and checked and replied to coven email.

Then, even though scanning the city for sparks of magic was one of Anson's duties, he did his own search as well. Every day he looked for threats or anomalies. Molly was such a statistical outlier, he didn't expect to find any disturbance of her caliber again.

No, if his quarry made a slip, it would be something subtle and possibly hard to define, so he quietened his mind and listened carefully. Beyond the robust roar of the city waking to a new workweek, he felt nothing. A very minor magic spark here and there, but that was all.

In fact, that was the most remarkable thing about Atlanta—the lack of a major magical presences. Looking out his window at the sunlit city, Josiah smiled. He didn't buy that kind of innocence for anything.

He pictured the face his quarry had worn over a hundred years ago, in a different place and a different life. But faces could be changed with plastic surgery. Josiah had altered his features, and so had Maria.

You're here, he thought. You're either in the city itself, or you're living somewhere nearby. And you've killed off any other major Powers that might have been here, or you've imprisoned them and are draining them to extend your own life, just like you did to me.

Maybe you're a sycophant, or maybe you're the governor. You might be a prison warden. That could have its uses. Maybe you're masquerading as a senator. You would like the taste of political power in Washington.

But no matter what you look like or what you call yourself now, I'm going to find you and finish what should have been done a long time ago.

I'll finally kill Grigori Rasputin.

Chapter Twelve

MONDAY WAS A bitch. Two cases left over from the previous DA came to a head while information came in about the weekend murders faster than he had anticipated.

Josiah navigated carefully through all of it. With staff members, he maintained a calm, laid-back facade. He asked to be copied on every report relating to the weekend activity and directed several interview requests from the press to one of the senior assistant DAs.

But when a phone call came in from Sherman & Associates, he chose to take that personally.

Russell's deep voice boomed over the connection. "Josiah, good of you to take my call."

"Russell." He shut his office door. "What can I do for you?"

"I hate to bother you on a Monday, but I've just had some detectives here asking a lot of questions about Austin and his wife. They wanted to go through his things, but of course I had to turn them down. Like every other lawyer, Austin has privileged information in his office." When Russell chuckled, he sounded like how

Josiah imagined a toad would when it cackled. "They'll have to come back with a warrant, I'm afraid. But I wanted to let you know, man to man, it's nothing personal. We want to cooperate with whatever they're investigating. We just have to follow the rules."

Josiah swung his chair around to look out his window. Like any lawyer with magical aptitude, he had developed a highly refined truthsense. He was interested to note that Russell had told only one lie so far.

Russell had no intention of cooperating with any investigation. That meant he was calling to pump Josiah for information.

"None taken, Russell," he replied easily. "I'm sure the detectives will return shortly with the right paperwork."

"Do you know what's going on? Or perhaps you know but you can't say?"

There it was: the ask.

"You know I can't speak about ongoing investigations…" He let his voice trail away reluctantly. "But I'm surprised the detectives didn't tell you."

"Tell me what? Austin's not answering his phone, and he hasn't shown up for work today." Russell paused, then chuckled again. "So I tried calling his wife, but I'm not sure she's on speaking terms with me after that party. Austin's been miserable over the past few weeks. Between me and thee, I think she might have left him for good."

None of that was a lie either. Josiah picked up his

pen and twirled it between his fingers as he injected a note of concern into his voice. "I shouldn't say anything, but some reports have crossed my desk this morning. Brace yourself. It's bad."

"For God's sake, man. I know it's just after lunch, but should I be drinking a scotch?"

Josiah replied gently, "This is not the kind of conversation to have over the phone. Let the detectives do their work. After they come back with a warrant and make everything official, maybe you and I can meet for lunch."

"All right." Cautious pleasure entered the other man's voice. "Let me treat you to the best steak you'll find in the state. How about lunch on Friday? I'll email you the details."

"You bet." As he hung up, he was sure about one thing—the detectives might not have told him yet, but Russell already knew Austin was dead. What the man really wanted to ascertain was what the DA's office knew.

And he wanted to find out what happened to Molly.

Josiah was ready to leave the office hours before he finally did at six thirty. By then the urge to drive out of the city beat like a drum underneath his skin. He needed to see for himself that Molly was okay.

It was a warm, late-spring evening. He mentally swept his car for devices. He didn't find any, but things had ratcheted up to a new level of tension, so he implemented the next stage of precautions and drove his car to a local YMCA, where he parked and kept a sharp eye on his surroundings as he strode to a Camry parked down a neighborhood street.

Within minutes, he sped down the highway in the new vehicle. After stopping at the country store for more supplies, it was close to eight o'clock by the time he pulled up to the safe house.

He parked behind the house, then gathered the shopping bags and strode to the back door, picking up speed as he grew closer.

Part of him had waited all day for this moment. Before he could fit the key into the lock, the back door opened and Molly stood on the landing. She smiled warily. "I got worried when I saw the strange car."

He was unprepared for the spike of fierce gladness that drove through him at the sight of her. As he stepped inside, it brought them close together on the small landing. He looked at the empty coffee carafe she gripped in one hand. "Were you going to try to brain me with that? It's not much of a weapon."

"There aren't many options lying around. I grabbed what was available."

He kept weapons in the locked safe, but she didn't need to know that. He looked her over. She had washed her clothes and wore her jeans and shoes from Saturday along with another of his T-shirts.

Her blond hair was sleek and clean, and the dark circles that had hollowed out her eyes looked lighter. She still needed a couple of weeks of rest and good nutrition, but she looked worlds better than she had yesterday.

She stood close enough that he could feel her body heat. He leaned closer, narrowing his eyes. "Are you wearing makeup?"

"As it so happens, yes, I am." Frowning, she leaned backward and pivoted in one neat, fluid movement, heading down the stairs to the basement. "I wanted to see if I could make the last of the bruises disappear."

"Good. I need to take some photos."

"Why?" She put the carafe back in the coffee maker and stepped out of the way as he approached the fridge.

He knelt to put away the new food—two Cobb salads, garlic and butter dinner rolls, containers of yogurt, more sandwiches, and a bottle of wine along with an opener. As he straightened, he noticed a few wrappers from the chocolate bars in the small wastebin nearby and smiled to himself. "For your new passport and driver's license. Do you have a preference for your new name?"

"Let me think about it." She regarded the wine bottle with obvious yearning. "From the country store?"

"Yes." He regarded the bottle too and said drily, "They didn't have the best selection."

"I don't care." She sighed.

"Let's get business out of the way first. Afterward, we can open the wine and eat some supper." He frowned at how the neck of his T-shirt gaped on her and then looked down at himself. He still wore his work clothes, a dark suit with a blue dress shirt. "But first I think we should change shirts. What I'm wearing will still be too big for you, but I think we can arrange the collar so it doesn't show."

She hesitated. "Okay."

He stripped off his jacket and shirt. The cool air licked his bare chest and arms as he held them out. Looking steadily into his gaze, her fingers brushed against his as she took the clothes.

Something electric and raw hovered between them.

He almost moved forward, almost reached to pull her into his arms, but then she spun to walk rapidly into the bedroom and slam the door.

He rubbed a hand over his face. His body felt like it had caught fire.

She's a new widow. You need to stay on track.

This can't happen.

A few minutes later she walked out again, wearing his shirt and dark jacket, and waited expressionlessly while he stared at her.

His suits and shirts were tailored to his frame, but she had rolled up the sleeves and her long, leggy body carried the look far better than he had anticipated. He was unprepared for how the sight of her in his clothes would hit. The electric, raw tension vibrated higher.

Finally she asked, "Well? Will it do?"

Blindly, he turned toward the stairs. "Like I said, I think I can make it work. We should use the blank wall in the living room as a backdrop."

She followed him. He listened to the soft friction of cloth, the sounds of her footsteps, light and graceful.

You can't act on this. You can't.

In the living room, the automatic timers on the lights had clicked on. She walked over to stand at the wall while he jerked out his phone and angled the camera for a headshot. Zoomed in. Watched the screen rigidly as she licked her bottom lip. Her gaze was shadowed with thoughts he could only guess at.

He had already taken a few shots before he noticed that the shirt collar had gaped enough to show the tip of her lacy bra. "Hold on," he said tersely.

She held still as he strode forward to adjust the collar. The back of his knuckles brushed the tender skin at her neck. The sensation of touching her shot straight to his groin. They both sucked in a breath.

"Take the damn picture." Her voice sounded low and strained.

He strode away, adjusted his camera again. This time when he looked at the screen, he saw the tension in her expression, the taut way she held herself.

Whatever else she thought of him, she felt this too. This inappropriate, all-consuming thing. How much more excruciating could it get?

"Try not to look like a felon," he advised.

Surprised laughter brightened her expression, and there it was, a sparkling glimpse of just how beautiful she would be when she found happiness. As he stared, his thumb pressed down. He clicked several shots.

Her laughter faded. "Did we get it?"

He came back to himself and scrolled back through

the photos. "Yes. These will do."

Tension returned to her features. "Good." She left the room.

He glanced out the window. Darkness had fallen some time ago. There was nothing like a dark night in the country. It felt like the house was surrounded in velvet.

They had barely touched, and it had still left him struggling for self-control.

I can't stay, he thought. Having made that decision, he went downstairs. She had shut herself in the bedroom again. A moment later she reappeared, wearing his T-shirt and carrying his suit and dress shirt.

She held out the clothes. This time he carefully avoided any contact with her fingers.

Their eyes met.

He lunged forward the same moment she stepped toward him, and they didn't kiss so much as collide together. He hauled her against his chest while she wrapped both arms around his neck, mouth slanting under his.

Her lips parted. With a deep sense of relief and excitement, he delved into her. Her mouth was soft, wet silk. The curved heat of her body shifting against his bare skin made hunger spike uncontrollably.

He couldn't get enough and ate at her while cupping one of her breasts. The soft mound filled his palm, and he stroked her nipple through the barrier of her bra and the T-shirt, making her gasp. As he fondled her, she ran her hands down his chest, igniting him everywhere. The hardest erection he could remember having strained against the zipper of his dress slacks.

This was insanity. A recipe for disaster.

He was damned if he was going to stop it now.

✧ ✧ ✧

THAT DAY MOLLY had slept late, eaten chocolate for breakfast, and read some of the thriller. Then she slept some more. Even though most of the day had gone by in a blur, she was glad when Josiah arrived and even more glad when he pulled a bottle of wine out of his shopping bag.

Oh, yes please, wine. The fact that he'd bought it showed he was starting to think about things other than what was useful or what furthered his objectives. If she had learned one thing over the past twenty years, she knew life should be about so much more than meeting one's ambitions. Or, in his case, being driven by revenge.

Then he took off half his clothes. When he shrugged out of his suit jacket, she saw where he was going and had a moment to brace herself. But then the material of his shirt fell open as he unbuttoned it, and everything inside ground to a halt.

He had whipcord strength bound with heavy muscles on a big frame. His shoulders and arms flexed along with the accordion shadows of lean ribs as he stripped off his shirt. He was deeply tanned everywhere, not just his face and neck, and his broad chest and flat stomach were sprinkled with dark hair that glinted in the basement light.

Her throat went dry. God, she wanted him. He glanced at her, eyes glittering, the bones of his face tight. He looked at her like she was his only meal for miles around, and she wanted to say *come and get it.*

She thought running away to change in the bedroom would help, but then she slipped into the clothes that were still warm from his body. Immediately, she was enveloped in his scent, and it made things worse. Made it unbearable. Needing him became a scratch under her skin that she couldn't reach.

Watching him watch her, take photos of her while he wore nothing but the dark slacks of his suit. Could he see through the lens of his phone how she fought to hide her erratic breathing?

She ran away the first chance she got, tore off his clothes only to put on his T-shirt again, and tried to give the shirt and jacket back. All the while the need for him was running fast and liquid in the back of her mind like frenetic music she couldn't silence.

Until she stopped trying and a force greater than she was drove her forward.

Coming into full contact with his body caused an explosion of sensation—the taste of his mouth, his hard muscles sliding against hers, his heat, his scent, my God, those big hands roaming over her with such shaking greed.

Tearing her mouth away, she rubbed her face against

the crisp hair of his chest and gasped, "I'm still leaving."

Aggressively, he walked her back until her shoulders hit the wall. "You're still leaving," he agreed roughly. "I'm not. We both know what this is."

Do we? What is it?

She was glad at least one of them was clear about where things stood. The only thing she knew for sure was that she couldn't stand to have a single piece of clothing between them, and she yanked the T-shirt off again. While she struggled to get free of the soft cotton material, he put his arms around her to search for her bra clasp.

He found it, her bra fell away, and he stopped, chest heaving as he stared down at her. When his gaze came back up, his expression had turned molten.

It stabbed her, that look, somewhere deep where she had been bruised and hurt. She had needed somebody to look at her as if she were the only thing he had ever wanted—even if it was just for this moment.

"You can change your mind and walk away," she whispered, testing the threads of desire that tied them to each other.

"*Like hell I can*," he growled, pressing her against the wall with his bigger, harder body. But then he paused as he sank a fist into the hair at the nape of her neck. He muttered, with difficulty, "I understand if you're not ready for this, but you'd better say something now."

That was… thoughtful. Winding her arms around his neck, she whispered against his lips, "I'm so ready for this."

Grabbing her hips, he ground against her and hissed, "Birth control."

"On the pill." She brushed his hands aside and yanked open the fastening of her jeans.

He pulled out his wallet and withdrew a foil-wrapped package. "Condom."

"Safe sex *and* protection. We're good." Coping with wall sex and a condom seemed like more than what she could handle. She slid away and walked into the bedroom, then wiggled out of her jeans.

When she turned, she wore only her lacy panties. He had opened the fastening of his slacks. Underneath, his large erection strained against the confinement of sleek, black shorts. The unruly wave of dark hair had fallen on his forehead, and his Power radiated like a furnace.

She felt like she was going crazy. The surface of her skin *needed* his like her lungs needed air. She snatched the condom out of his hand and ripped the packet open. He put the flat of his hand against her collarbone and shoved her so she fell back on the bed.

Then, swooping like a hawk, he dove on top of her. A sound broke out of her as their bodies collided. She curled one leg around his waist while he pushed his cock against the bowl of her pelvis.

He angled his dark head so that he could bite and suckle at her nipples, quickly teasing them into reddened peaks. Stabs of pleasure rocked through her body. The need to have him turned painful.

Pushing his shoulder, she muttered, "Let me get this on you."

Growling, he lifted his head. A flush had darkened his cheekbones. Bracing his weight on both hands, he held still while she yanked his slacks open farther and reached into the black shorts to pull out his erection.

They both looked at her hand gripping his cock. He muttered, "I'm close to spilling all over you."

"Don't you dare," she told him breathlessly. "I want you inside me when you come."

A small, sensual smile tugged at his strongly molded lips as he looked at her with approval and heat. "You know what you want. I like that."

So did she. Austin had always tried to exert control in the bedroom, and while she didn't mind giving up control sometimes, she also wanted to take control too. With shaking fingers, she smoothed the condom over the broad head of his erection and rolled the edges down. He was beautiful everywhere, and large enough the condom didn't reach to the root. While she worked it on, he jerked in her hands and swore under his breath. She paused to give him a few moments.

Then, with sly gentleness, he teased his fingers under the edge of her panties and stroked her. With a strangled sound of surprise, she climaxed.

His clenched expression softened. Gently, he stroked her in a rhythm that helped her further along while he watched every shift in her expression. Riding the waves of the climax until it eased, she gave him a twisted smile.

"Well, that was a bonus," she told him unsteadily. "Normally I don't come that easily, or even every time."

"You can change that expectation right now," he said as he eased one finger inside her. "Because you're going to come every time you're with me. Every time, Molly, and more than once."

"Those are some bold words." She gasped, rocking to his penetration. "Are you sure you can live up to them?"

He laughed, a soft and wicked sound that ran over her like caress. "I don't make claims I can't fulfill. Lift up, *milaya*. I don't want to destroy your only pair of panties."

Milaya. What did that mean? As she lifted her hips, he pulled the panties off and dropped them to the floor beside the bed. Then, holding her gaze, he settled between her legs and rubbed the petals of her intimate flesh with the head of his cock.

When she was ready, he pushed in, stretching her wide with his entry. It felt so incredible she tilted back her head and closed her eyes to savor every moment.

"Look at me," he commanded.

Startled, she opened her eyes.

Watching her closely, he pushed harder until he was in all the way. "You chose this. No regrets, no turning away."

He looked fierce, possessive, his expression taut. Surprised by his insistence, she gripped his biceps. "No regrets, I swear it. I'm enjoying this too much. I only closed my eyes because you feel so damn good."

"That's all right then." The clenched line of his jaw eased. Then, as he pulled back and slid in again, her eyelids fluttered shut again.

"Still here," she murmured as she arched up. "Still with you all the way."

"You better be," he growled. "God, I hate condoms, but I love how you feel."

"I love how you feel too," she gasped.

Tension coiled higher as they found a rhythm together. He stroked her hair back off her face as he moved inside her, and somehow the wordless gesture conveyed something she needed. Sliding both hands down the long, strong curve of his back, she rose up to press her mouth against his shoulder, and in response, he gripped her hip and increased the power of his thrusts.

When he pulled out, she grumbled in protest. A quick white grin flashed across his face.

"Turn over," he told her.

Eagerly, she complied, and he guided her into position on her hands and knees and covered her from behind. When he entered her, the angle made him feel bigger than ever. Bonelessly, she collapsed onto her elbows, which raised her hips higher until at last he was buried to the root.

He braced himself on one hand while he curved the other arm around her torso to stroke at her entrance. When he found her clitoris, she shuddered everywhere from the piercing burst of pleasure.

He growled against her neck, "There it is."

"God!" Reaching blindly for a pillow, she buried her face in it. "It feels amazing, but I don't know if I can come again."

"Oh, you can," he told her. He bit her neck as he fucked her, and the relentless circular motion of his fingers drove everything else out of her head.

It was indescribable. She felt empty and he filled her. She wanted to focus on everything about him—his big body, the taste of his skin, the grace and power in his movements—but he kept the focus on her with those wicked, wise fingers. The pleasure spiked higher and higher until a climax crashed through her again. This one was deeper, stronger, and she cried out at the intensity of it.

He growled again and cut loose. Gripping her by the hair, one arm wrapped around her hips, he drove into her. "I can't get enough of you."

"Me neither." She felt crazed, outside her own head. What the hell were they doing? Nothing existed except this overwhelming drive to mate. Reaching above and behind her, she cupped the back of his neck.

With a muffled groan, he twisted and held rigid. She could feel him pulsing inside, and it was gorgeous, glorious. His roughened breathing sawed in her ear. Gently, she released the back of his neck and stroked his cheek.

We both know what this is.

Except… she didn't.

She only knew one thing for sure. No matter what this was between them or how deeply it shook her, she was still leaving.

Chapter Thirteen

AFTER HOLDING AGAINST her for a long moment, he withdrew slowly. Shaking, she collapsed on the bed. He stroked callused fingers along the curve of her spine.

"All right?" His voice sounded hoarse, as if he had been running for miles.

"Yes," she gasped. What else could she say? No? How much fun would that be after he'd just treated her with such consideration?

She couldn't admit that he had shaken her to the core and tossed her emotions head over heels. *We both know what this is.*

He rolled away to sit at the edge of the bed, and she pulled up the blankets and curled on her side to look at him. God, he was beautiful. They hadn't even gotten his pants off. She rubbed his back as he pulled the condom off. His dark head angled as he looked down, and he froze.

She lifted her head. "What is it?"

"The condom broke." His voice was expressionless.

She took in a deep breath, absorbing that. Then she

sighed. "Don't worry. I got tested after I left Austin. I'll need a retest, but I think I'm good."

He turned his head to one side as he listened. "I didn't pick up anything when I scanned you for damage after the attack. I'm safe too. And you're on the pill."

"Yes."

Reaching behind him, he captured her hand and pulled it around to press his lips to her fingers. Then he stood, gathered his clothes, and strode out. A few moments later, she heard the water running in the bathroom.

His absence was deflating, and she curled into a tighter ball. She felt inappropriately raw. What an inconvenient time to discover she might not be any good at casual sex.

But there was nothing casual about what happened. She might feel unsure about almost everything else in her life, but she felt certain about that. They hadn't committed to anything, and they had been very clear they were going their separate ways, but this lovemaking hadn't been casual.

He was fully clothed when he strode back in. Desire stabbed at her again, and this time it was stronger than ever. Now she knew what those sophisticated clothes covered.

His gaze burned as he looked at her, and a muscle flexed in his jaw. He said tonelessly, "I won't be coming tomorrow. I've got too much to do, and I can't develop predictable habits."

Something dark pulsed in reaction. Disappointment? She sat up, holding the sheet up to her chest. "I understand."

"Two of my colleagues will be delivering your new car tomorrow. They'll park it at the end of the lane. I'll have them leave a cooler with supper in it."

"There's more than enough food," she said drily. "You brought two Cobb salads, and it looks as though you're leaving—and how many sandwiches did you bring? I think there's six now in the fridge."

"This was unplanned." The muscle flexed again. "Now it's grown late, and I can't stay."

"Josiah, I wasn't complaining," she said in a gentle voice. *Because we both know what this is.* "I was simply pointing out there's already more food here than I can eat."

His expression clenched. He strode forward, clamped one hand at the back of her neck, and his mouth crashed down on hers. After a long, blistering kiss, he tore away.

"We'll have your documents day after tomorrow," he said and walked out.

God. She felt as if something inside tore away to follow him when he left. A moment later, the back door slammed. She touched her mouth with unsteady fingers. Her lips were shaking too.

She whispered to the empty house, "I'm leaving Wednesday."

Sometime later, she roused herself enough to open

the wine and pull out one of the salads. As she sat cross-legged on the bed and mechanically picked at the supper, flashbacks of the evening played through her mind.

His face, his hands. The sensation of his body moving over hers, in her. Her inner muscles were already sore. How he had stilled when he said, *The condom broke.*

Thank God she was not just on the pill. Because of the upheaval, she carried the container in her purse. She always took it first thing every morning without fail, except…

The salad went flying as she exploded off the bed and lunged for her purse. After digging frantically for the container, she opened it and checked three times for evidence of the answer she already knew in her heart.

She always took the pill first thing, except she hadn't taken it yesterday morning after the attack. What were the chances that it would matter?

She wasn't on the regular pill. Because of side effects, she took the mini pill—and the mini pill was the one you had to watch out for. But still, the chances had to be low. And she was almost forty, and she'd never been pregnant.

"It's all going to be okay," she whispered. "Because we know what this is."

After a while, she stood and picked up her mug of wine. Even though she knew the science for how unlikely it was she might get pregnant—or even if she did, how safe it was to drink the wine before a fertilized egg implanted—she took it into the bathroom to pour it down the sink.

✧ ✧ ✧

JOSIAH'S MOOD WAS savage as he drove back into Atlanta. Away from Molly. Away from what they had done together.

It never should have happened, yet he wanted to do it again and again, because apparently whenever he got near her every firm decision he'd ever made about his life flew out the window.

Once he reached the YMCA, he left the Camry down another neighborhood street, walked back to his Audi, and drove to the apartment. Then he flipped through the photos he had taken of Molly, selected a few, and forwarded them to Steven with the message: `FedEx the documents to my attention at the office on Wednesday.`

`You got it`, Steven responded.

After that he poured himself a scotch and checked coven email. Henry and Maria were delivering a Subaru Outback by midday on Tuesday. Henry and Steven's research on the Seychelles file had led them to a Russian bank. Anson continued to monitor the city for flares of magic while he built a file on the governor of Georgia's background. It would be, Josiah knew, as meticulously researched as every other file Anson had compiled.

Everything was proceeding smoothly. Nothing was on fire except for him.

After years of living with a dormant sex drive, it had

come roaring back to life. He strode through the quiet apartment, half erect. The need to take her pounded in his temples. Even at half past two in the morning, he wasn't sure he wouldn't drive back to the safe house to make love to her again before morning.

She had been so sexy, aroused, and yes, caring when they had made love. Worlds different from any other woman he had ever had. A universe different from his dutiful, treacherous wife.

And Molly had been so goddamn calm when he had told her he was leaving. She had torn his focus into tatters and watched with perfect composure as he had left. She was the most dangerous woman he had ever met, and she didn't yet know a fraction of what she was truly capable of.

He threw himself onto the bed and stared dry-eyed at the darkened ceiling until his alarm went off. Then he hauled his ass through his morning routine and went to work. By midmorning people were beginning to avoid him, and he realized he needed to dial back some of the savagery.

He didn't give a damn about the job. It was just a means to an end, but he shouldn't abuse the people who worked for him. Not only did they not deserve that kind of treatment, but it wouldn't get him reelected. So he reined it in.

Maria and Henry texted when they were about to drop off the Subaru, so he texted Molly. `Your new car is about to be delivered at the end of the` lane.

She responded almost instantly. Amazing. Thank you!

They'll tuck the keys in the visor. Don't approach until they're gone. That way you can't ID them.

I won't get close.

He paused. He should put down his fucking phone and get back to fucking work. Instead, his fingers moved almost reluctantly over the keyboard. Everything good?

Everything's fine, Josiah.

He gritted his teeth. His office was up to its eyeballs in cases that had turned red-hot. He could have Anson deliver the package of cash and documents. He didn't technically need to see her again.

But a wave of rebellious anger rose up to quell that. Avoiding her would be taking the coward's way out, and she deserved better than that.

Besides, he wasn't going to pass up the chance to see her again. The fever running rampant in his blood wouldn't allow it. As he sat at his desk, fighting an inward battle with himself, several emails came in at once.

One of them was the autopsy report for Sullivan. Another was the report on Rodriguez.

He clicked on the report for Sullivan and scanned it before sitting back in his chair. Then he texted Molly again. You didn't kill Austin. Cause of death: smoke inhalation. The bruising on his body is attributed to the collapse of the ceiling over him.

Long moments passed with no reply. He imagined her reacting to the news in the solitude of the quiet country house. Just as he was about to call her, a text appeared. What about Nina?

Hold on. He opened that report and scanned it too. Same cause of death. There were no signs of struggle. The coroner stated it's likely she died in her sleep. He thought of how upset Molly had been at the news of Rodriguez's death, almost more upset than she had been about Austin. A sense of responsibility weighed heavily on her, so he added, She didn't suffer any fear or pain.

Another long pause, then: Tough news, but I'm glad you told me. Thank you.

You're welcome. He waited, but she didn't text further, and he couldn't think of how to maintain the connection, so he set his phone aside and got back to work.

Maria and Henry delivered the car just before noon. He alerted Molly, and fifteen minutes later she confirmed that she had driven the car back to the house.

A little after two in the afternoon, he received a memo stating the police had issued an APB for Molly, listing her as a person of interest in a murder investigation. Photos of her had been distributed to all the local television statements. She would be featured on the evening news.

So they had connected Nina Rodriguez to Molly and Austin Sullivan. That had only been a matter of time. He called the lead detective on the case for an update. Afterward, he texted Molly again. `What size clothes do you wear?`

This time it took her a few minutes to respond. `Size eight, long in pants, 34B bra. I have about $60 in cash, and I still have money on some prepaid Visa cards. I thought I'd go to the country store to see if I could pick up some new clothes. Where is it?`

Adrenaline kicked in. Goddamn it, she had keys and a vehicle at her disposal now. She could do anything. Go anywhere. She didn't have to listen to what he said.

Rapidly, he sent back in all caps, `DO NOT GO.`

Silence stretched out long enough that he charged to his door to slam it shut, then he dialed her number. When she picked up, she sounded wary. "Hello?"

"You know it's me," he snapped.

"Of course," she replied irritably. "But God forbid we actually talk on the phone anymore. You made it quite clear before that you're very busy."

"I am busy," he growled. Striding to his window, he yanked at the confining tie at his neck. "But you didn't respond to my latest text."

"No, I didn't." Her voice turned cool. "I was still thinking about it. I don't like somebody else dictating my actions. It was different when I was too hurt to go anywhere. The bruises on my face alone would have drawn attention, but I'm past that point now."

"Or when you didn't have a car and couldn't?" he bit out.

"For Christ's sake, it's just the country store. It isn't a bank branch with security cameras. What's wrong, they don't have clothes?"

"They have TVs," he hissed. "And internet, and they can stream news channels. The police have just put out an APB on you. Your photo is going to be featured in the evening news tonight."

He heard the breath go out of her. She said in a choked voice, "Well, that complicates things."

"Yes, it does," he snapped. Then he made an effort to corral his wayward temper and said more calmly, "Look, you're not a suspect. The current theory is that Austin killed your lawyer and then died trying to set the fire in her office."

"That's ridiculous. Why would he do that? It wasn't as if he could stop her from filing the divorce papers. She had already done that the Friday before."

"I know, but I just talked with the lead detective. With her office records destroyed, I don't think they've discovered that yet. Even still, it looks too pat. They aren't convinced, but they don't have anything else to go on right now. They want to see if you can shed any light on what might have happened, but the concern is that Austin did something to you and you're dead too. You should be fine when you drive far enough away from the area, but you're not there yet. So wash what you've got and stay fucking put. I'll bring you a few outfits when I deliver the documents tomorrow."

"Fine. Do you have to get back to work?" she asked abruptly.

He craned his neck from side to side to ease the tension in his shoulders and made himself relax. "No, I can take a few minutes," he said. At least he no longer sounded like a crazy man. "What do you need? Are you all right?"

"I'm frustrated and going stir-crazy, and I feel a little stupid about insisting I go to the store, but I'm fine."

He pinched the bridge of his nose. "You didn't know about the APB," he replied. "It just went out, so I know what you said sounded reasonable from your point of view. But I don't issue arbitrary orders, Molly. You need to trust me when I tell you to do something. Or not to do something, as it were."

"Okay." She sounded calmer too. "You're right."

He wanted to put his arms around her. Goddamn it. "I'm sorry for biting your head off. I'm on a rampage today. It's not you."

"What's wrong?"

Aside from the fact that I'm losing my fucking mind over you?

He clenched his teeth and didn't say it. "I didn't sleep. Too many things running through my head."

"Ah. Me too."

Curiosity stirred. "Was there something you needed

to say to me?"

"Yes," she said carefully. "But we don't have to talk about it right now." Her measured tone said it wasn't a lightweight subject.

"What is it?" Someone knocked on his door. "Hang on." Holding the phone away, he raised his voice. "I'm on the phone! I'll be with you in a few minutes." Then he turned his attention back to Molly. "What were you saying?"

"Nothing," she told him.

He frowned. "That's not true. If it was nothing, you wouldn't have brought it up."

"Bad impulse," she replied crisply. "What I have to say isn't urgent, and you've got people waiting for you. Go back to work."

"Fine, see you tomorrow." He hesitated, reluctant to break the connection. "Don't hesitate to call if something does turn urgent."

"It won't, Josiah," she said gently. "Everything is fine here. Bye for now."

He frowned as she disconnected. She was the polar opposite of a needy woman. He ought to be glad. Relieved, even. Instead, he felt like she kept shutting a door in his face—a door he should never walk through but also one he couldn't seem to keep away from.

The knock sounded on his door again, and reluctantly he pocketed his phone and got back to work.

Around a quarter after three, he received Sherman's email about lunch on Friday and responded to confirm.

He had a feeling some of Sherman's questions would get answered by the evening news. Still, the luncheon meeting should prove interesting. Sometimes people gave away things by what they didn't say as much as what they did.

That evening he stayed even later than usual and left the office after seven.

When he approached his car, he scanned it. He'd been taking precautions for so long, they had become automatic.

This time he found something.

He stopped. In case his actions were caught on CCTV, he bent to tie his shoe, and under the guise of that he checked again. A glimmer of magic hovered around the license plate. It was too small and subtle to be a bomb, but he clicked his key fob from where he crouched, just in case. Nothing blew up.

Only then did he approach. Opening the trunk, he set his briefcase inside while he examined the glimmer of magic up close. It was a tracker.

Somebody had decided to keep an eye on his movements.

On the way home, he stopped at an ATM. Then he went to a big-box department store to buy a variety of different things—household cleaners, groceries, paper products, travel-sized toiletries, and a soft-sided carry-on bag.

He also strode through the women's clothing section to grab a couple of outfits in Molly's size along with some underwear, a sleep set with a short nightie, a pretty thigh-length robe and matching slippers, and a jean jacket and a baseball cap. He selected a checkout lane far away from any others, and as the cashier rang up his purchases, he checked his surroundings carefully. Nobody paid any attention.

As the cashier rang up the women's clothes, he smiled. "Why don't you go ahead and tuck those into the carry-on? I'm surprising my wife with a getaway weekend."

"Lucky wife." She returned his smile. "Sure thing."

When all his purchases had been tallied, he paid with cash and whistled as he took his cart out to the car and loaded everything into the trunk. While he did, he conducted another sharp, detailed scan but didn't find anything new.

Back at his place, he hauled everything, including the new go-bag, into the apartment. Once he had everything inside, he scanned the rooms, first magically, and then he swept for mechanical bugs. Nothing. Only then did he shrug out of his suit jacket and pour himself a scotch.

This changed everything. *Goddamn it.*

It was almost ten when he called Molly. He listened to the phone ringing. When she answered, she sounded sleepy. She sounded so fucking sexy, he hardened in an instant.

Huskily, he asked, "Did I wake you?"

"No," she sighed. He heard something rustle, perhaps the sheets. "Well, almost. I wasn't quite asleep.

What's going on?"

Suddenly so much rage flooded his body he wanted to punch a wall. "There's been another development."

"What is it?" she said sharply. "What's wrong?"

"Someone put a tracker on my car." As he spoke, he opened the blinds at the wall of windows in the living room. The view of the city was why he had picked this place. "I can't come to you tomorrow."

"What about the other car you drove? The Camry?"

"Here's the thing, *milaya*." He stopped.

It was only in that minute that he realized he had been intending to spend the night with her on Wednesday if she would have him again. Despite all common sense, he had been counting on being with her one more time before he let her go. Giving up that precious, rare opportunity caused a mental outcry that felt like physical pain.

"Josiah?"

He snapped back into focus. "The tracker could be good news. It means I've come to somebody's attention, and they want to see what I'm up to. But I don't know what triggered it. Maybe it's something about my movements. Maybe somebody noticed I drive in a way that shakes loose anybody who might be trying to tail me. Maybe they found my car where I parked it at the Y. Maybe they know about the Camry."

"What if you remove the tracker?"

"I don't want to. We need to see if we can find who put it on my car. This is an opportunity we can't ignore.

But that means coming to you is out. We're going to have to set up a meet in town. I've got a go-bag for you, and I withdrew a thousand dollars from an ATM tonight. Tomorrow morning I'll take out another thousand on my way to work."

"Two thousand in cash?"

"Yes. That won't be enough, and it's not what we agreed on, but it will get you out of town and far enough away that your photo won't be in the news. I'll figure out how to get you the rest. I'll also be getting your new ID delivered sometime tomorrow." He paused. "We need to set up a meet where you can drive straight in, pick up the package, and then leave right away. Somewhere public and easy for us both to get to but with enough space for privacy."

"Grant Park," she said.

"Where the zoo is? I haven't been there yet."

"Yes, and the Oakland Cemetery is close by. The park has over a hundred acres with plenty of places to meet, and it gets busy when the weather is nice—there are plenty of chances for anonymity. It's also accessible from downtown." She added, almost wistfully, "It's quite beautiful in the summer."

He thought it over. He could leave his car somewhere, catch several Ubers quickly in a row, meet her to deliver the package, and make his way back to his car. "That will work. Where do you want to meet inside the park?"

"I think one of the pavilions will do." She described

the area while he made a mental note.

He told her, "I'll text you when to meet me. Do something to pin up your hair or pull it back. The photo they used on the news tonight was with your hair down. I bought you a baseball cap. It's in your go-bag."

She had looked beautiful in the photo as she laughed at someone off camera, but she looked beautiful in all the photos he had taken. He didn't think she could take a bad shot.

He should delete them from his phone, but he hadn't. And he knew he wouldn't.

"Thank you." The expression in her voice turned complex. "It feels like I've been treading water for so long, but I'm really leaving tomorrow."

"Yes, you really are leaving," he replied quietly. "I've got to go. Talk to you tomorrow."

She hesitated, but then all she said was, "Good night. And thank you again for everything."

"You're welcome, Molly."

Before she could say anything else, he disconnected.

She had quickly exploded into such a large presence in his life. He needed her gone to keep his head in a dangerous game. More than that, he *wanted* her gone, for her sake. But in privacy, he was forced to admit she would leave a big hole behind when she went.

He stood for some time looking out at the vibrant city lights and drinking. Feeling a host of unwelcome things… regret, frustration, loss… but feeling none of the elation he would have six months ago at reaching another milestone on the way to his ultimate goal.

When he finished his scotch, he went to email news of the latest development to his coven.

Chapter Fourteen

SHE WAS LEAVING.

Leaving. It repeated in her mind like the rhythm of train wheels turning.

If she got safely away, it would be thanks to the man who had carefully crafted an identity over forty years, all so that he could patiently enact revenge for an outrage that had happened before her parents had been born. Perhaps before her grandparents.

He had saved her life more than once. He had climaxed inside her, and she might never know his real name.

She was leaving a place where she had lived all her adult life, leaving her only surviving family, her acquaintances, friends. Her favorite restaurants and bookstores. Her body still ached in areas from Austin's attack, and she'd hardly had a chance to process the news of his death. She certainly hadn't had any chance to process Nina's. She needed to buy a pregnancy test kit, and unknown forces of malign intent wished her harm.

But Josiah dominated every other consideration. She was eager to drive far away from everything else, except him. Thinking about leaving him behind caused her to… ache.

Leave it to her to get inappropriately attached to a man who had never asked for it. Who had, in fact, warned her to do the exact opposite.

She still tired too easily and couldn't wrap her brain around everything. Hopefully she would survive long enough to process it all. Closing her eyes, she slept.

The large old Victorian house settled around her like a well-worn cloak. She walked through it, soaking in the peace and the airy quiet. She badly needed some peace and quiet.

This time the woman sat in a square of sunshine, looking out a large picture window. As Molly glanced outside, she noticed a white stone labyrinth in the middle of a beautiful garden.

"There's been some drama, but I'm finally leaving tomorrow," Molly said.

"Are you?" The woman turned to smile. "I'm glad. That means we'll get a little time together."

Why only a little bit of time? She frowned. "How do I find you?"

"The spell is still active, so watch for signs. You'll see them." The woman sighed. "I'm too tired to hold this dream together for long. Good journey to you."

"Wait—what kind of signs?" Even as she asked, the dream faded, and she slipped back into darkness.

She woke just after five. After trying unsuccessfully to get back to sleep, she stripped the sheets off the bed to wash them along with her single outfit. There wasn't anything she could do about needing one of his T-shirts, so she shrugged and picked her favorite, a black one so old the aged cotton felt soft as silk against her skin.

Then she showered and laundered the towels and washcloths, made the bed, cleaned the bathroom, washed the coffee maker, and tucked the rest of the uneaten chocolate bars in her purse, until finally there wasn't anything left to do but read upstairs in one of the armchairs, bathed in the quiet morning light.

Just after lunch, her phone chimed, making her pulse leap.

`Meet me at one thirty sharp.` He added directions for how to get from the safe house back to the city.

`I'll be there.`

`If I don't show by one forty, leave but don't panic. It means something came up. I'll contact you with another meet time.`

God, she hoped that didn't happen. She was wound up enough as it was. `I won't linger.`

She had remained on task and hadn't fretted, but he still texted, `It should be fine, Molly.`

`Understood. Everything will work out. See you soon.`

After time had slowed down excruciatingly for the entire morning, suddenly it sped up. She gathered up her purse and looked around. She wouldn't miss the outdated, empty house, but she had grown sensitive enough to Josiah's magic to recognize his signature in the protection spells in the basement. Those she would miss, perhaps badly.

While the afternoon was sunny, there was a sharpness to the air that made her glad to run the heat as she drove. At 1:29, she pulled into the parking lot beside the pavilion and waited with the engine running while her gaze roamed restlessly over the scene.

The next few minutes trickled by. Her phone remained silent.

Then a tall, powerful man strode into sight along one of the park paths. He wore a dark suit and sunglasses and carried a bag. Josiah had made it.

She turned off the engine, climbed out and walked toward him. He saw her and picked up his pace. After a few steps, she started running.

As she drew close, he reached into the bag and pulled out the baseball cap. It was plain blue with no identifying markers.

He slipped it on her head as he looked around. "Keep your sunglasses on."

"You're such a mother hen."

When he gave her an astonished look over the rim of his dark glasses, she burst out laughing and put her arms around him.

Dropping the bag, he clenched her against his hard length. The ferocity jettisoned her into an emotion so powerful she had to blink back tears.

Pulling back, she said, "You've done so much for

me, I really don't know how to—"

"Shut the fuck up." He kissed her.

They both went up in flames. She wound her fingers through his hair, kissing him back with everything she had. When he finally lifted his head again, they were both shaking.

She stared into his glittering gaze. "Truth is, I wouldn't be so eager to leave if I didn't have to."

"And I wouldn't be so eager to see you go," he muttered. He grasped her by the hips and pushed her away. "That doesn't do either of us any good. This isn't goodbye. I need to get the rest of the relocation money to you."

She pulled his T-shirt back into place with hands that still shook. "What were you thinking?"

He glanced around again, hard face wary. "Meet me in New Orleans weekend after next. We'll transfer funds then."

Her stupid heart, which had been languishing in a gutter, rose up and began a Gene Kelly tap dance. "You sure you can get away?"

That brought his attention back. There was a banked heat in his expression that made her feel weightless, not quite connected to her surroundings. In that moment, they were the only two things that existed in the world. "I can get there safely. Just be sure that you do."

"I'm headed out now. I have a full tank of gas, and I'm not looking back."

He rubbed his thumb along her lower lip. "Drive the

speed limit. Your new license may have a different name, but the police have your photo. If you get in an accident or get stopped, you'll be charged with a felony."

She heaved a sigh. "That's one of the things I love about you. You're such a bundle of sunshine and joy. You must have been a shih tzu in a former life."

An unwilling smile tugged at the corners of his mouth. It vanished a moment later. Pushing back the edges of his suit jacket, he rested his hands on his hips. "Remember, without serious training, your power will remain undisciplined. Don't be surprised when it leaks out in new and unusual ways. Self-discipline and meditation will help to calm it down, but mostly you need a teacher. You need to find someone."

"I'm already working on it," she said steadily.

What flashed across his features? Jealousy? Possessiveness? Whatever it was, she was pretty sure she shouldn't feel quite as good about it as she did.

"You'll never find anyone else who can teach you the things I can," he said. His voice had deepened and grew quieter. Sexy.

It was a good thing there wasn't a bed nearby or she might have collapsed into it. She swallowed hard. Whispered, "You're going to miss the shit out of me."

He didn't have many tells, but he had one big one—that muscle in the hard line of his jaw when it bunched. "Text me tonight when you decide to stop," he growled. "I want to know where you're staying and how you're doing."

She nodded. "You text me when you make it back to the office."

"I will." He muttered something under his breath and swooped in for another fierce kiss. Then he bent to pick up the bag and thrust the strap into her hand. "Go, damn it."

Turning, she strode back to the Subaru. This time she was the one who walked away, but she still felt raw and empty, like she was leaving a vital organ behind. Setting the bag on the passenger seat, she climbed in the driver's side and buckled her seat belt as she looked back at the path.

He still stood there, watching. Somehow she knew he wouldn't leave until she did. Lifting one hand, she started the car, pulled out, and drove away without a backward glance.

This isn't goodbye, he had muttered. *Although it should be.*

The sensation of Josiah's mouth lingered as she drove through the city streets. It only faded when she reached Interstate 20.

She had a week and a half to get to New Orleans, which meant she had time to kill. And she had a teacher to find. Should she check the centers of the Elder Races demesnes? That would take a huge amount of driving since they were scattered all over the US.

She ran through all seven demesnes in her mind. The seat of the Wyrkind demesne was in New York City, the Elven demesne in Charleston, and the Dark Fae's demesne was centered in Chicago.

There was also the Light Fae demesne in Los Angeles. Demonkind, like the Wyr and Nightkind, consisted of several different types of creatures that included goblins and Djinn. Their seat was based in Houston. The Nightkind, including Vampyres, controlled the San Francisco/Bay Area and the Pacific Northwest, while the human witches demesne was based in Louisville.

She knew from her research that witches were considered part of the Elder Races due to their command of magical Power. Heading for that demesne would make the most sense, but the dream woman had told her to follow the signs.

As she approached the entrance ramps, the westering sunlight hit a bank of clouds just right and illuminated a feathery line of fiery light. Well, damn if that didn't look remarkably like an arrow. It pointed straight toward the setting sun.

"Okay," she murmured. "I'll take that as my first sign. West it is."

Josiah texted as promised when he had returned to the office. `All is well here. You?`

She sent him a smiley face.

Don't speed, he had said. That was harder to do than she had at first thought. She set the cruise control and let the Subaru take over, watching the mileage gauge and taking note of each milepost as it passed.

Fifty miles away.

Seventy-five miles away.

A hundred.

When she crossed into Alabama, she thought, I may not know where I'm going, but I do know one thing. I no longer live in Georgia. That thought set wings to her mood.

Originally she had intended to drive only far enough to cross the state line, then look for a motel, but when she crossed over, she changed her mind.

It had cost so much to get to this point, and she had worked so hard. She couldn't quit now. She stopped only once to fill her gas tank and go through a drive-through. When she grew too tired to drive safely, well past dusk, she stopped at a motel.

As she turned off the car, exhaustion settled in. Using one of her prepaid Visa cards and her new driver's license, she checked in. There was only one awkward moment when she needed to sign her name and she had to check her license first. (Felicia Johnston? Really?) But the sleepy desk clerk had turned away to swipe the card, so he didn't notice.

Ten minutes later, she carried the bag Josiah had packed for her into a cool, dark room. After latching the security chain, she dumped the contents onto the bed. Clothes, a toiletries bag, and the manila folder with the rest of her personal documents tumbled out.

She set the manila folder aside to explore later and looked through the clothes. Nothing was expensive, but he had a good eye and had picked things that would look nice on her.

He had also thought of details like a small travel bottle of mouthwash, a stick of organic ChapStick, a woman's deodorant, and a razor. Feeling warmed, she touched the short black nightgown and matching robe. They were tastefully simple with a small edge of lace around the border.

Her phone chimed. She checked the screen.

Josiah: `Check in, damn it.`

`Everything's fine,` she replied. `I just checked into a motel, and I'm going through the bag.`

`You must be tired. You pushed it late.`

`Once I started, I couldn't stop.` She wanted to hear his voice, and her thumb hovered over the Call button.

Before she could make up her mind, he texted, `Get some rest, and check in tomorrow night.`

Of course, it was late for him as well, and he had been pulling double duty ever since she'd called after Austin's attack. Reluctantly, she replied, `Will do. Have a good night.`

`You too.`

Heaviness weighed her down. She was too tired to shower or take the tags off the clothes, so she brushed her teeth and climbed into the strange bed. Despite how badly she needed to rest, she felt naked and exposed without the basement's protection spells. It took her some time before she could fall asleep.

The next day she left shortly after dawn and stopped

only for food and fuel and to make a quick stop at a pharmacy to buy a pregnancy test kit.

The odds were vastly against it. It was ridiculous to think she might be pregnant after missing one pill. Worse than ridiculous to hope for it.

But when she thought of her rage and pain when she'd considered the childless bedrooms in that big, soulless house, she knew she would welcome a pregnancy if she was gifted with one. The timing couldn't be more horrendous. Still, she wanted it with all her heart.

She didn't see any cosmic signs urging her to go in another direction, so she continued to New Orleans and arrived later that morning.

The weather had turned warmer, and there was just something about the scarred, beautiful city that spoke to her. The crooked streets of the French Quarter were steeped in a very old Power that was gracious and deadly. It whispered at the edge of her mind, *You may visit, but leave me alone.*

Respectful of the warning, and more than a little freaked out, Molly did nothing to seek it out. After walking through the French Quarter, she checked into a motel.

That evening she was happy to leave contact with Josiah to a simple text. Apparently he felt the same. After their brief exchange, she read the instructions on the pregnancy kit and realized she needed to wait a few more days before trying to take it.

Nobody knew where she was. There was nothing she needed to do. Nowhere she needed to go. No crisis that she needed to avert. Everything caught up with her. Everything everything everything.

She went to bed. Aside from a brief exchange of texts with Josiah and leaving her motel room when hunger drove her to find food, she slept for three days.

On the morning of the fourth, her brain and soul rebooted. She was hungry, well rested, and her body had rid itself of the last of the residual aches from the attack.

It had been over a week since she and Josiah had made love. Waiting ten days would have been better—or even waiting to see if she missed her period, but she couldn't make herself wait any longer.

She went into the motel bathroom, unboxed the pregnancy test, and reread the instructions.

It was simple enough. She had to pee on a stick and wait for the results.

She took care of business, sat on the floor, set an alarm on the phone, and closed her eyes.

Concentrate on your breathing.

Four-seven-eight. Stay calm.

There's less than a ten percent chance. You know you're not pregnant. It was just the perfectly bad timing and how it all came together…

You're only doing the responsible thing by making sure.

The alarm shrilled in the silent bathroom, making her pulse kick. She held up the stick.

The sight of the + sign hit her like a roundhouse punch. As she stared at it, the world shook around her.

After a while, she flushed the rest of her birth control pills down the toilet, showered and dressed, and headed out. Sure, the result of the test was a shock, but… she felt good about it. Really good.

More than that, she felt eager. Every minute, every mile, every new experience took her further away from the unhappiness of her past, and she wanted all of it. She went exploring, listened to jazz music, ate seafood gumbo.

Then she took a walking tour through the Garden District and bought new clothes that Austin and her mother would have hated and the clever, wealthy residents of their neighborhood would have labeled as regrettably flamboyant, but that she loved.

Tie-dyed dresses, organic cottons, midriff shirts, soft things with color that breathed and flowed with her body. Previously, her chic jewelry had been worth tens of thousands of dollars. Now she bought sterling silver bangles and dangly earrings with moons and stars.

She painted her fingernails and toenails a dark blue, wove small braids into her hair, and for the first time in her life tried eyeliner. After some practice, she managed to create wings that gave the familiar bones of her face an exotic slant.

And when she looked in the mirror, she whispered to the miniscule fetus, "You're beautiful."

The next day, she met a handsome musician who

tried everything he could to get her to sleep with him. While she appreciated his enthusiasm—and let's face it, you've got to love a man who's willing to work hard for what he wants—she laughingly turned him down.

But for the space of one evening, she danced with him and felt the heat of her healthy body moving gracefully on a sultry night. They argued about politics and religion while she watched the too-long blond hair flop on his forehead and appreciated his sinewy beauty without feeling the slightest desire to have him.

After staying up all night and eating beignets together before saying goodbye, she took a walk to the Saint Louis Cathedral in Jackson Square and thought to herself, This is what happiness feels like.

I'm happy.

She'd never said those words before with such simple purity. Always before, she had felt cramped, incomplete, and anxious, like her happiness existed on the edge of a precipice and she could lose it any moment.

Now, for the first time, she expanded. As she did, she felt her Power grow. It lay curled on itself like a dreaming beast, as if it allowed her this respite to heal and find her footing before it woke to demand the rest of her life.

But she had to meet with Josiah first.

What was she going to say to him? What if the test had come back with false results? Was that possible? Most pregnancy kits came with two applications, so she tested herself again. This time, as she stared at the +

sign, she *knew* it was accurate. She could feel the knowledge rising up from her Power.

I'm not going to tell him, she thought with complete and passionate certainty as she threw the test stick away. He didn't ask for this either—and he certainly wouldn't welcome the news if I shared it.

Forty-five minutes later, she did a one-eighty with as much certainty and passion as the first decision. He deserved to know the truth whether he welcomed it or not. He had the right to know he was about to become a father again.

Five hours later, she knew she couldn't tell him. He lived a hard, dangerous life, and he made hard, dangerous decisions. Giving him the news could split his attention and lead him to make a fatal mistake.

Flip: It wasn't her place to look out for him. He wouldn't welcome that, and she didn't want to do it. She would tell him. She was sure she would.

By the time Friday came and he texted her with his plans, her reawakened body remembered how much she wanted him, and her mind blew every which way like a weather vane in the middle of a hurricane.

She had no idea what she was going to do. The only thing she knew for certain was that Josiah would be flying in to NOLA that evening.

And over the weekend she was either going to serve him up a hefty dose of the truth or feed him a terrible lie.

✧ ✧ ✧

JOSIAH HAD NO fucking business flying to NOLA.

He could overnight a cashier's check to wherever she was staying—or several cashier's checks, as it were, each one under ten thousand dollars to avoid triggering whatever bank she used into sending a report to the IRS.

Worse, he had no intention of telling his coven. He and Richard butted heads too much already, and he didn't want to deal with any of the objections he knew they would hammer him with.

So he told them he needed to take a few days off after the drama and energy expenditure of the past few weeks. They accepted that readily enough. They could all use a weekend for some R & R.

Then Josiah Mason booked a flight to the Bahamas for the long holiday weekend. Close to the same flight times and under another name, he booked a weekend trip to NOLA.

As he laid his plans with damnable intention, the workweek smoldered to an end. Anson continued conducting intensive research on anyone that looked likely to be involved with their quarry. Richard joined them in Atlanta to see if he could catch anyone tailing Josiah. So far, he'd come up with nothing.

The police discovered Rodriguez had filed Molly's divorce before she died. After returning to Sherman & Associates with the appropriate warrant, they confiscated everything from Austin's office.

The Friday morning after Molly left, Frank Williams, the lead detective, briefed Josiah on the latest on the investigation. In the confiscated files, they found papers on how to set fires using the same techniques that had been used on Rodriguez's house and office. Meanwhile, Molly's face and name were in the news almost nightly, but the exposure drew no credible leads on her current whereabouts.

"It appears more and more likely that Sullivan might have done something to his wife," Frank told him in a face-to-face. "Unless or until we uncover any new evidence that says otherwise, the whole crime looks like a revenge killing gone wrong."

Josiah tapped his lower lip as he listened. Someone had gift wrapped what had happened and put a bow on it. "Papers on how to commit arson in his office? Pretty damn obvious, don't you think?"

"I'm just reporting on what we found. Not offering a commentary." The detective gave him a cynical smile.

It did not suit Josiah to have this go quietly into a cold-case file. "That theory doesn't explain what happened to Sullivan's BMW. Why would he sign the divorce papers only to kill Rodriguez and bomb her office later?"

"He let his wife take him to the cleaners." Frank shrugged. "So he might have changed his mind?"

"You're right, there's motive," Josiah murmured, watching him closely. "The settlement was for a lot of money."

The other man scratched his chin. "But yeah, you've got me on the car. We don't have a reason for it, and according to the timeline, his car blew first. Could he really have been such a fuckup that he accidentally blew up his own car, then got himself killed later that night? I also don't like that we haven't found the wife, so we've got to keep digging."

"Do you see her as a suspect?"

"At this point, there's nothing to indicate that," Frank said. "She might be up for torching his car—because by all accounts he was a cheating asshole—but she already had him. And she had absolutely no motive for killing her lawyer. She met her real estate agent at the house that Saturday night, and she hasn't been seen since. She was staying at an Airbnb and she just vanished. The owner contacted us when she saw the news. Molly Sullivan's possessions were still in the apartment—her personal papers, clothes, a laptop, and her new car was parked outside with a box full of mementos. And at the house, the trash cans had been knocked around and there was a pile of bedding left outside. When you put it together, it looks like she was taken against her will."

Josiah murmured, "The trash cans could have been raccoons, but the rest of it doesn't look promising." And the police's continued efforts to find Molly was the price they had to pay for scrutiny on the case. "Thanks for the update."

"You're welcome." The detective stood. "I'll email you if there are any further developments."

"You do that. When you've got a moment, I also

want a list of the client files Sullivan had in his office."
Not that he expected to find anything in them. The same person who had planted the arson instructions would have had plenty of time to pull compromising files before the police searched them. But still, they might have let something useful slip through the cracks.

"Sure thing," Frank said.

Josiah shook the other man's hand and walked him out of his office.

That afternoon he met Russell Sherman for a steak lunch at one of the best restaurants in the city. For several minutes they engaged in neutral conversation while the waiter took their orders and brought them drinks.

Once they were alone again, Russell took a hefty swallow of his bourbon. "Now I know why you couldn't comment earlier when I called."

Josiah nodded. "Had to wait until the news broke or the police told you."

"The whole office is in shock over the fact that Austin killed his wife's attorney." Russell shook his head. He had a blunt, powerful head like a bullet, situated on a thick neck.

Josiah's truthsense pinged. *Lie.*

His whole fucking eighty-hour workweek had been worth this single moment. Russell did, in fact, know the truth of what had happened that night, and he was working hard to cover it up.

"It must be a lot to take in," Josiah said.

"None of us saw it coming. Is Molly still missing?"

Their steaks arrived. Russell dug in, carving up his meat with the polished dexterity of a butcher.

"The police don't know her whereabouts," Josiah replied with complete truth.

"I hope they find her soon." *Truth.* Russell looked at him. "This is a bad business, Josiah."

"That it is, Russell." Josiah held the other man's steely gaze with a cold, steady smile. "And it's likely to get a lot worse."

Chapter Fifteen

THE NEXT WEEK shot by, filled to the brim with investigations on all fronts.

But whenever he thought of the weekend ahead, time slowed to a crawl. Finally he headed to the airport straight from the office.

He went through airport security as Josiah Mason, but then he boarded a different flight under a separate identity. All he took was a weekend carry-on. As the plane took off, he felt like an arrow shooting through the air.

When he landed, he got a text from Molly with the address of where she was staying. `Do you want to come here or meet somewhere?`

`Stay put`, he replied. `I'll come to you. We've landed. See you soon.`

`Okay. Have you eaten supper?`

He paused, breathing quietly. There she was, thinking of him again. It was like she had reached out across the distance to touch his cheek. `No.`

`Do you like pasta?`

`I like everything`, he told her truthfully. He'd

gone through too many tough times to be picky about food.

`I'll put something together.`

The plane taxied to the gate and he disembarked, threading through the holiday-weekend crowd at the airport while automatically checking his surroundings. It was unlikely that anybody was monitoring his weekend plans and even more unlikely that he'd been followed.

And yet.

And yet he took three taxis in quick succession to random, busy places in the city before he finally allowed himself to go to the address Molly had given him. In his last taxi, he checked the traffic as the city lights flashed past his window.

The taxi pulled up in front of a tiny Creole-style cottage in a quiet neighborhood. It was painted bright colors, the small yard draped in foliage. Through the lush greenery, he could see Molly's slender form through open french windows as she moved around inside.

He felt like he was on fire as he strode through the open picket gate and up the path.

She might not welcome what he brought. Hold back, he said to himself. Hold on.

He knocked on the door, and a moment later she opened it. She was… He lost his breath. She was vibrant. Wearing new, colorful clothes, wearing makeup, bangles, and radiating health and feminine Power. The scent of something delicious hung in the air. Behind her, he saw a bistro-style table set for dinner.

She gave him a small smile. "Did you miss the shit out of me?"

He dropped his bag and reached for her with both hands. Cupping her face, he kissed her fiercely. Making a muffled noise, she kissed him back just as fiercely.

Insanity set in. He pushed her back against the wall and plunged as deep as he could into her mouth while she wound her arms around his neck and arched against him. He couldn't get enough of her mouth, her body. He ran greedy hands down her curved form. Was the door shut?

He checked. It wasn't, and he kicked it.

"The pasta's going to boil over," she gasped.

"I don't care," he growled. Wait. Maybe he should.

Pulling away, she spun around a corner. He followed her into a miniscule kitchen, watched her turn off the small, apartment-sized stove, and then snatched her close again.

They had made love once. Once. And there were so many things he needed to do to her. Crouching, he ran his hands up her fabulous legs, underneath the gauzy skirt. Her breathing sawed unsteadily in the peaceful place. She staggered backward to lean against the cabinet while she ran her fingers through his hair.

She wore a pair of the panties he had bought for her, simple and white. He knotted both fists in the material and yanked it down.

"Say no if you need to," he said. "Say it now."

"God, no!" she exclaimed. Then, when he reared

back his head, her face flooded with sensual laughter. "I meant I'm saying no to no… Damn it, *yes*."

That was all he needed. The waistband of her skirt was elastic. He yanked that down too. Her body was beautifully made everywhere, the bone structure graceful and flowing. He rubbed his face in the tuft of tawny hair at the juncture between her thighs, inhaling her unique, feminine scent before exploring her with gentle, greedy fingers.

The breath left her hard, and the silken wetness of arousal coated his fingers. Wordlessly, he urged her to drape a leg across one of his shoulders. When she complied, it opened her up to him, and it was everything he had wanted over the past ten days, everything he had thought about.

She cried out when he put his mouth on her and licked along the tender, soft petals of her intimate flesh with careful urgency. Locating her clitoris, he suckled, teased, and stroked while inserting a finger into her tight sheath. He was ravenous for every inch of her, for every response.

"Josiah!"

<Reason number one why you should get over your phobia about telepathy,> he said in her head. <I can do this to you while I also tell you how delicious you taste. You're gorgeous, unbelievably sexy, and you feel like silk. I can't wait to get inside you.>

"Then do it," she growled, yanking at his hair. "Get up here!"

<Not until you come,> he purred.

She swore, and he laughed and licked her harder until she hung over him and the slender muscles of her inner thighs trembled.

"It's too intense," she moaned. "I can't take it."

<You'll take it, *milaya,*> he told her. <I'm not going anywhere. I can keep this up all night. Same rhythm, same pressure. All night long. Open up, lean into it. This—and this—and this—until you come.>

As he talked, he inserted another finger, stretching her gently and then fucking her with his hand to the same rhythm of his words.

"I can't do it," she whispered unsteadily. "I-I've got to lie down."

As she spoke, she listed to one side, then caught herself with a jerk.

Bed. What an excellent idea. He stood and swept her into his arms. "Where?"

She pointed to an open doorway. As he strode into a shadowed, simple bedroom with a double bed and two nightstands, a waft of fresh air blew in from the open french windows in the living room.

A lifetime of habit proved impossible to shake. Kneeling on the mattress, he eased her down onto it. "I'll be right back."

She nodded. The dark sparkle of her gaze followed him as he walked out. In the living room, he turned on a wall air conditioner and moved to secure the windows and pull the blinds into place. Then, unable to leave it at that, he cast quick spells over the windows and the door, enough to sound an alert if they were disturbed.

When he strode back into the bedroom, he found her sitting up in bed, arms wrapped around her knees. After a slight pause, he yanked off his tie, stripped off his suit jacket, and sat beside her.

"I've missed your protection spells."

He absorbed that. "Not the basement though, eh?"

"No, not the basement." She rested her cheek on one knee, her face angled toward him.

In the space of time it had taken him to secure the cottage, something critical had changed. He thought to ask what was wrong, but it seemed too heavy-handed in the delicate atmosphere. Instead, he stroked her back, waiting.

"I needed to see you," he said in a quiet voice. "I didn't welcome it, but I needed it."

"Same here," she whispered.

She hadn't said no, or that she had changed her mind, so he stripped off his shirt, removed his socks and shoes, and stretched out on the bed. It felt as if he was putting down something he had been carrying for a very long time, and he let out a long sigh.

Playing the tips of his fingers down her spine, he said, "Or, if you want me to, I can go."

She shook her head, and a lock of her hair fell over her eyes. "No, I want you to stay. I have something I need to tell you, but I don't want to talk about it."

He raised his head off the pillow to squint at her.

"That sounds tricky."

She bit her lip. "I should have kept my mouth shut. But I just want a weekend. Just one weekend with you, without drama or stress. Can we have that? Can we agree to talk before you go home on Monday?"

He thought about it. His body felt as unruly as a plunging bronco. He ached to find release with her, but…

She wouldn't need to tell him something so badly if it wasn't critically important.

And she wouldn't want to put off having the conversation if she didn't dread what might come next.

"No," he said.

✧ ✧ ✧

HIS VOICE WAS soft but implacable.

She buried her face in her knees, longing to return to the simple, urgent passion they had shared just moments ago. She had meant to wait, to steal the time with him and let her weather vane spin in the wind all weekend. And then she would go whichever way it pointed before he left.

But apparently she wasn't a secret baby kind of girl.

He pulled the curtain of hair back from her face. Even more softly, he asked, "Is what you have to say so terrible?"

"That depends on you."

She drew away from his touch, crawled off the bed, and went back to the kitchen to pull her skirt back on.

Then she picked up her panties. Oh, why the hell bother? She dropped them on a chair.

He had followed her silently, moving like a panther. When she turned back, she confronted the sight of him bare-chested, shirtless, and shoeless. The beauty of his body made her mouth go dry. She swallowed hard.

Crossing his arms, he leaned against the doorway of the bedroom. "I can wait all night if I have to, *milaya*."

Her hands shook. This was so much harder than she had imagined—and she had a vivid imagination. "Do you remember what happened after Austin attacked me?"

His amber gaze narrowed. "Of course I do. Every damn minute of it."

"Sunday was hard. Rough morning. Rough day." She couldn't watch his expression and let her gaze wander elsewhere.

His big body was out of focus. She tracked him out of her side vision as he came across the room and put his hands on her shoulders. He said quietly, "I went through it with you. Nobody knows that more than I do."

That was enough of an opening to allow her to give him a direct look. "I didn't take my pill that morning."

His eyes dilated, a fast, involuntary reaction. "And the condom broke the next day."

She nodded.

"Milaya." His expression, his eyes, his Power blazed.

Before something unbearable happened, she clapped both hands over his mouth. "Listen to me. Just listen.

I've got the advantage here—I've had a little while to absorb the news." Her eyes flooded with moisture. "And I want this, maybe more than anything I've ever wanted in my life. *And I'm okay with it.* And I wish… Oh, there's no point in talking about what I wish. But I'm going to do everything in my power to keep danger away from this little one. She—or he—is going to be brought up with all the love and happiness and safety and security I can provide. So I think it's best if you and I don't see each other again after this weekend, because we both know what your life is about."

He pulled her hands away from his mouth and bit out, "You can't do this on your own!"

"Watch me." It was harder than ever to meet the dark fire burning so furiously in him, but she did. "I'm on my way to find a teacher. I'm going to build a good life, and I'm going to be so damn happy it will make malcontents nauseated to look at me. I'm *excited* about my future. And… and you would be so welcome to be a part of this baby's life if you ever chose a different path than the one you're on right now. But the way you live—you're consumed with revenge. I don't know, maybe that's why you want power and why you want to become Georgia's next governor. This mysterious, terrible person who hurt you so badly all those years ago has eaten you up inside, and I'm not judging, Josiah. I'm really not. You get to be whoever you need to be. But you can't live that life you've chosen and bring it here to me. Not after this weekend."

"Goddamn it," he bit out. "Don't you think I fucking realize that?"

"Okay then," she whispered. Her gut hurt, and she realized she had clenched everything up in anticipation of an emotional blow, so she tried to relax her muscles and take a breath.

He strode into the bedroom. When he came back out, he had pulled on his shirt and shoes, and he carried his jacket in one clenched fist. His expression was severe, mouth clamped tight.

On his way to the door, he snatched up his carry-on. He said tersely over his shoulder, "I need some air."

She pressed the fingers of one hand against her mouth as she watched him go. That had gone every bit as badly as she'd been afraid it would.

But then, just before he stepped out, he paused, head turned to one side as if he could hear her silent anguish. Hell, he probably could. Her energy was crazy, all over the place.

In a more measured tone, he told her, "I'll see you in the morning?"

"Sure, if you can," she said jerkily. "I would really like that."

He nodded. Then he stalked out.

Silence settled in the little cottage. The hurricane had passed, leaving devastation in its wake.

Four-seven-eight.

Four-seven-eight.

At last her internal earthquake subsided. When she

felt calmer, she went to see what could be done with the half-prepared supper. The pasta had congealed, so she drained off the water and threw the clump in the trash. And the sauce looked tired and brown around the edges.

"I know how you feel," she said to it. She threw that out too. There wasn't a dishwasher in the rental, so she washed everything up by hand. She had bought Josiah a bottle of wine, and she set it aside on the counter.

When the little place was sparkling clean, she went to take a shower, washed off her makeup, and put on the black nightie. After the buildup and anticipation and then the raw intensity, the world felt flat and colorless.

It was too early to go to bed, and she was too tired to go out. Plus she should eat something.

She had made a beautiful green salad topped with delicately fried squash blossoms. Dumping some into a bowl, she went into the living room to slouch on the couch and channel surf while she ate pieces of the salad with her fingers like popcorn.

A quiet knock sounded at the door. Her heart thumped. Setting the bowl and TV remote aside, she went to look out the closed french windows.

Josiah stood on the doorstep, his white dress shirt stark against the yellow outside light. He had rolled the sleeves up. His bag sat at his feet with his suit jacket and tie draped across it. He turned and saw her looking at him. Said nothing. Just waited, watching her.

She went to open the door. His brooding gaze raked down her figure clad in the short black nightie and robe.

"I shouldn't have walked out."

"Don't be stupid." She stepped out of the way. "Given the circumstances, I think you were remarkably restrained. But I hope you're not back to fight, because I'm too tired to oblige tonight."

"I'm not back to fight." He met her gaze with a level look, then strode inside.

She watched him take in the bowl of salad on the couch, the muted television screen, and remote. "There's more salad in the fridge. And the wine on the counter is for you. And there's cheese and bread, and some beignets from Café Du Monde in the pastry box. Help yourself to whatever."

"Thank you." He looked down at her bare toes with their dark blue-painted nails. She wore a little sterling silver ring on the middle toe of her right foot. "Mind if I take a shower?"

"Knock yourself out." The wall air-conditioning unit was overpowering the little space, but she didn't want to turn it off and let the muggy warmth back in, so she went into the bedroom to grab a blanket and curl back up on the couch.

Nature channel. Reality TV show. A sitcom. The news. She chewed salad and flipped through channels, not really paying attention. Most of her focus was on what Josiah was doing. The shower ran for a while, then switched off. Shortly after, he came out wearing black shorts that showed off the sinewy strength of his muscled legs and a T-shirt that strained across his wide chest and biceps.

Damn, was there anything about him that *wasn't* sexy? What he had done to her with that firm, stern-looking mouth… She closed her eyes as her body pulsed.

She would be so lost over him if he had chosen a different life than the one he was living—*any* kind of different life—so, in a way, she should probably be grateful that he kept everything so crystal clear for her.

After some silence, he asked, "Is that all you're eating?"

She lifted one hand in an indifferent shrug.

He approached to bend over and stick his face between hers and the TV screen. Their gazes collided. His soft, even voice was at odds with the volcanic force in his eyes. "Would you like a grilled cheese sandwich if I made one for you?"

Silently, she nodded. She watched as he went into the kitchen and found everything he needed. He knew his way around a kitchen, his movements purposeful and economical. His expression gave away nothing of what he was thinking.

When he returned, he carried a plate piled with grilled cheese sandwiches, another bowl of salad, and a glass of wine. She scooted over to make room, and then they sat and watched the news while they ate.

Once she took her first bite of sandwich, her appetite roared in and she ravenously ate the rest. He took away the plates and bowls, poured himself more wine, and when he came back to the couch, he put an arm around her and propped his feet up on the coffee table.

She held very still, but the warmth of his body was too much to resist. Melting against his hard length, she let her head rest tentatively on his shoulder. He cupped the side of her head and drank wine.

Was this all right? The experience flowed into places she wasn't sure she wanted it to go. It felt too warm, too good. It felt too right for her to give in to it entirely. She turned her cheek into his shirt and closed her eyes. "Why did you come back?"

"Because I want this weekend with you more than I want to react or fight." His chest moved in a sigh. He drank more wine and stroked her hair. "Don't think about it too hard, okay?"

She nodded. Sometime later, she said telepathically, <I still don't know your real name.>

Just when she thought he wasn't going to answer, he said, <Alexei.>

Ah. That suited him. She smoothed the T-shirt over his chest. <I'm glad you came back.>

He kissed her forehead. <I am too, *milaya.*>

Toothy leviathans swam underneath the calm, peaceful surface they created, but if he could restrain himself from poking them, she could too. Gradually the tension eased out of her body and she dozed. She only woke when he turned off the television and picked her up to carry her into the bedroom.

"I have two perfectly sound legs and feet that work quite well together," she remarked in a sleep-blurred voice.

"Yes, you do, but I've discovered I like carrying you around. Don't rob me of that enjoyment."

She clearly heard what he had left unspoken. *Don't rob me of that enjoyment while I can have it.*

When he eased her onto the bed, she laid a hand to his cheek and kissed him. He made a sound at the back of his throat, settled the weight of his body on hers, and kissed her with so much passion and hunger it was almost enough to reshape their futures.

Almost enough to reshape everything.

Heat and light exploded between them. It was sex mingled with a gush of Power. His, hers. He swore, a guttural, foreign-sounding word, gripped her hips with both hands, and thrust her legs apart with his.

A fine sweat broke out over her skin. She felt fevered. In that moment she needed him more than she needed anything else. More than air, than light. Than food. How excruciating, dramatic. It was unsustainable. They would burn themselves out on each other.

But they hadn't burned out yet. She raised herself up on her elbows to lick and nip at his flat male nipples while he fingered her, preparing her for his entrance. He grabbed her by the hair and pulled her head back to plunge down for a searing kiss, his hardened lips slanting over hers while he invaded her with his tongue.

His roaring, sensual drive shook her. She had originally thought he was so cold, so calculating. How could she have been so mistaken about him?

When he positioned his cock at her entrance and pushed in, she rose to meet him, and the empty ache at her core turned to a sharp spike of pleasure. As he took her, she took him. He conquered her senses, and she gave over control, allowing herself to go boneless and submissive as he spun her around, wrapped an arm around her throat, and fucked her from behind.

She had never felt this way before, so out of her mind with need. The rhythm he built made her crazy, crazy—she had to do something to get at him the way he was getting at her. She reached back for any part of him she could touch, raking her nails along his shoulders, sinking her teeth in feral response into the bunched muscle of his forearm. He felt massive inside her, hardened everywhere, his body clenched on hers in an unbreakable hold.

Then he reached down to touch her between her legs, and she exploded with such force she saw white stars against her closed eyelids. She cried out sharply, bucking underneath him, while he held suspended over her, in her, rubbing, rubbing… Jesus, she thought she would never stop climaxing…

Even as the waves still rippled through her body, he stiffened and swore again, his mouth pressed to the soft skin at the nape of her neck. She felt his thick, hard length pulse inside, and oh my God, she had never climaxed *with anyone* before. She grabbed his hand and pressed his fingers against her.

He understood immediately and rubbed her harder

as his raw breathing sawed in her ear. The second wave hit, clear and piercing. She twisted back against him, straining for that last tantalizing peak, and he buried his face in her hair as he spilled the last of his own pleasure.

Afterward came the mental and physical collapse. She couldn't talk even if she wanted to. Apparently he felt the same. As he pulled her back around to take her in his arms, the heavy muscles of his biceps trembled. She gave in to simple, animal need and burrowed against his larger, heavier frame, her head resting on his shoulder, one leg hiked up to drape over his hips. He tangled his fingers in her hair, and she plunged asleep.

Only to wake again sometime later as he pushed her onto her back and entered her. She made a sound, a cross between surprise and incoherent delight, and wrapped arms and legs around him, cradling him with her whole body while he fucked her.

He brought her to climax that time too, not quite as sharp and high as the first ones, but a fuller, deeper sensation that rewrote the pathways of her circuitry as she locked everything on him and realized just how much he could give her. How deeper, higher, further they could go.

Nobody had *ever*—her ex-husband had *never*... She held such distaste for him she couldn't tolerate his name in her mind in that moment and let the thought spin away.

The weekend blazed like tissue paper, disappearing in a bright flash of sex, heat, and need. They slept and made love in the shower, on the couch, on the living room floor.

Those times when they needed food, they moved around each other warily, like animals that had been stripped of their protective layers. They avoided talking about anything controversial or difficult—the future, the past—and concentrated on small, domestic things.

Everything was raw and heightened. When she drained the cooling water off hard-boiled eggs she had cooked and forgotten, he trailed the tips of his fingers along the back of her neck. She dropped the pan into the sink, shaking. That was all that was needed to set him off again.

He lifted her so she sat perched on the sink. She hooked her ankles eagerly around the back of his thick, muscular thighs, taking his cock in both greedy hands, fingering the broad head and stroking along the rigid length until he hissed between his teeth and entered her again in a slow, liquid slide.

By that time she was so sore and sensitized that when her swollen little bud came against the root of his erection, she made a muffled sound and twisted in agonized pleasure. This time he rocked against her gently and took his own pleasure a few moments later in a quiet, liquid gush.

Don't come, she said to Monday.

But time was the most measured, inexorable force in the universe, and Monday dawned anyway. Lying sleepless beside *Alexei* she witnessed the day's arrival alone.

Even at rest, his angular face was hard, but this was the most relaxed she had ever seen him. He had laced his fingers through hers before drifting off, and they still held hands.

I don't want you to go, she thought as she watched his sleeping profile. But this was never something we meant to sustain. And you can't stay.

She had known that all along. *She* had been the one to set the ground rules.

But—oh, what a stupid thing to do—she had gone and fallen in love with him anyway.

✧ ✧ ✧

WHEN THE TIME came, he packed his belongings in the carry-on bag. It took less than ten minutes. The pure gold of a hot afternoon shone in the open french windows while Molly sat outside at a patio table, drinking iced herbal tea.

Denial hadn't worked, so he had gorged on her. He should have worked her out of his system by now. Watching her profile from the shadows of the cottage interior, he thought of everything she had taught him.

She was diametrically opposed to his dutiful, traitorous wife from that long-ago past life.

Molly's eager excitement at her pregnancy.

The way she reached for him, both giving and receiving physical affection and sexual pleasure. His wife had been the kind to turn her face away even as she presented her cheek for his kiss.

Molly had destroyed his sovereignty of solitude. Laid waste to his cold purpose.

He had loved his sons, and they and their mother had betrayed him, but he had accepted a very long time ago that a portion of the blame must lay on him. If only he had been a better father. If he had just taken a closer involvement in their raising. If he had only known then what he knew now.

But that innocent spark of life that nestled in Molly's body… It would grow up with her as a role model and mother. It would know her deep, abiding sense of loyalty, decency, and her affection, and he wanted to claim it more badly than he had wanted almost anything else in a very long time.

The only thing he wanted more was Molly herself.

He called for a cab. Setting his carry-on by the open windows, he withdrew an envelope and walked out onto the patio. Turning, she smiled at him.

As he looked at the small, telltale marks he had made on her skin with his teeth and hands, his body flooded with desire again. Maybe he could call in sick and steal another day. But her sunglasses couldn't hide her exhaustion, and now, more than ever, he needed to avoid deviating from normal behavior.

He handed her the envelope. "There's five checks in here, all under ten thousand. Movement of anything over ten grand gets an automatic report sent to the IRS, so be sure to deposit them one at a time."

"Thank you so much," she said as she took it. "I'll pay you back as soon as I can."

"It's not a loan anymore, Molly." When objection flashed across her features, he went down on his haunches in front of her and said harshly, "I will support the mother of my child, and I don't want to hear any arguments about it."

Her expression closed. "Money will be one more thing that ties us together."

He cupped her hands in his. "You've trusted me this far. Trust me a little further. I will keep you both safe." Safe from me and the life I lead. Out of the corner of his eye, he saw a yellow taxi approach. Huskily, he told her, "This isn't goodbye."

Her tight mouth softened. "Oh Josiah, it is." She smoothed the hair back off his forehead, her fingers gentle against his skin. "I don't want to see you again."

Her lie shrieked at him. He pressed her hands to his mouth. "You do."

She gripped his fingers so tight it cut off the circulation. "Yes, I do. But as long as you're living the life you live, *I won't.* You and I are not a couple. We had an affair—we haven't even dated. We're not together, and I'm not waiting for you. This baby and I deserve someone who will always put us first."

The ferocity in that rocked him back on his heels.

Just as fiercely, he growled, "*This isn't goodbye.* But there are several other people involved, along with those who have already been killed, and remember, careful investigations take time. I have to finish what I started for everybody's sake—including this new young life you carry—and then I will find you."

"Am I supposed to believe you'll walk away from your plans for building power, just like that? Well, I don't. You've had a long damn time to become who and what you are, and people don't change on a dime even if they might want to." She yanked her hands out of his. "Your taxi is here. Just go, will you?"

Fucking hell. He lunged forward and kissed her with all the wild hunger raging inside. It rocked her back in her chair. When he pulled back, he said through gritted teeth, "See a doctor, *milaya.* Let me know how you're doing."

Looking devastated, she nodded and whispered telepathically, <Goodbye, Alexei.>

If she had stabbed him in the heart, she couldn't have dealt a more effective wound. Blindly raging, he grabbed his carry-on and stalked away.

This baby and I deserve someone who will always put us first.

They did. Goddamn it, they did.

And he could not walk away from his coven, not after the decades they had put into their mission. He could not simply walk away from what he had started.

As he waited to board his flight, he texted his coven. `We have got to do whatever it takes to finish this.`

Chapter Sixteen

THE NEXT DAY, Molly left New Orleans. She still had another night booked in the vacation rental, but Josiah… *Alexei*… had put his stamp on everything. He was everywhere she looked. She couldn't rest on the bed without his reclining body to curl against.

And her Power finally unfurled, fueling a sense of restlessness. It was time to start the search again for her teacher. When she started to drive, another sign leaped out, this one in the shape of a key pointing west.

Over the next three days as she drove toward Los Angeles, she began to sense when the moon rose. It was waxing toward the full moon. Each evening the glowing, ivory orb grew larger, like a vast night-skinned goddess slowly opening one eye to contemplate the world spread below.

When the full moon came, she felt so sensitized to the pale light pouring like cream over the shadowed landscape she couldn't sleep. Leaving her motel room, she walked outside while Power leaped and coursed underneath her skin, reaching for the moon. The next morning, disturbed and exhausted, she left for another hypnotically long drive.

She almost picked up the phone to call Josiah but managed to stop before she followed through with it. They had left things too raw at the end, but even so, he had spoken from a place of realistic, severe self-discipline.

If there was the possibility that she might be in danger, so was the baby, and like he said, careful investigations take time. When there were any relevant updates, he would get in touch. Besides, hearing nothing from him meant there was nothing to say.

That evening her phone lit up with a text. All thoughts of self-restraint went out the window as she lunged for it.

`People may not change on a dime, but they do change when they are ready.`

She sat on the bed, elbows on her knees as she stared at the phone she held in a death grip. Don't answer. You're not behaving rationally.

Her phone lit up again. `Molly.`

This time she could feel him waiting. He might be in Atlanta while she was in SoCal, but he felt close enough to touch. Carefully, she typed out a message and read through it. `I meant what I said. If you ever chose a different path than the one you're on right now, you would be so welcome to be a part of this baby's life.`

So welcome to be a part of mine. She didn't add that.

She read through the text again. Did it sound sane

enough? Like she was a lot more balanced than she really was? Oh, for Christ's sake, stop second-guessing yourself.

She hit Send.

She and he were linked by an invisible wire. It drew taut, vibrating tension.

`I meant what I said too. This isn't goodbye. Be patient.`

Be patient for what? So much dangled unresolved between them.

All he had ever said was that he would come find her. And that he wanted to support the mother of his child. He had enough decency that he didn't want to be a deadbeat dad—and she had opened that door when she had told him about the pregnancy.

He didn't know she had fallen in love with him, and she didn't need to go flapping her damn mouth about it.

She typed out another text, read through it. Sent it. `I saw a doctor today in a clinic in LA. I told her I was on vacation and just discovered I was pregnant. She took a blood test and will call me, but she said that's most likely a formality since pregnancy kits are very accurate these days. Everything looks good. I got prenatal vitamins.`

`That is really good news. Thank you for telling me.` She could almost hear the words spoken in that quiet, husky way he had when his voice gentled. `And you're safely in for the night?`

Should that be any of his business? She was wearing herself out by overthinking everything. Yes.

Excellent. Get a good rest. Where are you headed in the morning?

There was the boundary she was looking for. She knew it as soon as she saw it. She might trust him to do everything he could to keep her and the baby safe, but as he had pointed out once already, you couldn't divulge what you didn't know.

I'm going to enjoy the coast. Good night, Josiah.

Alexei.

Her phone was dark and blank for a long moment. He was doing the same thing she was, thinking things through, deciding whether or not things were okay. This was a strange new reality for both of them.

Good night, Molly.

✧ ✧ ✧

OVER THE NEXT several days, they fell back into their habit of texting at the end of the day. At first she was afraid he might want to talk, and she wasn't ready to go that far. But he didn't suggest it. Gradually she grew to look forward to their nightly exchanges.

He didn't share details about his job, and she didn't ask.

She didn't share details about where she was going. And he didn't ask again.

The clinic called with the results of the blood test,

but by that point it was just a formality. She was, indeed, pregnant.

Meanwhile, the signs pulled her north. Now that her Power had woken, it pressed her forward with barely understood impulses and urges.

The inside of her ears itched. The moon disrupted her sleep, and an ocean of magic filled her body. She could hear the tide washing underneath her skin. It spilled out of her eyes, nose, and mouth and dripped invisible ectoplasm from the palms of her hands.

She went to extremes to avoid accidentally brushing against anybody. She couldn't settle to meditate. She felt unpredictable, undomesticated like a feral cat, and she didn't know what she was capable of or what she might do. If she didn't find her dream teacher soon, she would sell the Subaru and catch the first flight she could to Louisville, the seat of the witches demesne.

Eight days later, the sun edged close to the horizon as she drove into a town called Everwood in Northern California. Her eyes felt dry and itchy, and an ache had set in between her shoulder blades from so much driving.

She was tired of trying to interpret random signs, and she was beginning to feel discouraged. All she wanted was a room she could rent for longer than a few nights. She needed a shower and her clothes were dirty, so she needed to find a Laundromat as well.

She wanted to order pizza delivery. Hell, she wanted a massage.

Just after she had crossed the city limit, she found a gas station and filled up. Then she paid with another prepaid Visa and walked inside.

"Can I help you?" asked the girl at the cash register.

"I'm looking for a place to stay for the night. Got any suggestions?"

"Nothing in Everwood is too far away." The girl grinned. "It's a pretty small place."

"How nice." It wasn't nice. It meant she might be staying in another roadside motel. She hadn't felt a twinge of morning sickness yet, but if she looked at one more cheap polyester bedspread, she might hork all over it.

"The closest place is a motel off the highway. Turn right at the next light and you can't miss it."

Uh-huh. "What other options are there?"

An older man walked in from the back. He nodded to her. "How you doin'?"

Her tired mind seized up. It was getting harder and harder to pretend to be normal. She hesitated too long as she groped for the right pleasantry.

Both the man and the girl watched her, their attention hooked. The girl paused in chewing her gum.

Molly said cheerfully, "It's going to be summer solstice soon."

Soon as the words left her mouth, she winced. That didn't sound crazy at all, did it?

Oddly, the man seemed to relax. Smiling, he said, "Did I hear you're looking for a place to stay?"

"Yes." She eyed him warily, unsure if she wanted to trust anybody who relaxed at her strangeness. "Got any recommendations?"

He nodded. "Follow this road north about a mile and a half. It'll curve to the right. Turn left onto Muir Road. That will take you up the hill. There's an old bed-and-breakfast at the top. You can't miss it. It's the big house that overlooks the bay. There's a widow's walk on the roof."

A widow's walk. That meant the house was built sometime in the nineteenth century, it would be large, and it had an ocean view. And the thought of a real breakfast acted like a siren's lure. They might even let her do her laundry.

"Sounds interesting, thanks." She returned the man's smile.

"Sure thing." He told her, "Sarah Randall runs the place. If you decide to go up there, tell her Colin and Tallulah say hey."

"I will. Have a good night."

"You too."

Back in the Subaru, she drove slowly through the town. It looked well kept, with a main street filled with charming shops painted different colors and several side streets that held more utilitarian buildings such as a post office and a courthouse.

The road wound up an incline that lifted her over the rooftops of the town she had just passed through. She could see the Pacific. Sunlight sparkled off the calm surface of the water. The approaching sunset would be a kaleidoscope of fiery color.

Clusters of houses in cul-de-sacs spun off either side of the road like fractals, interspersed with clumps of redwood forest. When she reached Muir Road, she turned left. The road took her along the curve to the top of a hill where a large Victorian house with a widow's walk sprawled, limned with the gold of the setting sun.

Even to her cranky, tired gaze, it was beautiful. Signaling, she turned into the short drive and pulled up to the house. The grounds were attractively landscaped with areas of bright green lawn bordered by lilac bushes and flower beds and large pots filled with lemon trees.

A man walked around the corner of the house. She summed him up in a glance. He was either a gardener or a handyman, maybe thirty, with broad shoulders, shaggy blond hair, sun-bronzed skin, and strong features. He wore faded, dirty jeans and an equally dirty white shirt. As he strode toward the Subaru, he stripped heavy-duty gloves off large-boned hands.

"Evening," he said as she climbed out of the car. He had a great face, intelligent and friendly. Flecks of dirt dusted the bronzed skin at his throat. "Can I help you?"

"A man suggested I come up here," she told him, shading her eyes from the brilliant westering sun. "Is this Sarah Randall's place? He told me to watch for the house with the widow's walk. He said it was a bed-and-breakfast."

"This is Sarah's place." The man held out a big,

callused hand. "I'm Sam, her great-nephew. I keep the weeds beaten back for her."

Forgetting her recent aversion to touching anyone, Molly took his hand. His long fingers closed around hers gently, then he let her go.

"Love the lemon trees."

His hazel eyes smiled as he looked around the property. "Thanks. I don't know if Sarah's still taking guests, but you can always ask."

He didn't mean the bed-and-breakfast was full, did he? She looked around. The parking lot was empty, and that view was really spectacular. "I think I will. The worst she can do is tell me no."

"That's what I figure." He smiled into her eyes. "Good luck."

That straight look held just a little too long. He'd done that on purpose. Apparently a ten-year age difference with an older woman didn't bother him very much.

"Thanks." Smiling, she turned to walk up the path with a little extra bounce in her step. Her life might be the definition of complicated, but there was nothing wrong with a little ego boost.

The top half of the door was beveled glass. She admired the handiwork as she knocked and waited. Through it, she caught a blurred glimpse of an old woman moving toward the door just before it opened.

She revised her impression immediately. The woman was not so much old as she was frail. A scarf of soft blue cotton wrapped around her head, and Molly's heart sank as she took in the implications.

She glanced away at the large foyer. One of her mother's friends had gone through chemotherapy the previous year, and she had been very sensitive about her hair loss and appearance.

"Well, hello," the woman said.

"Good evening. I'm Molly. I'm hoping you might have a room available to rent?" she asked. "Colin and Tallulah say hi."

She offered her hand. The other woman took it, and as their palms came in contact, she sensed an immense Power. It was quiet and strong, honed like Josiah's, and deep as a well.

She fell into it. And fell, and fell…

Her shocked gaze lifted to the other woman's face, which was thinner and more lined than the witch's face from her dreams. But it was indisputably the same woman. Molly stared into her dark, powerful eyes.

"I'm Sarah Randall." The witch smiled. "It took you long enough to find me. You'd better come in."

Over the past several weeks, she had gradually lost faith that she would ever meet the witch from her dreams. Now here they stood, face-to-face, and excitement and fear jostled for dominance. "I can't believe this."

Sarah Randall laughed. "Moving from the dream world into the physical can be a trip." She opened the front door and called out, "Sam, would you bring Molly's luggage in?"

Sam straightened from his weeding. "Sure thing."

She called over Sarah's shoulder. "It's unlocked. Thanks!"

He grinned. "You bet!"

Closing the door, Sarah turned around. "He's a good boy."

"Boy?" Molly raised an eyebrow. The mature man outside was nowhere near a boy.

"I held him on my lap when he was not yet a day old," Sarah told her, eyes twinkling. "So yes, to me, he's still a boy. Come with me."

Molly followed her back to the kitchen. She looked around with fascination. "This isn't like the kitchen in the dream."

"No? What was that like for you?" Sarah went to the refrigerator and pulled out a pitcher of tea.

"It was yellow and green, and there was a huge, antiquated gas stove." Molly glanced over the thoroughly modernized space with stainless steel appliances, cream-painted cabinets, and granite countertops.

"Funny how the magic chooses to manifest," Sarah said. "I haven't had that kitchen since the fifties."

Molly accepted the tea with a murmur of thanks, eyeing the older woman sidelong as she slid into the opposite chair at the breakfast nook. Despite her illness, Sarah looked barely old enough to have been born in the fifties, let alone old enough to have had a kitchen.

"You're one of those witches who's older than you

look."

"One of 'those witches'?" Sarah raised her eyebrows. "How many have you met?"

"One, before you." The tea was delicious, and she drank thirstily. "I think he was born at the end of the Russian Empire. He taught me a few things that kept me from going crazy."

Sarah regarded Molly curiously. "What kind of things?"

"My Power started to manifest telekinetically, so he showed me how to focus and use it at will. He also said at some point I would have the ability to slow down my aging, which he has done. I assume you have too?"

"Yes, I'm much older than I look." Sarah's expression turned dry. "And with the kind of Power you carry, you'll be able to make the same choice, but I would encourage you to think hard about it. While you might gain a prolonged life, you'll give up a lot in order to get it."

"I wondered about that. The witch who helped me said he watched his children's children die of old age, and he still looks like he's in his midforties." She looked down at her glass, reluctantly acknowledging how much she missed Josiah.

Sarah nodded. "If you use the spell of youth, eventually you'll be saying goodbye to all your loved ones, their children, and their grandchildren. It is a hard choice, and at some point you will still die. We're all human, after all, but you won't face death until all the people you know and love have been dead and buried for a very long time."

"I see."

"Don't look so stricken on my account," Sarah said gently. "I'm not a victim. I knew what I was doing when I cast the spell. For all that I gave up, I gained a very long, fruitful, and interesting life. This is just the consequence of that choice. Besides, I'm not checking out quite yet."

"No, you're not." Sam spoke from the doorway. "You made me a promise. You're going to stick around for at least another year, hopefully two."

"You know I can't promise anything," Sarah replied. "We'll see how much time the chemo buys me."

"I'm not letting you off the hook," Sam told her. "I want to have you in my life for two more years at least, so focus your intention and make it happen. You've always said you could achieve anything with enough focus."

Sarah smiled. "I'll see what I can do."

Sam helped himself to a glass of tea and drank it down while standing in front of the sink. His warm hazel gaze met Molly's while he said, "I put Molly's luggage in the seaside turreted room. Is that okay?"

"That's perfect. Are you going to stay for dinner?"

He shook his head. "I'm rank as a buffalo. I need to shower, and I have some contracts to go through this evening, as well as an early-morning appointment."

After he took his leave, Sarah said, "Sam's a

landscape architect. He runs a very popular business."

Molly told her, "It's nice how he looks after you."

Sarah's expression softened. "I call him my great-nephew, but the reality is there's a few more 'greats' involved. He and I are the last of our direct family line. He's a good person—strong, kind, and committed to doing wonderful things." She pushed to her feet. "Come with me, and I'll show you the house."

It was a spacious place. From the outside it looked like it had three stories, but Sarah only took her through two. There was a door at one end of the second-floor hall that was closed. She guessed it led to an attic.

Curiosity had her lingering. In her mind's eye, she could feel/see sparks hanging over her head like stars. "What is that?"

"That's my workroom," Sarah replied. "Some things up there are dangerous. I keep it locked so strangers won't go poking around up there."

"Gotcha," she murmured. What would a workroom of a very old witch look like? Maybe if she was lucky Sarah would show it to her sometime.

Upstairs, there were eight bedrooms in total, counting Molly's turreted room, which she adored the moment she set eyes on it, and two upstairs bathrooms, one on either side of the house. The bedrooms were small, but the bathrooms were spacious and modernized with showers installed in claw-foot tubs, the shower curtains hanging from oval metal rings suspended overhead, and white-painted cabinets and floors tiled with Carrara marble.

On the first floor, there was a large entrance hall, a comfortable reception room, Sarah's bedroom that had once been a library, a formal dining room, the large main kitchen with a breakfast nook, and another large back kitchen that had been built as an extension off the main house.

That room had windows on three sides and would be an ideal place to do the hot, heavy work of canning in the summer without heating up the rest of the house. The area underneath the counters was filled with boots, gardening tools, and odds and ends.

Last, but not least in Molly's view, there was the walk-in pantry, the laundry room, and a water closet that had been recently renovated into a tiny bathroom with modern fixtures and a compact shower with a small bench upon which to sit.

Like all Victorian homes, it was an enormous and expensive beauty, and other items and areas glowed with magic, not with the attic's bright, dangerous sparks, but with a soft, gentle subtlety.

A stained-glass piece hung in a kitchen window, with a circular, repeating design that seemed to go on forever.

A small, rustic-looking broom, tied with a blue ribbon and decorated with spring colors, hung on the wall near the front door. A wrought iron candelabrum sat in the clean fireplace in the reception room, filled with lavender-scented beeswax candles that looked homemade and felt gently, deeply magical.

Outside the french-style doors in the breakfast nook, there was a patio with a round table and chairs. The tabletop was a mosaic of a pentagram, made with pieces of bright polished glass and stone. The pattern was repeated in the flagstone floor of the patio. Farther out in the yard, a large labyrinth made of small white stones spread out over a large yard.

The house would have been a work of art all on its own. With the magic that had been woven over the years into wall art and the everyday furniture and items, there was a complexity about the place, both visually and mentally, that Molly found compelling.

Moving as though her joints pained her, Sarah sat at the kitchen table again. "You're welcome to stay while you and I get acquainted. I might not suit you as a teacher, and Everwood has its quirks, so not everyone feels comfortable here. You're the only guest, so please clean your own room and keep up with your bedding and towels. If you find a place in town where you'd like to stay, we can work out when you'll come up for lessons."

"Of course. How much do you charge per night?" She frowned. "And would you consider a monthly rate?"

The other woman waved that away. "I'm not going to charge you anything."

She shook her head. "I can't stay here for free. I have to pay you something."

"I don't need your money. If I did, I would charge you." Sarah considered her. "I'll be blunt. We don't have the luxury of taking years for me to teach you or for you to study in your free time. You would do better to stay here. It will be cheaper than having to pay for room and board. Then you'd only have to work part-time."

"I don't need a job right now." Molly smiled. "If I stay, I can get groceries and cook, and I'll help with cleaning as well. If you're going teach me, I can help you in return. It's only the right thing to do."

Sarah nodded. "We can always change our minds if it doesn't work out." She eyed Molly. "What do you think?"

Molly tapped her fingers on the table, considering. "I think you should know the whole story before you decide to take me on," she replied. "My real name is not on the ID I'm carrying. My husband tried to kill me, and now he's dead. The police want me for questioning, and no, I didn't kill him. That witch I told you about… It's complicated. I'm pregnant with his baby. He and his coven are hunting down an ancient, dangerous witch who steals other witches' Power to prolong his life. That may or may not have something to do with how my husband died, and whoever it is may or may not also want me dead. We're not really sure at this point."

She paused to give Sarah a chance to react. The older witch said nothing, just regarded her with a calm, nonjudgmental gaze.

"Want to kick me out?"

Sarah said gently, "It makes me want to help you more."

Her face softened, but then her own words caught up with her. "Wait. Josiah said eventually every witch faces a choice. Either they exit their lives with integrity, or they steal what is forbidden—someone else's Power. But why isn't there a third choice?"

Sarah's gaze narrowed. "What do you mean?"

"The way I see it, we have two urgent issues," Molly said. "The first one is time. You need to teach me how to prolong your life. You don't need to steal my Power. I've got too much to control right now as it is. As long as we can avoid draining me completely, I'll gladly help to sustain you."

"You would do that?" Sarah's expression opened with wonder. "What a kind heart you have. I'm afraid I've advanced too far for your gift to do much more than buy me a bit of time, but I would love to give Sam as much time as I can and to be here as long as I can to teach you."

"Then we'll do it."

"What's your second urgent issue?"

She gave Sarah a grim smile. "Nobody's hurting my baby, and I'm not going to wait around for someone to rescue me if I get into a tight spot. So I need to learn how to fight if it comes down to a battle with another witch."

Chapter Seventeen

IN ATLANTA, MULTIPLE investigations marched on.

Even though Josiah did everything he could to make Molly disappear without a trace, none of the other members of the coven trusted the safe house now that she could potentially expose its location.

So Richard scrubbed it. He eradicated the spells, filled in the tunnel and repaired the hole in the basement, stripped out the security equipment, and methodically wiped the house of prints from top to bottom. When he finished, Josiah would sell it and buy another, and they would undertake the laborious task of setting up a new country safe house within driving distance of the city.

In their forensic accounting, Henry and Steven traced multiple paths to and from the Russian bank, the Seychelles islands, and Sherman & Associates, but a discernible pattern had yet to emerge.

It wasn't clear if the law firm was laundering money or taking payment for services rendered. Perhaps both? They only knew one thing for sure. The connection between Sherman & Associates and a Russian organization or company was strong and unmistakable.

Anson and Maria continued to painstakingly build files on each person of interest in Atlanta—anyone who might possibly be their quarry. Josiah would have suspected Russell himself if that hadn't been patently impossible. Bodies changed over time, and cosmetic surgery could easily alter facial features, but Russell was a good four inches shorter than Rasputin had been, and while he wore various magic items, he had no intrinsic Power himself.

Josiah read files, created scenarios to meet each individual they had researched, processed cases, and ordered an extensive audit of the Sullivan estate. But his head wasn't in the game. It hadn't been since he had returned from New Orleans.

One night Anson was waiting for him in the apartment after work, sitting on the couch with the living room lights on.

Josiah paused, then locked the door behind him. They rarely met in person, preferring to conduct most business via email, text, and the occasional phone call. "Anson. What do you need?"

"To talk to you. What are you doing about that tracker on your Audi now that Richard's scrubbing the safe house?"

"Nothing." Josiah carried his briefcase, suit jacket, and a bag of takeout to the kitchen counter. "I'm going to work, and I'm coming back to the apartment, and I'm doing normal things the DA would do. If somebody wants to waste their energy tracking that, let them. If we remove the tracker, it will alert the watchers that we know about them."

Anson stood and followed him. "You had good reason to put Richard to watching your back before. Now it's okay that he isn't?"

"We don't have enough people," he said tiredly. "So I'm watching my own back."

"What's going on?" the older man asked. "You've always been the sharpest barracuda in our stream, and you've *always* been on everybody about every little detail. You trained the rest of us to be patient and methodical—in fact, I'm sure that's how we've gone undetected for so long."

He skewered the other man with a hard look. "I'm still the sharpest barracuda in the stream."

"Okay," Anson said grimly. "Look, I can't fault your logic—logic isn't the problem. And no, we don't have enough people, but there's something different about you. That's why I'm here. It's been different ever since you got tangled up in that mess involving the Sullivan woman."

"What do you want me to say?" He yanked his tie off and threw it on the counter.

"I want you to tell me what's going on, because I know something is! We've known each other a long damn time, Josiah."

He rubbed the bridge of his nose, abruptly sick of answering to that name and holding everything back. "Molly's pregnant. It's my baby. I went to meet her in

New Orleans for the holiday weekend. And I want to meet her again as soon as possible. I just have to find a way to talk her into it."

Anson's eyes widened. "You're the last person I would have expected that from. Out of all of us, I thought maybe Maria or Steven would be vulnerable to the lure of a new life."

"They would have been my guess as well. They're more balanced and open." Josiah went for the scotch bottle, poured a few fingers into a glass, and held the bottle up in silent question to Anson, who nodded. He poured a second glass and thrust it across the counter.

Anson swallowed down a hefty gulp. "We've all lost something precious to that bastard. My wife, Maria's daughter, Steven's parents, Richard's platoon, Henry's fiancée. But you—you lost years. Nobody's hate has burned hotter than yours, and none of us have been more driven."

"Oh, I still hate him." Josiah knocked back his drink and poured another. "And I still want him dead. But what if I'm starting to need something else more than I want that?"

This baby and I deserve someone who will always put us first. And I'm not waiting for you.

"You're tired," Anson said quietly, his gaze keen.

"She said this mysterious, terrible person who hurt me so badly all those years ago has eaten me up inside." He sighed. "And she was right. I made him my mission. *I let him* eat me up inside. I gave him decades of my life, and I don't mean just the ones he took when I was in prison. I need this to be over."

Anson looked down at the amber liquid in his glass and swirled it around. He murmured, "I would have given up everything for my wife. Our lives didn't lead us down that road, but I would have if I'd had to."

What was Anson trying to say? Josiah frowned and yanked himself back on course. Lately the need to do that happened all too often. "Maria's visions have consistently led us to Atlanta, Anson. He's here. He's got to be."

Anson finished his scotch. "Maria's made mistakes before, and he's too good at covering his tracks. If something doesn't shake loose soon, maybe we should think about doing something to shake it."

"Maybe," Josiah said. "All I know is, I believe I've acquired an expiration date."

"What does that mean?" Anson studied him closely. "You're not just our coven leader. You're also our bankroller."

"I don't know what it means." He gave Anson a reassuring smile when the other man hesitated. "When I have it figured out, I'll let you and the others know. Don't worry, I'm not going to pull the rug out from anybody. The mission still matters."

When the older man left, Josiah thought about eating his takeout, but he'd lost his appetite, so he went to take a hot shower. Later, when he finally dumped cold food onto his plate, his phone lit up.

The highlight of his days was texting with Molly. Smiling to himself, he checked the screen.

`I found my teacher. And it's too soon to tell for sure, but I might have found the baby's and my new home.`

Jealousy seared him. He punched her number, listened to it ring. And ring.

She finally answered. "I don't know how I feel about this. Texting and keeping you up to date about the baby is fine, but where's the line?"

Don't hold a line against me! he almost roared. His body clenched. Gently, go gently now. "Don't hold a line against me, *milaya*."

"Josiah," she whispered.

Just as she had whispered too many days before, pressing her lips against his skin. His body caught on fire. Closing his eyes, he whispered in reply, "I respect your boundaries. I am asking you to change them."

He listened to her breathing. Don't hang up.

She didn't hang up.

"Tell me about your teacher," he coaxed.

"She's very old and nearing the end of her life. She's a good person. We're going to help each other out a lot, I think. And my bedroom tonight is in a turret in a grand old Victorian house."

He dared to relax a little. "Describe it to me."

"There are four tall windows, and either the house sits at an angle, or the shoreline curves, because I can see the ocean from all of them. There's a double bed with a walnut frame. It's made with a homemade quilt with faded colors, and I've got a comfortable armchair. I'm sitting in it right now, looking at the water. I'll be able to listen to the surf when I go to sleep."

"Beautiful," he murmured, his voice husky. Muffling his phone for a moment, he flung his plate viciously across the room. It shattered against the wall. "You sound happy."

"Well, that's complicated," she said dryly. "But I'm happy to be here, and I feel safe."

"That's very good to hear. You should have always felt safe—always been safe."

Truth was, she was better off without him. *He had always known that.* He was a morose son of a bitch. He didn't know how to be anything other than cold, brooding, and driven.

Hesitantly, she asked, "How are things going for you?"

"Well, that's complicated too," he told her, matching her dryness.

"I imagine it is." She fell silent.

"It's not that I don't want or need to tell you things, *milaya*, but I'm not sure how much I should say over the phone," he said gently.

"I… see." Suddenly she asked, "Are *you* safe?"

A startled warmth spread through him. "Tonight I am very safe."

"Right. You are for tonight. Maybe we shouldn't talk anymore."

Her sudden intensity jolted him. *"Don't hang up."*

"Why? What are we trying to do here—sort of carry on a relationship but not really, while you get to be in danger and embrace a vendetta, or sometimes not, and I can't know about any of it? I already told you once. I can't be the mistress to your wife."

I'm not waiting.

His scotch glass broke. Looking down, he found he was clenching the pieces hard enough to drive one of them into his palm. Blood dripped onto the granite counter. He said, "Meet me next weekend."

She coughed out an incredulous laugh. He heard the stress threading through it. "You're kidding. Right?"

With rigid self-control, he kept his voice even, deliberate. "I have things I need to say to you, and I believe they should be said in person. I will be at the Venetian Resort in Las Vegas Friday night, and I will wait there for you until Sunday evening. It's your choice whether you show or not, but I hope you do, *milaya.* Just know I will be there."

"What are you trying to do now?" she whispered.

"Show up and find out."

"I'm hanging up now." Abruptly, she disconnected.

He stood contemplating the messes he had made. The shattered plate of food, the blood on the counter, his life.

A text came in from Molly. `I don't know if I'm coming. I need to think, so give me some space. Don't call or text.`

`Acknowledged`, he replied.

Instinctively, he knew now would not be a good time to push. As hard as it was to give up those evening interchanges, he turned his attention to work and kept it there, only taking time enough away to lay the elaborate travel plans that would hide his true destination from any potential onlookers.

Would she come? Thoughts of her consumed him. Belatedly, he realized just how much of a danger he had become, to himself and his coven.

Friday evening, after he had checked in at the Venetian, he texted her the suite number. She didn't respond. She was staying somewhere on the coast, so it was possible she was still in midflight.

He showered, dressed in jeans and a T-shirt, ordered a steak from room service and let it grow cold while he cast protection spells around the suite. Then he paced the spacious cream-and-taupe interior like a caged animal, raging at the restrictions he had set on himself.

He would not text her again. He would wait, as he had promised.

Close to nine o'clock, a knock sounded at the door. Lunging, he yanked it open. She stood in the hall with a handbag on her shoulder, wearing sandals, a loose cotton shirt, and flowing capri pants. She did not have a weekend bag, and her expression was strained and white.

He soaked in every detail, his mouth held tight. The things she put him through. She was here, but just barely. She was the most gorgeous thing he had ever seen.

Finally he asked with a grim smile, "Did you miss the shit out of me?"

Her eyes blazed. She looked like she didn't know whether to laugh or hit him.

He stood back, holding the door wide. She stalked in like a tigress and flung her purse onto a chair.

Then she rounded on him. "What?" she snapped. "Why am I here?"

She was very angry. But she was still here.

He told her gravely, "Only you can answer why you came, *milaya*."

She gestured impatiently. "There were things you needed to say in person. So say them."

He wanted to leap at her, drag her to the carpeted floor, bite her neck. At the unruly thought, his cock hardened, and he turned away. Every inch of her body shouted she would not welcome a physical overture right now, as she had in New Orleans.

He was so close to losing her, if he had not done so already. She didn't have a bag with her, which meant she wasn't here as a lover. She might only be present as the mother of his child.

Instead of approaching, he paced restlessly through the expansive suite. "You said you weren't waiting. Have you started to date?"

She exploded. "What the fuck is wrong with you? I'm pregnant. You and I were just together a couple of weeks ago. *My husband died last month!* Who do you think I am? And anyway, it's none of your business."

He had reached the floor-to-ceiling windows and crossed his arms while he stared out at the evening lights. Las Vegas sparkled at night. Even in his faint reflection in the glass, he could see how his eyes burned.

Don't turn, don't let her see what is in your face.

When he could trust himself to sound restrained, he replied, "You get to date who and when you want. You said yourself that you and Sullivan hadn't been in a real marriage for a long time. As far as who I think you are, I think you're a beautiful woman with strength and integrity. You're a woman of your word. You told me some pretty sweeping and important things, and I'm asking you for clarification."

Silence throbbed. "I have no interest in dating," she told him, her voice stilted with held-back emotion. "I've barely begun my training with Sarah, and as I just pointed out, my life is complicated."

He nodded. His hands were clenched into fists underneath his crossed arms. "Would you be interested in dating me if our lives were appropriately arranged to do so?"

"They're not," she said flatly.

He watched her reflection. She walked over to sit at the edge of the bed and put her head in her hands.

"Because I would date you," he said quietly. "I would see you every opportunity you would let me. I would go with you to the doctor appointments, sit in on every ultrasound, listen to the baby's heartbeat with you. I would make love to you in the morning while we shut out the rest of the world, and I would kiss the back of your neck while you cooked us breakfast."

He had done that in New Orleans. He could tell the moment she remembered it as her head lifted.

She wiped her face and whispered, "What do you want from me?"

"I want a timeline," he said immediately. "I want a negotiation. We've both said things in moments of high emotion, and now I want to know what it means. You're right. You do deserve someone who always puts you and the baby first, and I want the opportunity to apply for the position. If it were a matter of simply quitting my job, I would have already done so and moved across the country, but I have five coven members who depend on me. We've all suffered terrible injuries from the individual we're hunting. They lost people they loved to him—a wife, a daughter, a fiancée, coworkers, parents—and I'm the one who convinced them to join me on this quest. I owe them something, Molly. I don't think I'd be the kind of man you would want to be with if I just abandoned them."

"Okay," she said, sounding calmer. "I can see how important that is, and you're right. I wouldn't think much of anyone who could drop those obligations and run, so I understand why you wanted to talk."

The pinched tension between his shoulders began to ease. "Thank you."

She walked over to put a gentle hand on his back. "Look at us, sounding so reasonable."

He spun to grasp her upper arms. The suddenness made her flinch. "Nothing about this is reasonable. The feelings I have for you *aren't normal.* I'm obsessed with you. I can't stop thinking about the way your skin tastes, the sound of your laugh, the way you face life with such fierce anticipation."

Her lips shook. "I can't stop thinking about you either."

"Thank God for that." He passed a hand over her hair. "Because thoughts of you are interrupting my work, my decisions. I can't sleep. Is this love? I don't know. I've never been in love before. All I know is I'm ready to abandon almost everything just for the chance to be with you."

"Josiah…"

"Don't call me that," he hissed.

"I have to call you something." The pragmatic words were at odds with the way she touched his face. "I want to fling everything I've got at you, and if it were just me, I would do it and take my chances. But my life is not just about me anymore."

"*I know.* I get it." He caught himself up, then added more quietly, "Because my life isn't just about me anymore either."

"How much danger are you and the others in?" She searched his expression.

"I don't know," he told her truthfully. "It varies, depending on the situation. From things he said when he had me imprisoned, this witch is over a thousand years old—he's dangerous, canny, and unprincipled, so we're obsessive about covering our tracks. The only thing I know for certain is that it's going to get more dangerous the closer we get to him. Our seer believes he's in the Atlanta area, and we've seen other indications that something dangerous is hiding there, such as spells layered over the local internet hubs."

And he had been taking the most dangerous position of all of them, always at the forefront, in the public eye, initiating face-to-face contact with likely suspects. He did not offer that statement. Molly was already aware of it.

"He must have hurt or killed so many people," she murmured. "Can your coven defeat him?"

At that, he had to serve up another dose of truth. "We think so, but we won't know until we fight him."

She shuddered, then gave him a clear-eyed look. "You said you wanted to negotiate. So tell me what you want and lay it out in specific detail. Then I'll let you know if I can give it to you."

"I want eighteen weeks," he said. "Four and a half months. From what I've been reading, you should be due for your first ultrasound. I want to make that trip to the doctor with you."

She tilted her head. "You're asking for that to be our first date?"

There was a certain wry amusement in her words. He touched her lips with a forefinger. "Your first ultrasound is only one part of this negotiation. Dating is another matter. When we go on our first date, there'll be no doubt that it's just between you and me."

Heat smoked along the edges of her expression and her mouth softened, but then she asked, "What would you do with the eighteen weeks?"

He could see that what he said next mattered a great deal. But just as he was willing to make massive changes, he also couldn't water himself down to make things more palatable.

He said without hesitation, "Try to find the witch. You should know, we intend to kill him. That's the best solution to everything. The Elder Races have a tribunal, but we have no intention of pursuing justice that way—not when there's a chance he might go free. As a district attorney, I can pursue certain legal strategies, but we have only ever intended those as one possible method to reach a final end."

She closed her eyes. "You've been hunting him a long time. What if you can't do it?"

"I would also use the time to extricate myself from the coven in a way that won't harm them. If it looks like we've hit a dead end, one of the coven members mentioned doing something to provoke a reaction that might get him to reveal himself. But whether we finally manage to take him down in that time frame or not, I'll give them notice I'm leaving."

Angling her jaw out, she tapped her fingers on her chin as she thought it over. She looked remarkably unpredictable in that moment, and he tensed.

"You've got eighteen weeks," she said. "After that,

all bets are off."

"What does that mean exactly?" He narrowed his gaze. She had thought of something, and suddenly he felt certain he wasn't going to like it.

She gave him a thin smile. "You're not the only one with loose ends that need to be tied up before this baby is born. In eighteen weeks, I'm coming home to meet with the police and to claim my estate."

✧ ✧ ✧

IF SHE'D THOUGHT she'd seen Josiah angry before, it was nothing compared to the rage that transformed his face now. He snapped, "The hell you will!"

"Yes. I will." She stopped to consider him. "Did you really think this was all about you—*your* coven, *your* needs, *your* enemy, *your* transformation, *your* timetable? Oh, bless."

"Of course it isn't all about me," he said savagely. His eyes flashed yellow fire. "Why do you think I needed to talk to you? But *this* idea is unacceptable!"

"Then you and I have a fundamental difference of opinion," she bit out. "Because I think it's the only thing that makes sense. I'm not going to live out the rest of my life in hiding, and I'm not going to idle passively on the sidelines when I can do something to make the world safer for this child. And I have material assets I need to claim, not least because they mean independence."

"The money doesn't matter," he snarled.

She raised her eyebrows. "I've found that's easy to

say when you have money. It's not quite so easy when you don't—and when you start thinking about things like the medical cost of giving birth and needing to put a child through college."

"You don't need to pay medical bills, and I will never let our child want for anything!"

She sighed. "It speaks so well of you that you have no intention of being a deadbeat dad. But on the other hand, that would foster an even greater dependence on you, and I don't want to need you because of your money." She rubbed her forehead where a headache had started to bloom. "Also, I have a mother who's been a bitch to me, but she's getting elderly. Maybe she's thought better about how she's always taken Austin's side. I don't know, because I don't have my old phone, and I haven't dared to access my email. And I lived in Atlanta a long damn time. I have friends, and I know people. They deserve to know what happened to me, and I should be able to use my real name again."

"You'd be putting both yourself and the baby in danger!"

Breathing hard, she glared at him. "Let me see if I've got this right. You'll be actively courting weeks of continued danger that I'm supposed to accept without question, because… what, I'm supposed to be happy that you want to date me—later—at a time that is more convenient for you and your coven? But when I want to assert my right to take back control of my life, you get to dictate that it isn't okay? You say you want a negotiation, but I'm not buying what you're putting on the table."

He roared, "You can't defend yourself—you haven't any training yet!"

"Well, I'd better go back and start getting some, hadn't I?" She wanted to touch him so badly it almost broke through her resolve, but she stiffened her spine and held her ground. "You want time? Great. You've got your eighteen weeks to clean up your shit, and then I'm coming home. And if you think you're good enough to take out this mysterious bad guy of yours, then you're good enough to keep me safe while I'm there, so maybe this will be what you need to shake something loose. It will sure as hell be your opportunity to step up."

"I'm too angry to talk right now," he said over his shoulder. His voice had gone hoarse. "Get the fuck out of my face."

Her lips tightened. "Right. I've got a plane to catch anyway."

"Don't go," he whispered.

She had planned it all carefully. She would fly in only to see what he had to say. She wouldn't stay, she wouldn't weaken and sleep with him again no matter how much she was tempted, and she would be back in her wonderful turret bedroom before dawn.

But now she hesitated. What if this was the last time she saw him? He would be pushing harder than ever to finish what he had started before she returned to Atlanta.

Not stopping to second-guess the impulse, she flung herself at him. He pivoted, and arms like iron bands closed around her.

He knew her body so well already. He knew how to shape himself around her, how to tilt her head back, how to plunder the depths of her mouth until they were both shaking. He kissed her as if he almost hated her.

"I could stop you," he said against her mouth.

"You could try." She strained to hold him tighter. She knew his body too, and God, it felt so good to feel his larger, muscular frame taut against hers. "But I don't see how confining me is going to get you any closer to a first date."

"Goddamn you." He leaned his forehead against hers, eyes closed.

"Well, goddamn you," she told him. "Because if you think the next eighteen weeks of worrying about you are going to be easy, you can think again."

They stood together, breathing quietly, in sync. She could tell when, gradually, his anger eased. She put a hand on his chest, feeling his heartbeat underneath his broad, hard sternum. He was a difficult man, but she knew a few things about him now, and he had a strong, good heart.

Underneath it, his Power shone dark and smooth like the depths of a bottomless lake. After starting to wrestle with her own unruly Power, she had begun to understand a little of what he must have gone through to achieve that even, polished balance.

Then he said more gently, "Thank you for the eighteen weeks."

"I've got my first appointment with my new doctor next week." She cleared her throat. "We'll work out a schedule of visits. I'll let you know when the first ultrasound is."

Because that would begin the eighteen-week countdown.

Chapter Eighteen

IT WAS HIS turn to nod. "I'm still furious. Don't expect me to be rational if you need to talk further." His voice turned husky. "But I really want you to stay."

God, she was so tempted. Just throw everything to the winds and wreck herself on him.

She shook her head. "I just… I can't."

Oh, who the hell was she fooling. She had already wrecked herself on him. She might make it sound like she had a good game going, but inside she was a twenty-car pileup.

Would leaving right now save her the tiniest bit of anguish if he was killed in Atlanta before they could see each other again? Or would she be haunted by the time they could have had if she had only opened herself up to it?

She only realized she was opening and closing her hand over his chest when he pressed his hand over hers. "Molly."

Need melted the stiffness in her limbs so that she sank to her knees in front of him. Wrapping her arms around his thighs, she held him there and he let her.

She had never understood the tyranny of physical passion before, how the need for another person could drive someone to disregard every sensible instinct they owned, until now.

He was going to hurt her, maybe even badly. The light of real life would be pitiless on them both, and if he made one more attempt to manipulate her, she knew she would take a wrecking ball to every bridge they had managed to build between them.

They probably wouldn't make it past the second or third date.

Once you accepted the inevitability of impending disaster, things usually got a bit easier. This time they grew crystal clear. Resting her cheek against the zipper of his jeans, she savored the thick bulge of his erection through the material. He couldn't hide his need for her either.

He bent over her kneeling form, stroking her hair, her jaw, running his hands over the curve of her shoulders. "What do you need?"

"I don't understand how we got to this place," she murmured, almost dreamily. "I didn't even like you when I first met you."

Laughter shuddered through him. "As I recall, I wasn't being very likable, but I loved everything about you. I knew you were going to be a colossal inconvenience."

"You were right. I was, wasn't I?" She unbuttoned his jeans and drew the zipper down.

"You don't even know the half of it, but I wouldn't trade away a minute with you for anything." Long gentle fingers hooked underneath her chin. He lifted her face until she looked at him. His amber gaze was intent. "You still haven't told me what you need."

"I need to take what I want."

Reaching inside the opening of his pants, she pulled his cock out. She knew his body just as he knew hers. She knew the pattern of veins along the side of his shaft, the velvety, sensitive skin over the hardened muscle, his scent, the way his sac tightened underneath when she cupped him.

He hissed as she stroked and fisted him, spreading his legs apart to brace himself, the muscles of his thighs rigid. She had grown obsessed with him too. The way his skin tasted. The sounds he made when he lost control.

When he wasn't saying sexy things to her, he liked to make love quietly, in near silence. It made her zero in on every moment, like a series of flash photographs. This. This. This. Until he couldn't stay silent any longer. God, she loved when that happened.

She took him in her mouth, widening her lips to fit around the broad head, for a while content to simply hold the tip inside her, she stroked her tongue in a gentle pulse against the most sensitive part of him. The tension in his body grew tighter until it fractured in micro tremors. He started to pump gently, and she took him in farther, opening her throat until she encompassed all of him.

She took and he moved, silently intent until the very end. Then a sound broke out of him, harsh like a hawk's cry. He shuddered, spilling into her, and she closed her eyes and swallowed every drop down.

Because we know this dance, don't we, my friend? We've been here before in this private place.

You push harder, and I give in. You fall into your animal while I rise up to meet you.

And we might break our hearts, but we'll say it will have been worth it.

To bathe in this fire one more time.

Just to spark the fire.

One more time.

✧ ✧ ✧

AFTERWARD, HE KNELT and held her. She rested her head on his shoulder and drifted until he picked her up to lay her on the bed. As he stretched out beside her, she rolled away and looked out the window at the wild array of lights. Eighteen weeks.

Lifting aside the heavy fall of her hair, he said against the nape of her neck, "I would love to return the favor, but suddenly you feel like you're a million miles away."

She shook her head and said telepathically, <It doesn't have to be quid pro quo, Alexei.>

<You are so wrong, *milaya.* Lovemaking always has to be quid pro quo.>

Her lips pulled into a smile. <Okay, but it doesn't have to be all at once, you know? Sometimes it's okay if I

give, or you give, and we can let it be at that.>

He kissed her earlobe. <I don't care what it has to be, as long as you stay here. Come back from wherever you went.>

<I can't.> She looked over her shoulder at him. <You asked for time, and I'm going to give it to you.>

His expression tightened. <Every time I see you it gets harder to leave.>

She nodded, unsurprised, then pushed to a sitting position. <Same for me. That's why I don't want to see you again until the eighteen weeks are over. We both need to stay focused on what we need to do.>

<But not right now.> He sat up too and gripped her by the back of the neck. <We can take the fucking weekend, Molly.>

She winced and said aloud, "I think I'm at my limit, and I don't want to get into another argument. You're exhausting when we butt heads. You need the time you asked for, and I've already said I'll give it to you, but I'm not going to change my mind about returning to Atlanta."

When his gaze narrowed in quick, disingenuous reaction, she knew she had struck a chord. He'd been strategizing how to argue her out of that decision.

He said, "Let's start another negotiation."

"I'm all lawyered out, babe." She pushed the dark hair off his forehead. "I miss you already, and I'm worried about what the next eighteen weeks will do to you. There's only one thing we can do to make this better, and that's both of us getting through this intact."

Sinking his fists into her hair, he kissed her until the muscles in her thighs shook. When he finally lifted his head, his eyes were bleak, and his expression had settled into grim lines. "I've got a rental car. I'll take you to the airport."

It was getting late. "You don't have to...," she began.

His composure cracked, and something volcanic and frightening flashed across his face. "I will take you. To. The fucking airport."

Speechless, she nodded. Releasing his grip, he rolled off the bed, his movements quick and tight. She escaped into the lush bathroom to straighten herself. There was nothing she could do about her rumpled clothing or the stark look in her eyes. She drank some water, finger-combed her hair, and shrugged off the rest.

When she emerged, he had his phone out and had turned brisk. "Did you miss your flight?"

She didn't know what time it was. She shrugged. "It doesn't matter. If I have, I should be able to fly standby. I can sort it out at the airport."

His mouth tightened, and he pocketed his phone. "Fine. Are you ready?"

He had turned distant. She nodded.

They made the drive to the airport in silence. When they drew close, he clamped a hand hard on her knee and didn't let go until he pulled into a spot to drop her off. She unbuckled her seat belt, and as she turned to say goodbye, he rounded on her.

"I am not okay with total silence," he said savagely. "Text me every night. One word. Just let me know you're safe. And tell me when you make it back okay."

"Yes," she agreed in a whisper. "And you text me back too. Just a quick word. I want to know you're safe too."

They both leaned forward at once to share a searing kiss, until she couldn't take any more. She tore herself away, climbed out, and walked blindly into the airport.

Even if they both survived what came next, feelings change and evolve, and they hadn't had enough time together to establish a solid basis to their relationship.

The disaster no longer felt like it was impending. She was pretty sure it was already insidiously here.

She hadn't missed her flight. She had already checked in, and she didn't have any luggage, so she was soon winging back to the Bay Area. She had to drive north from there, and it took longer than she had anticipated, so dawn had broken by the time she pulled into a parking space at Sarah's old Victorian home.

The peaceful surroundings wrapped around her raw, abraded nerves. Something ungovernable welled up, and she screamed in the confines of the Subaru. Then, for the first time since the night she had left Austin, she sobbed wildly until she was completely emptied.

She texted Josiah, `I'm back safe.`

He responded immediately. `Good. I'll text every night at 8 pm EST/ for you—5 pm.`

She sent him a thumbs-up.

When she walked inside, she went into the kitchen for a piece of fruit to quiet her gnawing stomach. She found Sarah sitting in the breakfast nook with a cup of herbal tea. When Sarah looked at her, her expression softened with kindness. "Was it as hard as you thought it might be?"

"Yes and no." She rubbed her face, grabbed a banana, and went to sit opposite Sarah. "It wasn't as bad as it could have been, but that somehow made it worse. I don't have the right words." She peeled the banana and looked at it. "We swore and yelled at each other and came to a compromise of sorts."

"It looks like you hate it."

"I think we both do." She poured out the details of what they had decided while Sarah listened sympathetically. "So I have eighteen weeks to train for a possible confrontation with an evil, potentially thousand-year-old witch. In the meantime, I can always hope that Josiah and his coven find and kill him first." She twitched a shoulder. "And survive."

Other than a small wince, Sarah took the news with the appearance of calm. "I see. It looks like we have our work cut out for us."

"Thank you for not saying it's impossible." She looked outside. The morning was sunny with a mild temperature and another cool breeze blowing off the jade-colored water. Outside, the sky was a clear, bright aquamarine blue. Golden light streamed in from the windows.

"I thought I would avoid stating the obvious," Sarah said dryly. "I hope you enjoy studying for long hours. Do you need to go to bed?"

She had napped on the plane, so she shook her head.

"All right. Have you finished reading the books I gave you last week?"

Molly nodded. The week before, Sarah had given her a pendulum to work with along with the books.

"How is practice with your new pendulum going?"

"Would you like to see?"

"Please."

She pulled the amethyst on a sterling silver chain out of her purse and held it steadily in front of her, in the position described in one of the books. The pendulum started rocking back and forth. Then it began to spin until it whirled in a circular movement perpendicular to the table.

Sarah's eyes widened. Molly tilted her mouth in a wry slant. When the pendulum began to spin so fast it whistled through the air, she clapped it between both hands. "You tell me. How am I doing?"

"Oh dear," Sarah murmured. "Well, it can take students several months to master how to use a pendulum, so don't feel discouraged. Let me show you how it's supposed to go."

Molly handed it over. Sarah propped her elbow on the table and held it in the same position as Molly had, by pinching the end of the silver chain between thumb and forefinger and letting the stone dangle freely.

Sarah said, "This is the right way to hold it. You did a good job with your positioning."

Sarah held her other hand palm up and directly underneath the pendulum so that the dangling amethyst and chain drew a line from her raised right hand to the left hand down below. Her expression was calm, even serene. She hadn't bothered to wear a scarf that morning, and her strong, almost aquiline face was accentuated by the smooth, round dome of her bald scalp.

At first impression, she had seemed rather plain, but as Molly had gotten to know her, she could see there was a harmony to Sarah's features, along with the lines in the soft, tanned skin bracketing her mouth, that was pleasing to the eye. Even with the illness, she carried a sense of vitality lacking in many other people.

Sarah told her, "Now watch."

At first nothing seemed to happen. Then the stone began to move. It swung back and forth at an angle. Sarah's hand, she saw, remained perfectly steady, her elbow propped on the table.

"At least it's not spinning wildly like it does for me," Molly muttered. "But why is it doing that?"

"It's responding to my energy, like it was responding to yours," Sarah replied. Slowly she tilted her hands, first one way and then another, and the amethyst tilted with her, straining from the fingers of one hand to the palm of the other.

As Molly watched, there was no doubt in her mind.

No matter what position Sarah held the stone in, she maintained complete control.

Molly sighed. "I'm never going to achieve that."

"Yes, you will. When you gain mastery over your Power, the pendulum will calm down for you too. Now, let's ask a question. Can you think of one that can be answered with either a yes or a no?"

"Am I pregnant?"

"Perfect. Is Molly pregnant?" Sarah asked. The stone began to swing in a clear clockwise motion. "That's my positive. When the pendulum swings in a counter-clockwise motion, that's my negative."

Molly stared in fascination. "You said *my positive* and *my negative*. What does that mean?"

"A pendulum doesn't respond the same way to everybody. Your positive might be when it swings back and forth in a north/south direction, with the negative at east/west. My teacher's positive was when her pendulum always angled toward her heart. It's also possible your positive might be my negative."

"So counterclockwise isn't necessarily bad?" She rubbed her dry, tired eyes.

"Not at all. Historically, several cultures considered widdershins to be going against the sun, which was unlucky or unfortunate, but other cultures see widdershins as a very mystical and positive thing. In Judaism, circles are often walked counterclockwise in affirming rituals. It all depends on social context and flow of energy." Sarah withdrew her lower hand, and the pendulum stilled. "I wasn't going to suggest this until later, but I think you should walk the labyrinth today."

Surprised, Molly said, "The one in the yard?" When Sarah nodded, she shrugged. "Okay. What am I supposed to be looking for?"

"Just walk through it sometime today." Sarah handed the amethyst back to Molly and stood. "Then come tell me what you discover. For now I think you could use a break, and I'm going to do some gardening before it gets too hot."

"But I don't need a break…" Her voice died away. She *was* tired.

"You've set quite an agenda for yourself, but you need to learn how to walk before you can run." Sarah tapped her gently on the shoulder as she walked past. "And you need to look after that miraculous body of yours, not just for your sake, but for your baby's as well."

After Sarah had left, Molly sat thinking in the empty kitchen. Sarah was right. Her pregnancy was so new she didn't even feel it yet, but that was no excuse to put her body under unnecessary strain.

She fixed herself a proper breakfast and did some quick prep work on what she would make for supper. When she was through, she showered and took a nap, then woke sometime later to a fresh ocean breeze moving in from an open window.

She lay for some time, soaking in the peace. Thinking of Josiah. Alexei. His eyes, his hands. The way his cold demeanor covered an intense, passionate nature. In that moment, she didn't miss him in the slightest.

God, she was such a liar.

After dressing in clean capris and a T-shirt, she went outside. Some distance away, Sarah knelt, weeding rows of baby vegetables. She wore a wide-brimmed hat that protected her vulnerable head and shoulders.

In the opposite direction, the labyrinth waited. Not wishing to disturb Sarah, Molly strode toward it.

Up close, it was larger than she had first thought, at least fifty feet in diameter and as well-tended as the rest of the property. The paths were white gravel, while larger rectangular stones, perhaps five or six inches in height, set the "walls." The entrance was marked by two gargoyles carved out of white marble. They stood about four feet high.

It was a charming landscape fancy, but she couldn't sense any magic, or why Sarah would be interested in what she thought after she walked it. Shrugging, Molly stepped between the gargoyles and onto the path.

After the first few steps, she paused. Hadn't that first turn curved right instead of left? Confused, she looked over the patterned stones and paths. They wound in spirals around the center, twisting and turning back on themselves like snakes.

Her left hand tingled while hot gold sunlight poured down on her head. Then she started forward again. She had to watch where she stepped to keep from tripping over the larger border stones. The pattern of the labyrinth was hypnotic.

Going left, always going left. Against the sunward path. *Widdershins.*

Going left felt good, felt correct. Whenever the path twisted to the right, she resisted for a moment, and somehow it changed to take her left. As the circles narrowed and she approached the center, the world around her aligned into a patterned whole. The sun and the moon danced together while the ocean played a rhythmic song.

Sunward was clockwise. The moon was her mistress, and she followed it. The ocean joined in, its music swirling with the tide. She was walking in a vortex. Her Power rose in response to spin around her, a vortex within a vortex, and the scene expanded. The stone walls grew to towering heights while the path shone ivory-bright, as wide as a highway.

She had so much magic her body couldn't contain it. It poured out of her eyes and streamed down her arms. For once she didn't try to dampen or contain it. Letting it flow felt so good, she almost sank to her knees.

She had used her left hand to throw Power at Austin and his car. Remembering, her palm tingled again. She shook out her fingers to release the tension, and magic like argent fire poured from her palm.

She lifted her hand and swirled it in the air. The magic responded by curling around her wrist. She shook it out again, and it unfurled with a snap like a whip.

This is mine, she thought. This beautiful, deadly thing is my Power.

Widdershins is my positive, my correct path. Everything aligns when I walk my correct path.

As she neared the circle, her magic grew higher, more intense. Her vortex of energy overrode the vortex of the labyrinth. Her magic swallowed the stones and gravel until they rose in a column around her, spinning in her vortex, spinning, spinning, spinning.

Letting her magical whip trail loose, she stepped into the center of the labyrinth and turned in a circle, keeping her left hand to the center, in the heart of her magic.

Then she looked up. The labyrinth stones spun above her head as high as she could see, whirling like mad constellations in the cloudless, cerulean sky.

Out of the corner of her eye, she saw Sarah standing in the vegetable patch, holding her hat to her head. The edges of the brim flapped wildly. Several yards away, a copse of trees whipped back and forth. The vortex Molly had created was affecting everything in the vicinity.

A tree branch broke and flew through the air to smash into one of the downstairs windows. Sarah shouted something. Molly couldn't make out what she said.

She called out, "What?"

Sarah shouted again and pointed to the ground between her feet. "You've got to ground yourself! Release your Power into the earth!"

"How?" she shouted. Her hair rose around her head in a nimbus, and strands blew across her face.

Sarah's hat tumbled from her head as she held out

both hands, palms down. She mimed pushing something invisible down.

Watching her, Molly copied her stance. Power flowed from her right hand too, but it wasn't as concentrated as the deadly line of Power that poured from her left. As it dripped from her right hand, it fell harmlessly to the earth and disappeared, soaking into the turf.

The whip of light pouring from her left palm was less cooperative. It twisted and turned on itself and called to Molly to play with it. Lifting her hand, she flung it out. It snapped at the air like a crackle of lightning.

Thunder roared out of the cloudless sky like a sonic boom. It shook the ground, and nearby, a maple tree cracked and toppled over with a crash.

Oh shit.

Through the roar of the vortex, she gradually grew aware of Sarah's chanting. It ran too low for her to hear the words, an entirely different Power from hers, deeper, much older, and more anchored to the earth.

Only when her feet landed on the ground did she realize she'd been levitating several feet in the air. The reconnection jarred her back to her senses. Giving the whirling stones overhead a leery look, she fell to her knees, planted her hands in the lush grass, and concentrated on pouring the magic into the ground.

She poured and poured. It gushed out of her in a seemingly endless flood until finally the flow eased to a trickle. As it stopped, the stones and gravel dropped randomly over the yard.

The wind died down. Molly and Sarah stared at each other from across the distance. Sarah's eyes had rounded. Molly was still on her hands and knees.

"Sorry," she called out. "Was it supposed to do that?"

Abruptly, Sarah clapped both hands over her mouth and bent at the waist. The sound of her guffaw echoed over the yard.

Chapter Nineteen

MOLLY AND JOSIAH'S agreement didn't last eighteen weeks.

Every evening at eight, his phone lit up with her message. `Safe.`

And he texted in reply, `Safe.`

His enjoyment of his days had narrowed down to that single word.

The next Saturday, he called another coven meeting at the safe house in Birmingham. After ditching his Audi and taking evasive maneuvers, he picked up the Camry from the new neighborhood where Anson had parked it. This time Steven attended the coven meeting in person. After they cast their circle, Josiah looked around.

Anson wore his usual mild expression. Maria stood with her arms crossed, looking ready to do battle. Richard kept his gaze fixed on the floor while he sucked at his teeth and looked like he was swallowing back a whole hell of a lot. Steven glanced around the group too, thin face friendly behind heavy-framed glasses.

He didn't strictly need the glasses, Josiah knew. Steven wore them to keep people at a distance.

Of them all, Henry was the only one who appeared preoccupied. He stood reading through some papers with a frown.

"When you're ready," Josiah said to him.

Henry replied, "I've been ready for days." When he looked up from his papers, his icy gaze speared Josiah.

That confirmed what he had already expected, and he nodded. "I see that Anson has given you all advance warning of what this meeting might entail."

Richard's face flooded with furious disgust. "So Molly Sullivan is pregnant… Really?" He barked out an angry laugh. "We've had our differences, but I didn't expect you to be so goddamn typical."

"I'm not so goddamn typical." He kept his voice calm. "She's that goddamn extraordinary."

"If this devolves into a shouting match, I'm going to step out." Henry sounded bored. He was already looking over his papers again.

"No shouting match on my end," Josiah said. He stared at Richard, who flipped him off.

"I only want to know one thing," Maria burst out. "How can you live with yourself if you walk away from us now? That's like pulling out of everything we've worked so hard to achieve."

He reached for patience. They deserved their chance to vent and react. "I'm not walking away now. Molly and I came to an agreement. I hate it, but she won't budge. We've got eighteen weeks to try to find and take down that bastard. Whether we've achieved mission completion in that time frame or not, she's coming back to Atlanta to talk to the police and claim her property."

Everybody reacted.

Henry's eyes narrowed. "Interesting."

Maria's voice turned shrill. "Tell her to stay away if she wants to carry that baby of hers to term. There's *nothing* like the pain of losing your child."

Richard laughed angrily again. "She's a total fucking stranger, and you're letting her dictate what happens to us? After all the time we gave you… Un-fucking-believable."

Josiah's resolve to keep hold of his temper vaporized. "You didn't give me jack shit, Richard, not when I've financially supported all of you, and not when this has been your mission too. I've given you the time and opportunity to pursue your revenge—that's why we all started working together in the first place. And she isn't a fucking stranger *to me*, and I don't *let her* do anything. Even if I don't agree with the decision, she has the right to return home. If we try to stop her, that would be criminal confinement. She won't be back here for four and a half months, so we need to pull our heads out of our asses and finish what we started."

"But this might be perfect," Anson said. He smiled at Josiah. "Look, I know you've got all the messy personal stuff to deal with… but remember when I said we might need to try to shake something loose? Molly's return could do that very thing."

"Christ almighty," Josiah muttered in disgust.

Henry rubbed his jaw with the side of his thumb as he stared at a vista only he could see. "I like it." His gaze snapped to Josiah. "But what if that fails too? What then?"

"She and I haven't discussed the details of what comes next." Other than the most important things of all. Her first ultrasound. Their first date. "But I'm putting her first. That means if she needs me to pull out of the coven, I'm going to pull out. I'll set up a trust fund so you can keep going." He gave Richard a hard look. "I won't leave you in the lurch like some of you seem to think I might."

Richard started to look somewhat mollified.

Then Steven spoke up with a smile. "I think we should break into Sherman & Associates. Or Russell Sherman's house. Or both." Everyone else fell silent and stared at him. "What? I'd love to get a shot at what they've got on their servers."

If they did break in, nothing they found would be admissible, but pursuing a successful legal strategy had always been just one potential plan they might use to get at their opponent. And this would give them the opportunity to harvest a list of the firm's real clients, not the bogus, partial list someone had planted in Sullivan's office for the police to find.

"That's perfect," Josiah said. "Let's do it."

`Safe`, he texted at eight o'clock that evening.

`Safe`, she replied.

In Everwood, after the incident with the labyrinth,

Sarah called Sam to tell him they'd had a "magical mishap." He whistled when he stopped by the next week to check out the lawn.

"I'll pay whatever it costs to fix it," Molly offered, heat washing over her face.

Both Sam and Sarah looked at her, amused. "I don't think that will be necessary," he said. "Sarah's got a lot of social collateral in Everwood. I'll round up some volunteers."

Sarah underwent her next chemo treatment. Sam took her and stayed with her for the four-hour appointment. Afterward, Sarah took to her bed for three days. Unable to keep solid food down, she watched TV and napped while Molly brought her cups of tea made with turmeric, ginger, mint, and magic.

Molly's pendulum began to respond properly after two more days of practicing. As she suspected, it spun widdershins as her positive answer and clockwise as her negative. She started using it to figure out which meals would be the most advantageous for Sarah to eat and focused all her energy on cooking those. After only a week, Sarah began to look and sound as robust as she had before the treatment.

"I've never recovered so quickly before." Sarah gave her one of those smiles that lit her face. "And I have you to thank."

"Truly, it's my pleasure," Molly said. "I'm so glad I can help."

After her experience with the labyrinth, she had been

afraid she might be imbalanced, but with Sarah's direction, she began to learn how to cook foods, healing potions, and cast healing spells with her right hand, and to practice offensive spells with her left. The more she practiced with both, the more even and balanced her Power became.

"Because you're both things," Sarah told her, smiling. "Both healer and fighter."

When Sarah grew strong enough to walk up the stairs again, she took Molly up to the attic, and Molly got the chance at last to see what Sarah's workroom looked like.

The attic floor ran the length of the house, and it was massive, airy, and well-organized. The smell of herbs was pervasive, all coming from a tall set of shelves that covered half the room on one side. On the other side, bottles of unknown substances lined the shelves, some of them carrying liquid that seemed to swirl and twist restlessly within the glass.

An extensive library, along with cabinets that were closed and appeared to be locked, covered the shelves in the other part of the workroom. A large fireplace dominated one wall in the middle of the space, and a few Bunsen burners sat neatly to one side of a long table.

As Molly stood in the middle of the room, sparks of magic came from every direction. She felt drunk with possibility as she turned, soaking everything in.

Watching her, Sarah laughed. "I have no cauldron, as you can see."

"It's all so perfect." She gave a happy sigh. "I love

how organized you are."

"I don't like confusion in any state, not mentally or emotionally, and certainly not physically." Sarah walked over to the shelves that held potions and candles. "See how I have everything marked here?"

Molly walked over, noting the labels on both the shelves and also on the items themselves. "Yes."

"Think you can find anything if I send you up here on your own?"

She grinned and nodded. "Oh yes."

"Good. The cabinets are the only thing off-limits for now, and those are locked with a separate key. We'll get to what's inside them eventually." Sarah led the way back down out of the attic. Molly followed, and Sarah carefully locked the door behind them. "Always lock this door behind you when you leave. Most of the dangerous things are in the cabinets, but to be on the safe side, I don't want anybody up here I don't trust."

That sent a small glow of pleasure through her. "I understand."

After that, she began to run errands for Sarah, delivering herbs, simples, and unguents to nearby residents. On her errands, Molly met Alyssa, a young single mother with a five-year-old boy named Evan who suffered from a rare lung disease. The potion Molly delivered helped Evan breathe almost normally from full moon to full moon.

She also met Charles and Bertrand, a retired married couple from San Francisco. Charles's muscular dystrophy was held in check by Sarah's simples and unguents. And she grew acquainted with seventy-five-year-old Homer, whose rheumatoid arthritis was eased by one of Sarah's ointments.

And when she stopped to buy gas from Colin's gas station, he came out to chat. He told her that Sarah had saved his daughter Tallulah's life while his wife Sonja was still pregnant with her. Tallulah was a bright, healthy young woman now because of her.

Molly said, "The more I meet and talk to people, the more I realize how important Sarah is to this community."

"That she is. Heard she's taken a shine to you." Colin squinted in the bright morning light as he leisurely washed the windows of her Subaru. The sun highlighted the gray threading through his short, curled hair and the good-natured lines that marked the mahogany landscape of his face. "It's going to be a hard day when she leaves us."

Sam rounded up a group of high school students to gather the labyrinth stones and rake the lawn clear of the scattered gravel. Once that had been done, Sarah taught Molly how to set the labyrinth, beginning with the portal stones, which acted as reservoirs to hold the actual magic. Walking through the portal activated the spell, but if someone stepped into the labyrinth at random, the magic remained quiescent.

Re-creating the labyrinth took multiple volunteers and a long, sweaty day of work. Sam showed up along with Colin and Tallulah, Bertrand, Alyssa, three students, and several witches from the local coven—Delphine and her younger brother Remy, Lexie, Sylvie, Tasha, Cara, and Lauren.

Bertrand's husband Charles couldn't contribute in physical labor, but he kept everyone supplied with cold drinks, watched Alyssa's son Evan, and laid out the lunch Molly had prepared ahead of time.

When they finished, the labyrinth sprawled across the lawn as pristine as before, and Molly felt she had made friends with almost everybody present except perhaps for Sylvie, who was skittish as a feral cat and avoided direct contact with her.

Molly especially liked Delphine and Remy. The family resemblance between them was unmistakable in their regal bearing and long-limbed, muscular bodies. Delphine let her dark hair flow free in corkscrew curls and wore a pentacle on a leather thong at her neck while Remy had a spiderweb tattoo that covered most of his muscular back. Molly had come to realize how difficult it was to guess a witch's age, but even so, she thought they might be in their late twenties.

What she mostly noticed, however, were the closed, wary looks they gave her that gradually melted into friendliness as the day wore on. By the time everyone left in a flurry of good-nights, Molly felt exhausted but happy.

She belonged. In under a month's time, she had managed to fit in here better than she had in nearly forty years back in Georgia. There was something depressing about that, or maybe it was uplifting for what it said about the future. As she fell asleep, all she knew for sure was that her life felt better now than it ever had. She wanted to grab hold of it with both hands and never let it go.

The more she saw of Everwood, the more she loved it. It was a small town with a population of around fifteen thousand with a greater population in the swirl of neighborhoods and shopping areas that sprawled farther outside the town limits. She loved to walk the boardwalk and shop in the small boutiques by the water.

There was only one vital piece missing. Countless times she struggled with the urge to call Josiah to tell him something. But no. She was the one who had made the rule, and she needed to abide by it.

So every day at five o'clock, she texted the one word they had agreed upon.

`Safe.`

`Safe`, he replied.

In Atlanta, Josiah and his coven prepared painstakingly to break into Sherman & Associates.

They expected to run into complications, possibly even magical traps. Josiah let them decide how they wanted him to help. For his part, he would just as soon stay on the front line, but if something happened and he was caught committing a crime, he would lose his position as DA.

After some deliberation they decided the power of

the district attorney's office was still too useful and he should work with Maria to provide backup surveillance. Steven, Henry, Richard, and Anson would do the actual breaking in.

They would execute the break-in on a Sunday night. After they had finalized the plan, Josiah worked with Anson on where to leave the Camry so he could pick it up when he ditched his Audi in another public place.

"I'm starting to feel uneasy about this," Anson muttered. "You're vanishing too much. If you had no idea someone was trying to track your movements, you wouldn't be disappearing at all."

"We always knew this would come down to violence and risk." Even as he said it, he frowned. Like his old ambitions of political power, violence and risk no longer felt as acceptable as they once had.

If this were just a matter of revenge, he would have already given it up, set up the coven trust fund, and headed to California. But revenge was the simplest part of this. He could even give up the possibility of ever getting justice for what had happened to him. But Rasputin would keep victimizing witches, destroying not only their lives but the lives of their families, unless he was stopped.

He almost missed the eight-o'clock exchange that night, but at the last moment he whipped out his phone to text.

`Safe.`

She replied, `Safe.`

Back in Everwood, Sarah wanted to have a gathering on the summer solstice. "At first I didn't think I'd be up for it, but I feel different with you here. Do you mind helping?"

Even with Molly's gifts of energy and healing, they both knew this summer solstice was likely going to be Sarah's last.

"Of course not," Molly told her instantly. "I'm happy to do whatever I can."

They worked hard to prepare. Molly found a blessing in a grimoire she'd been studying. With Sarah's approval, she said the blessing over the food dishes she prepared the night before. It sank in over the night to provide extra nourishment and luck to anyone who ate the food.

When the day itself dawned, over three hundred people showed up to visit, eat, dance, walk Sarah's labyrinth, and take turns sitting in on a drum circle that played for hours. After enjoying a bonfire that lasted late into the evening, Molly was pleased to see Sarah's evident happiness as she said good night to the last of the visitors.

Then they called the day done. Right before Molly fell asleep, she whispered, "I love my life."

The house seemed to be listening, because it gave a sigh and settled around her like a worn, much-loved jacket.

Molly kept delivering herbs, simples, and unguents to people in the surrounding area, and Sarah began to teach her how to create uncomplicated medicines.

At first Molly didn't understand why certain medicines were better as a "simple"—which included tinctures—as opposed to an unguent, which was a thicker substance like an ointment or lotion that could be used for lubrication, because they weren't categorized in a way that she could recognize.

"Magic is an entirely different ecosystem from what we've created through science," Sarah told her. "Just because Tylenol and ibuprofen need to be taken orally, that doesn't mean the magical equivalent for a headache medicine will be the same. Certain spells are only effective in combination with certain herbs. And some of those herbs can only be taken orally, and others can only be absorbed through the skin. In a modern drugstore you can find pills to take for an upset stomach. In magic, you can rub a tincture on your abdomen and the magic is absorbed through your skin. Different systems mean different ways of delivering relief for the same ailment."

Once Molly understood that, her lessons on healing went much faster. She loved those, because they called out a nurturing side in her that blossomed and grew—but she studied offensive magic with the same single-mindedness that she had practiced back in Atlanta, as if her life depended on it, because one day it very well might.

Just as every witch had a positive and a negative, they also had a greater affinity for certain elements than others. Molly's two strongest affinities were to the moon and the ocean. At Sarah's direction, she went down to the beach to gather fresh, foaming ocean water under the light of the full moon, whispering over the jars until they glowed with Power.

There were defensive and offensive spells she could memorize. The most Powerful spells would be ones she created for herself. Most of those took at least a few minutes to cast, so if she became embroiled in an actual battle, her two main weapons were the telekinetic blasts and her Power whip that came out of her left palm.

She practiced spellcasting on the lawn with Delphine, who smiled with sharp-eyed pleasure as their combined Powers called in thunder and lightning while below the cliff, the ocean surf roared.

For practice with the telekinesis and the whip, she spent countless hours with Lauren, one of the Everwood coven witches who owned a yoga studio in town. Lauren looked like she had come into her Power around menopause, but her body was in immaculate condition, and she could spin and kick like a ninja.

"You've got one of the strongest Powers I've ever met," Lauren gasped once after a long session that left them both streaming with sweat.

Molly nodded, unsurprised. Josiah and Sarah had each told her the same thing. She muttered, "I hope it'll be enough if I run into trouble."

When I run into trouble.

Because as Sarah had once said to her, witches were lightning rods for interesting and unusual events. And she intended on living a very long and interesting life.

When they sat to drink some water, Lauren gave her a sidelong smile. "You know she's grooming you, don't you?"

"What?" She shook herself out of her preoccupation. "Who is?"

"Sarah. She's grooming you to take over running the Everwood coven when she… You know, when she passes."

"She is?" Astonishment threatened to floor her. "You must be mistaken. I'm the least experienced witch in Everwood."

"Delphine and I've talked about it. We both think you have the kind of combination that would matter most to Sarah—the healer side and the fighter side, and you're extraordinarily strong in both. Everwood is a sanctuary to some people who really need it, and the leader of our coven has to be strong enough to protect it. But the healing matters too. And I've known Sarah for a lot of years, and she's never invited any of her students to live with her."

Molly blew out a breath. "I thought she let me stay there because I offered to help, and because…" She had as much difficulty saying it as Lauren had. "Well, because time is short."

"Before you arrived, each witch in the coven was going up to help out a few hours every day." Lauren laughed. "Don't look so crestfallen. Your magic-infused foods have done far more for her than any of us could. But… yes, you should give it some thought, because sooner or later, I think Sarah's going to have The Talk with you."

Next to Sarah, Lauren was the most senior witch. Pursing her lips, Molly asked with care, "How would you feel about that?"

"I think you'd be a good choice, Molly. You have a lot to learn, but you also have a solid head on your shoulders. I like the fact that you're not too young but you're still willing to learn and cooperate with others. I also appreciate the kindness you've shown to Sarah, but more importantly, to others who don't have any way of paying you back. If the coven has an overwhelming objection, you might find the position hard to hold on to, but I'd back Sarah's decision. I'll be here to support you if you choose to take us on."

She was thoughtful when she drove away from Lauren's studio. How ironic that she might be in a position to acquire power after all. Not that it mattered to her. But she did like the idea of investing in her new community. She loved helping people who needed it, and if they needed her protection too…

She could see herself doing it.

The alarm on her phone went off. It was five o'clock.

Pulling over to the side of the road, she almost called Josiah to tell him about it and see what he thought. She was pretty sure she knew what the Josiah she had first met would have said.

But, no. That's not what they were doing.

So she texted, `Safe.`

And he replied, `Safe.`

In Atlanta, the Sunday-evening B & E didn't go off without a hitch.

They executed it close to midnight. The Sherman & Associates main office was located in a downtown high-rise, but they didn't need to break into the main office. As the most prominent law firm in the state, Sherman & Associates would pay a fortune for data protection, so they would almost certainly use an off-site server with encrypted security anyway.

But the coven had yet to discover an electronic encryption that Steven couldn't breach. Steven said all they really needed was to get him access to the internal network, so they chose to target one of the firm's smaller auxiliary offices located north of the city.

It was physically more accessible, located in its own building separate from other businesses. Also, if things went south, they had a marginal hope of gaining a minute or two more before either the police or some other form of security showed up.

But when the team of four went in, something happened, some elusive magical thing that shot off into the night. None of those who went in caught what it was, and Josiah and Maria were positioned at road points too far away to identify it.

"Get out," Josiah said into his mic.

"Roger that," Anson replied.

Steven might have difficulty with social situations, but at that moment he sounded entirely calm. "I just need forty-five seconds to finish casting this malware spell. Hold on."

Josiah heard fast-approaching sirens and got the sense of something huge, magical, and ugly approaching fast.

Maria said, "*Jesucristo.* Incoming."

"Twenty-two seconds. Almost there." Steven sounded like he was discussing the weather.

Two cop cars hurtled past Josiah's sentry position, but that wasn't what worried him. He was worried about that huge magical thing. Josiah said, *"Get out now."*

"Goddamn it." Richard uttered a foreign-sounding name.

Another immense magical thing hurtled in like a cyclone. A moment later the cyclone appeared in front of Josiah. It resolved into the form of a tall, stern-faced Djinn with sparkling, diamond-like eyes. He had with him the four who had gone in.

A hint of strain etched Anson's distinguished features, while Richard looked pissed. As usual.

Henry held a laptop in one hand as if he were about to place it onto a table. "I guess I can't put that back anymore."

Steven fist-pumped the air. "Forty-seven seconds. Got it."

"Yeah, and they know you've got it," Josiah muttered.

"My debt to you from years ago is now paid," the Djinn said to Richard. Then it vanished.

Richard glared at the space where the Djinn had stood. "Do you know how fucking rare it is to get a favor from a Djinn—for a *human* to get a favor from a Djinn? I was trying to hold on to that."

"Bitch later," Josiah said grimly. "Get in the damn SUV." He spoke into the mic again. "All the eggs are in my basket."

They poured into the car Anson had stolen just for that evening's work. As Josiah drove sedately away, Maria replied, "Good to hear. I'm headed out."

"Meet you at the rendezvous."

Ten minutes later, they converged behind the darkened building of a chain store that had gone out of business eighteen months previously. While Richard wiped down the interior of the SUV, Maria hugged them. She hung on to Steven for several moments.

The sense of something malicious and ugly still hovered at the edge of Josiah's senses. "Do you feel that?" he asked Maria, and she nodded, her gaze hard and shiny with visions. "Do you know what it is?"

"Some kind of demon, I think. But I don't believe they have a fix on us. Our obfuscation spells held."

He turned his attention to Steven. "You know that whatever team they've got guarding those off-site servers are working on that malware spell."

"Doesn't matter." Steven gave him a sunny smile and snapped his fingers. "I've already got it, baby. Even as we speak, a shit-ton of their info has bounced through a half dozen IP addresses and is downloading onto my server. Of course, it's going to take me a couple of days to break through the encryption."

"Everyone's clear we can only pull this kind of stunt once, right?" Josiah arched an eyebrow as he looked around the group.

"I'm just glad we lived through it this time," Maria said softly.

Josiah was too. He said to Steven, "First priority is a list of their clients. I want that as fast as you can get it to me."

Henry said, "A close second—get me their financials."

Steven bounced on the balls of his feet. "You got it."

After that, they split up. Total meet time: less than five minutes. Josiah went through the laborious task of winding his way back to his Audi and eventually back to the apartment. He was too wired to sleep for a long time afterward.

Everyone else had been relieved, but he knew better than to relax. Only time would tell if they had really gotten away with it and had gleaned the information they needed.

His attention turned to Molly as his thoughts did too often these days. He wouldn't have shared the stress in any case, but she'd been smart to insist on minimal contact.

The next morning he headed to work, already strategizing his way through the various meetings and decisions on the docket for the day. As he slowed to a stop at an intersection, he caught movement out of the corner of his eye.

A semi, approaching too fast. It roared toward him. He spun the steering wheel hard, gunned the Audi. A gigantic force T-boned him from the other side and spun him around. Not the semi, he realized, dazed.

The door on the driver's side was smashed in, immoveable. Not enough time to find his phone. He flung a communication spell.

Molly's voice, sleepy and confused, "What… Josiah?"

He should have said it before, but he was so often his own worst enemy. He should have done so many things differently. "I love y—"

With a scream of metal, the semi hit his car from the other side. He felt a gigantic jolt, and then everything went black.

Chapter Twenty

FORTY-TWO HOURS LATER, Molly's plane touched down at the Hartsfield-Jackson Atlanta International Airport on a sultry, late-summer afternoon.

Thirteen weeks into her agreement with Josiah. Over four months after the death of her husband. She was fourteen weeks pregnant.

Two plainclothes detectives from the Atlanta PD met her as she deplaned. One of them, a world-weary man in a gray suit, introduced himself as Frank Williams. "Good afternoon, Mrs. Sullivan." His tone was polite as he eyed her with a penetrating gaze. "I've got two uniforms appropriating your luggage from the airline. If you would kindly come with us to the police station."

"Of course." She kept her expression closed to scrutiny, her voice calm. "I expected as much. That's why I called you."

The drive to the station was riddled with pleasantries. How was her flight. Had she missed the Atlanta summertime. The air felt like pea soup today. Frank liked sweet tea on a hot day. His partner, Molly believed his name was Rubio, drove in silence. Apparently Rubio didn't feel the need for pleasantries.

Neither did she. She stared out the window at the scroll of familiar scenery and answered questions when they were asked. At the station, they took her into an interrogation room and tucked her luggage into a corner.

Was she under arrest? No, of course not, but Frank didn't mind if he said so himself: he thought it was exceedingly odd she would disappear for such a significant amount of time when her husband had just died and so many personal issues were unresolved.

Could she tell them what happened the Saturday night her husband died?

Would she mind going over that again?

They just needed a little clarification… Could she narrow down the timelines in her story a bit more?

She told them a deeply edited version of what had happened and stuck to it no matter how often they circled back around to question various points.

What happened the night of the doomed party. How she had emptied out the house safe when she left.

How Austin had found her at the hotel and chased her into the elevator. How she had filed a restraining order, hired Nina, found a place to stay, filed for divorce. She had given her hard copy of the Seychelles file to Nina, whose office files had burned in the fire, but she had kept a copy of all relevant documents in a zip file in her email account.

She left out any mention of Josiah completely. Funny. He was the most important part of it all.

Her composure cracked when she told them about the attack. Her memory had grown foggy on the details. (True enough.) She got away from Austin, drove her car back to the Airbnb rental, and realized she was in way over her head and needed to disappear.

True, true, and true. After spending months under Sarah's tutelage, she knew the importance of telling at least some version of the truth. Even if they weren't aware of it, many people had a rudimentary truthsense.

"About that," Frank said. "How did you disappear so completely?"

At that point she stopped feeding them information. "I don't have to explain that," she said. "I felt like my life was in danger, so I did what I needed to in order to hide and survive."

They didn't like that, so they circled back around again, taking turns and questioning her for several hours. She asked for water and bathroom breaks when she needed them. Her pregnancy wasn't showing yet, but she did have to pee a lot.

At one point, they brought her a cup of coffee that she left untouched, and later a sandwich from a fast-food place. She ate some of that.

As far as why she stayed away for so long… she had heard the news that her lawyer had been killed and her husband had died.

Frank had stepped out for a moment, so Rubio asked, "Why didn't you come back when you first heard the news?"

"Because the money in that offshore account didn't appear out of thin air," she said flatly. "And Austin attacked me for a reason."

"Had he ever been violent with you before?"

"No."

"Where do you think the money came from?"

As Rubio asked those questions, the door opened and Frank returned, followed by another man who redefined the room when he stalked in.

The newcomer wore dark slacks and a white shirt that was open at the throat and rolled up over the arms. He had a muscular, spare frame and moved like a wounded panther, limping slightly, his hard face expressionless. His amber, catlike gaze sparred with hers.

She had been leaning forward, elbows on the table. Now she sat back to tuck her hands underneath the scarred tabletop to hide how they shook.

Her hungry gaze soaked in details. He'd lost weight since the last time she'd seen him. He looked leaner. He looked mean.

Mottled bruises marred his deeply suntanned skin. A new scar slashed along the knife-edge of his jaw, curving around to the back of his neck to disappear into his collar. It looked as if…

Abruptly, she pressed her mouth hard with the heel of one hand. It looked as if he had almost been decapitated. Her stomach heaved. While she hadn't suffered any morning sickness, for a moment she thought she might vomit up the few bites she had eaten of the chicken sandwich.

The two detectives didn't notice her reaction. They had focused on the newcomer. Rubio looked shocked. "DA Mason. Good to see you. We hadn't heard you'd been released from the hospital, or that you'd already returned to work."

"I left the hospital this afternoon. Officially, I'm on medical leave." Josiah turned the laser beam of his attention away from her to focus on the two detectives. "But I'm making an exception for a few special cases."

"I see. Well…" Rubio gave Frank a look that clearly said *now what?*

Frank responded with an infinitesimal shrug.

Josiah's hard gaze swung back to Molly. "Mrs. Sullivan, I was one of the guests at the party the night you and your husband had difficulties."

Hearing her name spoken in his deep voice after so many weeks was like touching a live wire. He was so angry at her. He hadn't tried to speak to her telepathically. She didn't dare reach out to him either. Her control felt precarious enough as it was.

"I remember." She met his gaze steadily.

"Frank has filled me in on things." Josiah crossed his arms. "If you were so afraid for your life that you've stayed away all this time, what made you come back now?"

You. I didn't know if you were alive or dead. I had no way to find out. Hospitals don't give out information to anyone other than family. I had only the news to watch.

She waited until she could speak again without losing her shit. "I was tired of waiting and wondering when it might be all right to claim the life I deserve. I decided I needed to have my questions answered about *what had happened* more than I needed to hide in safety. That I needed more than anything else to confront this." She spread out both hands, indicating him and the two listening detectives.

His cold expression hadn't warmed in the slightest. He said to the detectives, "Go grab some coffee."

"But, sir…" Under the pressure of Josiah's icy stare, Frank's protest fizzled into silence. He muttered to Rubio, "Come on. Let's do as the man says."

As they filed out, Josiah pulled out the chair across the table from Molly and sat. Holding her gaze, he deliberately put his hand over the recorder that was stationed in the middle of the table and switched it off.

What was he doing now?

Even as she opened her mouth to ask, he said, "The audio might be turned off, but the camera isn't. They're watching everything you do."

"Understood." More than anything, she wanted to reach out to touch him. She clenched her hands together under the table. "How will you explain wanting to talk to me without the recorder on?"

"I'll tell them the truth, that you've been my CI and you've given me what information you had that's pertinent to another investigation. They won't like it, but they'll have to accept it." Anger blazed in his expression. He said fiercely, "The only reason I'm not biting your head off right now is because you look like shit."

"Likewise, because you do too," she muttered. Her gaze fell and skewed left to the new scar, and sudden wetness blurred her vision. "How are you walking around after an injury like that?"

"Magic. My coven called in a trauma specialist who arrived in Atlanta this morning."

She folded her arms and gripped her elbows tightly. "But how are you standing upright? You shouldn't be out of the hospital, not after an injury like that. I don't care what kind of magical healing you've had."

"As far as the rest of the world is concerned, I'm still in the hospital." He planted his fists on the table and leaned forward, the knuckles showing white. "What the hell are you doing here? You're weeks early."

A fine tremor shook through her. Pulling out her phone, she activated the screen, scrolled to the call log and held it up at an angle that allowed him to see but obscured the view from the camera mounted high in one corner. "Two days ago, you woke me out of a sound sleep around four a.m. Then I couldn't get in touch with you. All I got was an error message."

His hot gaze dropped to the phone, and the muscle in the side of his jaw tightened. She must have dialed Josiah's number a hundred times, only to listen to the same message over and over.

The number you are trying to reach is not in service at this time.

The phone trembled in her hand. He looked like he might leap across the table at any moment. He said tonelessly, "I lost my phone in the crash."

"Hospitals have telephones." She whispered so she wouldn't shout. She wanted to hit him. "You didn't call. Not even to leave a message."

His expression tightened. "I couldn't. I wasn't conscious until this afternoon. When I got back to my place and looked through my work emails, Frank had emailed to say you had called and were on your way back to Atlanta. I got here as fast as I could. You shouldn't have come, Molly."

She had been eviscerated two days ago. Now her raw emotions spilled out. "Your accident made national news. Did you know that? I scoured every online news service I could find, but none of them offered any real updates. All they said was that Atlanta's district attorney was fighting for his life after being in an accident involving multiple vehicles. Staying away was not an option."

"It wasn't an accident," he hissed.

Her lips went numb. "Somebody tried to kill you?"

"That's why you shouldn't have come back."

The words blasted her. Feeling buffeted, she flinched and then jumped up to pace erratically. "I don't care. I don't care. I'm done with this shit. You woke me up. You were trying to say something. Then your presence settled on the bed, and I could see the outline of your body. You looked like you did in New Orleans when you would lay beside me, only you were transparent." Backing into the corner underneath the camera's pitiless lens, she shouted, "*I thought you had died!*"

He sprang up, knocking his chair back, and launched at her. Pushing her against the wall, he leaned the length of his body on hers. Tears spilled over as she felt his taut, muscular length pressed against her. His scent was strange, overwhelmed with something antiseptic.

She knew so much more now about how to read a person's Power and physical state, and she used those skills to scan him. His Power was seriously depleted, his body under tremendous strain as he recovered from massive injuries.

But his heart, that sturdy, good heart, was still beating strong.

He buried his face in her neck. "You didn't catch what I said?"

Her arms locked around his waist. "No," she said hoarsely. "I was sound asleep, and whatever it was shot by too fast. By the time I had woken up enough to figure out something had happened, you'd fallen silent. Then you faded away."

"I said I love you," he whispered. "I should have said it before. I shouldn't have waited until impending death dragged it out of me. You were talking about your mother, remember? You said she'd always been a bitch to you, but she was getting elderly and you wanted to be available in case she changed. I thought, how like you to be so loyal to someone who doesn't deserve it. I'd fallen in love with you long before then, but that was the moment when I knew for sure."

She released a shaky breath. "I love you too, but you sure don't make it easy sometimes."

"I will," he said into her hair. "I swear it."

She snorted. "Don't make promises you can't keep."

"I'm keeping this one. Sometimes you're too loyal for your own good, and sometimes I hold on to my promises for too long. I should never have asked you for more time. It was easy to risk my life when I was the only one involved. Then it became unbearable."

"I understood." Her fingers couldn't stop roaming the expanse of his wide, tense back. "It made me frustrated and angry, but I got it. You've had other people depending on you, and you were right—you wouldn't be the kind of man I would want to be with if you could abandon them so easily."

"Fuck this fucking camera," he muttered viciously. Shoving away, he stalked around the room like a caged animal, then rounded on her. "Go back to California."

She shook her head, mouth grim. "That genie's out of the bottle."

His eyes flashed yellow fire. "It isn't. You flew back under your own name. That leaves your new ID intact. We can get you out of the city, to another airport."

"I'm not leaving." God only knew what their watchers were gleaning from this furious confrontation. She walked toward him but stopped with her back to the camera, keeping her expression obscured, because God only knew what it revealed. "I meant what I said. The agreement we made has blown up in our faces."

He slashed at the air with a hand. "That's not acceptable!"

"I don't recall asking for your permission." She searched his expression as his anger boiled higher. "You said it wasn't an accident."

"It wasn't!" he snarled.

The sick feeling returned to the pit of her stomach. "What happened?"

"I got T-boned," he bit out. "Twice. First on one side, then on the other. If I hadn't already started to swerve and accelerate, I would have been crushed. I threw the communication spell to contact you just before impact."

She felt the blood leave her face again. "Who did it?"

"The two trucks are licensed to a local shipping company. We know they were stolen, but our seer said there's a direct connection between the drivers and our quarry. She said he's here everywhere she looks. The drivers disappeared. We collected what evidence we could find, swabbed the steering wheels, and now we're searching through law enforcement databases to see if we can find a match." His mouth tightened. "*Milaya*, you need to reconsider. You're a corroborating witness." His fists opened and closed while frustration twisted his features. "Right now my magic is more depleted than it has been in decades. I can't protect you."

"I didn't ask you to. *I thought you were dead.*" At his expression, she rubbed her face and reached for patience. "I didn't return without taking precautions. This time you're going to have to trust me."

✧ ✧ ✧

JOSIAH STARED AT her in angry incredulity.

The time when he had pressed against her had been all too brief. Every raw, stressed cell in his body screamed for more contact. But as desperate as he was to touch her again, he had to confront this reckless, dangerous naïveté.

"You've gotten a couple of months' training under your belt, so you think you can handle whatever might come your way?" he said harshly. "I never would have guessed you'd be that naïve."

"I'm not!" Anger made her eyes flash with blue fire. "Give me some credit here."

The door opened, and Frank and Rubio walked in warily.

Frank said, "Everything okay, chief?"

Josiah rounded on them, his expression savage. "I'm not finished."

"Too bad, because I am," Molly said. She looked at Frank. "*I* contacted *you*, and I've just spent several hours cooperating with you fine gentlemen and answering your questions."

"Actually, that's not quite true." Frank raised his eyebrows and scratched at his chin with a thumbnail.

"We still have a few questions you've refused to answer."

"Is that so?" she snapped. "Tough shit. You don't have cause to hold me. I've done nothing wrong other than leave my affairs in a mess, which may be irritating, but it's not illegal. I'm not responsible for spoon-feeding every detail of my private life to you, *especially* when it doesn't have any relevance to your case."

"Says you," Rubio remarked.

She glared at him. "And it's not my job to speculate about what may or may not be going on. That's *your* job."

Verbally, she was on fire, but Josiah suddenly realized how dark the circles were underneath her eyes, how brittle the damp sheen was in her blue gaze. She had been through hell these past few days.

He needed to take her in his arms again so badly he had to turn away.

He was so close to blowing their subterfuge. For a blinding moment he couldn't think of any reason to continue with it. Almost he opened his mouth to spill everything and lay claim Molly and the baby. It would feel so damn good to finally say it.

If he did, it would shoot him to the top of Frank and Rubio's suspect list, but who the hell cared? He had alibis all over the damn city with the emergency responders he'd talked to throughout that endless Saturday night. He might need to go on administrative leave until he was cleared, but the DA position didn't mean shit to him anymore.

Both he and Molly were already in danger. They should be together. Face whatever came next together.

One thing stopped him. His injuries, and the subsequent healing, had taken every ounce of stamina he had. He was only standing out of anger, fear for her safety, and sheer, bullheaded determination.

And while the danger to him had made its presence known loud and clear, so far only he, Frank, and Rubio knew that Molly had returned to town.

Trust me, she had said, but damn, that was hard to do when her life, along with the life of their baby, was at stake.

"She's right," he said to the detectives. "This has gone on long enough. Wrap it up for tonight. Will you give her a ride to wherever she's staying?"

"Yeah, we can do that," Frank replied.

Josiah pivoted to confront her angry, exhausted face. "If you can provide us with a copy of the Seychelles bank statements, I'll consider that enough cause to believe there's a credible threat to your safety. Can you do that before you go?"

Her mouth tightened, but she replied readily enough, "Absolutely. Like I said, I've got copies stored in a zip file in my email account. All I need is a few minutes with internet access."

Frank said, "We'll stop at my desk on the way out."

Josiah reached out telepathically. <I'll get a new phone first thing so I can apologize for being an asshole. I'll use the same number.>

Her expression softened, and the damp sheen returned to her eyes. <Forget about the damn phone for now. Just go somewhere safe so you can get some rest. It hurts to look at you.>

<I would not leave you, *milaya*.> Josiah held her gaze. <Not for anything, except right now you're better off without me.>

Her mouth worked. She shook her head but didn't try to argue.

"Are… we done?" Rubio asked, looking cautiously from one to the other.

"We're done," Josiah said. "At least for the moment. After you get a copy of the zip file and verify everything, have a squad car stationed outside wherever she stays tonight. I want a police presence on her twenty-four seven. Is that clear?"

"Crystal," replied Frank.

Josiah leaned back against the table, ostensibly to wait as the others left, but mostly because he wasn't sure his legs would hold him up any longer. His body ached all over, especially in his hip and neck where he had taken the most damage.

Molly wasn't fooled. She gave him a grim look as she followed Frank. Rubio was the last to leave and wheeled her luggage out.

When Josiah was alone, he rubbed the back of his neck and let his shoulders sag. He'd broken into a light sweat from the effort to stay upright.

But his night wasn't over yet. He had to convince his

coven that watching over Molly was the right thing to do.

He could hear their arguments already, and they were all valid points. Right now they were stretched too thin. They had other urgent matters to attend to, like following leads from the crash site as quickly as possible before they went cold. And protecting Molly wasn't in their mission.

But keeping watch for any suspicious activity that might happen around her… that might just sell it to them.

After catching his breath, he pushed upright and limped out. As he passed through the squad room, Molly sat at a desk while Frank leaned over her. Their attention was focused on the computer screen in front of them.

As Josiah's gaze lingered on the pair, she sat back, and Frank let out a low whistle. "I thought my inbox was bad, but yours takes the prize. People cared about what happened to you."

"I guess they did," she said. Her voice had gone husky with emotion. "There's the zip file."

"I'll take it from here," Frank told her. Once she moved out of the way, he palmed the mouse. A moment later, his eyes narrowed, and he straightened. "Okay lady. Like the DA said, looks like you've got a credible threat."

Josiah didn't wait to hear more. He stopped by the scheduling desk to see if he could catch a ride from a squad car. The desk sergeant assured him they could take him back to his apartment, and he limped outside to meet the patrolmen.

Half an hour later, when he unlocked his front door and walked inside, he found his coven waiting for him. All of them.

He gave their tense, unhappy faces a thoughtful look as he limped over to the nearest leather armchair and eased into it with a grunt. Everything in his body hurt.

"What?" he said.

"What are you doing, running around all over the place?" Maria strode over to glare at him point-blank. "You nearly died. The specialist said to take it easy!"

He closed his eyes. Gods, what he wouldn't give for the chance to simply rest until he woke up naturally. "I know."

"You can't keep pushing yourself like this. Maybe the crash didn't kill you, but a heart attack could." She squeezed his hand.

"I need a new phone. Then I'll go to bed, I promise."

"I'll get you one," Steven offered.

Josiah nodded his thanks. "What else? You didn't gather here because I ignored doctor's orders."

Anson said grimly, "I've been sensing magic sparks. Several discernible ones have appeared throughout the afternoon and evening."

He raised his eyebrows and looked at Maria. "People?"

She nodded. "I think so. They haven't appeared all at once, and they haven't converged, but I think there's a gathering of some kind going on. I mean… other than us, of course. We've gathered too."

His breathing suspended as he absorbed the news. "Are they friendly or unfriendly?"

"That's unclear."

"Do they connect to our mission?" Richard asked.

At that, she didn't hesitate. "Very much so."

"Doesn't sound very friendly to me," Henry muttered.

"We need to take turns keeping watch," Josiah said. "See what kind of activity occurs and if we can get a lock on their locations."

Anson said, "Agreed."

"I regret I can't help with that at the moment," Josiah told them. Sick exhaustion dragged at him, and he raged against it.

"Nothing's more important than you recovering your energy ASAP," Henry said. "We need you for whatever comes next."

"Agreed," Richard said.

He didn't have any other choice. The sooner he recovered, the sooner he could reunite with Molly to face whatever came next. Damn the subterfuge and the lying. He was *done.*

But there was one last thing he needed to attend to before he could fall into bed.

"There's something else you should know," Josiah said. "Molly's returned to Atlanta. She heard about what had happened to me, and she was worried I might have died. So far the only people who know she's back are the detectives working the case surrounding her husband and, of course, me. I went to the station to see what was going on. They were questioning her this evening."

He paused to look around, gauging their reactions to the news. Richard glowered. Anson and Maria looked noncommittal. Henry wore a more skeptical expression. As always, Steven looked friendly. It was his go-to face. That and his heavy-framed glasses camouflaged his dangerous, lightning-fast brain.

Then Maria sighed and rubbed her eyes. "I would have flown back too if I were her."

"We need to keep watch on her too," Josiah told them.

"To do what, exactly?" Richard asked. "It's not our job to babysit her."

"Hold on now," Henry interjected. "We have the arrival of unknown magic users, Josiah's been attacked, and now Molly's here. It's all got to be connected. I think we should take turns keeping watch in her vicinity. And Josiah shouldn't be left alone either, not until he's back on his feet."

"I agree on both counts," Anson said. "Josiah and Molly are our two known hot spots. If things are reaching a boiling point, it's likely they're going to boil over in either one of their directions."

Steven pushed his glasses up his straight nose and smiled. "And also! Since we're all together and Josiah didn't die, I have news too. I broke the encryption on the data we stole. We now have a full client list from Sherman & Associates."

Chapter Twenty-One

THEY ALL TURNED to stare at him.

"You couldn't lead with that?" Richard snapped.

As Steven's clever gaze touched on their expressions, he shrugged. "Everybody had a lot to say, and we've been busy."

Anson rubbed his face. "True enough. Do you have it with you?"

"Yep." Steven held up a flash drive. "I also have their financial records."

"That settles it," Henry said. "I'm staying here. I need to comb the data to see if I can find matches between clients and the financial activity we've uncovered."

"And you need to get me another phone, activated to my old number," Josiah said to Steven. "ASAP. I want it functioning and in my hand whether I'm awake or not."

"Right," Steven replied.

Anson, Richard, and Maria looked at each other. The whole coven knew it was better to keep Richard and Josiah separate when possible. Maria said to Richard,

"You and I can take turns keeping watch on Molly."

Anson added, "I'll stay here with Henry until Steven gets back. Then I can run interference between you and bring you what you need."

Josiah felt the weight of decision fall away. The coven had sorted themselves out without him. Frank and Rubio had given him the address where Molly was staying, so he passed that on to them and pushed to his feet. "Looks like I'm not needed for now."

"Yes, you go to bed," Maria said.

Like Molly when she had been injured, what he really needed was a couple of weeks of good nutrition and rest, but he didn't think he was going to get it.

What the hell, he'd settle for his Power returning. He could rest when he was dead.

"Wake me if anything breaks loose," he told them.

Limping to his darkened bedroom, he stretched out his aching body with care. He didn't remember when his head hit the pillow as unconsciousness washed over him in a dark tide.

FRANK AND RUBIO escorted Molly to a motel and stayed until a squad car arrived. The two uniformed police would remain stationed in the parking lot until morning.

Frank handed her a card before they left. "Keep us apprised of your whereabouts. We can't provide a police presence if we don't know where you are."

"Understood." She took the card.

Once they had stepped out and she could latch the security chain, she breathed a sigh of relief. She was tired, and the sandwich hadn't given her a lot of mileage. She needed real food, but it was also late enough she didn't want to leave the room. She had a bottle of water in her purse and some dried fruit and nuts in her suitcase. That would have to do until tomorrow.

It was all logistics. She didn't care. The only thing that mattered was that Josiah was alive.

Sitting sat at the edge of the bed, she called Sarah, who picked up on the first ring.

"There you are. We were getting worried."

"Sorry, this is the first time I've had a chance to call. The police questioned me for hours. I only just got to my motel room." Now that she was in private, she let tears spill over. "Josiah was hurt badly, but he's alive. His coven brought in a magical trauma specialist. He came to the police station—he said the crash wasn't an accident."

"That's… complicated," Sarah said. "It's such good news that he survived and he's all right, but are *you* safe?"

"For now, yes. Nobody knows where I am, and they put a police car outside."

"I'll let the others know. You've got to be exhausted."

"I am. I'm going to get some sleep. Then I'll start tackling my to-do list."

"I want you to check in often after you wake up."

"I will," she promised. "Sarah, thank you for everything. Please thank the others again for me too."

"Of course. In this coven, we look out for each other. Always remember that. Now get some rest."

"You too."

After washing and getting ready for bed, Molly rummaged in her carry-on for the new tablet she'd bought at the airport. She went through the setup instructions, connected to the motel's Wi-Fi, and logged back into her old email account.

She had over a thousand emails from friends, acquaintances, old coworkers and volunteers she had worked with, Tanya Martin. So many people, offering condolences, asking for her to get in touch, sending good wishes. The volume was overwhelming.

There wasn't anything from her mother, but email was not Gloria's preferred method of communication. She had an email account that she checked from time to time, but the phone was how she chose to reach out, and Molly knew her old phone number had been deactivated after the bill had gone unpaid.

Julia had sent dozens of emails. Dozens. Molly covered her mouth as she scrolled through them. She opened some at random and read through them. The first ones sounded calmer, but the later emails were more erratic. She let her head hang and sighed.

She was a bad friend. Julia had listened to her so many times over the past several years, and Molly had dropped her without so much as a word.

And she was here to confront everything she had left dangling from her old life, not just to deal with legalities, possibly confront bad guys, or claim her estate.

First things first. She composed a blast email that was warm and reassuring but not apologetic. She would not apologize for doing what she needed to do to stay safe. She also didn't go into details. The fact that she was a person of interest in an ongoing police investigation was nobody's business.

She sent the blast email off to everybody except for her mother, Julia, and her real estate agent, Tanya. For each of them, she composed personal messages and added her new phone number. After sending those, there was nothing more she could do that night, so she went to bed.

Where was Josiah resting? Was his coven looking out for him like Molly's was looking after her? She stared sightlessly at the darkened ceiling until her eyelids closed and she drifted into a doze.

Her phone shrilled. Josiah. Bolting to a sitting position, she snatched it up. "Hello?"

Julia's choked voice sounded on the other end. "Molly, is that really you?"

Disappointment plunged her eagerness into a downward spiral. She glanced at the motel's luminous red bedside alarm clock. The time was just after midnight. It was stupid to think he might have called. If he was anything like she was when she'd been injured, he must be deeply asleep. He might not wake up until the next afternoon, if then.

"Yes," she said. "It's really me."

"Oh my God." Julia started sobbing.

It took several minutes of disjointed conversation to calm her down. It sounded like Julia had been drinking, but Molly stuck with it.

"I still can't believe I'm talking to you," Julia said. "I have to see you in person. When can we get together?"

"I don't know," she replied. "There's so much going on right now. I spent hours at the police station. They wanted to question me about what happened the night Austin died."

"Why did you disappear without a word? Not even your mother knew where you'd gone."

"Austin attacked me that night," she said bluntly. Not everybody needed to know every little thing about her life, but she was also done with pulling her punches or sugarcoating reality. "I got away, but I was afraid he might try again."

"Oh. My. God," Julia breathed. "Where are you? I really need to see you."

"Now?" She glanced at the clock again. "It's almost one in the morning. What about Drew and Philip?"

"A lot has changed since you left. I left Philip and went into therapy, a-and my parents have taken Drew for the summer so I can get my shit together. They're taking great care of him." Julia sounded bitter. "They're taking him to s-swim lessons and riding therapy, and he loves it. He's better off with them than he ever was with me."

"I don't believe that," Molly said in a gentle voice.

"I do." Julia laughed wildly. She sounded

dangerously unsteady. "I don't know what I'm going to do, Molly."

"Well, speaking for tonight, I don't know that you should come here. It sounds like you've been drinking. You shouldn't be on the road."

"Yes, I've been drinking, but so what? Who cares!" Julia exclaimed. "I can get a taxi. Come on. I've got things I need to say to you, and I've had them bottled up inside for months. Please?"

Ugh. She let her head hang again as she considered. It might be one in the morning in Atlanta, but her body clock thought it was three hours earlier, and now she'd napped she felt wide awake. "Sure, come on over." She gave Julia the address of the motel and her room number.

Julia promised, "I'll be there soon."

Once they disconnected, Molly climbed out of bed. She didn't want to meet Julia in her pajamas, so she dressed in jeans, athletic shoes, and a comfortable pullover sweater. After twitching the bedspread back into place, she brushed her hair and ate a large handful of dried fruit and nuts.

A knock sounded at her door. Looking through the peephole, she saw Julia standing with one of the uniformed police officers. It had started raining at some point, and the parking lot was full of puddles.

The officer wore a severe expression. When Molly opened the door, she jingled a set of car keys. "When Miss Oliver pulled up, I came over to make sure everything was all right and smelled alcohol on her breath. Do you two know each other?"

Molly looked at Julia's familiar Volvo parked at the wrong angle, and then she confronted a miserable-looking Julia. "You promised to take a taxi."

"I know, but I didn't want to wait for one," Julia replied tearfully. "I thought, what could be the harm? Everybody would be in bed. How could I know there would be a cop car sitting in the middle of the parking lot?"

Molly bit back another sigh. She asked the officer, "Is there any way you can let this go?"

"Yes. Take her keys and don't give them back until she's sober. It's not my job to book her for a DUI while I'm on another assignment." The officer gave her a significant look.

"You got it," Molly promised. She accepted the keys and stuck them in her pocket. Then she turned to Julia, who slammed into her, hugging her tight.

"My God, it's so good to see you!"

Molly returned her hug and pulled her inside. After locking the door, she ran her gaze over Julia.

Julia didn't look good. Normally she wore makeup, but not now. Stress lined her pretty face, and her skin was puffy.

"I can't believe how great you look," Julia said when they separated. "You're so tanned, and your hair is amazing. The weather here has been awful."

"You look good too," Molly said.

"Liar," Julia said without heat. "I know I look horrible. But hey, I brought us some pinot noir. It's not a lemon drop martini lunch, but at least it's something."

As she fished two bottles out of her leather tote bag, Molly told her, "I won't have any, but I've got your keys now, so you go ahead if you want."

Looking disappointed, Julia squinted at her. "Are you sure? It's not like you to turn down a good pinot. Red wine was always your favorite."

"I'm sure."

"Well, I'm going to have some."

Looking defiant, Julia went into the bathroom to grab a plastic motel cup while Molly sat at the small dinette table near the window. Julia opened the wine, poured herself a full cup, and sat in the opposite chair.

She asked, "What are you doing that's making you look so happy? And is there any chance you've got any left over that you can give to me?"

Julia took a big gulp of wine. Her smile looked sharp and desperate, and after that first tight hug, she had avoided looking directly at Molly.

Molly replied carefully, "I don't think happiness works like that, Juls. Everybody's got to work things out for themselves. You said you started therapy. When did that happen?"

"About a month after you disappeared, and… and… and Austin died." Julia drank more wine. "I really felt it when you were no longer around to listen to me vent, you know?"

Molly watched her pour more wine into her cup. "How's therapy going?"

"Hell, I don't know." Julia's chuckle sounded unamused. "I hate it actually, but nobody promised me it would be fun. I'm seeing the guy Janet went to. You remember when she and Todd went through their rough patch? Janet strongly recommended this guy and said he was in network. Since we all have the same insurance through the firm, I thought I might as well give him a try."

It felt jarring to discuss old acquaintances from her past life. Todd was an associate at Sherman & Associates. While Molly hadn't been close to the couple, she knew Todd had missed making partner the previous year, and it had put a strain on his and Janet's marriage.

"I hope seeing someone helps."

Abruptly, Julia set her cup down and gave Molly the first direct look since she had arrived. "We don't have the same connection anymore, do we? You're not drinking with me, and I can see that you're wondering why I had to come in the middle of the night."

She tried to be diplomatic. "Don't take it personally. Things have really changed for me, but it means a lot that you wanted to get together."

Julia clasped her hands together on the table and looked at them. "I actually needed to tell you something."

"So you said. What's going on?"

"I owe you an apology. A really big one." Julia's

knuckles whitened, and her voice shook. "I guess it's one of the biggest apologies I've owed anybody in my life. Robert—my therapist—insisted I needed to talk to you as part of my healing. At first I resisted, but when he wouldn't let it go, I realized he was right. I had to do this in person if I could."

Molly frowned. "Okay, just spit it out. What's wrong?"

Julia's reddened gaze lifted to meet hers. "I'm the one who slept with Austin."

For a moment the words didn't sink in. Then Molly shook her head sharply. "*You* were the other woman? You always said you detested him."

"I did!" Julia swiped at her nose and sniffled. "He was an asshole. He was never good enough for you."

Molly's stomach lurched. "This doesn't make any sense."

Julia barked out another wild, unsteady laugh. "That's par for the course. Nothing I've done over the past few years has made much sense. I told myself it didn't mean anything. He was going to cheat on you anyway, and I said it was just sex. Nasty sex, the kind you don't ask your h-husband for, not when you're a mother and your husband is chronically short on sleep from working too much and your five-year-old boy sleeps across the hall, and God, this is coming out all wrong."

"Unbelievable," Molly muttered.

The purple panties would have looked good on Julia, with her petite, rounded figure, pale skin, and dark hair.

Remembering how Molly had found the panties that afternoon brought back an echo of the sharp, desolate pain.

Julia had been the one in her bed, cheating with her husband.

Tears spilled down Julia's pale cheeks. "I am so, so sorry. If I could take it all back, I would. I never meant to hurt you. None of it was ever about you, at least not until the end."

"You always did say you envied us." Molly felt herself grow distant, as if she were watching herself talking with Julia from a great distance.

Julia eagerly latched on to that sentence. "That's exactly it. It all got tangled together in my messed-up head. I felt trapped in my marriage, and I always needed to be available for Drew, and I never found time for myself. That turned into looking for ways to escape. I began drinking too much. I still drink too much. Then, after a few months, the affair started to make me feel sick. I thought I could keep it separate from our friendship, but I couldn't. You deserved better. You deserved to know."

"It lasted a few *months*?" It took a few moments before she could speak again. "And instead of facing up to what you did, you pretended to lose your panties so I would find out that way."

She felt like an idiot. All the supposition she had gone through when she had held that imaginary conversation with Austin's mistress. She had been right on some things, but mostly she had been wrong. Austin had acted against his "type," and she had never once suspected Julia.

Julia wiped her cheeks and searched Molly's face. "I can't tell what you're thinking or feeling right now."

Mindful of how thin motel walls were, she bit out quietly, "How do you think I feel? I'm over what Austin did. That's old news. But *you* did that in my bed, and *you* met for me lunch afterward. I was gutted that week. You looked me in the eye, and you never said a goddamn word. What the fuck is wrong with you?"

"I know." Julia started crying again. "I just didn't want to lose you."

"You know what I keep hearing you say? It was always about what *you* wanted, what *you* needed." Breathing hard, Molly stared at Julia until the other woman's gaze fell. She said, almost conversationally, "I'm tired of people trying to take things that don't belong to them."

Austin and Julia with their infidelities. The witch who had done so much damage to Josiah and others.

Julia straightened. "Just because I'm ready to apologize doesn't mean you're ready to forgive me. I understand that."

Molly stared at her like she was a bug. "You think?"

Julia flinched. "I deserve everything you've got to say, and you deserve the chance to say it. I only hope you can find it in your heart to forgive me. I still don't want to lose your friendship."

"Again, that's all about you." Molly fought the urge to slap her. "Did you see him after we met for lunch?"

The other woman recoiled. "Only once or twice, and then I ended things. I didn't even do it in person. I broke up with him over the phone the Friday before he… before he died."

Only once or twice…

Suddenly Molly felt done with the whole conversation, done with talking with Julia, done with living through the old, bad feelings from the breakup of her marriage. Done.

She wanted to be back in Everwood, cooking healing foods in Sarah's large, serene kitchen. She wanted to eat lunch at the seafood restaurant on the pier while watching the moody, restless water. She wanted to practice spellcasting with Delphine and train with Lauren. She wanted Josiah to come join her. She wanted to live her new, good life.

"I don't want to see or talk to you again," she said abruptly. "I don't want to think or speak your name. I may never forgive you, and whether I do or not is none of your business. I hope you get your shit together—because that's a lot of shit, and Drew deserves better from his mother. And I hope this conversation did you some good, because it didn't do a goddamn thing for me. Maybe I did deserve to know, but I deserved to know months ago. Right now all this did was pull up a lot of old bad stuff I'd left behind me. Get out."

"No, please. Wait!" Lunging forward, Julia grabbed

Molly's hand.

Such a tiny lunge forward. Julia liked to touch people. Molly had seen her do it a dozen times before.

When Julia's palm connected with the back of her hand, something flared to life and burrowed underneath Molly's skin.

A spell.

An unknown spell penetrated her body.

Shock made the rest of the room recede. She snatched her hand away. *"What did you do?"*

Looking pale and bewildered, Julia stood too. "I didn't do anything. What do you mean?"

"You touched me!" Molly stared at the back of her hand. Was it poison? Would it kill her? The spell was so subtle, and her skin looked unblemished and smooth.

"I-I just didn't want you to leave."

Molly barely listened as the back of her mind ignited. Someone had set a magical trap and laid it quietly. Now it was locked on her. She could feel them. They knew where she was now, in real time, which meant they could track her.

Which meant, if they were close by, they could find her quickly. And they had found her using magic.

She raced to the bathroom to scrub her hands with soap and water. It didn't help. The spell had entered her bloodstream. She could feel it coursing through her veins, alien and unwelcome.

Julia had followed her. "What's wrong? Are you okay?"

Molly rounded on her. "What was on your hands?"

"What do you mean?" Julia's expression was pinched. "You're starting to scare me."

"Your hands!" she snapped. "You had something on your hands!"

Looking completely mystified and more than half-panicked, Julia stared at her own hands. "I used a hand lotion from a toiletry basket the firm gave the partners' families at the Memorial Day picnic. That was before I left Philip. I was impressed. It's high-end stuff, and they gave us a lot of different things. There's face cream, and body and hand lotion, and shampoo and conditioner. They even had hair spray. Why, are you allergic?"

If the spell had been hidden in the unguents Julia was using, why hadn't it activated before, when they'd hugged?

But Julia hadn't actually made contact with her skin earlier. They both wore sweaters, and Julia had worn a jacket.

And the searchers were local, very close. They had never gone searching for Molly. Instead, they had planted traps and waited. Julia and Molly had done the rest.

Julia, who apologized to Molly at the insistence of her therapist, whom she had found through people who worked at Sherman & Associates. Maybe Julia's therapist wasn't really a therapist. At that point, Molly was willing to believe anything.

"You fool," she whispered to herself. She needed to

leave, now, as fast as she could. She told Julia, "We're done, but I need your car. Go home."

"What do you mean, you need my car?" Julia followed her. "We can't leave things like this. We need to work through our feelings."

"Fuck your feelings!" She didn't have time to waste. The spotlight of attention was traveling closer.

She needed her phone, her purse, and her kit of magic items from her suitcase. And she already had Julia's keys. Grabbing everything, she raced out the door, unlocked the Volvo with the key fob, and jumped in.

The parked police cruiser was visible in the rearview mirror. As she glanced at it, the doors opened and both officers began to climb out.

She didn't have time to deal with them, and if they followed her, they would be sitting ducks in a magical confrontation. Whispering a sleep spell into her fingers, she flung it at the cruiser. Both officers collapsed back into their seats.

Julia had followed her out. She yanked the driver's door open. "You can't just leave like this—"

Molly shoved her away, slammed the door and locked it. Then she started the car, reversed, and accelerated out of the parking lot. In the few minutes it had taken to extricate herself, the searchers had gotten even closer.

The wet streets were slippery and reflected light from halogen lamps, so she drove as aggressively as she dared. A van up ahead was moving too slowly. Stomping on the gas, she drove around it.

Where could she go? She needed to buy some time to try to remove the spell. Failing that, she would need to get ready for a confrontation, and she didn't want to have one near a neighborhood where people lived.

Grabbing her phone, she thumbed to Sarah's number and punched it. Sarah answered on the second ring.

Molly said, "I'm in trouble."

Sarah's voice was calm and crisp. "What's happened?"

"I saw an old friend. There was a spell buried in the lotion she'd used, and she touched me. She had no idea. She doesn't have any magic. Someone used her to set me up."

"How close are they?"

"Maybe twelve, fifteen minutes." She swerved sharply to avoid a twisted piece of scrap metal. Her mind was in hyperdrive, the edges of her vision delineated. "I'm not sure. I've never sensed anything like this before. The spell's in my bloodstream. How can I counteract it? Can I make it stop working?"

"Yes, but it would take time and materials you don't have. Depending on the strength and complexity, you would need to soak in Epsom salts and a cleansing spell for a good hour. If the magic is strong enough, sometimes it can take multiple cleansing baths over a few days to dislodge it completely."

Molly could hear the stress in her own voice as she

said, "You're right, that's not doable."

"We've prepared for this, so don't panic. I'll wake the others and get them ready. In the meantime, pick your battleground and let me know where it is as soon as you can. I need a focal point, and Lauren, Delphine, and Sylvie need to know where to find you."

"Okay." She paused. "If this doesn't work, I want you to know how grateful I am—"

"Shut up and drive fast. Try to gain as much time as you can." Sarah hung up.

She shut up and sped through the city streets as she sifted through various ideas for where to go.

The best place she could think of was an old airstrip northeast of the city. One of the charities where she had once volunteered had stored local historical documents, photos, and maps of the area.

Atlanta had several old, abandoned airfields that had gradually disappeared from the public eye. Molly had spent an enjoyable summer driving to each airfield and taking modern snapshots of each one to place in their files. Some had been repurposed into new housing developments or used for strip malls, expressway interchanges, or roads, but a few areas still lay fallow and unused.

This airstrip was one of them, located in a large, overgrown field. No one lived nearby, and it was surrounded by a dense cluster of forest.

She called Sarah again. "I've got the place."

"Tell me everything you can."

Rapidly, Molly filled her in while she pushed the Volvo to a higher speed. It helped to have a destination in mind.

Sarah said, "Excellent. Have they fallen behind at all?"

She checked mentally. "A little. Not by much."

"What's your best guess?"

"I've still got only about fifteen minutes' head start."

"Go faster," Sarah told her. "I'll update the others. I love you."

"I love you too." She hung up.

Her phone rang again. She was going forty over the speed limit and couldn't take her eyes off the road, so she answered without looking.

"Molly," Josiah said. His voice was hoarse and gravelly. "Where are you?"

Her pulse leaped with gladness and surprise. "You got a phone. What are you doing up?"

"One of my coven woke me. We had two people watching the motel. They said you knocked out your police escort. They'd checked into another room and ran out in time to see you drive off. They tried to follow, but they lost you. What's wrong?"

"An old friend wanted to get together, and I was stupid." Using broad, quick strokes, she sketched everything in. "I can't shake the spell, and I don't dare stop until I get to the airfield."

"I'm on my way. Keep your phone on and tuck it somewhere, like under a bra strap against your skin. It'll give me a focal point until I get there."

Pressing her phone hard against her ear, she listened to him breathing, oddly comforted by the sound. "Even if you break every land-speed record on the books, you're not going to make it in time."

"You don't know that," he said fiercely. "*I'm coming.* In the meantime, hide if you can. I can use our connection as a conduit to place some defensive spells on you."

Biting her lip, she considered that. Much like medicines, spells often interacted with each other. Sarah called it *relative contraindication.* It was possible Josiah might do more harm than good if he happened to throw a defensive spell that counteracted any of the offensive spells she'd been practicing.

"Don't throw any spells on me," she told him. "But I'll take any strength you and your coven are able to send my way."

"I'll give you everything I've got." Lifting his voice away, he said to someone else, "Get Richard on the line. I need to talk to him."

She was so focused on him she almost missed her exit off the highway. Signaling, she swerved right just in time and shot onto a two-lane country road. This one was winding, wet, and dark, and it forced her to slow down.

The Volvo's headlights threw images into the dripping trees. She caught a glimpse of a raven, a wolf. They had borne witness months before when she'd left her old life. It felt right that they had shown up for this.

Her trackers started to gain on her.

"I'm back." Josiah's voice came through loud and clear. "We're exploring an idea to get to you faster."

"I've got hairpin turns coming up," she told him. "I have to put the phone down."

"Don't hang up yet." He sounded so calm, so steady. "What's the name of the airfield you're headed for?"

He was working his heart out to find ways to protect her and join the fight, but meanwhile he hadn't had a chance to recover from life-threatening injuries. This upcoming confrontation might not kill her.

But it might very well kill him, because he would die before he let anything happen to her.

Except he couldn't join her if he didn't know where she was.

"Josiah?"

"Yes, *milaya*."

"I love you," she told him.

She didn't wait for a reply. Pushing her phone's power button, she turned it off. Then she tossed it into the drink holder and concentrated on the dark, solitary road ahead.

Chapter Twenty-Two

THOSE HAIRPIN TURNS cost her.

Maybe she had ten or fifteen minutes at best before they caught up with her.

It wasn't worth trying to get to the airfield. She had to stop now, before she lost any more time. Anyway, she was tired of running. Months tired, in fact, and she was more than a little pissed.

So okay. It would have been better if the area was by the ocean, or—she glanced at the clouded night sky—if there was a full moon. She was missing the presence of her two strongest elements, but she had to play the hand she was dealt.

She passed around another curve and reached a relatively straight length of road.

This was the place.

She spun the Volvo into a tight U-turn. There was just enough room on the two-lane road to turn around. Then, putting the vehicle in park but leaving the engine running, she ran to the narrow shoulder and searched until she found a rock that was heavy enough she had to lift it with both hands.

Jogging back to the Volvo, she set the rock on the floor on the driver's side, poised on its narrowest side in front of the gas pedal. Then, leaving the driver's door open, she dug through her kit of magic items for a piece of consecrated chalk and a vial of the ocean water she had harvested on the beach by the light of the moon. At least she had some form of her two strongest elements with her.

In the vial, the liquid shone with an ivory light. The blessing she had used when she had taken the water made it glow with Power. Jamming it into her pocket, she slammed the door.

How much time had that taken? Three minutes? Five?

Falling to her knees in the middle of the road, she drew a pentagram. As she reached each point, she chanted.

"Holy Air, I implore thee, attend to me.
Hallowed Water, I implore thee, attend to me.
Come, Fire.
Rise, Earth.
I beckon you, Sacred Spirit.
Banish all weakness and fill my well.
Power within, power without,
Bless my vortex,
Fill my hand,
Bathe me in the Moon's white light,

As I make my stand."

With each phrase, she brought herself more into alignment. Here was her placement in the cosmos, exactly here, with the elements gathering around her like friends around a warm fire… if those friends were as ancient as the universe and as essential as gods. Her vortex spun slowly at her feet, acquiescent for the moment, and magic poured from her left hand.

A wave of Power hit—elegant, sharp and distinct. She recognized Josiah's magic as it poured over her. He had found a way to reach her without using the phone as a conduit. She wanted to reject it. He had been running on sheer strength of will at the police station, but she also thought she might need all the help she could get, so she opened herself up to draw it in.

God, he was so strong, and she could sense he was boosted by the full force of his coven. The magic poured in until she felt as if she were floating above the pavement. "Okay, enough," she muttered. "I can't take any more. Ease up, love."

The magic eased slightly, as if he could hear her, or more likely, he could sense she was full to the brim. She anchored herself back into her body.

Another massive wave of energy hit. This time she recognized Sarah's rich, abundant magic buoyed by the Everwood coven. The ends of Molly's hair lifted. This time, when she felt her awareness floating up, she tethered herself only lightly to her body.

She marveled at what they had achieved and basked in their combined Powers like bathing in rare wine. “Holy shit. I owe everyone flowers and chocolates.”

Sarah’s laugh ghosted through her head. She thought she heard Josiah whisper, <Survive until we can get to you. That will be thanks enough.>

Then her own magic rose to match theirs. Lightning gathered at the edge of her vision. Her sight splintered, and she seemed to see several things at once.

There was Josiah, standing bare-chested in sweat pants with his feet planted wide, catlike eyes flaring yellow as he pulled energy up from the earth and poured it into her.

And there was Sarah’s dark gaze, watching her over a wide silver bowl filled with consecrated water. She thought those things were happening in the present, but she saw other things as well, shards of the past and possibly hints of the future.

Josiah, standing beside a grave. His hair was much longer, and his black suit looked like it belonged in a different time. There were tears on his bitter face.

A much younger Sarah, screaming in pain and joy as she gave birth.

And Molly saw herself as Austin swung a baseball bat and struck her with all his strength. She collapsed, and when she stood again, a night-skinned goddess settled a dark mantle of Power like a raven’s wings across her shoulders.

Sarah said clearly in her ear, “*Focus.*”

Molly's snapped back to the present, and her vision became singular again.

The approaching witch was very near. Molly moved to the driver's seat of the Volvo and sat halfway in, one foot on the brake while she shifted to drive.

Up ahead, a car growled around the bend in the road. It was some foreign model, racy and expensive. Just as when she had felt the search lock onto her, conviction settled into place. This was her adversary.

Taking her foot off the brake, she knocked the rock onto the gas pedal and jumped out. The Volvo roared forward. She wasn't quite fast enough, and the car knocked her off her feet. Hitting the pavement, she rolled, twisted, and came upright again in time to see what happened next.

The expensive, racy car swerved sharply to avoid the Volvo. The road was too narrow. The car plunged over the shoulder into an adjacent, four-foot-deep ditch. Molly saw airbags release while the Volvo continued straight off the curve and crashed into a tree.

Light from the tilted headlamps of the witch's car threw everything into exaggerated relief. The fancy foreign car wasn't getting back on the road anytime soon.

The driver's door opened, and a man spilled out.

She felt a brief, intense warmth, as if Josiah had put his arms around her. He said in her ear, <Kill him now.>

She knew all the reasons why she should, but preemptively killing an unknown person felt very wrong.

Maybe they could come to some kind of truce. She shook her head. "My rodeo. My decisions, my mistakes."

Yellow cat eyes blazed. <*Milaya*! Save your life!>

While they argued, the warlock climbed out of the ditch and straightened. He was beautiful with a striking Slavic bone structure and long, dark hair pulled into a ponytail.

He felt Powerful too, but with a sudden conviction she couldn't explain, she knew he wasn't as strong as she was. He wore jeans, sharp-toed boots, and a black cashmere sweater pushed up over tattooed forearms. She caught a glimpse of a blue pentacle and a sun atop a pyramid.

The man's dark gaze glittered. He said in accented English, "I was fond of that car."

"Who are you?" She studied him. She was all but certain he was Russian, but she couldn't reconcile this young man's brash confidence with the slyness of the ancient witch in Josiah's story. "Why are you doing this?"

"That is none of your business. I have been given a job to do, and I will do it." He strode toward her.

"Killing me isn't going to solve anything," she told him. "I've already given all the information I know to the authorities. People know where I am."

"I have had this conversation before with others." He smiled. "Next, no doubt, you will beg. It is all useless. I do not change my mind, and I have no pity. I will make sure you aren't alive to testify to anything in this ridiculous country's court of law."

She turned cold and calm. "I don't want to hurt you. I don't know who you are, and I have no grudge against you. Go now before you do something you can't take back. Book a flight, get out of here, and never look back. This is not worth your life."

The strange warlock smiled. "Do you think I am the only one you have to worry about, that you can send me slinking away with my tail between my legs? You may have acquired some Power, but you have a lot to learn, Molly Sullivan."

A rush of raven wings touched the edge of her hearing, and she smiled too. "You've been warned."

He threw his hand out toward her, fingers splayed. She recognized the gesture. She had made it herself many times over the past several months. His palm was tattooed. She didn't have time to decipher what the image was.

She dove to one side. Again, she wasn't as fast as she needed to be. The invisible edge of a massive blow clipped her right shoulder.

Spinning, she staggered and went down on one knee. Damn. That was going leave a hell of a bruise.

Watching him warily, she shook magic out of her left hand. When it formed a whip, she lashed out. His eyes bulged as the whip caught him around the neck, and he staggered and went to his knees too.

It was hard to do, but she closed her fingers, and the magic whip tightened around his neck. He made a choking noise and clawed at his throat.

Could she kill him this way? She'd never so much as killed what she ate for supper, and this felt intimate and ugly, as if she were pressing her own fingers to his flesh. Her intention faltered, and she swallowed hard against a wave of nausea.

Digging into his pocket, he pulled out something black and threw it at her.

As it flew through the air, it unfurled and grew larger and larger until it blotted out the night sky. I need to learn how to do that, she thought, staring at it. She didn't try dodge. She couldn't have outrun it in any case.

The black net settled over her head. Corrosive, burning pain flared everywhere as the spell ignited. She screamed, lost focus, and her Power whip fell apart.

<It's a death curse, Molly.> Sarah's telepathic voice sounded urgent. <You have to stop it from absorbing completely.>

<How?> The pain turned excruciating as it lit all her nerve endings.

If either Josiah or Sarah tried to answer, she couldn't hear them. Falling to her knees, she hunched over. There was nothing she could do to stop it. The curse had seemed physical at first, but when it touched her, the dark net had already melted through her clothes.

She didn't know enough about how to dissipate spells… she had no Epsom salts, no tub of water to soak in, no time…

The only thing she had was her vial of ocean water.

Ocean water, blessed by the light of the full moon,

and filled with nature's salt.

It was growing hard to breathe. The inside of her lungs felt wet. Coughing, she spat out a mouthful of blood.

She dug into her pocket, pulled out the vial, and poured the liquid over her head.

Nothing happened. There wasn't enough of the liquid to bathe in, and it wasn't imbued with a cleansing spell. It wasn't going to work, but she didn't have anything else to try. Sagging, she planted a palm on the pavement and tried to keep herself upright.

The water from the vial soaked through her hair and touched her scalp, and a cool, white Power washed over the corrosive pain, soothing it. Gasping, she looked up at the sky as the clouds parted to reveal the moon.

The Power grew stronger. Her magic rose to connect with it, and they fit so perfectly together. Of course they fit. Molly had created the blessing when she had gathered the ocean water. She had put herself in the vial, and as Sarah had told her, all the strongest magics were created when you gave of yourself.

Moon's light, ocean water, and her magic.

The Power of Three.

The pain vanished. Raising her head, she looked at the warlock. He stood, hands on his hips, watching her with a slight smile, unaffected by the pain he had inflicted or the fact that he thought he was watching her die.

Lightning filled her eyes and mind. Pushing to her

feet, she spat out another mouthful of blood. "*Now* I've got a grudge."

Astonishment bolted over the warlock's expression. He opened his mouth and raised his hands. Molly didn't give him time to cast another spell. Reaching deep into her core, she called up her vortex and let it take over.

It roared out.

She had called so much Power—from the elements, from the strength given to her by Josiah and Sarah, from her own well of magic—that she lost control. She was a holocaust, and *she didn't care*. Opening her arms wide, she embraced the madness.

The whistle of Air rushing in sounded like a freight train.

The vial of Water she had poured over herself multiplied until it became a gushing flood that spun widdershins around her.

Earth rumbled underneath her feet, and the pavement cracked.

The foreign, racy car exploded, and a gigantic ball of Fire billowed up. It roiled in a massive red thundercloud overhead.

The warlock, she saw, was still standing. That was an offense.

She was the Spirit that united the other elements. She flung the vortex at him.

It picked him up and spun him high into the air. He screamed as his body was swallowed by the cloud of Fire. After a few moments, the screaming stopped.

<Jesus Christ,> she thought she heard Josiah say.

Suddenly, Sarah's presence winked out.

The abrupt loss of so much Power unbalanced the maelstrom. Molly lost touch with Josiah. The cloud of Fire dissipated into black, billowing smoke. The ground underneath stopped shaking and grew firm again. The burned body of the warlock plummeted to earth, and the lightning left Molly's vision as the vortex died.

Pushing to her feet, she looked at the destruction she had caused. A spiderweb of cracks ran through the pavement of the road, out from the epicenter where she stood. The witch's car still burned, and an acrid, oily smell filled the air. The witch himself was no longer recognizable in the burned piece of meat sprawled on the pavement.

She had never killed anybody before. She stared at the body. His face was gone.

But he had tried to kill her first. Notching her chin to one side, she straightened her aching shoulders. She planned on living for a very long time. She would have the rest of her life to come to terms with how she'd killed him. Right now she was just glad she had survived.

And she needed her phone. Limping to the Volvo, she climbed into the ditch and searched the lopsided car until she found it underneath the steering wheel. As she thumbed the button, she looked around. The area was remote enough, there might not be a cell phone tower to connect to.

As soon as the phone powered on, it started ringing.

Lauren's name lit up the screen. Molly answered, and Lauren said, "We're almost there."

"Oh good." The ditch was rough and uneven, and the muscles in her legs shook. She braced herself against the side of the car. "Sarah was with me for most of the fight, but then she dropped out. I'm worried about her."

"She reached her limit and couldn't hold everyone's Power together any longer, but she's all right," Lauren said reassuringly. "Lexie and Remy are with her. What about you? You were just in midbattle. Where's your assailant?"

"He's dead." She looked back at the body and shuddered. It had started to rain again, and the drops hissed as they hit the flames. From where she stood, it looked like the earth had cracked open to let hell spill out.

Do you think I am the only one you have to worry about? What had he meant by that? Were others searching for her?

An SUV appeared around the bed and approached at a cautious speed.

Molly asked, "Are you in that SUV?"

"Sure am," Lauren replied.

She climbed out of the ditch and waved when the headlights caught her. The SUV pulled to one side, and Delphine, Lauren, and Sylvie emerged.

The copper tones in Delphine's corkscrew curls highlighted her rich, tawny skin as she stared at the scene. "We all felt when you released that, but daaaamn.

It's one thing to sense it from a distance and another thing altogether to see it. Remind me to never piss you off, *cher.*"

Usually the skittish one, Sylvie looked around, eyes gleaming with Power. While she was entirely human, she was Elven slender and wore her hair back in braids. "This place feels alive with possibilities. We can bury the body here. The forest won't mind."

Delphine gave Molly a round-eyed look and mouthed *oh em gee.* Then she said in a light, easy tone, "Nobody said anything about burying the body, Syl."

Sylvie blinked at them. "We've got to do something with it… don't we?"

"First things first. Everybody take a breath." Lauren's classically beautiful features were lit with relief. She pulled Molly into a tight hug. "I'm so glad you're okay."

"Thank you. You have no idea how much it means that you guys came back to Atlanta with me." Molly returned the hug with one arm as she held up her phone. "I have to call Josiah. I lost touch with him too. He's got to be worried."

As she scrolled through her list of contacts, a mechanical growl caught her attention. That wasn't the purr of an individual engine. Several vehicles approached. She met Lauren's gaze.

"Emergency responders?" Lauren suggested.

"That was a hell of a fireball," Delphine remarked. "It had to have been visible for miles."

Biting her thumbnail, Sylvie muttered, "Told you we should hide the body."

Or maybe that was Josiah and his coven? Molly held her phone to her ear as she watched car after car speed into sight. Two, three, four, five… six… Their headlights turned the shadowed stretch of road as bright as day.

She hit dial.

Josiah roared in her ear. "There you fucking are! Don't you ever fucking hang up on me again!"

Oh, yeah. She'd already forgotten about that. "Is that you, baby?"

"What do you fucking mean, is that fucking me?" he demanded. "If you have time to chat, the other guy better be dead."

"Yeah, he's dead."

"Good. I was bargaining for transportation with a Djinn."

A *Djinn*? "You mean you haven't left yet?"

"I've been a bit busy directing coven resources your way," he bit out.

She started the four-seven-eight technique. "You're not going to let it go, are you?"

"God no. Wait until I see you in person."

The vehicles pulled to either side of the road, and silhouetted individuals climbed out. A crawling sensation ran up Molly's spine, and the other women drew close. Delphine said uneasily, "I'm feeling a lot of magic, *cher*. Didn't you say this area didn't have many magic users?"

Do you think I am the only one you have to worry about?

"Josiah, remember when I said I took precautions?" Molly breathed. She counted silhouettes as they approached at a leisurely pace. Seven, eight, nine… "I meant to tell you at the police station, but I didn't get the chance. A couple of friends came back to Atlanta with me, and we're in trouble. At least thirteen more witches have arrived."

The silhouettes raised Power that snapped together to form a seamless web.

"Right," Josiah said. The connection went dead.

Ooo…kay. She pocketed her phone and shook out her Power whip. Delphine flicked open a switchblade and positioned the razor tip at her elbow, preparing to use her unique form of magic, while Sylvie started to whisper, making the edges of the forest rustle.

The silhouettes stopped advancing, and a man's deep, thickly accented voice said, "I suggest you drop those spells if you wish to live. No need for all four of you to die when I only want one."

That voice. It held the complex patina of countless years. That was Josiah's tormentor. Molly had no proof, but she felt it in her bones.

"Oh, well, if you only want one of us." Delphine's voice was thick with sarcasm. "Fuck you."

She cut into her skin, and as blood welled, it released a deluge of Power. In the same moment, with a snap of her fingers Sylvie finished her whispered spell. Vines whipped out from the trees to wind around the silhouettes. That broke the group's seamless web of

Power, but not before a blast of magic hit all four of them.

The world tilted as Molly and the other women collapsed. The magic looped back on itself, sophisticated and complex like the stained-glass piece hanging in Sarah's kitchen window, except Molly couldn't turn her attention away from this spell. Couldn't concentrate to use her Power.

Lauren gasped, "Mind trap."

Molly lifted her head, squinting hazily. Several silhouetted figures fought off the entangling vines, but still others approached. Every movement spoke of unhurried confidence.

A vast roar of alien Power coalesced on the scene. It landed a few yards away from Molly and the others' prone figures. Blinking, she tried to get her eyes to focus on this new development.

Seven new figures stood in the road, one at the lead and the others spread out on either side of him.

One of them said, "I will collect my favor at the time of my choosing," and blew away, leaving six behind.

The one in the forefront was Josiah, still half dressed.

She caught a blurred glimpse of his hard face. He looked inhuman.

He opened his hands, and a gigantic force exploded out from him like a bomb. It lifted everything into the air and blew it back. Everyone standing. All thirteen vehicles. The only ones it didn't touch were Molly and the others who were still sprawled on the ground.

Screams filled the air as bodies were crushed. Josiah and his coven hit the survivors with more individual blasts while one broke away to kneel by the incapacitated women.

It was a small Hispanic woman. She cupped Molly's head with hands that glowed with Power and broke apart the mind trap. Her hard, shiny gaze met Molly's. "Help him! He gave you everything—he doesn't have anything in reserve."

Right. Molly rolled up onto her hands and knees.

If there was one thing she'd learned how to do well over the past three months of helping Sarah, it was how to give someone else strength.

Locking her gaze on Josiah's broad back, she dug inside as deep as she could and poured all that she had at him. Briefly his head went back, and he staggered as the wave of Power hit. Then he sucked it all in and strode forward while his coven followed.

✧ ✧ ✧

ALL THE YEARS.

All the years of planning, training, preparing. All the years of patiently waiting.

They were all fuel for the holocaust of fury that drove him now. Grigori Rasputin's Power saturated the other group of witches. *Josiah could feel him.*

His roaming gaze took in everything at a glance. His initial blast had killed a few of them outright and injured more. Others were fighting to get free of vines that held them trapped like flies in a spiderweb.

But more were free and able to fight than not.

Buoyed by the bountiful flood of Power Molly offered, he drove at the enemy coven like a sledgehammer. Steven, Henry, Anson and Richard fought at his side while Maria freed the other women. Josiah coated both fists with a telekinesis spell, and those he struck didn't rise up again.

One guy, a lightning-fast son of a bitch, slammed a hard foot into his bad thigh. Gasping from the hot, stabbing pain, Josiah staggered back and almost fell. Then Steven body-slammed the enemy witch, and Henry angled in fast to land a brutal uppercut that lifted the other man off his feet and then left him crumpled on the ground.

At that point, Josiah looked up, across the narrow battlefield the road had become, and into a familiar dark gaze set into unfamiliar, handsome features. Grigori had done what Josiah had always suspected he might—he had changed his face.

The man looked thoughtful and stroked his chin where he had once worn a beard. He said, "*My ukhodim seychas.*"

We are leaving now.

"*No.*" Josiah roared, "*NO!*"

Even as he drove forward, determined to engage, a tangled wall of thorns sprang up between them. It grew rapidly to twenty feet in height. Richard screamed in agony. His body was wrapped in the wall.

Josiah could either batter through the wall with another massive magic blast, or he could free Richard. He couldn't do both, not at the same time.

He hesitated only for a fraction of a second. Then he ran to the trapped man and began coating the wall around him with dissipation spells. As he worked, he heard engines start from the other side of the wall. Some of the vehicles had remained drivable.

Furiously, he worked faster. The wall kept regenerating, but he kept recasting until enough of the sorcerous thorns melted for Richard to break free and collapse to the ground. Steven ran over to kneel beside him.

As soon as Richard was free, Josiah whirled to slam the wall of thorns with all the force of his and Molly's Power combined. Even as he did it, he already knew.

Rasputin, along with those of his coven who had survived, was already gone.

Chapter Twenty-Three

THE REST OF the wall of thorns fell apart and dissipated into thin air.

The fury that had driven Josiah forward dissipated as well. He looked around at the devastation on the road. Vehicles had been knocked at crazy angles, the beams from their headlights slicing through the scene at random.

Molly was safe. She crouched where he had last seen her while three unknown women surrounded her. The women had placed their hands on her shoulders and arms, their faces etched with concentration, supporting her as she fed him energy and Power.

Bodies lay strewn on the pavement. Turning, he counted six…

Anson.

Maria knelt by Anson's body, both hands flattened on his chest. No. No. Josiah lunged at them. As he fell to his knees on Anson's other side, Maria lifted her head. The rain had flattened her hair to her head, and tears poured down her mud-streaked face.

"He's alive, but just barely."

Josiah whirled to look at Molly. "*Milaya*, don't stop now. I need a bit more."

Her expression showed strain, but she nodded. The steady flow of Power pouring at him never wavered. God, she was so steady, so strong. A wave of love for her washed through him, so pure and potent, if he hadn't already been on his knees it might have brought him down.

He turned his attention back to Anson. Magic burns covered most of his face and chest. His breathing was labored and uncertain.

"If you still believe in praying, now would be a good time," he told Maria. He cast healing spells, holding his breath as each one hovered over Anson's body before slowly sinking in. Sometimes if the injuries were too severe, a body wouldn't absorb the kind of healing spells he knew how to cast.

A newcomer joined them. He looked up at one of the women who had been with Molly. "My name's Lauren," the woman said. "I'm a healer. Let me help."

He glanced again at Molly, who nodded as she watched.

"Yes," he said to Lauren. "Thank you."

Together they worked on Anson until gradually his breathing became less labored and some of the rawness had scabbed over. Josiah kept casting healing spells until Lauren grasped his wrist, silently urging him to stop.

"He can't take any more." Lauren's hazel eyes were kind. "But it's all right. Your friend's going to make it now."

He nodded and swiveled on one knee to look for Richard. Steven and Henry were with him, supporting him as he sat up. Tracks of blood formed runnels over his face and body.

"Enough," he said to Molly.

Her face was twisted with effort. She nodded and broke off the Power transfer with a gasp while the two women beside her sagged.

When the steady flow of Power stopped, spots danced in front of his eyes. He swayed and toppled onto his back. Everything felt black and raw inside, and he ached everywhere. His bad leg felt like it was on fire. He had nothing left. Nothing to resurrect, not even if their enemy decided to turn around and reengage.

"*Josiah*!" Molly fell to her knees beside him. She met his gaze, then closed her eyes briefly. "Thank God. You scared me when you collapsed."

He rested a hand on her knee. She'd been out in the weather longer than any of them and was soaked to the skin. Her lips had turned blue.

Lauren crouched by Anson's unconscious form while Maria and the other women checked Richard over and examined the other bodies. Quietly, Molly introduced Sylvie and Delphine to Josiah.

"I don't understand what I'm looking at," Maria said. She turned in a circle, staring from body to body. "What am I seeing?"

That drew everyone's attention. Steven asked, "What

is it?"

"They *all* feel like him. But he left. He was here… right? And then he left?"

"Yes," Josiah said hoarsely. "I saw what he looks like now."

"I know," she replied. When she looked at him, her gaze was hard and shining from visions, her voice sober. "And he saw you too—he saw every one of us. So none of these bodies can be him."

"Perhaps they're part of his family," Lauren said. "Family members can carry the same kind of energy."

Horror swept over Maria's expression. "That's what happened. That's what he did. He bred." Then she looked at Josiah. "All this time we thought we were looking for one adversary, but now there's a whole family of them."

Richard said roughly, "That may be, but we're not going to find or fight them anymore tonight. We have to get out of here."

"Do we put them all in one big grave before we go?" Sylvie asked. Her eyes darted around. "Yes? No?"

Steven rested his hands on his hips. "I think we should leave them. They fought and killed each other."

"That won't fly," Molly told him. "The Volvo in the ditch belongs to a friend of mine. An ex-friend."

Pebbles on the cold, wet pavement scraped the bare skin of Josiah's back as he struggled to sit up. Quickly, Molly put her arms around him to help, and he leaned against her strong, slender form.

"We set fire to the Volvo," Sylvie muttered. "No wait, that won't work. They'd still be able to read the VIN. We could always bury the Volvo with the bodies."

Richard barked out an abrupt laugh. "Lady, I don't know what planet you're from, but none of us can dig a pit in this forest that would be big enough to hide a car and six bodies."

"I can do it." Sylvie gave him a sly, sidelong glance. "If you wanted."

"Don't even go there!" Delphine jogged over to the Volvo. "I think we should try to get this car out of the ditch. If we can start it, we'll just drive it away. Right? There's nine of us, and our SUV is fine. We leave everything else the way it is, and we go." She looked around the group. "Come on, everybody who isn't injured and laid flat on your back, get over here and push."

"Let's get Josiah and Anson in the SUV first," Lauren suggested. "They should be out of the rain."

Henry, Steven, and Richard carried Anson's lax form to the SUV while Josiah got to his feel with Molly's help. "I can make it there under my own steam," he growled.

"Touchy," she muttered. She hovered beside him as he limped to the car and eased into the passenger seat. He had to lift his bad leg in with his hands. Afterward, he sagged back, and she leaned in to look at him nose-to-nose.

"I'm still pissed at you," he told her in a tight whisper.

She nodded, eyes darkened as she stroked his face. Her fingers were icy.

He moved when she did and clenched her to him while she buried her face in his neck. He said telepathically, <God, what you've put me through. I aged a decade while your phone was turned off.>

<What I put *you* through!> Her muffled laugh shook her shoulders until suddenly he wasn't so sure it was laughter anymore. <Let's agree to never go through anything like this week again.>

<Never again, *milaya.*> His mental voice turned husky as he pressed his mouth to the side of her wet head. <That's a promise.>

He'd had his chance to kill Grigori. He missed it, and he wouldn't try again. Nothing was worth risking either his life or Molly's, or their unborn child. Nothing.

Because they would always come first.

✧ ✧ ✧

THE NEXT THREE weeks went by in a blur of activity.

After successfully getting the Volvo out of the ditch and starting it, the group went to the new safe house. The least exhausted and injured drove the Volvo back to the motel and collected bedding and supplies while the others tucked Anson into bed.

Josiah and Molly slept on a pallet on the floor beside him. The pallet was hard and uncomfortable, and they were in a basement again. But Molly settled with her head on his shoulder, and Josiah wouldn't have traded it away for anything. He fell into a black pit and only woke again when she nudged him up so they could settle more comfortably on one of the new air beds the group had set up.

He took the opportunity to use the bathroom and drink a huge amount of water before sinking back into healing darkness with Molly's arms around him. The next time he woke, he was alone. Her scent was still on the pillow beside him, and his phone had been plugged into a nearby wall outlet.

A quiet growl of frustration escaped him. Most of the time they had just spent together was while he'd been unconscious, and he missed lying next to her. Picking up his phone, he stared at the date and time and then surged upright. Aside from that one interruption, he had slept for over thirty-six hours.

The new safe house was as big, isolated, and ugly as the first one had been, and they'd had plenty of rooms to tuck people into. He dressed in clean jeans and a T-shirt that had been left by the air bed. Then he exited their bedroom and went in search of the others.

Voices sounded in the basement. He limped down the stairs to discover a couple of card tables had been set up. Several of the group were sitting on folding chairs, eating and drinking while they argued.

Anson wore his favorite old bathrobe, his skin patchy where the burns were still fading. Henry yelled something from the monitor/computer room. A moment later Steven chimed in. They were both in the same room. Richard's face and hands were scored with light scars. Maria and Molly sat together, a little apart from the men.

Everyone noticed his arrival. Molly's expression lit up, and she hurried over. Putting his arms around her, he sank into the miracle of her presence. "Coffee."

"Food," she told him. "You haven't eaten anything in days."

"All right. And coffee." He sat, and Maria put a fresh cup of coffee in front of him along with a full plate of sandwiches, fruit salad, and hard-boiled eggs. Suddenly starving, he dug in. Molly sat beside him, resting a hand on his back.

Relishing her touch in silence, he didn't stop eating until he had cleared everything off his plate. Then he reached for his coffee and looked around. "Where are the other women?"

"They went home," Molly replied. "They wanted to stay, but they have jobs and lives of their own. It wasn't fair for them to hang around any longer, especially since I'm sort of back in hiding again."

He gave her a long level look and sipped his coffee. "What do you mean by *sort of*? Either you are in hiding, or you aren't. And you'd better be in hiding."

"I've been in contact with Frank and Rubio," she said calmly. "I told them I was attacked again, this time by magic, which is why I ran from the motel. They confiscated Julia's toiletries along with the toiletries from the families of other partners who work for Sherman &

Associates. After a test for magic came back positive, they brought Russell and other management in for questioning. The firm is denying any knowledge of it."

"Of course they are," he growled. His gaze met Anson's. He asked quietly, "How are you?"

Anson smiled. "I'm good, thanks to you, Molly, and Lauren. Getting better every day."

He relaxed and turned to Richard. "And you?"

Richard nodded. "Nothing that a little aloe vera gel won't fix. Lauren said the scratches will fade." Telepathically, he added, <Thank you for freeing me.>

<You're welcome.>

Henry and Steven left the monitor/computer room to join them.

"And also!" Steven said with a wide smile. "Now that we're all together and you didn't die again, Henry and I have figured out that the money hasn't been coming and going from just one client or company but from several. The main links are the Seychelles and Russian banks. We're looking at an organized crime syndicate. Our adversary is the head of a prominent Russian crime family."

Maria looked down at her clasped hands. She murmured, "I keep going over and over everything. He might never have been here until the night of the battle. What I was picking up might have been family members the whole time, but we kept looking for an individual."

Josiah reached across the table to cover her hands. "I remember it differently. We kept looking until we found him."

When she looked up, tears glittered in her eyes. "I was so sure."

"You weren't wrong," Anson said gently. "We just didn't have the whole picture."

Sitting back, Josiah clasped Molly's fingers and held her hand against his thigh. He drank some coffee, relishing the rich black brew.

"I'm out," he said. "Officially, as of right now. We all knew this was coming. As long as Molly agrees with it, I'll keep funding the coven's efforts. I'll be glad to strategize with any or all of you, and I would like to provide shelter if any of you need it. But I will not actively choose to go into battle again."

Molly's grip tightened, and a sigh went through the group.

"He may not let you just walk away now that we've played our hand," Anson said. "But yes, we all knew this was coming, and it's about time it did. You've done enough."

"I'll do whatever I have to, to protect my family, but I won't initiate anything." He shook his head as he replayed his memory of what had happened. "He was right there. I almost had him."

After a moment, Molly stirred. "I have another suggestion. I've been talking with Sarah, the leader of the coven where I now live. A long time ago, she created Everwood as a kind of sanctuary for people who needed one. She has authorized me to offer each of you up to a year's probation. You may come and live in Everwood to rest and recover while you decide what you're going to do next—because taking on a large, powerful crime syndicate is a hell of a thing, and you'll want to consider carefully how you choose to move forward. If this appeals, there would be ground rules you'd need to follow."

Maria stirred. "That's very generous of her to invite so many of us. What are the rules?"

Molly smiled. "They're pretty simple. You don't bring this fight to Everwood. Not ever. There's a lot of vulnerable people in that town, and it must remain a protected space. Also, like every other coven member, you would tithe ten percent of your energy and finances to the coven while you're there. Then you would get to enjoy the community resources along with everybody else. Exceptions are made for those who can't afford to tithe. While you can discuss whatever you like, wherever you like, you don't actively practice your coven's mission in Everwood's space, and at the end of the year you either need to leave or you need to join Everwood for real." She made an apologetic face at Josiah. "You'd be under a year's probation too."

"Fair enough. Every coven has something similar in their bylaws." He raised her hand to kiss her fingers. "I accept."

As the others talked over the opportunity, Molly tugged Josiah's hand. He rose with her and walked outside to a warm, sunny summer afternoon. Breathing deep, he lifted his face to the sunshine. When he looked at her, she was waiting patiently for his attention, her expression sober.

His simple enjoyment of the summer day faded. Eyes narrowing, he asked, "What is it?"

Her jaw tightened. "I have to go back. I was only waiting for you to wake up so we could talk before I left."

"Why do you have to leave now?" he demanded, pulling her against him. "You were so insistent about getting here."

"Well, for one thing, you're alive," she pointed out as she nestled against him. "That's the most important thing. Also, I've been busy while you've been down. Steven and Henry helped me transfer the contents of my checking account to an offshore one that Steven swears is secure. And the dynamic shifted when the police discovered the magical sabotage in the toiletries. After talking with Frank and Rubio for some time on the phone, I've developed a… shall we say… cautious rapport with them. I created an email account dedicated to keeping in touch, and I've promised to return if they need me to testify."

"I see," he said grimly.

She looked baffled and frustrated. "You don't sound very happy. I thought that was what you wanted."

"It was, before I realized how much I love you and need you to be safe." He rested his nose in her clean, lavender-scented hair. "But go on."

"I also reestablished my connection with my real estate agent. She swears she can sell my house within a few weeks. If that's the case, I can sign everything electronically and the money can be wired to that secure account Steven set up for me. I still haven't figured out how to safely get rid of the Jeep I bought—I assume it's impounded?"

"Correct."

She sighed. "And I can't access the retirement accounts without paperwork, and I don't know how to get a box of mementos that I'm sure is also in police evidence, but I don't really have to be here anymore. And Sarah's sick. She needs my help."

He tightened his arms. "Yes, you need to go. You're safer and happier in California. No, I don't want you to return—but we can cross that bridge if and when we come to it. I just can't leave quite yet."

She lifted her head. "I thought you might say that, and I hate it even more than I've hated any of this—"

He put a hand gently over her mouth. "I wouldn't stay to engage. I would only stay to wrap up my affairs and see how my coven wants to proceed, and I can pretty much do all that from this safe house. I need to finish setting up the trust fund for them, if that's what they want, and Josiah Mason needs to resign while he's on medical leave. Then he'll vanish."

She gripped his biceps and asked telepathically, <That's all you'll do?>

<That's all,> he promised. <I swear it. I should be

able to leave in a week or so. If you want, I can see if Frank will let me have your box of mementos, and I'll bring them with me when I come. Forget about the car. You don't need the money as much as you need to stay safe. Remember how I said you wouldn't get out of this financially unscathed?>

She replied, <I remember.>

<And your retirement account is still earning money, right?>

She nodded.

"Then leave it," he said aloud. "Someday it will be safe for you to access it, but you've already proven you're not dead, and to the police, no less. Nobody can try to seize it without your permission."

"You're right." She straightened. "I don't have to do anything right now."

He searched her expression. "So, we have an exit strategy?"

"Yes."

"One of us will drive you to Birmingham, and you can use your new ID to fly out from there." He gripped her arms with a suddenness that made her flinch. "I just remembered how mad I am at you."

She raised her eyebrows. "Then it's probably a good thing that I'm leaving?"

"It's never a good thing when you leave," he snapped. "And don't you ever fucking hang up the fucking phone on me again!"

She tried to slide sideways as she mouthed at him

silently, *Fine. Just fine.*

But he couldn't let her go. His skin, his body, his hungry soul hadn't gotten enough of her, and he was already going to lose her again for days. Pulling her close, he kissed her until it left them both shaking.

When he finally lifted his head, he found that his unshaven beard had rubbed her sensitive skin to a bright red. He touched her cheek gently and cast a small healing spell to smooth the irritation away.

Her gaze grew fierce. She said, "Hurry up."

He promised, "I'll be as fast as I can."

Chapter Twenty-Four

ON THE LONG flight back to the Bay Area, Molly purchased Wi-Fi and plowed through some of the immense backlog of emails she had received. Genuine people deserved a genuine reply.

There were several new emails from Julia. She deleted them unread.

There was also an email from Gloria. Raising her eyebrows, she clicked on that to skim through it.

"… I don't comprehend how my own daughter could treat me so terribly… leave me alone to bury Austin all by myself… and after you had the gall to stay away for months, Molly Ann, all I get is an email…"

Some people clung to their nastiness. She only hoped it gave Gloria some satisfaction, because her own daughter never would. She hit Delete.

She was exhausted and out of sorts by the time she reached Everwood but pulling into the parking lot at the old Victorian house by the ocean caused her mood to soar. As she climbed out of her car, Sarah left the house to greet her with a bright smile and a tight hug.

"I was worried about you." Molly held Sarah

carefully. Such a fragile body to hold such a wonderful, powerful spirit.

"And I was worried about you," Sarah said. "I'm so glad to have you home."

Fretting about Josiah did no good, so she plunged back into her new, wonderful life. She bought every member of the Everwood coven chocolate and flowers in thanks for their help, returned to her healing and fighting lessons, and cooked strong batches of Power-filled foods and tinctures for Sarah.

`I'm home safe`, she texted to Josiah. `And I miss you.`

`I'm safe too`, he replied. `I miss you, and I'll be there soon.`

Nine days later, a newcomer came to Everwood. He talked to various people about acquiring space to set up a new law clinic that would operate on a sliding-scale fee, and he rented a furnished oceanfront apartment. Excited gossip ran through the town like wildfire.

He was an up-and-comer, people said. A man of Power and means who would be a real asset to the town. A man to watch.

Soon after arriving, he drove up to the Victorian house on the hill and knocked on the front door.

"I got it!" Molly called out as she went to answer the summons.

When she opened the door, she looked at the tall, imposing man. Amber, catlike eyes smiled into hers. "My name is Alexei Volkov," the man said. "Come have dinner with me?"

Pleasure expanded inside, light and airy and filled with a sunlit ocean breeze.

"I would love to." She returned his smile. "But you should know—I never put out on the first date."

"*Milaya*," he growled.

Laughing, she threw herself at him, and she was never so entirely at home as she was in that moment, standing on her tiptoes on the wide, airy porch as his arms closed around her. After a long, searing kiss, she pulled back. "Come meet my new mom."

"I would love to meet your mom."

Molly took him inside and introduced him to Sarah. Then she left them to talk over things, coven leader to new witch, while she went upstairs to get ready for their first date. She decided to wear a soft cotton tunic and a bright loose skirt because her stomach was finally beginning to show a slight baby bump. Scooping up a patterned shawl, she went back downstairs where she discovered the two loves of her life were getting along together famously. She and Alexei left to eat seafood at the restaurant by the pier.

Much to his frustration—and hers—she didn't put out on the first date. She said, "I deserve to be courted."

"So you do, my love." He tipped an imaginary hat at her.

After another chaste but searing kiss, he left her on the doorstep. She watched him drive away and then fumbled her shaky way into the large old Victorian house that settled around her like a well-worn cloak. Wandering through the shadowed downstairs, she soaked in the peace and quiet while two tears ran down her face.

She was pregnant. She was allowed to be emotionally overwrought now and then. Besides, it was all so good, so good.

She put out on their third date. They had gone together to her first ultrasound and watched the grainy black-and-white images of the baby.

The doctor asked, "Do you want to know the sex?"

"No," she said.

At the same moment, Alexei said, "Yes."

The doctor laughed. "Which one is it?"

"Tell me," Alexei said, his face creased with amusement. "Don't tell her. I'm good at keeping secrets."

He was, diabolically good. *That would be terrible.* Molly sat up, eyes rounded, and said, "NOOOOOOOO." As Alexei and the doctor laughed harder, she caved in. "I already can't stand it! You're going to have to tell us."

"Congratulations," the doctor replied with a smile. "You have a beautiful, healthy little girl."

But that wasn't the date. That was baby mama and baby daddy stuff.

After the appointment, they went out for ice cream to celebrate, and that was their third date. Alexei had coffee while she indulged in chocolate chip mint ice cream.

When she was finished, he asked, "Want to see

where I'm staying?"

"Of course!" she answered with enthusiasm.

He had asked it in all innocence. She was pretty sure he had. Either that or he was just that good. In any case, he took her to the apartment and showed her the wall of windows that looked out over the ocean, which she *loved.*

Staring out at the water, she whispered, "I didn't know I could be this happy."

He came up from behind, put his arms around her, and whispered huskily against her neck, "Me neither, *milaya.* I did not know such happiness existed."

When his lips touched the delicate, sensitive skin at her neck, a violent fireball of sensation exploded between them. With a sharp gasp, she twisted around, and their lips collided. He ran shaking hands up under her tunic. The rasp of his callused fingers on her bare skin caused a pleasure that was almost unbearable.

She pulled his shirt, yanked open the fastening of his slacks. He bit her neck, walked her backward, pushed her down on the couch and fell on top of her, his body a long, muscled arc of aggression. They never managed to get completely undressed before she wrapped her legs around his hips and he entered her.

"I want so much to take my time with you, but not yet," he muttered against her skin.

"Shut up. Whatever." She groaned, digging her heels into the cushions and lifting her hips for his thrusts. Greed turned her selfish. Sliding a hand between them, she fingered where he penetrated, pleasuring herself while he moved inside.

Knocking her hand away, he took over. When he touched her, she climaxed. Swearing, he followed soon after, twisting up with the force of his own climax while she watched his clenched face and tightened her inner muscles until he had finished.

He fell back down to her, face buried in the fall of her hair and chest heaving while she held him and let herself drift.

After a time, he stirred, lifted his head, and said, "Shut up? Whatever?"

A lopsided grin lifted one corner of her mouth. "You were maundering on about something. Blah blah, I want to be a courteous lover, blah blah I want to take time. There were too many words and not enough screwing."

He burst out laughing while his hard features were still flushed from the heat of what he had done. God, she loved the sight of him like that. "I wasn't being courteous. I want to savor you like a five-course dinner in a world-class restaurant and take all night. Don't tell me you want to go back to not putting out."

Chuckling, she ran her fingers through his hair. "I think that ship has sailed, don't you? But it was fun while it lasted."

"If you call excruciating fun." He pulled away, stripped with practiced economy, and picked her up.

"My two legs and two feet, they all work perfectly well together," she reminded him as she laid her head on his shoulder.

"Shut up," he said. "Whatever. This gets you into my bed as quickly as possible, and I'm hungry for my five-star meal. Don't plan on going home tonight."

She should text Sarah to let her know, she thought. Then Alexei swung her onto the bed and came down over her in one controlled motion, and all rational thought splintered.

She knew how powerful it was to be the sole recipient of his dedicated attention. Her body remembered too, and it ignited everywhere he touched her. She lost herself in a haze of sensuality and pleasure and only remembered she was supposed to text Sarah when it was well after two a.m.

Sarah always kept her phone on in case there was a coven emergency, and Molly certainly didn't want to wake her with an apology. After deliberating for some time, she decided to let it go and apologize the next morning.

When she did, Sarah laughed. "I didn't think anything of it. Honestly, I was surprised you waited as long as you did. The way he looks at you… I always like to tell the man that he's the lucky one, but he looks at you like you've hung the moon."

She bit her lip and then smiled. "He does, doesn't he?"

On their fifth date, he proposed. Out near the labyrinth by the light of a full moon, down on one knee as he held out a blue-diamond engagement ring.

"It's gorgeous," she breathed.

"The blue is for the ocean," he told her. "I love you. More than that, I like and admire you, and I will want and need you every day for the rest of my life. We won't get it right all the time—and I know I certainly won't get it right. But I can promise you this: I will support you in everything you want to do, and I will cherish and respect you for as long as I live in this body. And when I do something wrong, I will *make* it right."

She stared down at him. For someone who wasn't a romantic man, he had put so much thought into the proposal. The moon, the ocean, the labyrinth.

He was telling her so much more with his actions, not just his words, and it was so perfect.

So perfect.

She replied, "Absolutely, yes."

A keen smile lit his features. He surged to his feet, picked her up, and swung her in a circle. She threw her arms around his neck, holding him tightly.

She would have said yes if he'd mentioned the possibility casually over lunch at some point, but she didn't tell him that until much, much later.

Over the next several months, other newcomers drifted into town. First Anson came, and then Maria, Steven, and Henry.

But not Richard. Richard couldn't, he said. He was still too angry to settle somewhere, and he had taken over running the trust Alexei had set up. Everwood was not the place for him. Alexei and the rest of his coven talked about it in depth at Sarah's kitchen table while

Sarah and Molly listened.

From time to time, Sarah joined in the conversation, but Molly kept her own counsel. For one thing, her opinions weren't necessary, and in any case, she was selfishly glad that Richard had made the choice to stay away and continue with their mission while the others took their sabbatical to decide how they wanted to move forward with their lives.

Working with Sarah as intensively as she did, Molly could feel dark, seeking tendrils of magic slide along the edges of the cloaking and obfuscation spells that Sarah and the Everwood coven had cocooned the area in for the past several decades. Everwood's sanctuary still held, but Molly never forgot the price of what they would pay if that screen ever fell.

By actively working elsewhere, Richard would draw the attention of the Rasputin crime family away from Everwood.

At least for now. With what she now recognized was precognition, she knew another confrontation was coming—perhaps even several confrontations—but she wanted that future delayed as long as possible. They all needed as much time as they could take before that came.

Time for recovery, time for Molly to have her baby, time for her to finish her training.

Time for the all-encompassing business of living, time for joy.

As fall came, Sarah did have The Talk with Molly

early one afternoon over butternut squash soup. They had just sat down to lunch. Closing her eyes, Sarah inhaled the aromatic scent of the soup and smiled with pleasure.

"I hope you like it." Molly sliced a loaf of homemade bread. "I put some of that spelled oregano in it since it's been doing you so much good."

"Would you be my successor, Molly?" Sarah asked. "I have so much respect for everything you've gone through and everything you are. Everwood needs someone with your strength and kindness."

"Yes," Molly replied. "You teach me something good every day, even when you don't mean to, and I'm deeply honored you would ask me. I could never hope to fill your shoes, and I know I have so much still to learn, but I promise I will always do my best to carry on your legacy the way you would want."

There it was, so simply asked and so readily answered. Sarah's dark, powerful eyes smiled with so much love and acceptance from the other side of the table as she offered to give to Molly the life that she already adored. Just like that.

After that, some part of Molly knew that several big life events were going to come in quick succession. After she and Alexei discussed everything, they decided to have a quiet wedding that would allow them to really enjoy the day with their friends.

Molly baked her own wedding cake. Alexei asked Anson to be his best man. Sarah officiated. It rained buckets the whole day, and they rolled back the rugs downstairs so everyone could dance.

After they married, Alexei moved in. A few months later, Elisa May Volkov was born on winter solstice. Molly knew she was in labor hours before the evening gathering, but she refused to let Sarah or Alexei cancel it. She wanted to know people were enjoying themselves while she gave birth.

Frankly, it sucked. Labor was hard work and very painful, but when she finally pushed that baby out, the experience held more primal joy than anything she could remember experiencing before.

Alexei held his delicate, new daughter in his hands and said to her fiercely, "I will be the best father you could ever hope to have."

That moment. That one moment was everything.

After the first of the year, Sarah stopped accepting treatment of any kind. When Molly, Alexei, and her nephew Sam protested, she enfolded each in a hug.

"I'm done," she said. "I wanted to hold that new little baby and to ring in the New Year, and I'm so glad I did. But you need to understand I'm ready to go. Death has been waiting for me for a very long time, and there's *something on the other side.* I don't know what it is. None of us do, but I'm excited to see it."

"God, when you put it like that," Molly exploded. She had to walk away while her eyes sprang another leak. Once again, when she didn't mean to be, Sarah was still her best teacher.

Sarah died in late January, slipping out of her body from one breath to the next. Everyone knew it was coming. The coven had kept a bedside vigil so she wouldn't face the crossing alone.

No matter how Molly had tried to brace herself—no matter how well in advance she knew it was coming—she was still utterly devastated.

Everything had been decided, the end-of-life business done. The coven had accepted Molly as Sarah's successor. Alexei and Molly had already purchased the grand old Victorian house, and Sarah had transferred her liquid assets to Sam. Sarah had handed the mantle of the coven's protection spells to Molly. The only thing that remained was the hardest part.

They scattered Sarah's ashes just as she wished, on the bluff overlooking the ocean. Hundreds of people came to pay their respects and celebrate Sarah's life. Flowers, donations, and notes of condolences came from every one of the grand families in the witches demesne in Louisville.

Molly did everything she could that day to the best of her ability, all with a broken heart. At one point, Alexei found her hiding in their bathroom.

"Everything's all right," she sobbed. "I just can't stop crying."

He said nothing, wise man that he was, and just folded her in his arms.

Finally, when the day was over, Molly went to sit in Sarah's bedroom in the old chair by the empty bed while

Alexei took Elisa upstairs to tend to her.

A knock sounded at the open door, and Molly looked up. Sam stood in the doorway, holding a leather-bound book in his arms. He gave her a smile. He was as red-eyed as she was.

"I'm sorry, Sam." Molly wiped her eyes. "I thought you'd already left."

"Not yet—don't get up. I was just heading out, but I had one last thing to do." Walking over, he offered the book. "Sarah wanted me to give this to you once the memorial was over."

She accepted it with a murmured thanks. "You know, we might have bought this place, but you're still welcome here anytime, Sam. Come for dinner next week."

"That sounds good. I'd really like that. Get some rest, will you?"

"You too."

Sam kissed her forehead, then left, and the house settled into peacefulness. The floorboards creaked as Alexei walked with Elisa in her bedroom. Molly listened, breathing deeply. The house loved having a baby again, and it always knew when everything was all right.

After a time, she relaxed enough to sit back in the chair. Alexei walked in, carrying one of the chairs from the other room. Setting it beside her, he sat and rested a hand on her knee.

She gave him a lopsided smile, and then her attention turned to the leather-bound book in her lap.

She opened it to the first page. It was dated in the spring from two years ago, and written in Sarah's strong, steady hand.

My dear,

At some point in the future, you are coming into my life, and I don't know yet who you are, but I love you already. From time to time I can see glimpses of you. They shine like bright fireflies on a warm summer evening.

I wish I could tell you what I see, that you are stronger than you know, more kind than you realize, and so much more powerful than you believe. You are good, whole, and perfect, just the way you are. You always have been, and the people in your life—the people you are even now getting ready to leave—should have told you so. Their loss is my gain.

I've discovered we're not going to have as much time together as I would have wished, so I thought I would use this book to jot things down as I think of them. That way I can visit with you as much as possible before you ever appear. These are just notes, so use them or not as you need.

You're coming into your Power, and it is such a strange, lovely time of transcendence, but it can be frightening too. The most important thing—the only important thing—is to remember that your Power lies within you. It's not out in the ether, it does not belong to anyone else, and you can't give it away.

Nobody can steal that from you. No matter what

anybody else does, or what happens in the world around you, that Power is yours, completely and forever.

All you have to do is claim it.

All my love,
Sarah

With a light finger, Molly touched Sarah's signature on the page. Then, rocking gently in the old, comfortable chair, she turned the page and began to read.

Thank you!

Thank you for purchasing *American Witch*! One of the major themes of the book is how Molly comes into her own power, not only as a person but as a witch, and I hope you enjoy reading about her and Josiah's story.

Would you like to stay in touch and hear about new releases? You can:

- Sign up for my monthly email at: www.theaharrison.com
- Follow me on Twitter at @TheaHarrison
- Like my Facebook page at facebook.com/TheaHarrison
- Become my Patreon patron at patreon.com/TheaHarrison

Please take a few moments to post an honest review of the story. Reviews help other readers find the books they like to read. I appreciate each and every review, whether positive or negative.

Happy reading!
~Thea

Look for these titles from Thea Harrison

THE ELDER RACES SERIES – FULL LENGTH NOVELS

Published by Berkley

Dragon Bound

Storm's Heart

Serpent's Kiss

Oracle's Moon

Lord's Fall

Kinked

Night's Honor

Midnight's Kiss

Shadow's End

MOONSHADOW TRILOGY

Moonshadow

Spellbinder

Lionheart

AMERICAN WITCH TRILOGY

American Witch

ELDER RACES NOVELLAS

True Colors

Natural Evil

Devil's Gate

Hunter's Season

The Wicked

Dragos Takes a Holiday

Pia Saves the Day

Peanut Goes to School

Dragos Goes to Washington

Pia Does Hollywood

Liam Takes Manhattan

The Chosen

Planet Dragos

ELDER RACES SERIES COLLECTIONS

Divine Tarot

Destiny's Tarot

The Elder Races Tarot Collection: All 4 Stories

A Dragon's Family Album

A Dragon's Family Album II

A Dragon's Family Album: Final Collection

The Elder Races: Complete Novella Bundle 2013-2018

GAME OF SHADOWS SERIES

Published by Berkley

Rising Darkness

Falling Light

ROMANCES UNDER THE NAME AMANDA CARPENTER

E-published by Samhain Publishing

(original publication by Harlequin Mills & Boon)

These stories are currently out of print

A Deeper Dimension

The Wall

A Damaged Trust

The Great Escape

Flashback

Rage

Waking Up

Rose-Coloured Love

Reckless

The Gift of Happiness

Caprice

Passage of the Night

Cry Wolf

A Solitary Heart

The Winter King

Printed in Great Britain
by Amazon